ANNE McCLANE

THE INCIDENT UNDER

THE OVERPASS

BOOK ONE OF THE TRAITEUR TRILOGY

ISBN: 978-0-9977794-0-0
eBook ISBN: 978-0-9977794-1-7

First Edition

Library of Congress Control Number: 2016946883

Author photo by Matthew Foster
Cover and interior design by Shannon Bodie, BookWiseDesign.com
Cover photo of woman by Oleksii Zabusik/123rf.com

Published by McClane Fiction, LLC
P.O. Box 24778
New Orleans, LA 70184

www.annemcclane.com

THE INCIDENT UNDER
THE OVERPASS

ANNE McCLANE

 McClane Fiction, LLC

1

Ga-dunk.

The sound expanded in her head, empty at the moment except for a feeling akin to bliss.

Ga-dunk.

The heavy, rhythmic thud echoed like a church bell. *It's telling me I'm complete*, Lacey thought.

The breakdown would commence once she was aware. But in that final instant before cognition, the lovely density of the noise and the euphoric feeling teased at some great truth just outside Lacey Becnel's grasp. Unbeknownst to her, the memory of that feeling would be, at times, the only thing to sustain her in the month ahead.

Ga-dunk.

Her eyes opened to a soggy darkness. Another *ga-dunk*, a slight echo, and then silence. In the long pauses between the sounds, she could hear the trill of crickets. *Ga-dunk* again. It worked like an alarm clock.

It was the smell that finally roused her. The smell of fresh, dew-topped grass, and a faint scent of urine. She flexed her hand and felt a clump of earth yield to her touch. Her back was wet, tickled by the scrubby undergrowth.

She savored the feeling for a moment before she realized its meaning. She felt her sides, then her chest, and then her legs. Her clothes were gone. Not in tatters, or in half measures, simply gone.

She was lying somewhere outside, naked.

Fear paralyzed her. She crossed her arms over her breasts, but didn't dare sit up. She strained her neck toward the sickly glow of a light directly ahead. Beyond, about one hundred feet away, a faint pool of light shimmered around a sodium vapor street lamp. Lacey's heart broke as the vestiges of that rapturous completeness slipped away, replaced by a rising sense of panic.

Ga-dunk.

She looked up toward the sound. Huge concrete beams sailed high above her. *I'm underneath a bridge*, she thought. *Those are cars passing overhead.*

The air was warm and languid, but still she began to shiver. She tightened her arms across her chest and wanted desperately to find her clothes. She turned her head away from the light, searching.

Ga-dunk.

Lacey gasped and bolted upright. Inches away, a man lay on his back—fully clothed, eyes closed, a peaceful smile on his face. He had a laceration along his right cheek. His jacket was torn and bloody at the right shoulder. He looked familiar.

Her memory was patchy. Whatever had happened to her had shot holes through her faculties. What the hell had happened, and why couldn't she remember? She willed her brain to recoup and repair. Quickly. She took a deep breath, and her shivering slowed. The pungent smell of the outdoors revived her.

Her arms and legs twisted into a pretzel, Lacey looked at the man more closely. He looked tall…she knew he was full head taller than herself; she remembered that from speaking to him. Where? A handsome face, a full head of sandy blond hair, and a kind expression. How did she know he was kind?

She also knew he was strong. Broad shoulders and chest, no pudges peeking out from the T-shirt he wore underneath his linen jacket. Solid, lean muscles. He had a solidness her husband did not have.

Ga-dunk.

The memory of her husband at home crashed in on Lacey, another panic-inducing rear-end impact. Her heart leapt into her throat as adrenaline surged through her. She had an overwhelming instinct to flee. *Running away from here naked may complicate the situation*, she thought. She lay back down and took another deep breath.

Ga-dunk.

What time is it? Lacey had no concept of how long she had been in this state. It could have been forever. She tried to concentrate. Long intervals elapsed between the passing cars overhead. It must be very late or very early. She remembered the month. June. Whatever time it was, daylight would arrive sooner rather than later.

Where am I? She looked toward the area behind her and the sleeping man. She could just make out some picnic tables. Ashen concrete picnic tables. She knew where she was. The I-610 overpass, not three minutes from her house. She could slink away, try to slip into her house undetected, and pretend this whole…whatever it was…never happened.

What about Fox? Will he hear me come in?

Lacey took another deep breath. Her husband, Fox, wasn't home, she knew. She knew because he had died fifteen months before.

It still happened to her sometimes, usually upon waking. She would forget about his death and all its circumstances for just an instant, thinking he might be in the living room, asleep on the couch. All the burden of his legacy lifted for a moment of ignorant bliss when she returned to a time when she'd adored him unequivocally. It happened less frequently as time wore on.

Headlights approached from the direction of the lake. Her lungs deflated, and she was on the verge of hyperventilation as she waited for the car to pass. She exhaled loudly when its red taillights sped down Marconi, and then out of sight.

She wouldn't dare sit up again until she had some clothes. She was only about twenty feet from the roadway, easy enough to spot from any more passing cars. Whoever the familiar, sleeping, kind man was next to her, she needed his jacket.

Lacey reached out and placed a tentative grip on his right arm. She was blasted by an overwhelming déjà vu as soon as she touched him. Déjà vu and heat; an interior heat, radiating from the base of her sternum. A voice echoed in her brain: *This is it. This is what was always supposed to happen. This is where you were supposed to be at this very time.* The flash disappeared as quickly as it had come.

She pulled her hand away and rubbed her temple with her palm. The frustration of her memory loss manifested in a physical pain. *Nathan,* she thought. *The man's name is Nathan.* She didn't know how she knew it, but she was certain of it.

The sleeping Nathan adjusted his position so that his right side brushed up against Lacey. That made her ache even more.

Ga-dunk.

She tried to focus on her surroundings and develop a plan. She closed her eyes, and an amalgam of "Amazing Grace" and the Memorare prayer flowed through her head: *'Twas grace that taught my heart to fear, and grace my fears relieved… Remember, O most gracious Virgin Mary…*

Remember. That combination of song and prayer had helped her cope with Fox's death. Fox. The love of her life, and the source of her biggest heartbreak. Lacey let out a slight laugh. Considering her current situation, the impact of all Fox's actions felt small, or at least smaller, for the first time since his death.

Ga-dunk.

Another car approached on Marconi. She held her breath. It passed out of sight, just as the previous one had. Her exposure—their exposure—loomed as Crisis Priority One. It was time to wake Nathan up.

Lacey lifted herself on her side, pulling her legs up to cover her privates and crossing her left arm over her chest. It was a momentously awkward position. With her right arm, she gently nudged Nathan in his side, amazed again how he had no apparent body fat. She said his name several times, low but clear.

He roused, his peaceful countenance turning into a grimace. He moaned a bit and shooed off Lacey's hand.

"Nathan!" Lacey finally said more loudly. She instinctively looked out to the street to make sure no one had heard her.

"Lacey?" he asked in a raspy voice.

Lacey turned her head and saw the confusion on his face. *Okay, so at least I'm not full crazy. We know each other well enough to know names,* she thought.

"Nathan," she said. "That is your name, right?"

Still lying on his back, he said, "Yes. At least I think so. Where the hell are we?"

"Underneath the interstate," she said. "Do you think I could borrow your jacket?"

"Huh?" He looked at her, not understanding. Then her nakedness registered. He nodded, and tried to keep his eyes upward.

Something happened to both of us, Lacey thought. *Neither of our heads seems right.*

Nathan sat up, slowly. He tried not to look at her. Lacey tried to shrink herself out of sight. He looked down as he gingerly removed his jacket and handed it over to her.

"Where are your clothes?" he asked.

Lacey arched an eyebrow as she slipped into his jacket in a millisecond's time. "Good question. And, if I knew, I wouldn't have to ask you for your jacket, would I?"

He returned his gaze to her face, and this time smiled at the burst of feistiness. His amusement turned into a grimace, and he put his face in his hands.

"Why do I feel like I have the worst hangover of my life?" Nathan asked, lifting his head.

Lacey looked down at the bloody hole in the jacket, and a dark mark that ran down the length of it. "It looks like you were *run* over."

Lacey stood, the jacket coming just to the tops of her thighs. She tried to make herself smaller, to somehow shrink the surface area of her legs. She would have to make it work for the short walk home.

Nathan looked up at her and gaped. Lacey assumed it was because of the brutalized look of his jacket.

"Do you think you can take a short walk? We really need to get out of here. I live very close by," Lacey said. She tried not to sound as panicky as she felt.

Nathan nodded. He rose slowly, testing his unsteady legs as he stood. He went to roll his shoulder, and winced. His T-shirt was torn, but didn't look as bad as the jacket.

Lacey bounced on her bare heels. "We'll take a look at you once we get to my house. C'mon." She stood by his side, offering her arm in case he needed it.

He looked her in the eye and shook his head. "I think I'm okay. Lead the way."

Lacey made sure she didn't see any cars in either direction, and stepped lightly to the sidewalk. By the time she made it to the train trestle that paralleled the interstate, Nathan was twenty feet behind her.

She stopped behind one of the columns of the trestle and waited. She looked back at the interstate, and could see arcs of light from passing cars. She thought they were increasing in frequency. Her stomach tightened.

Headlights approached on Marconi, from the south. Nathan was visible from either direction, clearly impaired and sure to be seen. The chances that the oncoming car was a police cruiser were good—cops patrolled all over her neighborhood regularly.

Lacey ran to Nathan and pulled him to the concrete wall of the trestle. She turned her back to the street and put her arms around him. It was a reflexive action, born of a need to protect, to cover, to hide.

She regretted the embrace as soon as she made contact. She was nearly overcome by another electric feeling of déjà vu as she held on to him. The searing heat emanated from somewhere higher this time, a spot at the back of her neck. She longed to break free, but she was paralyzed by an overwhelming desire to know more, feel more, and explore what was happening to her.

Nathan wasn't struggling. He looked down at Lacey's face.

The feeling passed. She pulled away as soon as the red taillights were out of sight. It wasn't a cop car. She intentionally avoided Nathan's gaze, grabbed his hand, and continued walking. He held on to her hand.

"I'm sorry I'm so slow," he said in a low voice.

"It's okay. I hope I'm not making you any worse," Lacey replied in a voice equally low.

Lacey's breathing eased once they crossed onto her street, Florida Boulevard. Neither of her two neighbors would be out so early, although there was a good chance one of them might spy her from his window. Lacey hugged the curb, under the cover of a line of crape myrtles. The nosy neighbor had planted them, illegally, on the public right of way to obscure the view of the train tracks. It was their third year, and their branches were fat with buds.

Lacey found it hard to breathe. Nathan gripped her hand firmly, but it felt like he was clinging to her throat. She realized how utterly dependent he was on her at that very moment, and how easily he had surrendered to her. It freaked her out. She felt a fierce desire to be rid of him.

She broke her focus on the trees and stole a glance at Nathan. Pain and effort were evident on his face. Lacey cursed herself, the desire for him to disappear replaced with an entirely different feeling. He looked heroic, his hazel eyes fixed on completing this grim task, jaw set, body moving with marked determination.

"We're almost there," Lacey said. "We need to turn here. Just a bit more sidewalk and then we'll be there."

Lacey pulled away from Nathan and grabbed the key hidden near the side entrance of her house. She waited for him at the base of the steps. A deeper sense of recognition began to seep in as she watched him. Nathan reached for the stair rail and she turned away, ascending the six steps to the door.

Key in the lock, her hand on the doorknob, Nathan stumbled and fell against her, catching himself with a hand to her shoulder. In that moment, she remembered who Nathan was. She didn't turn around, but hesitated before opening her door.

She was overcome by an acute longing.

2

Forty-Two Hours Earlier

Lacey placed last month's accounting reports on the bookshelf and returned to her desk. She was alone in the office. Her dilettante of a boss, Clayton Charles Carriere III, or Trip, had showed up shortly after nine a.m., and after about four and a half minutes informed her he'd be out for the rest of the day.

It was Friday, and she did not want to be alone. Since Fox had died, she had come to dread Fridays. The threat of the weekend loomed, two days alone in the house they had shared—the walls, the floors, the furnishings rank with his memory. But she refused to sell the house. It suited her and her Saint Bernard, Ambrose, too well. So she had opted for a systematic redecoration project instead.

So far, it had helped the weekends go faster. The bedroom was complete, and she had decided to take a breather before tackling the living room. But now, sitting alone at work, with nothing to do, she regretted the decision. With nothing planned for this upcoming weekend, the wide-open time ahead preyed upon her mood.

It had only taken her an hour to produce the accounting

reports this morning, even using a game she had devised called Double Time. It was one of several she had created to fill the long hours alone with nothing to do.

There were three more Carriere properties that required reports, but they weren't due until June fifteenth. If she completed them today, it would make next week drag on mercilessly. Not even Double Time could help her then.

Contrary to the military sound of it, the aim of Double Time was to draw out the length of time it would take to accomplish any Trip-associated task. There weren't enough of them to fill a forty-hour workweek. Between managing the commercial properties that provided his only non-annuity income and overseeing his vintage book collection, she might spend ten hours a week, tops, if she used her full capacity.

The office phone rang, and Lacey was happy for the distraction. It was another new associate of Gus Savin's calling. The antiques dealer cycled through employees every six months or so. He was calling about a potential acquisition for Trip.

A sudden and immediate relief poured over Lacey. She was now *ecstatic* to be alone in the office. She would have to tell Trip about the books, but calling him simplified the process exponentially. And spared her the tale of the Great Tragic Season.

If Trip had been present, the stage would have been set for the recounting, in minute detail, of the year when all the stars had been supposedly aligned in favor of Clayton Charles Carriere III, only to implode with the horrifying revelation of Gustav "Gus" Savin being crowned Rex instead of him. If Trip had succeeded in his quest to be King of Carnival that year, he would have been the youngest on record. Now that chance was forever lost.

The Savin-Carriere rivalry had a delightful irony. The fifty-something bachelor, Trip, the last scion of an old New Orleans family, had only two evident passions: his antique books and his membership in the Rex Organization. Savin was the yin to his yang. He helped fuel one passion, while he was the source of Trip's greatest agony in the other.

Trip's enmity usually provided some amusement. Today, it only made her head hurt. Lacey took a deep breath and dialed him from the handset on her desk.

"Becnel, go," he answered.

Lacey rolled her eyes. "Trip, I just got a call about a set you might be interested in. Six of them. The theme is old cars, motor cars."

"Huh," he said. "Who's offering?"

"Savin."

Silence from Trip's end.

"They said one of them features a nice compendium of classic advertising," she added.

"Huh. I'll think about it. Thanks, Becnel, you're a sport. I'm out."

Lacey hung up and knocked her head against the desk three times. She cradled her arms and laid down her head, eyes toward the big picture window. It offered a panoramic view of the Mississippi and the West Bank beyond.

A huge freighter came into the frame of the window, headed downriver. She stood up.

She told herself not to play the game, but it was one of her favorites. She was already guessing the ship's registration before she could stop herself. The Philippines, she decided.

Having no insight into maritime affairs, the game was more of an indulgent daydream, requiring no particular skill.

She pictured herself on a beach on a remote Philippine island, where she would assume a brand-new identity, and no one would ever have heard of Trip Carriere, or Fox, or any Becnel.

She spied the flag on the ship. Korea.

Shows you how much I know.

✳

The ship from Korea was likely out in the Gulf of Mexico when Lacey returned from lunch. She discovered that Trip had lied. Or had ill-planned his day. Either option was equally probable.

"Becnel!"

She heard him before she saw him, the sound of his voice a familiar irritant. A small part of her was relieved to return to a non-empty workplace. Lacey walked to the doorway of his well-appointed office.

"Oh, hey, Trip. Change of plans?" she asked.

"Yes. No. Change of venue, really. I'm donating some of the duplicates for a fundraiser. I had to come by to pull them together," he said. He was standing with his back to her, perusing the floor-to-ceiling shelves that covered the back wall.

Lacey could have pulled the copies of the first editions herself, but she knew better. Trip would want to say goodbye to them.

"Do we have to deliver them somewhere?" she asked.

"No, someone's coming by to get them. Three o'clock. Will you be here?" He still had not turned around.

No, I'll be halfway to Korea with the money I embezzled by then, she thought.

"Yep, absolutely," she said.

"Becnel, can you come in here? And bring another container."

Lacey sighed. She was about to get the story of each book he was pulling, how hard it was to part with it, but how it was all for a good cause and that was why he bought duplicates whenever possible anyway.

"Sure, be right there," she said. She Double-Timed her way to the utility closet to gather an empty plastic storage bin.

When she arrived at his office two minutes and twenty-one seconds later, she saw one bin already full. That was good. It meant she would only get one bin's worth of self-absorbed prattle.

He silently handed her a volume. *Siddhartha*, Hermann Hesse. Lacey held her breath, waiting for the anecdote. None came.

It's because he's never read it, Lacey thought. *That figures.*

"You know, this is why I buy duplicates," Trip said.

One side of Lacey's mouth turned up in a smile. "What's the fundraiser for?" she asked.

"Oh, the homeless, I think. It's not through Pro Bono Publico, but it's something Evan Long's firm is sponsoring. I owe him."

Lacey bit her lip. Trip didn't mind altruism as long as it was quid pro quo. His charitable endeavors were either sanctioned by the Rex Organization's foundation, thus elevating his stature there, or a return favor within his Uptown old boy network, thus maintaining his status there.

Eight and a half minutes later, the task was complete. A pile of discarded clamshell packaging lay at Trip's feet.

"Do me a favor; tidy those up and put them in storage, Becnel?" he said.

Somebody needs to put you in storage, you anachronistic man-child, she thought.

She nodded silently.

He wanted to save the pricey archival boxes for things he really cared about. She gathered them up, and wondered how she might go about stowing away on an ocean-bound freighter.

✳

At three o'clock sharp, the buzzer rang on the office door. Lacey had been alone for an hour, her head mired back in dread of the weekend. Expecting the pick-up for the books, she pushed the button to unlock the door from her desk without screening. She caught her breath when the doorway filled with the form of a man dressed all in white.

"Good afternoon," said a deep velvet baritone voice.

"Good afternoon," Lacey said, rising from her desk. She chided herself for the thousandth time. *What good is the lock when half the time I forget to activate it, and the other half I fail to screen?* she thought.

The man in white was wearing a chef's coat, the name "Cecil" over the left pocket. The only splash of color on his black-and-white person was a red bandana, pulling back a copious amount of dreadlocks from a moon-shaped face.

"Can I help you?" Lacey asked.

"I hope so," he said. His voice sounded unreal, his projection and pitch more suited for a theater than a dead-end office. "I'm here to provide transport for something of value."

Lacey tilted her head, her eyes an unvoiced question mark. "The books are right over here. My boss didn't tell me—or didn't know—what the fundraiser is for."

"There is an event next Thursday night benefitting the Trinity Mission," he said. "We are trying to raise funds to expand the Women's Center."

"Oh. Well, I hope this donation will help," Lacey said. She stood across from the man, two plastic bins full of books between them.

"What is your name?" he asked.

"Me?" Lacey pointed at her chest and stopped herself from turning around. "It's Lacey. Lacey Becnel." She held out her hand.

The man reached out a giant oven mitt of a hand and returned Lacey's greeting with a firm, quick grasp. Lacey felt a spark, and a millisecond of déjà vu, easy enough to ignore.

"Lacey Becnel, I am Cecil," he said. "It is a pleasure to meet you. Young Lacey, I will be providing catering services for this fundraising event. I will be shorthanded. Are you available Thursday night?" he asked, as if he wasn't a complete stranger.

"Oh! Me? Thursday night? I don't know how to cater," Lacey said. She wished she could appear cooler when flummoxed.

Cecil's expression was inscrutable. "There is nothing to learn," he said. "Can you follow instructions?"

"I think so," she said.

"And are you available this coming Thursday?" he repeated.

"Um…" Lacey scanned her memory. Dinner with Fox's aunt was next Tuesday.

"Um, I think I'm free Thursday," she said. She wanted to invent something, like a sick relative, but was afraid of the karmic implications. *Stupid karma*, she thought.

"Very good," Cecil said. He bent down and picked up the two large bins. Stacked atop each other, they only came to his neck. They would have completely covered Lacey from her waist to the top of her head.

"Come to Mardi Gras World at six p.m., Thursday night. Dress in black. Functional clothes." Cecil walked to the door.

Lacey passed him to open it. "How should I contact you?" she asked. She had an instant regret for agreeing to sacrifice an evening to someone she had just met, and to cater, at that. She'd never even waited tables. "What if I can't make it? I'd like to let you know."

Cecil's face lit up in a smile that turned his moon of a face into the sun. "You will be there. You won't regret it. See you Thursday, young Lacey." Cecil carried the bins down the hallway as if he were carrying a tray full of cookies. He didn't turn around, even as he waited for the elevator.

Lacey closed the office door and cursed herself. How could she know if he was legitimate? What if he was a serial killer posing as a benevolent chef, luring naive, unsuspecting rubes to his Mardi Gras World lair? She thought of Buffalo Bill from *The Silence of the Lambs.*

She rushed—not Double Time—to her computer and looked up events at Mardi Gras World. Sure enough, Thursday evening, seven p.m.: *A Time to Shine, a Benefit for the Trinity Mission.* On the page were links selling tickets (*Less than thirty tickets left!*) and a call for volunteers (*No experience required!*)

Damn.

She resolved to check in with Angele before, during, and after, so if she wound up in a dark pit putting "lotion on its skin," she wouldn't have to wait too long for someone to know she was missing.

3

Sixteen Hours Earlier

Lacey hadn't expected such a quick response from her best friend. She had waited until Saturday morning to text her, a single line: GOT A STORY. She guessed Angele's production schedule might not be so tight on the weekend. Still, she was surprised to see Angele Lee calling her phone less than a minute after she sent the text.

Angele didn't ask about Lacey's story. Instead, she jumped right into a pitch for Lacey to meet her and her Hollywood-type coworkers out that night, at a bar on Harrison Avenue called Patton's. Angele feigned shock when Lacey agreed without any prompting or cajoling.

"If you're coming out just so you can draw me into your pity party, I'm revoking the invitation immediately," Angele said over the phone.

"Please! How long have you known me?" Lacey asked, a smile cracking her face for the first time that day.

"Long enough to know that given the opportunity, you could spend five solid hours moping about your dead husband and your dead-end job," Angele answered.

"Jesus. You're either the meanest or most judgmental friend a girl could ever have," Lacey said.

"I'm neither, just honest," Angele said. "You could use more honesty in your life."

"Amen to that."

"And because I'm so honest, I'll tell you that the Dakota Kid will be there," Angele said.

"You know I don't care about that stuff anymore," Lacey responded.

"Bullshit," Angele said. "I'm done talking. Wait. What's your story?"

"It's nothing," Lacey said. "I just got drafted into some volunteer work next week. I'll tell you about it when I see you."

"Good," Angele said. "Sounds like another chance to get you out of your grief cocoon. Can't wait to hear about it."

"I'm sure. See you tonight."

Lacey was proud of herself for being excited. She was sure Angele wouldn't believe her enthusiasm was authentic, but that didn't matter. She needed something to get her out of her dark funk. Meeting up with her best friend from childhood, and the exuberant young actor she had dubbed the Dakota Kid, stood as good a chance as any of breaking her melancholy spell.

Angele had hinted that part of her job was keeping an eye on the up-and-comer Kevin Horner, who was fulfilling a contractual obligation by appearing in a Lifetime movie being shot in New Orleans. It was the second of a slate of three movies he had signed on to before *Entanglement*, a big-budget, big-director, big-star picture Lacey had read about in *Entertainment Weekly*. According to Angele, Kevin Horner would be a star after it released at Christmas.

Lacey was secretly curious to meet him. She thought of the

marathon phone conversations she and Angele had as preteens, hours debating the merits of Zack over Slater and vice versa.

✳

That evening, Lacey applied her makeup in the guest bathroom; the light was better in there. Her giant dog, Ambrose, poked his head through the doorway. It was the only bathroom with a tub, and he enjoyed sitting and soaking, especially in the summer months.

"Sorry, Bro, no bath for you tonight. I'm actually going out!" she said.

He shook his massive head and nudged the door wide open as he left, disappointed. Lacey had long ago ceased to be amazed by the dog's comprehension. It was something she took for granted.

Lacey spent too much time staring at her closet, anxious about how she would appear to Angele's coworkers. She had lost fifteen pounds since Fox died, and her hair was longer than it had been in years. She had not done much to keep her wardrobe up to date. Her options were limited to a few things she had purchased on a recent shopping trip with Angele.

She pulled out the jeans Angele had made her buy: on-trend and long so that she had to wear heels. She had to admit they did fit like a glove as she pulled them on. She paired them with a V-neck, fitted T-shirt whose design was meaningless to her. It promoted the athletic department of a high school in Indiana. When she had protested the randomness of the message on that same shopping trip, Angele had turned Lacey to the side so she could see her profile, told her vintage was still in, and finally to "Get over it."

Lacey still didn't get it as she looked in the mirror, but she liked the way it gave her a sporty vibe.

She ran some product through her hair. Her tawny-colored waves fell just right, a rare occurrence. Staring at her reflection, Lacey felt she was looking at a stranger. Her patrician nose and green eyes stood out more on her leaner face. *I'm almost as skinny as Angele*, she thought. But it was an impossible comparison. Lacey had been five-five and curvy when she had started college, and five-seven by the time she graduated. Angele had been five foot nothing since she was fourteen, and had tiny proportions, like a doll.

Lacey went to the side table near the front door, where she kept her purse and keys. She opted against a purse and instead stuffed some cash and her ID into the pocket of her jeans, leaving just enough room for her car key. She could just carry her phone, or leave it in the car.

Ambrose shuffled up to her as she was arranging her things and giving herself one last check in the entryway mirror.

"Think you can take care of things while I go out for a little bit?" she asked.

"Woof," he replied in a low register.

"I know, I didn't even need to ask," she said, scratching his head behind the ears. His summertime shave-down recently completed, she was happy her attention wasn't repaid as it usually was, with a fistful of dog hair.

She went out through the side door, the one in the laundry room that opened onto General Haig Street. She had a good hiding place for her house key on that side of the house.

Lacey thumped her fingers on the steering wheel of her Honda Accord as she made the short drive down Marconi. The light was falling just the way she liked it, the oak trees forming dark silhouettes against an azure background. The sky that peeked out from the canopy was punctuated with silver clouds. It felt like a good omen. She almost wanted the drive to last longer.

Parking would be a mess on Harrison, what with the dinner crowds out at all the eateries. She didn't mind walking a bit, but any real distance might be a challenge in the wedge heels she was wearing.

She considered herself lucky to find a spot in the marked spaces on the neutral ground, right across from Patton's. Fox had insisted on calling the strip dividing the streets a median, like the rest of the country, instead of the neutral ground, like the rest of New Orleans, which Lacey always found peculiar, for someone so dyed in the wool about everything else concerning southern Louisiana. She reminded herself to let it go. It could be the neutral ground, now. She no longer needed to defend her choice.

She got out, pushed a button on her key to lock the car, and then turned around at the same time she was attempting to stuff the key in her pocket. She looked up at the gloaming sky—the faint outline of the new moon had appeared—and missed her pocket. The key dropped to the ground and skipped about a foot, just enough to land behind her in a ditch. Not just a ditch, but a gaping maw marked off with barricades and a few cones. Construction work on that part of Harrison Avenue was a constant.

"Well, shit," Lacey said to no one in particular as she turned on her precarious heels to see where the key had landed.

Fortunately, the pit was bone dry. It had been an unusually parched June so far. Lacey figured she could reach down and grab the key without getting too much of her new outfit dirty.

She stepped with her right foot into an innocent-looking part of the crevasse, bent over, and picked up the key. Pleased with the relative ease of the operation, she stood upright and found herself stuck. Her wedge heel must have caught on something.

"Well, shit again," she said as she strained to see if she could free her foot. She thought of bending down again and unfastening the strap on her shoe, but she began to question her every move. Suddenly the barricade she had previously ignored seemed to heckle her. She was feeling mightily self-conscious as she looked down at her foot, and looked across the street at Patton's to see if anyone was watching. Preoccupied, she was startled when she heard a voice behind her.

"You look like you could use a hand."

She whipped her head around and saw a man, alone, at the driver's side of the car next to hers. He was a little older—maybe ten years older than herself—and looked very sharp, in a summer-casual kind of way. Linen jacket and jeans, like he was dressed for an elegant dinner with elegant friends.

Feeling even more self-conscious than before in her trendy jeans and T-shirt and ridiculous predicament, Lacey didn't answer at first and just stared. The man removed his hand from his car door and walked toward her, a reassuring smile on his face.

"They always say the potholes in New Orleans are bad enough to swallow a person, but I think this is the first time I've seen it actually happen," he said.

Lacey finally spoke. "Oh, I dropped my key, and now I'm stuck. I feel really stupid. You don't have to help me."

"Well, what kind of douchebag would I be if I came over here to help and then didn't?" He bent his head to look at her foot and gave her a surreptitious once-over as he did.

"This is easy, you just need some leverage." He straightened up and looked her in the eye. "Did you get your key?"

"Yes," she said as she held out her hand, showing it to him like a child might. "Let me put it away." She looked down and stuffed the key in her pocket. She averted her gaze for a moment and tried to compose herself. She was afraid she was gawking. The combination of his charm and directness and easy valor was working a number on her.

When she finally looked up, he was smiling broadly at her. She blushed.

"Okay, now turn directly toward me," he said.

He watched her feet. "Straighten out your left foot. Good. Give me your hands."

Lacey caught her breath and looked reluctant.

The man laughed. "I promise I won't bite. And this will get you out of there. Give me your hands."

She hesitantly held her arms out. The man grabbed her by both forearms, lifting the ring finger on his left hand slightly. As soon as he had a hold, he tugged, and almost immediately Lacey felt her right foot purchase some air. She pulled it out of the ditch and lost her balance, falling right into him as she did.

They both laughed as it happened, and as he released his grip she steadied herself against him, her hands falling to his sides. His waist was rock hard to the touch, no love handles. Lacey quickly removed her hands and righted herself. Even standing straight, she only came up to his chin.

"I'm sorry, I should have given you some warning," he said to her.

"I'm the one who should be apologizing, for being so stupid," Lacey said, swiping her hand at the dirt on the right leg of her jeans.

Still standing where she had fallen into him, not looking like he was in any great rush, he held out his hand.

"I'm Nathan, by the way."

Lacey, most of the time, liked her name. It was unique, and feminine, and had paired well with both her maiden and married names. But there were times when she wished it carried a little more weight, had more of a ring of authority to it, like "Margaret" or "Samantha."

She sighed and took his hand and said nearly under her breath, "Lacey. And thank you, by the way."

He smiled. "Lacey," he repeated, drawing out the two syllables. He held on to her hand for an extra millisecond. "No thanks necessary. Glad I was able to help." He seemed at a loss for any more words.

"Me too," she said with a little smile. Lacey was also reluctant to end the exchange. Her sense of embarrassment eventually overpowered that feeling.

"Well, I guess I should be on my way now." Lacey would have started walking, but Nathan was blocking her passage between their cars.

"Oh, yeah, me too." He turned and walked toward the backs of their cars, and Lacey followed.

After three seconds, he stopped to face her.

"I had just come out here to get something from my car. Guess I found you instead," he said.

Lacey blushed again. She tried to stand a little taller.

"Well, I'm glad you did. Thanks again, Nathan." She paused after saying his name.

They exchanged a glance. Nathan seemed firmly cemented to the ground. Lacey finally moved past him.

"Okay, then. Well, bye."

She willed herself not to turn around as she walked the length of the neutral ground toward the crosswalk. Maybe she would see him again at Patton's.

*

Sitting with Angele out on the back patio of the bar, Lacey tried to keep her disappointment tamped down. The air was pleasant—unseasonably dry with a breeze, and some well-placed citronella candles kept the mosquitos at bay. But she couldn't help but feel that the anticipation she had reserved for meeting the Dakota Kid had been usurped by her encounter with Nathan.

An hour earlier, Angele had introduced her to a pack of five guys crowded around the bar. The one at the center of it all was Kevin Horner, the Dakota Kid. He was shorter than Lacey had expected, and the skin on his neck was broken out. He offered Lacey a perfunctory greeting, and then resumed holding court with his assembled jesters. If he had star power, Lacey must be immune.

Angele had never said, but Lacey had puzzled out that the Kid's handlers must have made an arrangement with her to provide some sort of reputation security—to make sure he didn't do anything now that would haunt his movie-star future. Or if he did, to make sure it was effectively erased. Lacey wondered how much money Angele was making from the deal.

A stocky guy with a shaved head came outside to talk to Angele. Lacey recognized him as one of those who'd been assembled around the Dakota Kid. She watched politely as they spoke, but tuned out their discussion. It sounded logistical.

Whoever he was, he was short but very muscular, the calves of a runner showing from beneath his khaki shorts. His black button-down shirt was utilitarian, full of pockets to hold useful things. A Bluetooth headset peeked out from one of them. Lacey didn't think he was security, but he definitely looked like movie crew. And someone important.

Lacey turned away and pretended to study the latticework on the patio gate. She whipped back around when she heard her name. Mr. Important Movie Crew must have said it.

"You might consider paying attention," he said. His eyes were hawk-like, but one of them floated, so she couldn't tell if he was addressing her or not.

Lacey looked to Angele for an explanation. Angele smirked and shrugged her shoulders.

Lacey was on her own. "I'm sorry, I didn't think your conversation concerned me."

"If it wasn't for you to hear, I would have pulled your friend away," he said.

Lacey couldn't think of anything to say. She sat staring, wildly uncomfortable. She couldn't read his expression. She fought the urge to follow the gaze of his floating eye toward the gate.

"You, especially, will be surprised what opens up to you once you start paying attention. I'll see you later," he said.

He turned his back to their table. Lacey was mouthing the words "*What the…*" when he turned around again.

"They have an outstanding wrestling team," he said. "But I suspect you have no idea."

"Who?" Lacey finally said.

He gestured at Lacey's chest, to her T-shirt of the once-meaningless design.

"Oh," she replied, looking down. "Okay." He had disappeared inside by the time she returned her gaze upward. Lacey erupted in nervous laughter.

"Jesus, Lee, who the fuck was that?" she asked Angele.

"That," she replied, "was Eli."

"What was all that about?"

"No clue," Angele said, and shrugged. "But not out of character for him. He's definitely a strange bird."

"What does he do?" Lacey asked.

"Special effects, among other things," Angele said. "He's incredibly good at what he does, though."

"Well, I would think he'd have better things to do than harass me," Lacey said, crossing her arms, concealing her T-shirt design.

Lacey kept her eyes on the patio doors for the rest of the evening, on guard in case the strange Eli came out again to pick on her some more. But also for another reason. She felt something had begun during her encounter with Nathan, and hoped she might see him again.

At the start of the evening, she had chosen her words carefully when she had told Angele about her foolish misstep and the man who had helped her. She didn't want Angele to know she was twitterpated. And she had not mentioned him again. On top of that, she had not spoken of Fox even once.

Feeling very proud of herself, Lacey was taken aback when out of nowhere, after a lull, Angele said, "He was probably married."

"Who?" Lacey asked incredulously.

"The old guy in the dinner jacket you've been fixated on all night," Angele answered.

Lacey pushed back in her seat and took a defensive posture.

"What? All I did was tell you the story when I first saw you! I haven't said boo about him again all night."

"Please. I know you," Angele said, perched in her seat, alert but relaxed. "You've been watching for newcomers all night, hoping he might magically appear. Did you notice a ring?"

Lacey tried to mask her exasperation.

"No," she said. "But then I never think to look. Plus, it all happened so quickly, I wasn't thinking about that."

Angele smiled like the Cheshire Cat. "It's a habit you should pick up, but quick," she said.

"What?"

"Checking for rings. It's not like college, when you can assume everyone's your age and not married."

"Look, I know," Lacey said. "But it's not like I was hitting on him or anything. He helped me out of a predicament."

"That's how you see it. I think he saw an opportunity to hit on a pretty younger woman and took it," Angele said.

"Oh, now I'm pretty, huh? That's rare," Lacey said.

"Sure. You look good tonight," Angele said, gesturing toward the clothes she had selected. "I have good taste."

"Yeah. Not sure what I would do without you," Lacey deadpanned.

"I guarantee that bastard of a dead husband knew to look for rings," Angele continued.

Lacey raised her eyebrows. "I thought I wasn't allowed to talk about Fox tonight," she said.

"You're not. But I can. It fits the situation. You *are* allowed to respond."

"Wow. Thanks," Lacey said. "Since you so graciously gave me the floor, yeah, he always noticed shit like that. Why do you bring it up?" Lacey folded her arms again and tried to shrink further into the patio chair.

"I'm sure he chose to fool around with married women whenever he could. It's easier that way. What do you think the percentage was, of married to single?" Angele made no effort to soften her words as she laid all this out on the table between them. The number and frequency of Fox's dalliances were no longer secret, but they were still seldom exposed to the light.

"I'd be lying if I said I'd never thought about it," Lacey said, stricken. "The woman he was with when he died was single. As for the rest, I have tried really hard not to dwell. What does it matter, anyway?" she added.

"Those who refuse to learn from history are doomed to repeat it," Angele answered.

Lacey found herself mired in familiar thoughts. "Say most of them were married. What kind of skanks must they have been? Women of any kind of bearing should know not to mess around with a married man. Now I'm getting repulsed," she said.

"Good," Angele said. She was wearing the closest expression to sympathy she could muster.

"Look, you've never been one to judge," she continued. "That's mostly a good thing, but in some instances, it can be really bad for you. Like this. I just don't want to see you hurt like that again."

"I don't want to be bitter. Ever," Lacey said. "I don't want to close myself off to the good things." She unfolded her arms.

"You don't have to," Angele said. "I just think you could stand to be a little less naive when it comes to romance."

"Point taken," Lacey answered.

"Just do a better job of paying attention, like Eli said," Angele said with a smirk.

Lacey shook her head. "Lee, I might be ready to call it a night," she said.

"But I'm just getting into my groove!" Angele said.

"I know. That's why I think I'm ready to go," Lacey said with a smile.

"Hold up," Angele said, turning businesslike. "We probably ought to wrap up the Kid, too. Give me a few and I'll walk out with you."

It was another half hour before Angele and Lacey walked out together.

"Where did you fall?" Angele asked as she looked toward the neutral ground.

"I didn't fall, I got stuck. Right over there, where that barricade is," Lacey said.

"You want to put up a plaque or some sort of monument?" Angele grinned.

"Shut up," Lacey answered. "Thanks for asking me out tonight."

They parted without touching. Embraces and other signs of affection were reserved for big occasions. They both knew this was not a hug-worthy night.

Feet aching, Lacey kicked off her shoes as soon as she was in the car. In the rearview mirror, she saw Angele wave as she turned onto Harrison headed toward Marconi. She gave a little wave back, but as soon as her eyes were fixed on the road, an intense wave of anger came over her. She was angry with Angele for being so blunt, angry with Fox for all the usual reasons, and angry with herself for all those reasons combined. She thought back to the start of the evening, and was mad for letting herself be so charmed by a complete stranger. But…

But it had been so nice to feel attracted to someone. It

was the first time it had happened since Fox's death. Whether it was shock or self-preservation, she wasn't sure, but in the past fifteen months she had been impervious to flirting. As she drove past the darkened soccer fields and tennis courts on Marconi, she tried to focus on the positive charge of that attraction. Maybe that was all the encounter was supposed to mean—a signal that she was ready to wake up and get on with her life.

As she approached the interstate overpass, something made her slow down. Her eyes might have played a trick on her, but something sent an overwhelming, visceral surge through her, stronger than the anger. She released her foot from the gas.

Her eyes hadn't played a trick. She could now clearly see someone stumbling about amidst the giant columns. There was something familiar about him. And definitely something very wrong with him. If she had been sensible, she would have continued on to the comfort and safety of her home, called 9-1-1 to report what she'd seen, and remained forever unlinked to the man who appeared to be in some sort of jeopardy under the interstate.

Whether it was Eli's admonition to pay attention, or something else buried deeper, Lacey could not pinpoint what made her stop the car.

Her heart beating fast, feeling like it was in her throat, she took the keys out of the ignition. Before she got out, she looked again in the direction of the stumbling man, and saw that it was Nathan.

He was about thirty feet away, near one of the concrete picnic tables that dotted the massive structure. Like a zombie, once he saw the car, he turned and started moving in Lacey's direction. He did not get but five feet before he crumpled to the ground.

No longer thinking, Lacey ran out of the car, barefoot. She barely noticed the gravel as she flew across the roadway. She looked around when she reached Nathan and saw that he was alone. He had passed out cold. He looked in pretty bad shape, like he'd been run over by something.

She got down on her knees and tried to see if he was breathing, or if she could feel a pulse. She felt neither.

4

Fifteen Seconds Later

Thunderous hoofbeats approached from the other side of the door. Lacey knew Ambrose would react when he saw the stranger at her side. She needed to let Nathan know before she brought him into her home.

Lacey finally turned around and looked at him, consciously noticing his left hand. Through the darkness, she saw a glint of metal on his ring finger.

Shit, she thought. She hated it when Angele was right, which was most of the time. Then she kicked herself for focusing on that one detail, skipping over the inconvenient fact of his apparent near-death experience. There was still much she didn't know.

"I have a dog," she said. "I'll need to introduce you before you come in the house."

Nathan nodded. He looked worse from the walk to her house.

Lacey opened the door and let herself in. Ambrose skipped right over his usual greeting, instead aiming one loud, deep bark in Nathan's direction. Then he planted himself firmly between Lacey and the doorway.

"It's okay, Ambrose. This is Nathan. He can come in."

The Saint Bernard sidled and let the stranger in, but kept a wary eye on him.

"His name is Ambrose?" Nathan asked as he walked into the laundry room and closed the door behind him. As soon as he did, his legs faltered, and he caught himself with both hands on the dryer.

"Oh God, I'm so sorry," Lacey said as she went to his side.

"Ambrose, go," she said, and pointed toward the kitchen.

He responded in a way very rare for him. He gave a low growl and bared his teeth, but obeyed anyway, walking out with his head hung low.

Hiding her shock, Lacey said to Nathan, "Let's set you down somewhere more comfortable. I hope the walk didn't do you in."

"I'll be okay, I think. I'm just weak."

Nathan accepted her offered arm this time without hesitation, and she led him out of the laundry room, through the kitchen, and out into the airy living room. She set him down on her sofa. It was a huge sectional, glaringly big for just one person.

Lacey thought for a moment of grabbing a towel. Nathan was covered in dirt that was going to transfer to her furniture. But she decided to deal with it later.

Ambrose returned and positioned himself directly across from Nathan.

"Nice dog," Nathan said in a strained voice. "Would you mind terribly if I lay down?"

"No! Please, go ahead," Lacey said, her panic beginning to crescendo again. "Should I call a doctor or an ambulance or something?"

"No, this is fine. I'll be fine." And before Lacey could fret any more about the possibility of his situation worsening and having to deal with a dirty dead man on her couch, he was fast asleep, the same way he had been underneath the overpass just minutes before.

After standing for a moment perplexed, she tiptoed up to him, and Ambrose followed, at the ready. She made sure she could see Nathan breathing in his supine position. He was, in deep, almost snore-like breaths. The cut on his face did not appear as bad as it first had. Maybe the harsh light from the street lamp had made his injuries look so severe. She remembered his shoulder, and how he'd winced when he tried to move it. She tentatively reached out her hand toward the tear in his shirt to see the skin underneath. Ambrose strained his huge neck behind her.

There appeared to be an old scar on his well-muscled shoulder, but it otherwise looked fine. Lacey stepped back and exhaled, trying to settle down and take stock of her situation.

Pull yourself together, she thought. She thought of her car, and had an overwhelming need to have everything in its proper place.

"Stay," she told Ambrose. "Watch him." Ambrose promptly sat back on his haunches to keep watch over Nathan.

Lacey darted to her bedroom and pulled on running clothes and shoes. She grabbed the spare key to the Accord and kept it in hand with her house key.

Lacey laid Nathan's linen jacket on the back of a chair. She caught her breath at the sight of it. It was covered in blood and dirt. She glanced at her own shoulder to make sure it was still intact.

She returned to Nathan, totally insensate on her couch. He appeared in much better shape than the jacket. Ambrose stood guard.

Before she slipped out the door, Lacey thought of what might happen if Nathan woke up. He would see that giant dog's head, a long line of drool dripping from his massive jaw. She felt reassured.

It took her less than two minutes to run back to the interstate. She didn't want to dally, she only wanted to prevent any unwanted attention. Her randomly parked car would draw just that, she was sure, once daylight arrived.

Ga-dunk.

She froze at the sound. *Don't dally*, she thought. *Move, move.*

Her body wouldn't follow her brain. Statue-like, she looked toward her car and saw something higher up, through the trees. Some sort of structure, the light from the street casting sparks off parallel lines and radius curves. Lacey thought of what lay in that direction. The dog park, a reception hall, Popp Fountain.

Popp Fountain.

Fuck, she thought.

Ga-dunk.

Of course. Whatever happened to me tonight would have to happen in the shadow of Popp Fountain. Fucking Fox.

Lacey looked down and blinked away a tear.

Ga-dunk.

The sound released her as quickly as it had paralyzed her. *Move.*

She cut a diagonal path to her car and passed directly by a column, roughly ten feet behind where she'd first awoken. She stopped when she saw something at the column base. Jeans,

T-shirt, underwear, bra, all in a neat pile. Her stomach jumped. She scooped them up and ran even faster toward her car.

✳

Lacey was shaking when she reentered through the laundry room, her clothes tucked under her arm. She locked the deadbolt and stood for several moments with her back to the door. She thought of the stranger lying on her couch and wondered if it was a good idea to be locked inside with him.

What if he raped me, and that's why I woke up naked next to him? she thought. *And why am I only thinking this now, after I left him alone in my house?*

A depraved sex fiend wouldn't leave her clothes like that, in a neatly folded pile. She knew she must have left them that way herself. And she had gone to him, and he had been badly injured, she now remembered that clearly. But she still had no memory of stripping down, or anything that had happened after. The blackout was like a shrinking inkblot, with reality slowly revealing itself from the edges.

She laid her clothes on the dryer. In the living room, Ambrose had not moved, only the line of drool dripping from his jowls had lengthened. Nathan had moved—he was lying on his side, not his back. Lacey positioned herself behind the dog and stood, arms folded and eyes intent. The clock on the side table caught her eye. It read 4:47 a.m. More than three hours had passed since she had left Patton's.

Where is his wife? Is she wondering where he is? Lacey thought of the evenings she'd spent alone, fully duped by whatever excuse Fox had given her. She had chosen that ignorance. Who did that hurt more?

Nathan's eyes blinked open. Ambrose moved to close in on him.

"Stay," Lacey said.

Nathan laughed. "Me, or him?"

"Both," Lacey answered, her arms still folded.

"Tell your hound I'm just going to sit up now, okay?"

Lacey called Ambrose to her side. Nathan moved deliberately. Lacey wasn't sure if it was out of caution or pain, and she didn't care at that moment.

"Do we need to get you to a hospital?" she asked.

"No!" he said adamantly. "No. I'll be fine. I just need to think. What time is it?"

"Almost five a.m.," Lacey said.

"And it's Sunday, right?"

"Yes," she said, her impatience bubbling up. "Nathan, what happened to you? Why did I find you underneath the interstate?"

He was sitting up, his hands on his knees.

"I was shot," he said, "and thrown out of a car, left for dead."

Lacey wasn't sure she'd heard correctly. "Jesus. Did you say shot?"

"Yeah. My wife and I were fighting last night, and…"

Marriage confirmed, Lacey thought. "Your wife shot you?" she asked.

"No, not my wife. Hold on, okay?" Nathan rubbed his face with his hands. He looked at Lacey and Ambrose. "This feels like an interrogation."

Lacey relaxed her stance, but didn't move.

"Well, it sorta is. Look, Nathan." She emphasized his name. "Last thing I remember is seeing you, thinking you're dead, and then I'm naked, and you're not dead. I'm figuring something major happened during that blackout."

He smiled at her. Lacey couldn't comprehend his expression, and it unnerved her further.

"And you seem pretty cavalier, for someone who supposedly just escaped the clutches of death," she said.

"I'm not cavalier," he said, the smile disappearing. "I don't know what I am. Everything feels unreal right now."

"Maybe you're in shock," Lacey said.

"Are you a medical professional?" Nathan asked, sarcasm apparent.

Lacey bristled. "No. But you won't let me take you to one, so I'm all you've got right now."

"Look, I know. I'm sorry," Nathan said. Tentatively, he stood.

"I just need to think," he said. "I'll finish telling you what I know, and then I'll think of what to do next." He let out a dry cough. "Could I have some water, please?" He choked out the words.

Lacey nodded and turned to the kitchen. Nathan followed with Ambrose at his heel.

She fetched two glasses and filled them with ice water. Without turning around, she said, "If you're up for it, have a seat at the kitchen table. Otherwise, I can bring this out to you in the living room."

Nathan took a seat before Lacey had finished speaking. She set a glass in front of him and then sat at the opposite end.

"Thank you," he said. "Look, I'm trying to piece everything together myself, so can you bear with me while I sound this out?"

Lacey remembered his dependency on her during the walk to the house, and felt a sudden pang of concern. She considered moving closer to him, but remained in her place, silent, and nodded for him to proceed with his story.

"My wife and I met friends for dinner at the Steak Knife. Our friends left, and we had a drink at the bar, just the two of us. It had been her idea. We got into a fight, and I stepped away, trying to cool things down."

Lacey suppressed the hundred questions that immediately came to mind.

"I went to the bathroom," Nathan continued, "and when I came back, she was gone. Took the car and went home, I assume. It was about eleven thirty when she left." He paused and sipped his water. "I figured I wasn't going anywhere for a while, so I had one more drink at the bar."

Lacey wanted to say something about how cavalier that sounded, but bit her tongue.

"That's where things start to get fuzzy. I was going to call a cab, but decided to take a walk first." Nathan fingered the toile runner on the table and looked at Lacey sideways. "I thought of walking over to Patton's, to see if you might still be there," he said.

Lacey felt her stomach jump. She wasn't sure if she was charmed or creeped out. She tried not to let it show.

"How did you know I was at Patton's?" she asked.

"I didn't. It was an educated guess."

"But you didn't go to Patton's," she said. She wanted him to finish his story.

"No. I started walking toward Argonne. A friend from college just finished building there; I thought I'd just pass by, see it from the outside, and collect my thoughts in the process."

Again, Lacey thought of how suspicious that seemed, but didn't say anything.

"It turned out to be a pretty stupid thing to do," he continued, his eyes cast down, both hands now on the table runner. "I got into a scuffle as I turned the corner by the gas station. Things went from bad to worse, and next thing I know I'm thrown out of a car, left for dead."

He stopped talking and took another sip of water. He avoided Lacey's direct gaze. The pause in his story stretched into an awkward silence.

Finally, Lacey asked, "A scuffle?" She knew the meaning of the word, but it seemed grossly inadequate.

Nathan sighed. "Yeah. Look, I know better, all right?" He looked her in the eye. "I guess this is how people wind up dead. When I turned the corner onto Argonne, there were some guys who looked like they were in the middle of something. I'm not sure if they thought they could take me for some cash, or if they thought I saw something they didn't want me to see."

Lacey was confused. And concerned.

"Shouldn't you tell the police about this?" she asked.

"Yeah, I will," he said. The weight of something was evident in his face. Something he wasn't telling her?

"Maybe," he continued. "Do you want to find out what happened with you, or not?"

His impatience set Lacey back. Her response was snippy. "Please, by all means. Continue."

"They overpowered me and threw me into the car. And they left my wallet untouched. That doesn't make any sense, does it?"

Lacey shrugged. She wasn't about to interrupt again so soon.

"There was one guy who would not stop talking. There were three guys altogether, but one just couldn't seem to shut up. Like a nervous talker. I remember him just babbling away, and then one of the other guys—one who was in the back with me—shot me."

Lacey shifted in her seat. She knew he was leaving something out, but she felt too vulnerable to push the issue. She made a gesture that Nathan couldn't see, and Ambrose responded and came to her side.

Nathan looked up at Lacey. "I don't remember much after that. I must have blacked out. I do remember getting thrown—hard—out of the car. I don't even think it stopped."

Lacey asked what felt like a pertinent question. "Was it where I found you?"

"No," he answered quickly. "I had been struggling—for how long, I couldn't tell you—to get somewhere where I'd have a better chance of getting help. I don't know where they dropped me, but I know I woke up somewhere that felt remote. I made myself get up and start walking. I know I passed the dog park before you found me."

Another pertinent question occurred to Lacey. "Is your phone dead?"

His eyes narrowed in response. "I don't have it," he said curtly.

Lacey pursed her lips to keep from responding.

Nathan added, more softly, "It was in the car. So my wife really left me stranded in more ways than one."

Lacey remembered how he was supposed to be retrieving something from his car when she first met him.

"Okay," she said in as flat a voice as she could muster.

"I didn't have much left in me by the time you found me," he continued. "I guess that was obvious."

"I thought you were dead," she said.

Nathan looked as serious as death, but something like awe

started to soften his expression. He paused for a long time before speaking again.

"I think I was. Or very close."

Lacey didn't respond. Her left hand reached underneath the table for the scruff of Ambrose's neck.

"You. You did…something to me," Nathan continued. "There was a light. Something that you had, or something that came from you. I don't think I was in any pain by the time you came to me…either shock or something…I was starting to slip. There was a very pleasant confusion as I watched you take off all your clothes."

Lacey was rapt. But the thought that Nathan might be mentally unstable occurred to her for the first time.

"The light became very intense, but it wasn't blinding," he said. "It was more like…sunlight…you know how you can feel the sunlight through closed eyes, when you're lying on the beach?"

Lacey nodded.

"You did something. Or whatever you had with you did something. I knew I was starting to slip, but then you came along, and my life was back."

Lacey wanted to ask, *Are you fucking crazy?* Instead, she chose her words carefully.

"What are you saying?" she asked.

He said, in plain words that did not seem at all unhinged, "You're the reason I'm not dead."

5

Lacey dropped Nathan off on Fontainebleau at Carrollton, careful not to ask him where he was headed. During the short drive to his neighborhood, she had discovered he had two young children. That made her feel even guiltier about her attraction, and about what had happened. Whatever it was.

Nathan was convinced she was the purveyor of some miraculous happening, a healing angel of light. Lacey's initial reaction to his confession, his confession to a belief in the impossible, was annoyance.

She was annoyed that he saw her as something she was not, and very annoyed with herself for not being able to remember a lick of anything that had happened. And annoyed that he'd used the word "angel." Lacey had never much cared for angels; they always seemed snobby in the Bible.

Lacey almost made a clean getaway, eyes straight ahead as she drove off. But as soon as she made a U-turn to go back in the direction of home, she couldn't help herself. She looked to her right and saw him, straight-backed with a slight strut to his walk, making slow progress into the rapidly lightening horizon. He turned just in time to see her, his eyes locking on hers.

Shit, she thought. *Everything about him feels messy.*

Lacey was charged up and unsettled the rest of the way home. When she turned onto Florida, the sky had lightened so that she could clearly see her neighbor, Max Kamenitz, framed against his weeping willow. She'd always marveled at how he still managed to spy on everything in spite of that unkempt tree, its foliage trailing the ground of his front yard.

He was in his summer uniform of boxers and sleeveless undershirt, cigarette in his left hand, leash and poodle in his right. Lacey's mom had deemed him "Kravitz" during the time she had stayed with Lacey after Fox died, and the nickname, unbeknownst to him, had stuck.

There would be no escaping, Lacey knew. He would be passing by as she turned into her driveway. Lacey thought of driving around the neighborhood to avoid him, but couldn't think of any excuse to explain it later. Because he *would* ask.

She was still in her running clothes. *Perfect.* That would be her cover. Lacey took a deep breath as she stepped out of her car, phone and keys in hand.

"Mornin', little Lacey. Where you coming from so early?" Neither his posture nor his voice suited his interrogations, incongruities Lacey had noted long ago: slightly stooped, friendly expression; a treble to his words, which sounded like they were raked over gravel before leaving his throat.

Here we go, Lacey thought. "I went for a run up at Audubon. Went a little ways along the river, too."

"You're too good for City Park, now?" There was a twinkle in his eye as he rasped out the words.

"Oh, come on, now. You know I've covered every inch of that park, between my runs and walking Ambrose. Sometimes I just need a change of scenery!"

Kravitz coughed out a laugh. "Sure enough. Though you sure are ambitious. There's a lot of park to cover. I heard from the city again," he continued.

"Oh, yeah?" Lacey was relieved. He must be referring to his beloved easement-planted crape myrtles, taking the attention off her.

Every year the city of New Orleans threatened to cut them down, and every year nothing happened. There were six of them, and each blossomed a different color, and they were magnificent. Lacey remembered the buds and thought of the bounty to come.

"Did they give you a date this time?" Lacey asked.

"Nope. Same exact letter as last year, just a different date at the top. No signature, no teeth, no problem." He took a drag off his cigarette without tapping out the ashes.

"I don't know, Mr. Max. Don't you worry about them rolling up unannounced and trying to cut them down?"

"I'll see them if they do. And Gabi here will scare them away if they try to touch those trees." He gave a slight yank on the lead, and the miniature poodle gave a little growl in response.

Lacey laughed. She knew he wasn't posturing. "Well, I can send Ambrose over in that case, to help out."

"I'm surprised you went jogging," Kravitz said, changing the subject again.

Lacey's heart started pounding wildly. Had he seen her in the middle of the night? He would say something if he had, she knew. Did he know this was a hastily constructed cover story?

"You know I have to get out early in the summer, to beat the heat."

"I guess it works, because you're not sweating at all." He

blew smoke out in a long blue line and jangled the leash, another twinkle in his eye.

Is that all he meant? Lacey wasn't sure. "Oh, yeah?" She looked down at her shirt. "Huh! I didn't notice. There was a great breeze at the river."

"Some breeze," he cackled. "Too bad it hasn't made its way out here yet."

"Maybe it will, before your walk is over," Lacey replied.

Kravitz started to move on, and then stopped. "Oh, hey. Tell your friend not to park by the trees."

Lacey panicked again. Was he referring to Nathan? No, that didn't make any sense.

He saw her confusion. "The little girl with the big truck?" He sounded like a frog.

"Oh! You mean my friend Angele." Angele had made a quick stop off at Lacey's the week before in a catering truck. Lacey knew Angele's job could call for her to do anything and everything, but she'd still looked funny, like a child behind the wheel.

"Yeah, I told her as soon as she did it," Lacey continued. "It won't happen again."

"Well, I'm sure a few minutes won't do any harm, just wanted to be sure it didn't become a habit."

"Yeah, don't worry, Mr. Max."

"I never do, little Lacey!" he replied as he resumed his walk.

Fat chance of that being true, Kravitz, she thought as she walked into the house.

Lacey only had occasional visitors, and most of them were related to her. Almost all of them knew not to park anywhere near Kravitz's house, or the illicit crape myrtles. If a tire rested on even a single blade of his grass, she would hear about it.

As Lacey walked into her laundry room, she began to shake uncontrollably. She was overcome with a chill.

"How the hell does this happen in this heat?" she asked as Ambrose approached her. He put his massive body up against her legs when he saw her shivering.

She let Ambrose lead her to the sofa, and she sat down and grabbed the cashmere throw that was perpetually draped over the side. She wrapped herself up and stared straight ahead, phone and keys still clutched in her right hand. Ambrose set his chin on the cushion beside her. She reached out her left hand and stroked his head.

She released her phone and keys when she couldn't stop her hand from shaking. She looked at the phone like it was infected, thinking of the new contact she had just stored. She and Nathan had exchanged numbers. It had seemed prudent at the time, like exchanging details at the scene of an accident.

How long had he been married? Did his wife often walk out on fights? How had he just happened across the people who had tried to kill him? How could he have survived being shot at close range? She knew he'd left something out. Several things, probably.

But she wouldn't call him. Hopefully, she'd never have to speak to him again. If he wasn't going to go to the police with his story, then her involvement in whatever had happened could remain hidden. Something just between the two of them.

And maybe just one other person for now. She had to tell Angele. It was still before seven a.m., but this warranted a wake-up call. Her teeth had stopped chattering enough that she thought she could talk. She called three times before Angele picked up.

The words poured out of Lacey as she gave her account of

the previous five hours. When she was finished there was a weighted silence on the other end of the line.

"You still there?" Lacey asked.

"Yeah. Jesus! Give me a minute," Angele responded.

Lacey felt the crush of remorse. She'd never imagined she couldn't tell Angele. Or shouldn't tell Angele. Why was it taking so long for her to say anything?

"If I didn't know you as well as I do, I'd think you had a psychotic break," she finally said.

That was not the response Lacey had hoped for. "You think I'm crazy," she said.

"No. Well, yes, but not that type of crazy," Angele said. "Maybe just temporarily that type of crazy. Maybe you're in a fugue state."

"A what?" The word made Lacey laugh.

"A fugue state. An altered state of consciousness characterized by delusions and unexplained wandering."

"I know what a fugue state is," Lacey said. It was partially true. "I don't think I'm in a fugue state."

"Don't dismiss it so quickly. Say you are. Your judgment would be so impaired that you wouldn't have awareness of it."

"But that's why I don't think I am. That's just the thing. I don't think I've ever felt more grounded," Lacey replied. She released her grasp on the blanket as her body temperature returned to normal.

"So do you believe Dinner Jacket, then?" Angele asked.

"About what part?"

"All of it."

"He's leaving stuff out, I know," Lacey replied. "But he didn't seem like he was lying when he talked about seeing me and a light. And he is very much alive now, but when I first saw him I thought he was surely dead."

Lacey thought of how crazy that sounded. She could picture Angele's reaction—a relaxed posture betrayed by tight lips and tapping fingers. Lacey cringed at the thought.

"So you say he didn't seem like he was lying," Angele said, "but you also said he seemed a little nuts when he told that part of the story. It's the level of conviction that draws the line between normal and crazy."

Lacey didn't understand what she meant, but didn't want clarification. "So you think *he's* crazy," she said.

"You don't? Do you believe you have magical powers? Because if you do, that's a different conversation, and we can leave Dinner Jacket out of it. That would put us back to the fugue state."

Lacey didn't respond.

Angele guessed what she was thinking. "Crap. If you do have some sort of mutant powers, and I'm only finding out about them now, I'm going to be really pissed."

Lacey shook her head. "Only you. I think I'll opt for crazy, just to not be a disappointment to you. And listen for a second, Lee," Lacey added. "Say I am a mutant, then this is the first time my powers—whatever they are—ever manifested. And you're the first person I called. You can't be pissed about that."

"Shit," Angele said. "You really *do* think something happened. Whether you're losing it, or whether you really are a mutant, this is huge either way."

"I know," Lacey said, her remorse notching down. She felt a strange level of comfort at having her crisis summed up so succinctly.

"The naked part's pretty weird," Angele said. "A fugue state might explain that."

Lacey's anxiety spiked again. "I'm trying to forget that part. So let's say, just to analyze, that I am going crazy. What caused it?"

"Grief," Angele said without hesitation.

"Why now? Why after so much time has passed?"

"These things don't follow a set schedule, Lace."

"I hate that," Lacey responded.

"Are you going to be okay? Do you need me to come over?" Angele asked. Lacey knew she wouldn't ask if she wasn't absolutely ready to follow through. But she also knew it would require a major restructuring of her plans. She had a rare day off from the production, and she had promised to spend most of the day with her parents.

"No, no, I've got to get some sleep," Lacey said. *Eventually.*

"Hey, what about Tuesday night? Could you do dinner?" It was unlike Angele to be so proactive.

She must really be worried, Lacey thought. But she was ready to jump on the offer until another familiar set of anxieties fell upon her.

"Shit," Lacey said. "You don't know how much I wish I could. But that's the Tonti dinner."

"Ohhh," Angele replied. "I'm sorry for you. But maybe you can see what she thinks about Dinner Jacket."

"Funny," Lacey said.

Fox's Aunt Evangeline, a.k.a. Tonti, was a small doses person. But Lacey was indebted to her for the invaluable assistance she had provided after Fox's death. More than anyone else, she had helped Lacey navigate the legal waters of the insurance proceeds, and the more complex matter of Fox's trust from his mother's side. The dinner date was nonnegotiable.

"Can't wait to hear how that goes," Angele said. "I'll definitely see you next Saturday, right?" There was another movie-crew night out in the works.

"Yeah. If I haven't fugued myself into another dimension by then," Lacey said.

"I won't let that happen. I want to hear from you every day," Angele said. Also atypical.

"Huh. Okay. You want to keep a record of my psychosis?" Lacey asked.

"Correction. Keep it *up*. I've got reams of data on you. Could be a bestseller."

"Glad you think so," Lacey said, taking a beat. "Hey. Sorry for calling so early."

"I would have been mad if you hadn't."

"Okay. Give your folks my love when you see them."

"They already have it. I'll check in with you tonight."

"Thanks."

Lacey set her feet on Ambrose, who had settled into a favorite spot between the couch and the coffee table. She thought for a bit about mutants. She liked them better than angels. She checked the skin on her arm to make sure it wasn't turning scaly and blue.

6

Lawrence LaSalle slipped into his office after nine p.m. on Sunday. He was a hardworking and astute businessman; no one who happened to be watching the quiet oak-lined Uptown street would have occasion to think anything amiss. "Poor Larry," Mrs. Von Lubbe two doors down might say, "can't seem to leave his work behind, even late on a lazy summer night."

Which is fine, he thought. Work and savvy had earned him a level of prosperity that finally justified his family's place in the upper tiers of New Orleans society. But it was this other pursuit that would secure his legacy. This other venture required his attention now.

He paused at Nathan's office door before he pulled out the mobile phone he had acquired earlier that day. He felt bile rise in his throat at the thought of the presence that typically occupied that small, unkempt space. It had come to that end—Nathan made him physically ill. That was why he was taking action. Indeed, the germ of the idea had come last November when LaSalle had not been able to come to the office, bedridden for three days with the flu. He had not missed a day of work (not counting vacations, when he typically closed the office, anyway) in over thirty years. He was less afraid of death than of the prospect of his son-in-law taking over the business. In a fevered imagining, his living pain was gone: a dreadful accident, a random violent crime, a mysterious disappearance.

When the fever had broken, and reason had slowly returned, it had been too late. The seed had been planted. There could be only one way to keep his business whole, to make sure his daughter and grandchildren had full rights to the fortune he had fought so hard for, scrimped and saved and measured so carefully for.

Once he'd made the right contact, the whole process had seemed suspiciously easy. So in a way, he was not surprised that last night had not gone according to plan. His contact had even hinted that it was a possibility. "We might have to put out multiple feelers" was the term he had used. "You have to surrender any expectation on timing" had been another hint.

Lawrence LaSalle did not think he was out of line in placing a call to his contact. It was a business arrangement, and he was merely checking in. He tried to keep a professional demeanor. He knew from experience that ultimate success is often comprised of many small failures. But the fact that his son-in-law was still in this world when he was already preparing his funeral was a grave disappointment.

He moved on to his own office. In sharp contrast to Nathan's, LaSalle's was spacious and tidy with a large walnut desk filling the center of the room. The Eames office chair was a conspicuous modern luxury amidst a setting that evoked a more genteel era. But he'd never found one that suited him better, so he'd learned to ignore the incongruity. He sat in the chair, assumed a posture that might suggest he was placing a call to his broker, and dialed the number he had memorized and never written down.

"Yes." It had taken eight rings for his contact to pick up.

"This is Roark," LaSalle responded authoritatively.

There was an audible sigh on the other end of the line. "I know who you are."

LaSalle did not want to waste any more time. "I just wanted to make sure another…feeler is in play."

The silence on the other end seemed interminable. And then, finally, "Yes. *Do not* call again. We will be in touch." Then dead air.

Lawrence LaSalle's face darkened. He stared at the phone and swallowed the urge to redial. Instead, he hurled the phone across the expanse of his office. It landed squarely against the pane of the second tier of his barrister bookcase. A spiderweb of cracks appeared, obscuring the twenty-year-old picture behind the pane, from his daughter's debutante ball.

7

Lacey stood paralyzed at Trip's massive oak desk. It was ironic that someone who did so little work required such a large desk. She stared at the ridiculous picture she'd seen a thousand times before. He stood alone, a towering papier-mâché creature in the background. It was affixed to the float he rode in Rex. Lacey was never sure if the creature was a duck or a dragon or some horrid combination. Trip was dressed in garish purple and orange satin, a mask atop his head like a headband, the Superman-style swoop at his forehead intact. Trip went to the same barbershop he'd gone to as a boy, where every time he received the same boys' haircut. Trip could be attractive, if he updated his look to this century.

The mask atop his head was the same one all the riders on his float wore, standard Mardi Gras fare, but their ubiquity didn't make them any less frightening. They'd always reminded Lacey of the mask Michael Myers wore in the *Halloween* movies. She wondered if Nathan rode in a parade. Maybe Nathan was Michael Myers. Maybe she had saved a psychotic killer.

A thousand thoughts flitted in and out of Lacey's mind on Monday morning at the office, but two feelings predominated.

One, she was relieved Trip was not in the office and likely wouldn't be at all today. Two, she didn't need Double Time. Between lack of sleep and a general sense of terrified awe over what had transpired during the weekend, she wandered around the office like a zombie, trying to focus on anything but accomplishing nothing.

She could have called in sick. There was something wrong with her, wasn't there? She still had amnesia. Not a lot of it, but enough. She thought of Kafka, and the salesman who couldn't go to work because he had turned into a giant bug. That was why she had come to the office. She felt fine. She felt very good, in fact. Just tired. And if she was turning into some freakish creature, she wanted to go about her normal life for as long as she could.

Lacey couldn't remember why she was in Trip's office. She had entered for some reason, and become fixated on the picture. It was an enduring symbol of his narcissism, a picture of his own self at his own desk. She knew it had been taken during the Great Tragic Season, because he never failed to mention that every time he recounted the story. Which had always seemed odd to her, but she had never given it much thought. Until today. She looked at it in a different way. Why would he keep a reminder of his greatest disappointment in such plain view?

A business card from Gus Savin lay conspicuously on the glass protector top, like a silent clue. It was the only other thing on his desk. Trip could not abide clutter. Savin's card had a new design, Lacey noted. An *S* stood out at the center of a fountain. It looked elegant, not overdone, if a bit old-fashioned. *Appropriate for an antiques guy,* Lacey thought.

While she couldn't quite figure out why Trip kept that

particular picture on his desk, she knew exactly why Savin's card was there. She predicted the conversation, once Trip was back in the office. He would want to know if he should get a logo, too.

"Should I get a logo, Becnel?" Trip would ask.

"I'm not sure, Trip. I kind of think your name is brand enough. Strong enough to stand on its own," she would say.

He would give a self-satisfied nod. And he would go on, entertaining what his logo might look like, even though he didn't need one. Several variations of triple *C*'s stacked or contained within each other.

But again she doubted herself. Maybe the conversation wouldn't go that way. Maybe there was more to Trip than she had ever realized. Or perhaps that was a bit much. Though she conceded that he could have motives that were hidden to her. That seemed more likely.

She didn't feel like she could trust her senses anymore. Not after the weekend.

What would Marva and Roland think about Trip's logo? she thought.

Jesus, Angele is right, she thought immediately afterward. She stepped away from Trip's desk toward the doorway.

I am in a fugue state, but I lost my mind long ago, even before Fox died. I have got to find another job.

It had started as another game. The name on the door read Carriere & Associates, plural; yet she was the sole associate, single. Thus, the invisible associates had been born. Marva was an older woman, brash with a foul mouth, and Roland was a young man of little means who had taken the job to help pay his way toward his Tulane MBA.

Get back to reality, Lacey, she thought. *Make a plan. Make yourself useful.*

She would punctuate her day by going home during her lunch break. And she would call her brother sometime in the afternoon. But there was still at least another hour to kill before lunch.

She suddenly remembered why she had gone into Trip's office. The settee. She desperately wanted to lie down. Trip used his settee for naps all the time, but she would never allow herself the luxury. She had thought that by staring at it, and picturing Trip there, she could will herself to stay awake, so repulsive was the image of Trip sleeping.

It sort of worked. The picture had distracted her instead.

She had never wanted to get too comfortable in this job. Nine years in, she realized how stupid it seemed to keep telling herself that.

She could afford to go a while without work. Between the life insurance and trust funds, she wasn't in dire need of money. The dread of nothingness was the only thing keeping her at Carriere & Associates. Having someplace familiar to go, and work that was rote, had been a blessing early on, in the throes of her grief. But now, especially after recent events, continuing in this torpor just felt ridiculous.

Make a plan, she thought. She considered looking for a new job, but didn't trust herself. If she went onto any search engine, she would start searching "healing powers / healing ability / superpowers" again. That was the rabbit hole she had fallen down last night, with her head ending up more muddled than it had been when she began. She'd found a wiki listing a bunch of superheroes she had never heard of, and plenty of websites for psychics.

She had promised herself that when she went to work, it would be business as usual; she'd put the supernatural stuff on the side. Easier said than done.

Lacey checked the time. She really wanted to talk to someone. She would risk a pre-lunch call to Jimmy. It was nearly eleven a.m.—nine a.m. for him—if he was home. If he'd had a show the night before, it would definitely be too early to get any coherent speech out of him.

Opening with a movie quote might be a safe bet. Neither the years nor the distance had diminished their fluency in their Esperanto-like language of film references.

"Hey, Budgie!" her brother answered. He sounded alert.

"Mav, you still got that number for that truck driving school?" Lacey asked.

"One-eight hundred-truckers, I think?"

"I know it's a little early," she said. "You sure I didn't wake you?"

"Nah, we're on the road. Actually I think it's almost ten here."

"Where's here?"

"Denver?" he answered. "So, what's up, Budge? How the hell are you?"

Lacey felt tears well up at the question. Ever since Fox had died, she'd found herself missing her profligate, rock'n'roll brother as acutely as she had when he'd first moved away fifteen years before.

She paced in front of the picture window, phone to her ear. She ignored the container ship headed upriver.

"Never been better, Chump," she answered with a lump in her throat. "Career is great, love life is on the mend, so at least I have that going for me."

"Which is nice," they answered in unison. Lacey choked out a laugh.

Jimmy picked up on her discomfort. "Trippy up to his usual shenanigans?" he asked.

"Nothing worse than usual," she answered. "No, it's not that. I had a weekend."

"Really? Ooh, I'm practically giddy," he said with the affectation of a teenage girl. "Do tell."

"No, nothing like that. I mean, nothing girly. Well, maybe a little, but that's not the important part."

"Okay, so a weekend that's got you worked up in some other way. Did you finally get blotto like I've been telling you to?"

"No, not that. Well, yeah, sort of, but not due to alcohol."

"Budgie! Do we need to have the drug talk?"

She laughed. "No!" One of Jimmy's many talents was that he could get her from crying to laughing in under a minute.

"No," she repeated, more relaxed. "Like some really weird, eighth-dimension stuff. Angele thinks I went into a fugue state."

"Are you okay? You didn't kill anyone, did you?" he asked, sounding a touch more serious.

"No, I'm fine, and no one's dead."

Thanks to me? she thought.

"Okay, that's a start," Jimmy said. "'Cause dead's pretty permanent."

"I know," Lacey replied, thinking of Fox.

"So give me the nickel version."

"All right." Lacey took a breath. "I met a guy, and I might have helped him out of a pinch, but I'm not sure how I did it, and I'm just kind of freaked out by it."

Jimmy took a few moments to respond. "You know, there's a lot of ways I could take that. Do you like this guy?"

"No! Well, yes, but I barely know him, and he's married, and I didn't help him out like *that*."

"Hmm. Seems like you definitely have more to tell me."

"Yes, definitely," she said. She turned her back to the

window. "But I'd just rather not do it on the phone. It's been too long since I've seen you. It feels weird."

As close as they were, and as much as she trusted him, he was still her big brother. The naked-in-a-public-space part of the story was something she would have to tell him about in person, if at all.

"Well, I guess it's good I'm going to be home in a few weeks, then," he said.

"Really?" It was the best news she'd heard in months. "Ma hasn't said anything to me."

"Reeney doesn't know," he said. "I'm not telling her or Joe."

Jimmy had never called their parents by anything but their first names. Lacey had never felt it was something she could pull off.

"Unscheduled tour stop," Jimmy continued. "We're doing a surprise set at the Publiq House. I won't have time to make it to New Roads, just in and out of NOLA in thirty-six hours."

"Okay, I'll keep it under wraps," Lacey said. "It'll be really good to see you. It's been way too long, and even longer since I've seen you play. What's the date?"

"Hold on." She could tell he was looking it up on his phone. "June twenty-fourth."

"Good. Good. I can't wait."

"You sure you'll be all right, Budgie?"

Lacey turned back to the window. She tried to make out the ship's registration, but it was too far away.

"I will be, Chump. I'm finding my way. I'll give you more details when I can. It's just really good to hear my big brother's voice."

"You can hear me in the backup vocals on our latest release."

"That's not what I meant, fool."

"I know. I was just trying to make you laugh."

Lacey set the phone on her desk after their call and stared at it for a few moments. She wasn't sure if she wanted to make her brother materialize immediately, or speed up time to June twenty-fourth.

Speed up time, she decided. Pulling a person out from where they were and what they were doing seemed inconsiderate. She closed her eyes and thought hard about June twenty-fourth.

She opened her eyes and looked at the date on her phone. Still June twelfth.

I guess that's not my power, she thought.

She threw the phone into her purse and left the office, deciding it was time to start her lunch break. Marva said she could.

8

"I'm fine, Ma, really," Lacey lied as her mother busied herself around her kitchen. Three minutes earlier, Lacey had shaken her head when she'd turned off Florida Boulevard and seen her father's truck in her driveway. She'd considered turning around and going back to work.

When Ambrose had met her at the laundry room door, she'd scolded him. "I thought we talked about not letting them in the house," Lacey had said as she gave his massive neck a strenuous scrub.

"I heard that!" her mother had yelled from the kitchen. Lacey had smelled the dreadful hazelnut-infused coffee her mother insisted upon.

Her parents had become very liberal with surprise visits. They at least had the decency to call first if they popped in on a weekend, apparently assuming if their daughter were to "entertain," it would only happen then. But weekdays were fair game. The excuses varied: sometimes her house was a pit stop on the way to one of the Gulf Coast casinos; sometimes her dad just wanted a safe house if her mom visited her aunt in Gentilly.

Ambrose left her to rejoin her father in the living room. He had found *Touch of Evil* on the TV and settled in to watch it from the recliner, the dog at his feet.

"Hey, Pop," Lacey yelled from the kitchen as she gave her mother a hug.

"Hey, pumpkin," he yelled back, not taking his eyes from the television.

Her mother broke off from the hug, returned to the sink, and started in.

"Everything in this kitchen is too neat. You're not eating."

"No, Ma. Do I look like I'm not eating?"

Irene Campo stopped rewashing the perfectly clean dishes from the dish drain and looked her only daughter over.

"You look too skinny. Beautiful, but too skinny."

"Ma, you know I like to keep things tidy now," Lacey said, grabbing a towel. She reached for the as-yet unmolested dishes from the rack to put them away. "I never realized how much I detested the mess that Fox seemed to leave behind in whatever room he entered," she continued.

Her mother responded by putting her hands on her hips.

"I promise you, I'm eating," Lacey said. She flexed a gym-toned bicep for her mother. "Look, healthy as a horse."

Irene sighed and shook her head. It was the exact same gesture Lacey had made five minutes earlier, turning into her driveway.

"Still, you spend too much time alone," she said. "Your Aunt Sue and half your cousins are right across the park in Gentilly. You could reach out to them, for company, you know."

Lacey smiled. She relaxed as she settled into the well-rehearsed blocking of a familiar argument.

"Ma, you can't pin your sister down with all the running

around she does for those grandkids. And the girls are all pretty busy. They all work, and they all have multiple kids."

Lacey wasn't sure what prompted her to go off-script. "And honestly, I think they find me threatening."

Irene looked aghast, as expected. "That's a terrible thing to say about your dear cousins! They love you!"

Lacey put an arm around her mother's shoulder and gently nudged her out of the way of the refrigerator. She grabbed an apple and a hard-boiled egg.

"You want anything?" she asked.

"That's all you're eating?" Irene asked, aghast expression renewed. She shook her head and grabbed a cup of freshly brewed coffee.

"I had a big breakfast," Lacey lied.

"You want some coffee with that?" her mother asked.

"That stuff?" Lacey asked. "No thanks."

"You're being so rude. What's gotten into you?"

Wish I knew, Lacey thought. "Sorry, Ma," she said.

They moved to the kitchen table, taking seats opposite each other. Her mother sat where Nathan had, just thirty-one hours earlier.

Lacey peeled the egg, placing the shell parts in the dish towel. She picked up the thread of Aunt Sue and her three cousins.

"Look, Ma, you know I love them all. We used to be pretty close. I just think they haven't figured out how to deal with me yet. With my situation, I mean."

"They should be sympathetic to your situation." Her mother dumped three packets of Splenda into her already sickeningly sweet coffee. Lacey wondered if Splenda ever went bad. She never touched the stuff, but she kept an ample supply on hand for these pop-ins.

"I'm sure they are," Lacey said. "But a young, childless widow is threatening enough. Add a cuckold to the mix, and I think it's all a little too close to their deepest fears." Lacey added a dash of Crystal hot sauce to the two halves of her egg.

"You're not a cuckold," her mother corrected. "A cuckold's a man. Fox would have been a cuckold if you had cheated on him."

"Really, Ma? That's what you've got for me?"

Her mother smiled, as sweet as the coffee in her cup. "Oh, La, in some ways I think you are your own worst enemy. And that only gets worse the more time you spend alone. Are you sure you don't need me to move back in?"

The script had circled back into familiar territory.

Lacey aimed her voice toward the living room. "Pops! Ma's threatening to move back in!"

"Get in here, both of you," Joe Campo hollered. He had a way of yelling without either elevating the volume or changing the inflection of his words. But you would still know it was yelling.

Lacey popped the second half of the egg in her mouth as she got up to humor her father. She and Irene smiled at each other, each of them thinking the same thing: *You're in trouble now.*

They stood together in the archway between the kitchen and the living room. Lacey and her father shared a sly smile. Ambrose was content at Joe's feet.

"Ree," he addressed his wife without taking his eyes from the TV, "I told you I'd divorce you if you didn't leave this girl alone and come back to take care of me. I still mean it."

"You'd never divorce me. You'd flounder without me around!" Irene returned.

"Exactly. That's why you can't stay with Lacey." He gave Lacey a wink. She rolled her eyes in response.

"Is that all?" Irene said.

"Yep."

Lacey and her mom returned to the table.

"Oh!" Irene looked as if she had just remembered she'd won the lottery and forgotten to tell anyone. "I actually *spoke* to your brother a few days ago. No emails, no messages!"

"Really?" Lacey decided not to mention that she had just talked to him.

"And, he actually told me about a girl he's been seeing, no prompting!"

Lacey raised her eyebrows. She was a little surprised that Jimmy had not said anything to her. But he was infamous for feeding their mother red herring.

"He said she has a good job, and doesn't seem to mind him going out on the road, and is very down-to-earth and not too California flaky. Has he said anything to you about her?"

Lacey's interest was piqued. This sounded like more than Jimmy just throwing Irene a bone.

She covered with more off-script dialogue. "No, but I'm not surprised. If he really likes her, he might not want to tell me about her yet. Because I can't be happy for other people who are happy."

Her mother's face fell. "Criminy, Lacey. Is that true?"

Lacey laughed. "Look at your face! No, Ma, it's not true. Listen," Lacey continued, "it's just that Jimmy has been really good about checking up on me, and I've been really good at dumping on him. That's been the tenor of our recent conversations. I can see how this might not have come up."

"Well," her mother continued, "I have to admit it has me mighty curious."

Lacey left after a half hour. Her parents were still there—

her father wanted to finish the movie—but she knew they'd be gone by the time she got home from work. The Silver Slipper Casino was calling out to them.

As annoying as their unannounced visits were, Lacey felt this one had been particularly well timed. It was the first time since the incident that Nathan, and the mystery of whatever had happened, had not occupied one hundred percent of her thoughts. The reprieve had lasted only moments, but she was still grateful for it.

When Lacey returned to the office, it took her more than an hour to complete another set of statements for Trip's properties. She was grateful for that, too. It was close to three p.m. before she found herself wandering the office again in a daze.

Screw it, she thought. *It's late enough, and Trip's not coming. Time to be productive.*

She sat at her desk, grabbed her phone from her purse, and had every intention of seeking new employment. But the specificity of her intended search made her think of something. Something about narrowing parameters for better results. Maybe it was because her brain and her fingers weren't communicating well, but instead of typing "production accounting California," she typed "Louisiana healers." And some light permeated the rabbit hole.

Amongst the results for voodoo practitioners and more psychics, she found a series of stories about a woman in Galliano, purported to be some sort of Cajun faith healer, or *traiteur* in the local dialect. Her name was Emmaline Bergeron, and she had died nearly twenty years ago. But Fox, and Fox's father, and all his aunts and uncles were from Galliano. Suddenly, tomorrow night's dinner with Tonti didn't seem so burdensome. She could ask Tonti about Emmaline Bergeron.

She would have to mention it casually, so as to not arouse any suspicion. That wouldn't be difficult—the challenge would be finding space to ask the question. Tonti talked a mile a minute.

Lacey read on about prayers for curing warts and healing hernias. Some accounts claimed the traiteur's abilities passed between generations from female to male to female and so on. That detail piqued Lacey's interest, though she couldn't explain why. She couldn't find any stories about Emmaline Bergeron waking up naked with amnesia or saving someone from the brink of death. But she figured healing was healing. It was a start.

9

Lacey padded around the house barefoot in a white sundress. Her resolve from the day before had dissipated. She was back to dreading dinner with Tonti. She thought of all the excuses she could give Tonti to get out of dinner. *My parents just came into town.* Believable, but Tonti knew them too well to believe that they would keep her from a prior engagement. *My brother just came into town.* Not believable, and Lacey didn't want to jinx his upcoming trip by lying about it.

She was worked up, and very hot. She held her wrist to her forehead. *Do I have a fever?* That would be a legitimate excuse. Lacey smiled in spite of her anxiety when she saw a car she didn't recognize pull up to the front of the house. Tonti was a drinker and not afraid to use a car service.

She gritted her teeth, grabbed Ambrose's head with both hands, and said, "Wish me luck, Bro!"

"Woof."

She slipped on her shoes, grabbed her clutch, and headed out the front door.

Tonti wore a regal expression in the backseat of the white

car. Evangeline Richard Becnel Schmidt was the only one of the eight Becnel children, a generation past, to leave bayou country. Her husband had risen through the ranks at Shell, and they had settled into a grand house in Lake Vista over twenty-five years ago. She had been a steady presence in Lacey and Fox's life together.

Lacey had always figured Tonti would be the perfect stand-in grandmother whenever she and Fox had children. Ever since Fox had died, Lacey felt a pang of guilt, right at the base of her throat, every time she saw Tonti.

She touched her neck as she opened the door.

"Look at us!" Tonti exclaimed. "We look like night and day. With matching feet!" Tonti held out her foot, and Lacey saw that they were wearing the same pair of silver sandals. Tonti wore an explosion of black and silver sequins and flowing layers, contrasting with Lacey's simple, A-line dress.

Lacey settled in. "Uncle John isn't coming?" she asked.

"Nope! We've got a girl's night!"

Tonti reached down toward an ice bucket nestled on the floor of the car, pulled out two plastic cups, and uncapped an unmarked container full of a fizzy-looking liquid. Lacey's eyes widened, and she looked at the back of the driver's head.

"Child, you have always been so afraid of the world biting you!" Tonti said. "I saw it the moment Fox brought you to us. I suppose once bitten, twice shy. We'll have to fix that."

She handed one of the cups to Lacey. "Fleurtinis: champagne, vodka, and pineapple juice. And don't worry, Hines is my go-to driver and knows I won't make a mess." She waved her free hand at the driver.

"Miss Evangeline's cool," Hines said. He smiled at Lacey from the rearview mirror.

"When's the last time you had a girl's night?" Tonti asked Lacey.

The fated events of the weekend loomed in Lacey's mind. She tried to appear nonchalant.

"Just this past weekend," she answered. "You remember my friend Angele? She's been in town working on a movie. I went out with her and her coworkers."

"The little Asian girl, right?" Tonti asked. "Your maid of honor."

"Right," Lacey said, avoiding Tonti's gaze. Fox's entire family, excepting those who still used the term "Oriental," referred to Angele as "that little Asian girl" or "your little Asian friend."

Tonti reached into the bucket and grabbed a piece of ice. "And those movie people," she said. "Were they fun? Did you dance with anyone new and interesting?"

Tonti held the ice to the back of her neck. Lacey wanted to pour the contents of the entire bucket over her own head.

"I didn't really talk to them much," she said. "Mostly it was just Angele and me out on the back patio. Patton's isn't really a dancing kind of place."

Tonti clucked. "Child, that isn't going to get you anywhere. You should broaden your social circle. You need a night of dancing and commotion 'til you walk out and the sun hits you in the face."

Lacey shook her head, holding on to her full drink. "Truly, Tonti. I think that's the last thing I need." Lacey thought of countless evenings with Fox. Too many memories tied up in places all around the city. "At least, not here," Lacey added.

Tonti looked at her sideways. "Are you thinking of not being here?"

Lacey took a deep breath. "Maybe. But not permanently. Maybe just taking some temporary work that gets me in a new place, a new environment, for a little while."

"Child, I *love* that idea," Tonti said.

"Really? I was a little worried you'd try to discourage me from leaving the city."

Tonti let out a long sigh. For an instant she was unrecognizable, as if she'd lifted a mask from her face. "Child, you are too young to be living the recluse life you have been. You have no exposure in your job, no social circle to speak of. You are going to come to flower and no one will see it. I can think of no better time than now to consider making a change." Tonti swallowed the remaining drink in her cup, and the mask returned.

Lacey stared out the window. What did she mean by flower? Was that what was happening to her? She watched houses pass from the car window, searching for a response that did not involve divulging the incident.

"Angele said she could probably get me in on a movie," Lacey said finally, her voice barely above a whisper. "It would be work that would just go for a few months at a time."

"Oh, how fabulous would that be?" Tonti said. "You could have a whirlwind fling with some arty type, work out some of your kinks, and come back here ready to get on with your life."

Lacey shook her head. "Geesh, Tonti."

"What, child?"

Lacey gave a half smile. "It's a tad awkward to hear my husband's aunt talk about me having a fling and 'working out my kinks.'"

"Your *husband's* aunt?" Tonti asked, aghast. "I became *your* aunt the moment you became Mrs. Marion Fauché Becnel Jr.

You could become Mrs. Husbands Two, Three, and Four if you want, but I'll always be your aunt. 'Til death do *us* part," she added.

Lacey thought of her Aunt Sue, her aunt by blood. She did not engender the same style of big, unconditional love as Tonti.

"Thank you, Tonti," Lacey said, eyes forward. "That means a lot to me, and I know you mean it."

"Of course, child. Why would I say something like that if I didn't mean it?" Tonti put her arm around Lacey's shoulder and relieved Lacey of the pressure of speaking for the rest of the car ride. Lacey got a full update on Tonti's son Jack and his girlfriend. Tonti enumerated all the reasons she wasn't convinced she was the right match for Jack.

Lacey felt a new sympathy for the girl, Amanda. She had met her a few times, when her head had still been stuck in her grief cul-de-sac. She marveled at how Tonti could be so accepting of herself, but so standoffish with her son's girlfriend. She resolved to be more welcoming the next time she saw Amanda.

When they reached the corner of Iberville and Telemachus, Lacey's drink was still three-quarters full. Tonti rattled around the ice left in her cup, and shoved the nearly empty container into the ice bucket.

"Here, child, give me yours." She held her hand out to Lacey.

She clucked when she saw how much was left. "That's shameful!" She thrust the cup back at Lacey. "Drink some more before we have to waste it. I think it's déclassé to take it into the restaurant."

But it's classy to drink out of a red Solo cup in the back of a car? Lacey thought.

"Really, Tonti," she said. "I don't want any more. I'll have something to drink with dinner."

"Of course you will." Tonti held on to Lacey's cup as she stepped out onto the curb. Hines held the door open for her.

Without looking, Lacey opened her door out onto the street side and nearly hit a car, a taxi, parked alongside. She shimmied out and plastered herself against the side of Hines' car. The driver of the double-parked cab glared at her.

Someone was struggling to open the rear door. Lacey glanced down and saw a wizened woman, tiny and frail, in the back seat.

"Don't just stand there, give the lady a hand!" the driver barked at Lacey.

Lacey held her hand to her neck and pointed at herself.

"You're the only one standing in the street, doll!"

Who is this guy? she thought. *East Coast transplant?*

Lacey stepped toward the door, now open a hairsbreadth. She pulled it open, leaned in, and introduced herself. "Hello, I'm Lacey. May I give you a hand?"

The old woman narrowed her eyes. Her shriveled mouth frowned, but she still accepted Lacey's outstretched arm. She stood and straightened to the best of her ability, supporting her ninety pounds on Lacey's forearm.

"Have fun, Miss Esther Mae!" the bossy and unhelpful driver called out. "I'll be back 'round in a few hours."

The woman's face transformed into childlike joy as she turned and nodded at the driver. When she turned her head back toward Lacey, it shriveled back into a small, annoyed grimace.

How does that dickwad get a nice smile, and I get this face? Lacey thought.

She escorted Miss Esther Mae toward the curb. Dickwad driver sped off down Iberville. Lacey felt the breeze of his wake, and the old lady wavered from it.

Once, about a month after Fox had died, when she hadn't been able to do much but stare out the front windows, Lacey had watched a snail traverse the entire expanse of her front porch. That snail would have already finished his dinner and been on his way home in the time it was taking Miss Esther Mae to move.

Tonti stood on the corner, outside the door, and sipped Lacey's drink. She beamed. "Talk about being in the right place at the right time!" she called to Lacey.

Lacey shrugged her shoulders. She didn't feel right. She felt the torturous weight of un-appreciation on her arm anchored by a cold claw. It was the only cool spot on her body. She was consumed by heat, and broke out into a full-body sweat in the ninety-five-degree heat.

Lacey wondered what she was supposed to do with the woman once inside Katie's. At their rate, it might be tomorrow before they made it.

One eternally long minute later, a drenched Lacey helped the woman up the step. Tonti held the door open. A host rushed up from the back of the restaurant and grabbed the woman from Lacey's arm.

"Miss Esther Mae!" the young woman with a backless blouse exclaimed. "Your friends are all here; we have your table set up."

Before Miss Esther Mae let go of Lacey, she turned to her and smiled. Lacey saw a glimpse of the woman she might have been forty years earlier: bright green eyes and a closed-lipped smile. In a voice that sounded much younger than she looked,

Miss Esther Mae said, "Thank you, Lacey. You have done me a wonderful service."

Lacey reached for the only thing she could muster, a rote reply. "Oh!" she coughed out in hoarse tones. "My pleasure. Any time."

Miss Esther Mae left her, holding the host's arm. She appeared sturdier, and speedier, than just moments before.

Lacey and Tonti stood at the host stand, mute. Lacey finally broke the silence.

"Well, that was weird. Why am I so hot?" She fanned at herself with her clutch. She looked down and saw sweat stains along the sides of her white dress.

Tonti was still holding the plastic cup. "Here, drink, you'll feel better."

This time, Lacey didn't hesitate and gulped down the rest of the drink.

"Tonti, I'll be right back. I'll meet you at the table."

Lacey didn't wait for a reply and ran to the bathroom.

The water came out of the tap lukewarm. She cupped her hands and splashed her face, and a cloud of steam fogged the mirror in front of her. She grabbed a paper towel from a faux-brass caddy to the right of the sink and wiped clear an oval in the glass. Her face, neck, and shoulders were bright red. "Jesus. What is wrong with me?"

I'm too young for hot flashes, she thought. She reached for another paper towel, wanting to fix her smeared mascara. In her peripheral vision she saw a small, orange flame growing exponentially in the caddy.

"Jesus!" Lacey said. She cupped her hands again and aimed as much water as they could hold at the fire. The resulting splash made a slapping sound against the wall. She dumped the contents of the caddy in the sink and ran water over them. A corner of one towel still smoldered, a small line of smoke trailing up to her nose. An acrid smell spread through the restroom.

Disaster averted, Lacey thought. She ran water over her fingers, afraid to touch anything else. She gripped the cool porcelain lip of the sink, and stared in the mirror.

"What the fuck is happening to me?" she said aloud.

A toilet flushed.

Oh fuck! she thought. *Pay attention.* She hadn't even thought to scope the bathroom first. She looked for a place to hide, but the only other stall was locked from the inside, an OUT OF ORDER sign issuing a highly personal taunt.

Just like me, she thought.

The woman who emerged from the stall looked familiar. Well-dressed, surgically altered, with spiny limbs and a protruding mandible that reminded Lacey of an insect.

She was someone's mother, someone from college.

She gave Lacey the elevator eyes. They finally settled on the paper towel caddy.

"Sorry," Lacey said, averting her gaze. She scooped up the sopping mess of paper and dropped it in the trash, and replaced the caddy in its original spot.

"I saw a roach," Lacey continued, ducking into the stall. "I'll fix everything when I get out."

She closed her eyes and remained motionless, standing over the toilet, until she heard Praying Mantis Mom leave. Her thoughts raced: Who was she, why did she look so familiar?

Doesn't matter. Pull yourself together first. Save the rest for later. Lacey unzipped her dress, careful to touch only the metal of the zipper, not the fabric. She let it fall into the crook of her arm, and welcomed the air circulating over her bare skin.

The lining of the dress caught her eye. The entire line of the zipper track looked scorched.

Maybe her eyes were playing a trick; the lighting was poor in the bathroom. Or maybe it had happened at the dry cleaners. She stood for a full minute, trying to empty her mind.

Lacey held her fingertips to her neck. Still warm, but they didn't feel like they'd catch anything on fire. She zipped up the dress and peeked out the stall to make sure the bathroom was still empty. She examined her appearance. There were no signs of damage on the outside of the dress, save the sweat stains. And as long as she kept her arms down, they were hard to see.

She grabbed some toilet paper and dabbed at her face. She still looked like she had just returned from a ten-mile run. She attempted to dry the wet wall with more toilet paper, with little success. *Will Tonti let me go home if I tell her I'm having a psychotic break?* she asked herself as she left the restroom.

Lacey was preparing her excuse when she saw Praying Mantis Mom standing over Tonti's table.

Fuck.

"Lacey!" Tonti said, her expression unreadable. "You know Dotty Trebuchet, don't you? Matt's mom? Didn't you and Fox know him at LSU?"

That was it. Matt Trebuchet was a fraternity brother of Fox's. Someone who was always a little too good for the likes of a boy from the bayou, much less a girl from Metairie.

"Oh, Lacey!" Dotty Trebuchet said. "I didn't recognize you! Did you find that creepy crawler? You should let the manager know."

No sign of elevator eyes this time.

"Oh, I sure should," Lacey said. "I had a little run-in in the bathroom," she explained to Tonti.

"Everything okay?" Tonti asked. Her eyes were saying something more.

No, I'm pretty fucking far from okay, Lacey thought. And she felt worse now that Praying Mantis had stolen her opportunity for a quick getaway.

"Yes, all good now," Lacey mustered.

Dotty Trebuchet perched over Lacey's chair. Lacey stood against the wall, her arms tight against her sides.

"I was just telling your aunt about the twins!" she said to Lacey.

Lacey attempted her most genuine fake face and said, "Oh my goodness, I didn't realize Matt had twins! How old are they now?"

Dotty Trebuchet proceeded to say many things about her grandchildren, including how old they were, but Lacey didn't retain any of it. Outside, a chorus of cicadas heralded the evening.

The chorus quieted, and Dotty Trebuchet looked at the Rolex on her bony wrist.

"Oh my goodness, I've abandoned my dinner party. Okay, Evangeline, I'll call to get that happy hour set up. We're overdue!"

"Oh, yes, too long overdue," Tonti answered. "Wonderful to see you, Dotty."

Dotty Trebuchet disappeared to the back of the restaurant, and Lacey grabbed her seat as soon as she had flittered off.

"Well, crap," Tonti said.

Lacey looked down along the sides of her dress. "What?" She sipped from her water glass.

"Looks like I have an *un*happy hour in my future," she said under her breath.

Tonti's choice of words triggered a spit-take from Lacey, and she felt her overloaded throttle finally ease up. Still laughing, she asked, "If you don't like her, Tonti, why do you hang out with her?"

"Child, you already know that being part of the world means sometimes having to entertain people you might otherwise choose not to. You can't expand your horizons being comfortable."

A server appeared with two glasses and a bottle of something bubbly.

"Oh, grand!" Tonti said. "I took the liberty of ordering this splendid prosecco."

Lacey took a deep breath.

"Forgive me, child, but you look like you could use it."

Lacey nodded. She felt marginally cooler. "Tonti, about"—Lacey motioned her head toward the rear of the restaurant and Ms. Praying Mantis Dotty—"well, once you reach a certain age, and a certain station, do you really have to entertain people you don't like?"

"A certain age, eh?" Tonti said, laughing.

"I didn't mean… I just, you know…"

"Don't fret, I know what you meant," Tonti said. "What I meant was this: an oyster needs an irritant to produce a pearl. Everything is connected in duality."

Lacey looked up from the menu, eyebrows raised, mouth gaping.

"Too many good things to choose from on the menu?" Tonti asked.

Lacey shook her head. "Tonti, maybe I have a fever or something, but you're just not making any sense to me."

"What's there to comprehend?" Tonti sipped her prosecco.

"Me and you, at dinner. You and the stately elderly lady. Me and Dotty. You and the menu. All dualities. Conjugates."

"Conjugates?" Lacey wiped a bead of sweat from her forehead.

"It's nothing. Just read the menu, child, make a choice. Produce a pearl."

"Fine, I'll have a salad. I need something cool. Maybe I'm having a hot flash."

"You're too young for hot flashes," Tonti said.

"My thoughts exactly." Lacey rubbed at her eyes.

Tonti motioned their server. "Your elderly friend looks like a different person," Tonti said, changing the subject. "Twenty years younger than she looked crossing the street with you."

Lacey turned her head toward Miss Esther Mae. She sat at a table of eight women, including Dotty Trebuchet. Lacey tried to imagine a scenario in which someone like her would find herself at such a mixed table, of both age and race. She came up short, and didn't feel like asking Tonti for fear of more confusing conjugate pearlspeak.

"I don't know," Lacey said. "She still looks pretty old to me."

"She's much more animated," Tonti said. "She must have gotten a shot of energy from somewhere." Tonti gave Lacey a pointed look and then launched into a full accounting and update on her younger son, Greg. And then an in-depth preview of her and Uncle John's upcoming trip to Brazil.

The rest of the dinner passed without any more meaningful glances or cryptic mentions, and Lacey was nearly overwhelmed by the tidal force of Tonti's verbiage. In an evening full of surprise encounters, Lacey was grateful for the familiarity of Tonti's chattiness. She had not forgotten about Emmaline Bergeron, but struggled to find the right opportunity to mention her. It didn't come until the ride back to Lakeview.

In the back seat of Hines' car, Tonti said, "You're being awfully quiet, child."

Lacey laughed. It was the first time Tonti had quit talking in the last hour and a half.

"Just thinking about something I read recently, Tonti. Something about Galliano."

"Oh, splendid. Do tell. Was it about the Becnels' long and enduring legacy?"

Lacey laughed again. She couldn't tell if Tonti was being sarcastic or sincere. "No, it was about a woman, some kind of faith healer."

Tonti's expression changed. She looked more serious, but her tone was nonchalant. "Hmm. What was her name?"

"Emmaline Bergeron."

The seriousness disappeared. "Never heard of her. You've got to be careful of what—and who—you read when it comes to there."

There being Galliano, Lacey assumed.

Before Lacey could offer anything more, Tonti went on about "country folk" in a way that did not sound complimentary, and also how Lacey should be mindful about which healers were sanctioned by the Catholic Church, and which were not, and how this woman must not have been Catholic because Tonti would have heard of her if she was.

Lacey labored to interject. "So, that's a thing?" she managed.

"Is what a thing, child?"

"Healers. Down there…in Galliano."

"Well, of course, child. And not just in Galliano. Everywhere. Were you not raised as a Christian?"

"Well, yes, but…"

"But nothing," Tonti continued before Lacey could qualify. "If you truly believe everything you've been taught, believe it in your heart, then you accept it as an article of faith that there are people put on this Earth with the power to heal."

Lacey stared at Tonti. She waited for the next words to come out of her mouth.

"Don't you think?" Tonti said in response to Lacey's stare.

Lacey couldn't form a response. She didn't know how to subtly declare that she'd woken up stark naked next to a man whose life she might have saved, and ask whether that was something Jesus had intended. Instead she said under her breath, "I'm not sure what I believe since Fox died."

It might have been the boldest thing she'd ever said to Tonti.

Tonti grabbed Lacey's hand. "I don't believe you, child. You know as well as I do that your faith—your faith in a greater good, never mind the particulars—has sustained you this last year. I don't want to hear you using Fox as an excuse to turn agnostic."

"It's not that," Lacey stammered. She thought of the strange and unexpected events of the past weekend, and realized, for the first time, how much they underscored how alone she truly was. She thought long and hard before she spoke again.

"I don't think I'm ready for life without Fox yet," she finally said.

Tonti tightened her grip on Lacey's hand. The look in her eyes was something like stern sympathy. Without her singsong cadence, Tonti said, "Child, ready or not, it's time. Fox's part in your life is over. You know I loved that boy, but Lord, did he have both God and the Devil in him. But God always wins.

And I *know*—truer than anything—that the very best part of him loved you like no other. There was a reason he brought you to us, and I have a feeling you're about to find out why."

A thousand questions rushed to the front of Lacey's brain just as they pulled onto Florida Boulevard.

"Oh my, I *am* tired!" Tonti said with a lengthy yawn. "Go on, child, scoot. I will call you this week."

Hines opened the door for Lacey. She looked back at Tonti. Her eyes were closed.

She shuffled out of Hines' car, mumbled a thank you, and stood mute on her sidewalk, watching the red taillights turn the corner toward Lake Vista.

10

"And what the fuck was all that talk about oysters and dualities?" Angele asked.

Lacey sat at her desk, phone to her ear. She was alone in the office—again. Trip hadn't even called or emailed.

"How the hell do I know?" Lacey replied. "This is why I told you, to help me figure it out."

Lacey had spent the past sixteen hours stewing over the events of her dinner, and especially Tonti's parting words. She had parsed out the story to Angele as best she could, over texts and staccato phone calls peppered throughout the day. This was the first opportunity Angele had to give her more than two minutes.

"I've been thinking," Angele said. "Didn't you say Fox's grandmother was crazy? Big Fox's mother?"

"I'm sure I've never said she was crazy," Lacey said, standing. "But from everything I've ever heard, it sounds like she suffered from bad depression, or was bipolar or something. What are you getting at?" She walked to the picture window. The Wednesday river traffic had been uninspiring.

"I don't know. Maybe the grandmother suffered from fugue

states, and somehow or other it got passed to you," Angele said. "And it was all like a plot," she continued, her voice elevating. "They knew the curse had to pass on to someone, and they set you up for it."

The thought of a protracted conversation with her best friend suddenly seemed less appealing to Lacey.

"Nice," she replied. "Look, the Becnels are far from perfect, but I really don't think they made me a patsy for some ancient family curse."

"Are you sure about that?" Angele asked, unwilling to let it go. "They didn't have any problem unleashing Fox on you."

Lacey rolled her eyes. Angele's timeworn distaste for Fox had not softened since his death. If anything, it had worsened once her suspicions had been proven right.

She blew out a breath. The phone vibrated in her ear, either an email or text coming through. "Look," Lacey said, "what if this thing's not a curse? What if it's a blessing?"

Angele ignored her. "What about that Creole healer lady? Maybe this is a regional affliction, and you picked it up like a virus on one of those ridiculous trips to Galliano."

"Like Lyme disease?" Lacey said. "I don't think so. And Fox didn't…never mind." Lacey stopped herself from defending Fox's penchant for Sunday drives. There was no reason to anymore.

"But I think there might be something to that woman, the healer," Lacey continued. "Even though Tonti was pretty dismissive of her. But not of healers in general…"

Suddenly intensely curious about the unread message she held to her ear, Lacey said, "Hey, think on this some more and get back to me. I have to go. How were your folks on Sunday?" Their shorthand meant neither needed to announce an abrupt change in subject or tempo.

"Good. Dad had a bug or something, so he stayed home while Mom and I went out," Angele answered.

"Is he better now?" Lacey asked.

"I think so. Just a twenty-four-hour thing, I think."

"You know my folks pulled a stop-by a few days ago," Lacey said. "They were there when I went home for lunch."

"I don't know how you tolerate that."

"I'm sure you don't," Lacey said. "I'll ping you later. Bye." She shook her head and checked her phone for the message that had buzzed her ear. A text: I NEED TO SEE YOU—NATHAN.

An instant knot formed in the pit of her stomach and tightened. Lacey stared at her phone. All the anxiety from the weekend returned and washed over her like the wake from an ocean liner. *Why does he need to see me? Should I ignore it? What if I have to go meet him?*

She gave a thought to what she was wearing for the first time since she'd dressed that morning and suddenly regretted her choice. Her pants were a little too tight, her blouse a little too sheer. It hadn't mattered in the office, which Trip kept at a frigid temperature—she wore a blazer that covered all her curves.

WHY? She finally texted back.

Several minutes passed. She built multiple scenarios in her head—she would go home and change clothes before meeting him, or she would keep her jacket on but melt, or she would try to postpone the meeting altogether.

The reply finally came: PLEASE. ITS IMPORTANT MEET ME AT REDDS ON MAPLE. 20 MINTUES.

The errors annoyed her. Why didn't he use autocorrect? She checked the time. It was late enough to close down for the day.

For precisely fifty seconds, she considered not going. In the other eleven minutes that passed before she finally locked the office door behind her, she looked up Redd's Uptilly Tavern on Maple Street to make sure she knew where it was, and then spent too long in the bathroom trying to adjust her appearance.

Less than five minutes later she was sitting in her car, outside the bar, nearly paralyzed. It was a lazy mid-June afternoon in New Orleans. Most of the students from Tulane and Loyola, right down the street, were gone for the summer. The rest of the city were probably away on their annual Gulf Coast vacation.

She stared at her phone again. It had not yet been twenty minutes since Nathan had sent his text. In no reality—real, mutant, fugue, or otherwise—would she walk into their meeting place earlier than anticipated.

The door to Redd's was closed and the sidewalk outside was quiet. The bar across the street from it seemed much busier. She wondered about Nathan's choice of venue. On one hand, a quiet place would allow for some privacy. On the other, the thought of being alone with him scared the hell out of her.

She couldn't put it off any longer. She checked herself in the rearview mirror, dropped her phone in her purse, and stepped out of the car. She left her blazer on the passenger seat.

Lacey walked in and instantly recognized the place. It had been more than seven years since she'd been in there, and it used to be called something else, but she knew it. She and Fox had gone there a handful of times in their adjustment period from young, single students to young, married semiprofessionals.

There was no sign of Nathan. Some grizzled men played pool; another group of slightly less grizzled men drank at the far end of the bar.

She stood near an empty booth and tried to look inconspicuous. She was plotting her escape when the bartender called out to her.

"C'mon over! I have a drink ready for you."

Without thinking, Lacey looked his way, and he gave her a crooked smile marked with dimples on either side. She wanted to pretend she hadn't heard him, but it was too late. She couldn't help but smile when he gestured toward the old men at the other end of the bar and mouthed the words, "Help me."

He was adorable, a grown-up baby with a mop of blond hair. Lacey moved to the empty end of the bar, and he smiled again. His dimples were almost too obvious.

He leaned toward her and said in a low voice, "It's been dead in here—the only customers in my last five shifts have been these good ole boys."

"They don't seem so bad. Doesn't seem like you have to break up many fights," Lacey said.

"Yeah, but I get to see them all the time, and not all their faces combined can come up with one half as pretty as yours."

Lacey rolled her eyes. She could tell two things about him: he was not from New Orleans—his accent sounded more Mississippi than anything—and he had that type of charm that put her instantly on edge. It was too much like Fox's.

"What'll you have?" he asked.

"I thought you said you had a drink ready for me?" she replied, pleased with her witty retort.

"I do! Fifteen seconds from now," Mississippi Charmer said.

He swept his hand above the bar in a grand gesture and said, "All you have to do is pick your poison."

"Fifteen seconds, huh?" Lacey was unimpressed. "How about an old-fashioned?" The drink was the only one she could think of that might take longer to concoct. She didn't time him, but she did find a drink before her in very short order. "You skimped a bit on the orange twist," she told him as she sipped. It was very strong.

"Oh, c'mon! That is a beautiful drink, if I do say so myself. Delivered in fifteen seconds."

"If you say so."

The good ole boys were trying to get his attention down the bar. "I think you're wanted," Lacey said.

"Yeah, I saw," he said. "Don't go anywhere," he said with a wink.

Lacey rolled her eyes again. She took another sip, and the alcohol went immediately to her head. *Get a grip*, she told herself.

She felt her phone vibrate in her purse. She pulled it out and saw another message from Nathan: I DINT THINK YOUD SHOW.

Lacey looked all around the bar. She typed a response, asking where he was. She triple-checked to make sure her message didn't have any spelling or punctuation errors.

An eternity passed while she waited for his response. She felt alone, exposed, and on the verge of a bad decision. She took another sip. Finally, her phone pinged: WAIT 2 MORE MINTS AND WALK TO BATHROOM.

Two minutes. What on earth for? She ignored his directive. She got up, drink in hand, and walked toward the ladies' room. She faced the door marked WOMEN and heard a voice behind her.

"Do you always bring your drink with you to the restroom?"

Nathan was sitting in a back office, inches away from where she stood. They were separated only by a halfway closed door. She pivoted on her heel, and before she knew what was happening, a firm hand clasped her by the wrist and pulled her into the office. The door shut behind her.

She found herself nose to neck with Nathan. He held tight to her wrist and braced his other arm behind her head, against the door. The ice in her drink clinked as her hand shook.

Whatever scent Nathan wore, she wished he didn't. It was all male, and it reminded her of Fox. An acute emotion pierced her. "Please let go of me," Lacey said.

Nathan released her, and stepped back as much as the cramped office would allow. Lacey was afraid to look him in the eye. When she willed herself to bring her chin up, she was surprised by the look of profound sadness on his face.

She folded her free arm across her chest and braced herself against the door. "You scared the shit out of me! Why would you grab hold of me like that?"

"I'm sorry. I didn't want anyone to see us talking. I'm sorry I scared you," he said. He sounded genuine.

"Some manners," Lacey said.

"Given the nature of our acquaintance thus far, I didn't think we needed to stand on ceremony. A thousand pardons, ma'am."

"Now you're just being a shit." Lacey's hand still shook.

Nathan's expression changed. He looked at Lacey with an intensity that made her feel like she was getting an MRI.

Lacey cocked her head at him and asked, "So, what is so urgent?"

"You mean other than narrowly escaping death a mere seventy-two hours ago?"

Lacey focused on a wall calendar behind Nathan's head. A Saintsation cheerleader heralded the month of April. She fought the urge to reach out and turn it to June.

"I would think on the other side of it, the sense of urgency would fade somewhat," she said, trying to sound steely.

"Not when you think your family might be in danger."

Lacey felt the knot in her stomach reappear at the mention of his family. She softened. "What do you mean?"

"I've been stuck in this vicious loop, ever since you dropped me off Sunday morning," Nathan said. He palmed the back of a rolling desk chair and sat. "Playing over everything that happened, everything I can remember, in my head. I think those guys were waiting for me when I turned the corner off Harrison."

Lacey nodded, remembering the conversation at her kitchen table. She knew Nathan had left something out.

"I guess I suspected something like that all along," he said. "But it seems too implausible. I know you have no reason—no basis—to believe me, but I'm not a trouble kind of guy. I have no idea why they would have been after me."

Her back against the door, still in a defensive posture, Lacey considered their close quarters in the back room of an Uptown bar and thought she'd never encountered more trouble than Nathan…What's-his-name.

"What's your last name?" the words escaped her lips before her brain could stop them.

"Huh?"

"Sorry. I was thinking how you're right—I have no basis to trust you. I don't even know your last name."

"It's Quirk. Nathan Quirk."

"Okay," Lacey replied. "That's a start." Her hand finally quit shaking. Lacey changed her focus to the cramped and tiny desk to Nathan's left. She tried to make out the total on a liquor invoice. An awkward silence grew.

"What did your wife say when she saw you?" Lacey asked. His face still bore the evidence of the weekend's events.

"Nothing."

Lacey raised her eyebrows.

Nathan shrugged. "That right there was about all she gave me, but more apathetic. She never asked. When the kids did, the story was that I fell."

"She didn't want to know?" Lacey already regretted the question when it was halfway out of her mouth. The less she knew about his relationship with his wife, the better.

"I don't know what's going through her head," Nathan said. "Her father is a different story."

"Her father?" Lacey asked, her eyes still focused on the invoice, but her mind elsewhere.

"Yeah. He's my boss."

"Oh. That can get…sticky." Her sense of trouble grew.

"He got one look at my face, practically sneered, and told me not to meet with any clients until I healed up." Nathan returned his gaze to Lacey.

"Well, that's awkward." She didn't know what else to say. She shifted her focus from the invoice to an outdated work schedule pinned on an ancient, crumbling corkboard above Nathan's head.

"Look." Nathan snapped out of some reverie. "I don't think I'm going to go to the police. But if I do, I wanted to be sure you would be on board with that."

Lacey finally looked at Nathan. "Yeah, of course," she said. "But I don't really see how I have much to do with it. I know less about what happened to you than you do."

Nathan rolled back a few inches in the chair and folded his arms. "I don't know what you told your boyfriend about what happened," he said. "He obviously wasn't home that night, and I don't know if you even mentioned anything about it to him."

"Nathan, what the hell are you talking about?"

"If the police came knocking at your door asking about it, I just wanted to be sure it wouldn't put you in a spot."

Lacey shook her head, resisting the urge to fling the door open and run away. "I don't have a boyfriend," she said. After a beat, she added, "And why wouldn't you go to the police? If you think your family needs protection?"

"I'm trying to figure this out." He stood, slowly. "And I'm trying to keep it contained. It might only get worse if I went to the police. Something tells me the less anyone knows about whatever happened, the better."

Lacey felt a pang of guilt about telling Angele. She masked it. "Look, I'm the one who woke up naked underneath the 610, next to a fully clothed stranger. I'm not looking to publicize this whole thing either."

Nathan's gaze returned to X-ray mode. "I figured that about you." He lightened. "If you don't have a boyfriend, then who was the guy in all those pictures at your house? Don't tell me he's your brother, because that would just be weird."

Agitated, Lacey fumbled about, wanting to put her drink down. Her hand was numb. "What the hell are you talking about?" She took a mental inventory of the pictures in her living room.

Nathan took her drink from her.

"There's a few pictures of my brother, I guess," she said, "but if you're referring to who I think you are, there aren't *lots* of pictures. I took down most of them."

"Whoa. Then what's left are very prominently placed."

Lacey struggled to put Fox out of her head. "He's not my boyfriend. Well, he was a long time ago, but he's gone. Totally out of the picture now."

"Interesting choice of words," Nathan said, eyes bright. It was the first time she'd seen him smile since he'd pulled her into the back room.

Lacey stood up straighter, still holding up the door. "I would think you have bigger things to worry about than if I'm going to get in trouble with my imaginary boyfriend."

"I can't argue that."

Lacey felt the walls closing in on her. "Nathan, why did you ask me here? It's not to get our stories straight, since you're not going to the police."

His face hardened. "I needed someone to talk to," he said finally. "I thought I might be losing it. Like maybe I had imagined everything that happened."

Lacey thought about Angele's fugue state theory, but thought better of mentioning it.

"Seeing you again has let me know that I'm not going crazy. It happened."

He took a step toward her. Lacey felt her will slipping. She realized that she had not succeeded in putting any distance between herself and the incident. Or him.

He stood in front of her, separated by less than a foot. He reached out and tucked an errant strand of hair behind her ear.

"I have to go," Lacey said in a quiet voice.

"You haven't finished your drink."

"I don't want it."

"There's something else going on here," Nathan said, his hand now planted right behind her head.

"I don't want to know. Please don't call me again."

She whirled around and shot through the door, leaving nothing but a whoosh of air in her wake.

11

Lacey arrived at Mardi Gras World at 5:47 p.m. She had spent the day trying to think of ways to get out of her commitment to stranger Cecil, and trying not to think of Nathan.

Her only option on the first would be to call the Trinity Mission and leave a message. Cecil had been wise not to provide a personal contact number. She convinced herself chickening out that way would make her irredeemably flaky.

She had no option on the second. She could not get her encounter with Nathan out of her head.

There were three other cars in the parking lot. Time crawled as she waited for it to get closer to six o'clock. *Screw it*, she thought. *Against all reason, I'm here. Might as well be early.*

Lacey checked her face in the rearview mirror, applied a little more makeup to her nose and chin, and mustered up the courage to walk in and report for duty.

She passed an impressive set-up: cocktail tables, white linens, all set under a faux starlit sky. The façade of a French Quarter street scene on the walls gave off the feel of a Parisian sidewalk. Impossibly young people, dressed in black like herself, ebbed in and out of a pocket door at the far side of the room. They seemed to multiply as she approached.

How is this shorthanded? she thought. *And where did they park?*

Lacey walked through the doorway, a stream of people flowing around her. She didn't need to look for Cecil. He stood in the center of the industrial kitchen, busy prepping something she couldn't see and voicing directions to everyone around him without looking up.

"Ah, young Lacey," he said in a stage-ready voice as he grabbed a summer squash. "You will stay here in the kitchen until you're needed otherwise. Silverware setup."

Lacey felt a hand at her elbow. A redhead with horn-rimmed glasses led her to a corner and issued precise instructions for rolling a fork and butter knife into a white cloth napkin.

Lacey was again of two minds. The first: relief that Cecil seemed on the level, and that she would spend a harmless evening performing simple, mindless tasks. The second: she might go insane spending an evening not knowing a soul and performing simple, mindless tasks.

Too much opportunity for her mind to wander. Would she know anyone attending the fundraiser? She knew Trip would not be there. But what about Nathan and his wife? It was the down time for New Orleans's social season; maybe it would draw a crowd for that reason. More relief that she would stay hidden in her corner for the foreseeable future.

Since no one from the teeming mass of black-clad youngsters introduced themselves, Lacey took up the task of applying names. The kindly redhead with the horn-rimmed glasses became the very unoriginal "Ginger." A male-female duo that she never saw apart became "Stuck on You." A young man with an intense expression, the one Cecil seemed to rely on, became "Duncan," because a man-at-arms should always be called Duncan.

Lacey invented a backstory for Cecil. He was a descendant of a voodoo priestess who had always used her powers for good. Cecil had joined the Marines on his eighteenth birthday, and was on the ground in Iraq during the first Gulf War. Or maybe some earlier skirmish. He could be forty or he could be sixty-five. It was hard to place his age. Whenever and wherever he'd served, he had earned multiple medals for saving his fellow soldiers on multiple occasions. He had never become an officer, preferring to serve in the noncommissioned ranks. He'd left the marines after ten years and returned to his ancestral home in New Orleans, where he had been quietly living his life and doing good works.

Lacey rolled her wrists and started on a fresh pile of utensils delivered in lockstep by Stuck on You. She checked the time—7:45 p.m. Better than she had expected. She had only fantasized twice about running into Nathan and his wife in the dining room.

Duncan, looking more intense than usual, went to Cecil and said something Lacey couldn't hear. Cecil left his post in the kitchen for the first time that evening. Lacey imagined everything would either grind to a halt or descend into pandemonium. Nothing did. The throngs of workers continued in and out of the door; everything hummed along. Lacey's wrists hurt. She wondered why on earth Cecil had recruited her.

"Lacey," an unfamiliar voice said. She looked up, startled to see Duncan. He had a cleft lip she hadn't noticed before.

"Cecil asked for you. Come with me out to the dining room," he said.

Lacey felt a glimmer of panic, and wanted to ask why she had to go to the dining room. But thinking it was best not to question a man-at-arms, she kept her head down and let Duncan lead her to Cecil.

A brass band played, patrons partied, and no one seemed to notice her. The crowd was thin.

Cecil stood at the far end of the room, by a café table with a faux sign above it that read CAFÉ AU LAIT & BEIGNETS. He was standing, talking to a man who was thirtyish, attractive, and very well groomed, his dark hair and clothing styled up to the latest minute. Seated at the table was the man's exact opposite. Thinning brown hair in need of a trim, jacket thrown over a wrinkled button-down in an attempt to dress it up. His five-o'clock shadow was evident on his pallid, fleshy face. Poor shlubby guy looked like he'd just been told his dog died.

"Ah, there you are, Lacey. Just in time," Cecil said.

"Just in time?" Lacey asked.

"Yes. You'll need to sit here with Jerry while we wait for help to come," he said.

"Thomas here will stay with you." Cecil indicated the natty man standing at his side.

Lacey stood motionless. "You'll need me to do what?" she asked. She looked at the seated Jerry and saw that his skin had turned gray and he was sweating profusely, all in the span of about ten seconds.

"Go sit with him, calm him," Cecil said. Now Jerry's breathing was labored, and he looked as if he might pass out at any second.

Calm him? I'm going to calm him straight past the point of consciousness, Lacey thought.

Lacey looked at Cecil and saw no chance of negotiation. She sat down next to the poor beleaguered Jerry. Deciding she might as well go all in, she took his hand and smiled, and tried to think of something soothing to say. Jerry offered her a weak smile and promptly went limp, falling sideways right into her.

Cecil and Dapper Thomas rushed over and moved Jerry's unconscious form onto the floor. Some of Cecil's black-clad minions had appeared, standing idle. Lacey realized they were blocking the view of the other party patrons.

Cecil knelt down and spoke sharply to Jerry. "Can you hear me?"

Jerry didn't respond. Cecil felt for his pulse. He pulled out a clean towel he had tucked away unseen, and gestured to someone in the human view shield. A spindly youth stepped forward. It was the one she had already deemed "Peter Parker."

Cecil told him, "Go wet this, fill it with ice, and bring it back to me." Next, he told Lacey, "Sit here with him while we wait for the EMTs."

Lacey again stood motionless. Cecil's face transformed, eyes bright, with a giant smile.

"Young Lacey, this hesitation is what is keeping you from your true self. Please, come," he said, patting the floor next to him.

Lacey once again sat next to the now-insensate Jerry. In a flash, Peter Parker appeared with the towel filled with ice.

"Jerry has a fever. Take this and hold it to his forehead and neck," Cecil said, handing her the towel.

Lacey arranged herself into a less awkward position on the ground. As she took the cloth to Jerry's grayish skin, the lifeless form of Fox filled her memory. The color was the same. But the unmistakable thrum of life was altogether different. There was sweat, there was a heartbeat, there was breath. She felt a slight shock through the towel as she touched his forehead, which radiated up her arm as she spread her touch to his temple and to his neck.

The pleasant warmth in her arm turned into an uncomfortable heat. She removed her hand—Jerry's pallor seemed already improved. Her hand hovered over his forehead, afraid to touch his bare skin. She felt Jerry take a deep intake of breath, and his eyes fluttered open.

"What happened?" Jerry asked with a faint smile and a creaky voice.

"You passed out. Help is on the way, though," Lacey said.

"I think it's already here," Jerry said, his eyes perusing Lacey.

"Nonsense," she said. "Try not to talk."

Dapper Thomas stepped up. Cecil was nowhere to be seen. "How's he doing?" Thomas asked Lacey.

She shrugged. "He's awake now."

"He sure livened up the joint," Thomas said with a wink. "The whole evening was a little too quiet for my tastes."

Jerry smiled and turned his head back toward Lacey. "Don't believe a word this guy says…"

There was a commotion as the wall panel behind them slipped away. Cecil was on the other side with two EMTs.

Jerry tried to prop himself up, but immediately lay back down. "Shit," he said as he put his hand over his mouth.

Lacey returned her hand to his temple. "Hold it there; I told you help was on the way."

Cecil said something she couldn't hear to the EMTs. A

stretcher appeared through the hole in the wall, Jerry was secured to it, and then disappeared.

Thomas scrambled to gather his things.

"Also take anything belonging to Jerry," Cecil said. "They are taking him to University Hospital. You should meet him there."

Lacey wasn't sure if he was addressing her or Dapper Thomas. She was relieved when Thomas grabbed everything under one arm, nodded, and held out his hand to Cecil. "Thank you," he said.

"Your friend Jerry will be fine," Cecil said.

Thomas disappeared, and the privacy wall of workers dispersed. Ginger and Peter Parker replaced the wall panel.

Cecil and Lacey stood alone together. Cecil laughed, a sudden outburst that rang like a sounding bell.

"Tom and Jerry," he said. "I used to love that show."

Lacey struggled, and then caught the reference. She chuckled. "You know, I always felt kind of bad for the cat," she said.

"Tom only reaped the consequences of his actions," Cecil said.

Lacey stood mute, unsure of how to respond or act. Cecil walked toward the kitchen. Lacey followed and aimed a question at his back.

"Should I go back to the silverware now?" She hurried her step to catch up.

Cecil turned around, and Lacey stopped short before running into him. They were standing in an uninhabited portion of the hall, near the silent auction table.

"No. You are done here. You can leave whenever you wish," he said. His arms were folded, and he looked down at her with an unreadable expression.

"You don't need me anymore?" Lacey said, sounding small.

"Not tonight. You did very well, young Lacey. I hope we get the opportunity to work together again."

Lacey wanted the opportunity to ask at least one of her million questions. What was wrong with Jerry? Why had Cecil asked her to tend to him? Why on Earth had Cecil asked her here tonight?

She wasn't able to voice a single one. She looked down, thought whether she had anything to retrieve in the kitchen, and realized she had everything she needed in her pockets.

"Okay, well," she said, holding out her hand, "it was very nice to meet you, Cecil."

Cecil grabbed her hand and held it for an instant. A flood of images made her immediately nauseated: a woman's face, a house that looked like the Becnel house in Galliano, a horrific accident, and at least seventy-two other things she couldn't identify but only sense.

Lacey stood stricken as Cecil let go. He smiled and said, "I was an infantryman, not a Marine. And my auntie was not a priestess, but she did practice light magic. Your talents are considerable, young Lacey, but you still have far to go." He turned around and returned to the kitchen.

Lacey was caught in some surreal frozen moment of space-time. Cecil was gone, the partiers were distant, their voices and sound muffled, her feet glued to the floor underneath her. The only thing she remembered before leaving was glancing at the silent auction table and seeing a first edition of *To Kill a Mockingbird* standing on its spine.

12

Sleep was elusive. Could Cecil read her mind? Or was he just amazingly perceptive? If he could read her mind, what else did he know about her? And what were all those images that had come to her when she held his hand? Those images, and more, kept playing in her head, blocking out anything as practical as rest. There was the house in Galliano, with visions of Fox leaving her at the doorstep like a baby in the bulrushes. Flashes of Nathan lying on the ground in a pool of blood, the sound of cars passing overhead a constant, deafening din. The mangled metal of a car crash. Miss Esther Mae, a young woman in a pillbox hat, window-shopping on Canal Street. Angele's coworker Eli on the back patio of Patton's, telling her to *pay attention.*

The image of a wreck was particularly difficult to block out. It was a fear nested in her subconscious for as long as she could remember. When Nick had called about Fox, she'd been certain it had been a car accident. She remembered her cognitive dissonance out by the lake, trying to match up his lifeless body with his neatly parked car, perfectly intact.

Getting up with the idea to use the bathroom, she paced the house. Ambrose kept a respectful five paces behind her.

Every picture of Fox she passed seemed to be outlined in bright yellow highlighter. Maybe Nathan was right. There was the one on the side table by the door, nestled in with several other family photos. The one behind the sofa, also one among many pictures of other family and friends. Maybe the one in the hallway by the guest bathroom was a bit conspicuous. But would Nathan even have seen that one? The one in the bedroom was a dead giveaway, but she knew Nathan hadn't seen that one.

Fuck Nathan. These pictures tell the story of who I am. I'm not going to take them down because of him. She returned to the bedroom with a renewed resolve to put all troubling thoughts out of her head. Ambrose, relieved, returned to his doggy bed in the corner.

Lacey tried to concentrate on the present. She stared at the outline of the full-length mirror a few feet away from where Ambrose slept. That freestanding mirror was the only holdover to survive the recent bedroom remodel. Everything else was new—a king-sized four-poster bed, vanity, and chest of drawers. A huge comforter in a shade of seafoam blue that was amazingly weightless. The bedroom was the one room in the house she could call completely hers. The mirror had been hers since high school. Hers since before Fox.

She looked at the clock. 3:27 a.m. Only three hours until her alarm would go off. She sat down on the edge of the bed and stared at the picture prominently displayed on the vanity. Lacey in her wedding dress, Fox in a tux, standing with the grandeur of Popp Fountain behind them. Easy to assume it was their wedding day. Except the light was perfect in that picture. Everything was perfect in the picture. Her mother had been the only one to remark on the difference.

"I don't remember that one from the proofs," she had said as she helped Lacey box up Fox's clothes.

"Huh?"

"This picture," her mom had said. It had been on a nightstand then. "It's so much better than I remember any of the other ones being. Definitely better than the ones in my book."

Lacey had played it off. She was determined to keep the secret solely between her, Fox, and the photographer. Even though Fox was dead.

"Wow, Ma. How do you remember looking at the proofs? That was almost eight years ago."

"Because I would have remembered this one. You held out on me!" She hadn't said anything more about it, and Lacey had let it rest.

But at 3:29 in the morning, it wouldn't rest. Three weeks before the wedding, Fox had shown up at her apartment, dressed in his tux. He'd stolen her breath away, all suited up like that.

"We're going to take our wedding photo, darlin'," he said, hands on the doorframe of her old bedroom. He filled up the space.

Lacey was in a camisole and shorts, and had been making her bed when Fox invaded. She stopped what she was doing and faced him. "No! You can't see me in the dress before the wedding. It's bad luck."

"Bullshit. I'm not superstitious."

Lacey gaped at him. "Oh my God! You're the most superstitious person I know. Who nearly threw me overboard when I brought a banana on your Dad's boat?"

Fox smiled his wide, crooked smile. "If I remember

correctly, it was my father who nearly threw you off the boat. But your point is moot, because no bananas on a boat isn't a superstition."

"Please. That's one of the biggest superstitions there is."

Fox took three steps forward and put his hand on Lacey's hip. "No, darlin'. It's not a superstition. It's a proven fact. Bananas will either sink the boat or scare the fish away. Either way, it doesn't matter. This is not a superstition, it's our future. Suit up."

"Fox!" she said as he pulled down the waistband of her shorts.

"Think about it, La," he said, lifting her camisole over her head. "You can't ask for a better day than today. And this will be just for us. No family, no friends, no commotion. This is about us."

He always knew just what to say to influence her. She stood naked in front of him, and he took off his jacket and laid it on the half-made bed.

"Who's going to take the picture?" she asked.

"Nick," he said, unbuttoning his pants. He was also never afraid to say the things that would set her off.

"Oh, Jesus," she said, hands on her hips. "So, this will be just about you, me, and Nick? What would you say if I got Angele to take the picture?"

"I know for a fact she's in California, working on a movie with Jeff Bridges. But it wouldn't matter if she were here. Her, Nick, either one, they're ciphers in this situation." His pants were now carefully laid on top of the jacket.

Lacey looked at him. "I thought you told me to suit up."

"We can suit up together. After I take care of something first." He smiled. He was already tumescent.

"Not so fast, Bronc. How do you mean, cipher? I'm still seeing we'll have this big secret between me, you, and Dickpuddle Nick."

Fox laughed. "That's a new one."

She arched an eyebrow at him. "You like that one? Dickpuddle?"

He stroked his hand down her side. "It's got potential. Nice shot at distracting me. But I'm focused."

Lacey stared at the reflection of his bare ass in her full-length mirror. He was still talking to her. He didn't seem to mind that she wasn't looking him in the eye.

"La, Nick's there to provide a service, nothing more. It would be the same for Angele, if she were here. We'd ask them to do this, and keep it a secret, trusting in our long friendship that they would." His hand moved to relieve her of her last item of clothing, her panties.

"Shit, Nick's not here, is he?" Lacey craned her neck to look out the doorway.

Fox shook his head. "No. He's gonna meet us out there." He could talk her into anything, especially after cunnilingus, and that's how their unscripted wedding photo happened.

Before they drove out to Popp Fountain, Fox helped Lacey into her wedding dress. She couldn't remember what he said, only that he made her laugh the entire time. She had to catch her breath so he could work the elaborate buttons up the back of the dress. For such coarse and clunky hands, he had amazing dexterity.

Fox phoned Nick after he helped Lacey into his truck. They covered the passenger's side with towels to try to protect the dress from the layers of swamp and sea accumulated there.

"I still have a bad feeling about this," she said as she saw Nick pulling into the parking lot behind them.

Fox leaned in and kissed her. "It only makes you more beautiful." High clouds skidded across the sky. The air was just cool enough so they wouldn't sweat. "Just wait, darlin'," Fox said. "Three weeks from now, we'll be out here for the full smash, and it's gonna be hotter than balls. And we can look at each other and know we've got it handled, because we had our secret practice run."

"Yeah, our secret. Just you, me, and Dickpuddle."

Fox laughed and touched his forehead to Lacey's. Nick was just walking up and may or may not have heard Lacey's new nickname. She didn't care if he had.

"You must be the happy couple," Nick said. He was playing stranger. He had a Nikon on a neck strap. Lacey had to admit he was actually a pretty good shot. They had considered asking him to be the official photographer, but his best man duties had won out.

"That's right," Fox said. He played along and shook Nick's hand. "My beautiful bride here is having some cold feet, so I need you to capture all that drama. Make this memorable."

Cold feet. Lacey had nightmares Fox would suffer from that, and leave her stranded. Was this pre-wedding charade part of his plan to leave her at the altar?

Lacey noticed for the first time that the fountain wasn't running. Fox caught what she was thinking and looked at his watch.

"Patience, darlin'," he said.

"What was I saying about a bad feeling?"

"Why don't we get some pictures by this oak while we're waiting?" stranger photographer Nick said.

"Great idea," Fox said. He caught Lacey up in his arms, threshold style, and took her over to the tree. Nick snapped several photos. None of them turned out.

Fox set Lacey down and looked at his watch again. He instructed Nick to go set up by the fountain. He scooped her back up in his arms.

"Fox! I'm fully capable of walking, you know."

"I don't want you trailing that dress on the ground. I'm sure you don't want that, either."

She put her hand around his neck. "You could walk behind me and carry it for me. Like a lady-in-waiting." She tugged on his ear.

"I'd make a terrible lady-in-waiting. When have I waited for anything?" He kissed her full on the lips, and set her down on the concrete in front of the fountain. He looked at his watch, snapped his fingers, and the fountain came to life. Lacey caught her breath.

"How do you do that?" she said, laughing.

Nick snapped a photo, and Lacey knew that had been the instant, the photo she kept on her vanity, the one her mom suspected she had held out on her about. It was her and Fox, completely candid, not posed, both laughing and apparently in conversation.

The feeling that burned in her memory was a result of what had transpired between them after that moment. It was the reason she held on to that picture, kept it on her vanity, chose to believe that the Fox of the afterlife was the Fox she loved, and who loved her back.

"Do you know why I proposed to you here?" he asked during a break while Nick adjusted some filters on his camera.

Lacey looked at him, confident in her response. "This is our place, our fountain. I love that you proposed here."

"But why is it our place?" he persisted.

"Jesus, Fox, this is unusually probing for you. I don't know, it just is."

"You know, out on the water, how you can tell anything's different about a spot? When everything looks pretty much just like everything else from up on the surface?"

"I don't know. I figure that's what all that high-tech gear your father has is for."

"That crap isn't worth much without what I'm talking about."

"What *are* you talking about?" Lacey asked. Fox looked about as serious as death.

"The pinging. Like on a radar, but internal." He placed two fingers in the center of Lacey's chest, right above the sweetheart neckline of her dress. "In here."

"A heartbeat?"

"No. Something bigger. Something more important. Like a sign. You know you're in a good spot because you get the ping, and for a little while after, everything is clear. You see the fish you're gonna catch, you see what you're going to do when you get back, you see what you mean to everyone around you. For a little while."

Lacey tilted her head. She felt a rush of emotion. He had an uncanny way of making her fall in love with him again repeatedly, relentlessly.

Fox had an unusual look on his face. A deep earnestness masked by his typical cocky swagger. "That's what this place," he swept his hand toward Popp Fountain, "that's what it is for me. For us. It's the only place, and you're the only person, I've ever felt the ping for. Coming here with you, everything is always a little clearer. For a little while."

Lacey felt like she might burst. Here was proof that her fears were unfounded. She swallowed her emotion, determined to play it cool.

She gave him a half smile and said, "So you're saying I'm a fish."

They had spent the rest of that day together. Gone back to Lacey's apartment and carefully hung up the wedding clothes. Made love again, ordered and picked up Thai food. Fox had been in an unusually sedentary mood.

At 3:34 a.m., in the very early June morning of her very present reality, a tear escaped Lacey's eye as she sat at the edge of her bed. She took the photo off the vanity and laid it face down in the top drawer of her dresser, atop her lesser-used underwear.

13

Lacey fixated on the Apache burden basket. It hung on the wall above her washing machine near the side door. It was a gift from Angele, acquired during a long film shoot somewhere in Arizona. The burden basket was supposed to contain any burdens you brought in from the outside, so that you didn't infect your home with them. *Maybe it could contain the trouble from inside, too,* Lacey thought as she pulled the door shut and walked down the steps.

If I'm supposed to leave my trouble there, then running past the spot where Fox died is probably not the best idea, she thought.

She ignored it as she set Saucony to pavement. Nothing was going to keep her from this run. She had spent another zombie day at work yesterday—from lack of sleep, too many unanswered questions, and overloaded circuits. She needed some miles on her legs and a good sweat. Ambrose had given her a cross look when he'd seen her walking out in running attire.

"You would overheat, Bro. You can't come because I love you too much," she said as she patted his head.

Lacey passed Kravitz's house and put her hand in the air in

silent greeting. He was on his screened-in porch, smoking. He croaked out an unintelligible greeting. She picked up her pace as she ran underneath the overpass at Marconi, attempting to make her mind a blank. She didn't succeed.

Looking straight ahead, willing herself not to think about the incident, the smell from Nathan's linen jacket suddenly came upon her. It was clean and spicy. She tried to bury it, but the memory it triggered was too strong. She wanted to see Nathan again. She cursed herself for that. But she also wanted answers.

There's nothing wrong, or immoral, with wanting answers, right?

Down, down Marconi. Past the tennis courts. It was late enough that she missed the packs of runners that took to the roads on Saturday mornings, but just in time to pose an obstacle for the packs of cyclists that came after. And the cars ferrying little soccer players to the playing fields just ahead. It would be less busy out by the lake.

This was her favorite route, she reminded herself. Was it weird that she still liked it so much? Lacey found that the more she passed the spot on the shores of Lake Pontchartrain, the less painful the memory of Fox's dead body became. That one six-foot spot of ground took on a reverential aspect. Now, when she passed, she would usually stop and say a quick prayer.

But there were several miles to go before getting there. Across the bayou, at the horse stables, Lacey could spot a horse grazing, but none were running. It was too hot.

She was hot. But nothing out of the ordinary. Her body felt like it usually did when running in eighty-five degrees with ninety percent humidity. But what was happening with those heat flashes? With Nathan, in the bathroom at Katie's, at Mardi Gras World. Nothing about any of that felt normal. Fugue states. And all in such a short span of time.

What was she missing about all this? What was she not paying attention to? She thought of Eli. "Pay attention." He'd made her annoyed and chagrined. She thought of her thirty-three years thus far, and wondered if all of them had been spent in ignorance of huge, important things.

Lacey approached the stop sign at Filmore. She jogged in place and waited for a car to proceed west. She thought of Popp Fountain. She had already passed it, more than a mile behind her now. *Pay attention.* But she didn't want to pay any more attention to Popp Fountain. Too much of herself wrapped up in there, too much love. Too much pain.

The car moved past the stop sign. The teenaged passenger shouted something, a garbled taunt she couldn't quite make out. The driver laughed, and then they were gone.

Even as recently as two weeks ago, Lacey might have obsessed over that minor incident, wondering why they were laughing at her.

Not today.

She let her mind wander back to her laundry room, and the Apache burden basket. She knew there was something she needed to pay attention to, and it wasn't the people in that car.

As her legs took her closer to the lake, she thought of another time in that laundry room.

Not quite spring, one year prior. She had just gotten home from the grocery, and was struggling to open the door while juggling the bags when her phone rang. It wasn't Fox; it wasn't his ring. Fox had gone to a crawfish boil, some work function, but he didn't expect to be late. He had said he would be home by sevenish. It was not yet 6:00 p.m. She entered the house and laid the groceries on the dryer, and immediately sensed something was wrong.

Nick was calling her phone.

That unfounded fear—a car accident—filled her head. As soon as she said hello, the tone of Nick's response confirmed her dread. "Lacey, you need to come out to the lakefront." The only question she asked Nick was where exactly on the lakefront she needed to go.

Lacey pictured it in her mind's eye. The sole swimming area on the south shore of Lake Pontchartrain. She was only about a mile from it now. The curve in the road, the pilings marking the swimming area, the kidney-shaped patch of grass on the bank.

Ambrose knew something was wrong, too. He didn't excitedly greet her with a nudge of the head and excessive wagging. Instead, he sat quietly in the doorway of the laundry room, a somber look on his face. Lacey put the quart of pecan praline ice cream—Fox's favorite—in the freezer. She left the rest of the groceries on the dryer.

Nick had said something about a heart attack. Lacey was certain Fox had suffered a heart attack as a result of a car accident.

When Lacey arrived at the lake, she saw Fox's car with no sign of damage, an ambulance, a cop car, and a small crowd of people gathered on the levee outside the swimming area. One thought filled her head: How was he thrown from his car?

She saw Nick break away from the small crowd and walk toward her. It seemed like he walked in slow motion.

He stopped her before she could go to Fox, his hands on both her shoulders. He looked her in the eye and told her the half-truth. That Fox had gotten a crazy idea to go swimming. True. The EMTs said he'd had a heart attack. True. A woman who happened to be walking the levee had seen him struggling and tried to save him. False. *Nick had been a few minutes behind and hadn't seen any of it.* False. *He'd arrived too late to make a difference.* True.

Lacey pushed Nick away from her and ran to the small crowd. Fox was lying at the center. He was naked, and he was gray. Lacey's one thought: that's not Fox. And that was when she realized he was dead.

Lacey was short of breath. She was remembering it all too vividly. Or she had taken the short bit of steep road that led to the lakefront too quickly. She stopped, bent forward, and grabbed her ankles.

Lacey had wanted to scream on that day in March, one year prior, but was afraid that if she did, she would lose her voice forever.

She knelt before Fox's supine, lifeless body and tentatively reached out a hand for the one part of him that still seemed like him: his hair. Dark and always a little unruly. She stroked the side of his head. It felt cold, and not like a head at all. More like a moss-covered stone.

One word escaped her throat, at barely the level of a whisper: "Goodbye." Silent tears poured out of her. Still kneeling, she removed her hand and covered her eyes.

She couldn't remember how long she had stayed that way. It felt like an eternity.

Lacey walked to a concrete bench, still about a half mile from the swimming area. She sat, and remembered her anger. Not at Fox's infidelities—that had come later. No, she remembered her anger on the grassy patch on the day Fox had died.

Someone came and covered the body with a sheet. That act snapped Lacey back to life. She rose up suddenly, intensely angry.

Why had these strangers been staring at her husband's naked body? Why had it taken them so long to show some respect for the dead? She scanned the small crowd of faces with narrowed eyes— strangers with various uniforms, a distraught woman with wet hair. She stopped on the one face she recognized.

"Why the fuck did you leave him lying out like this, for everyone to see?" Lacey yelled at Nick. Her voice had returned, and it was utterly altered from the journey.

Lacey never received a response from the stunned Nick. Instead, she felt a firm hand on her shoulder from behind. She turned around, and the hand did not move.

It was a police officer, a short and broad woman, her eyes bright against her brown skin and darker blue of her uniform. Her hand had stayed firm but gentle. Lacey's sudden rage settled down into something sadder under the woman's intense gaze.

"Ma'am, is this your husband?" she asked.

No, she wanted to answer. My husband is a vital, magnificent man who charms everyone he encounters. Whatever's lying there is a shell.

"Yes," Lacey replied instead.

"There are some things we're going to have to ask you," the police officer said as she led her away from Fox.

The blur of activity from that point forward softened the edges of the subsequent memories. Of those days that had led up to the funeral. But those days had been the last ones in which Fox remained the faithful, looming love of her life.

Lacey picked herself up from the bench. She had lost the desire to run. She would run home once she'd passed the swimming area, but decided to walk the remaining way there. She could feel a resolution forming.

Fox was still the love of her life, thus far, but less looming, and the faithful part had been obliterated. The truth had begun to emerge at the funeral: the distraught woman with the wet hair hadn't just "happened" across Fox at dusk on a warm March day that had turned suddenly blustery. No, she had been with him in the water when he'd died.

Lacey had pieced together the full story in the months after his death. Fox and the woman had left a crawfish boil in Lake Vista together, and Fox had somehow cajoled her into skinny-dipping. Lacey had discovered that had been a favorite gambit of Fox's—convince a woman to get wet, and any subsequent convincing became much easier.

His final gambit had had him suffering a heart attack as soon as he plunged into the still winter-cold water. His panicked companion had called the only person she knew to be connected to Fox: Nick. He had arrived minutes later, and helped the woman pull him from the water.

Lacey felt a profound sense of calm when she stopped at the swimming area. She thought of the immutability of death. And the ultimate mutability of living. Fox was dead and would remain that way. Who he had been with, what he had done while he was living, would stay unchanged. It was Lacey's perception of it all that was forever altered after his death. But this one immutable truth remained: Fox was gone, and the person most affected by the absence was, and always would be, Lacey.

When you boiled everything else away, it was that one truth that mattered. She closed her eyes and tried to focus on all the changes that had occurred, just in the past week. Whatever was happening to her, her burgeoning ability, she knew it had something to do with Fox. Or more precisely, she knew it had something to do with his family.

She thought of Nathan. Another man, the first one she had felt any sort of attraction toward since Fox, and he had also wound up lying dead. Or almost dead. Yet now very much alive; and, if one was to believe him, alive due to Lacey.

Had Fox needed to be absent from her life for any of this to start happening? She wasn't ready to think of that, yet. She opened her eyes. The resolve that had been lurking somewhere center-left in her brain crystallized in that moment.

She was done.

She was ready to move on from Fox. All those old feelings were clouding her judgment. Like why she couldn't seem to get Nathan out of her head. Yes, so maybe she had saved his life, and maybe the attraction was mutual, but he was married. End of story. Moving on from one philandering husband to become the object of philandering was not an option. She resolved to pay attention and figure out what was going on with her. And pay attention for more viable options in the relationship department.

Be done. Move on. Mutability. That was her option, not Fox's anymore.

Lacey focused on the patch of grass that had held Fox's body fifteen months ago.

Fox, I will always be the person you influenced the most profoundly. Nothing can change that now. And I loved you, maybe more than you ever realized. And nothing can change that, either. But I have some weird, crazy shit going on right now. And I think there's more ahead. I need to face it with a clear head and an open heart. That's it. I'm going to go now.

Lacey left the levee and didn't look back. And ran home at pace she hadn't been able to muster since high school.

14

"A definite fugue state," Angele said over her cuba libre. "Are your pupils dilated? They are, your pupils are dilated!"

Lacey sighed. "Maybe my pupils are dilated because it's dark in here?"

It was Saturday night and they were back at Patton's, but inside this time. The air outside was too thick, the unusually dry weather of the past several weeks threatening to end.

Lacey was attempting to get guidance from Angele. She had told her about her new resolution, her freakishly fast run that afternoon, how she was ready for a new start. Ready to make the most of whatever was going on with her. And ready, maybe, for a new relationship (but not with Nathan).

Angele had her own agenda, and it didn't seem to mesh with Lacey's. She was fixated on the flaming paper towel at Katie's. She had immediately drawn a comparison to Pyro. After a heated discussion around whether Pyro could still be called an X-Man, or whether Lacey was more like the Human Torch—because he acquired his power and had not been born with it—Lacey called it. She wasn't sure if she had been born a mutant, but she liked their story the best, so they decided to settle on the X-Men analogy.

"Great," Lacey said. "Now that we've decided how to categorize it, can you tell me what to *do* with it? Whatever this is, I don't think it's supposed to be all about me."

"Look," Angele replied, "so far, you've had an impact on how many people?"

"Two," Lacey said.

"We need to focus more on the second—Tom and Jerry," Angele said. "That's the only one with a witness, correct?"

"I guess." Lacey hadn't thought of it that way. "But a witness to what?"

"Cecil the Chef knows something," Angele said. "I think these are questions you should be asking him."

"I know he knows something," Lacey said. "He might know everything. But one, I don't know how to contact him and two, just what do I ask him if I could?"

"You'll figure it out," Angele said. "You know, out of this limited cast of characters you've introduced me to, Cecil the Chef seems the most interesting to me. He could be the cook for the commune!"

Lacey gave up on trying to get any advice from Angele. "What the hell are you talking about, Lee?"

"*Remember*, Campo, the Lakeway buildings? We were going to start a commune, base it there, and we'd have total control over who to allow in? Any of this ring a bell?"

"Shit," Lacey replied. "Way to bring up sixth grade. I doubt we were the only eleven-year-olds to ever come up with that type of plan."

"But I bet we were the only ones to plan it for the Lakeway buildings." The two skyscrapers were fixtures on the western horizon of their childhood. "And actually, this is a perfect time to bring up sixth grade," Angele said. "Jesus, I'm so brilliant."

"Please, enlighten me with your brilliance, because you've completely lost me."

"The impetus for starting the commune," Angele said. She folded her arms and nodded, self-satisfied.

"Still not making any sense."

Angele huffed. She suddenly looked like her eleven-year-old self. "We were going to start the commune after the world as we knew it had ended."

"I'm not remembering that part."

"Oh, it was key," Angele replied. "Why the fuck else would we start a commune unless we had no other choice in preserving humanity?"

"I guess I wasn't as focused on that," Lacey said. "I think I was more focused on the vengeful act of keeping all the people we didn't like out of there."

"That was a nice fantasy, wasn't it?" Angele said. "But back to the world ending. Seems kind of applicable now, doesn't it?" She arched an eyebrow.

"You're saying my world is over?" Lacey asked. She couldn't explain why this line of conversation irked her so. She had spent the evening asserting her resolve to start anew, or so she had thought. And Angele had brought up ancient, adolescent daydreams. Had she not been listening to anything she'd said?

"Jesus, you are so dense," Angele said. "That's exactly what I'm saying. One world, the life you relegated yourself to when you married Fox, is over."

Lacey felt a contrarian urge spring up. She was inspired to invoke Angele's ire. "I know how you felt about Fox," she said, "but at least my life with him was normal. Even finding out about everything he did, that's still normal stuff. It sucked, but there's nothing supernatural about dicking around on your wife."

"That's just it!" Angele said, standing up. "Who wants a normal life? You infuriate me, you know that?"

"You're no picnic yourself," Lacey said. "And what's wrong with wanting a normal life? I was happy with Ambrose on Florida Boulevard. I didn't ask for this naked mutant power thing."

Angele sat down again. Something was burning inside her, Lacey could tell. She tried to hide her satisfaction.

"Why do you lie like that?" Angele said, her tone ominous. "We both know you've been about the farthest thing from happy."

"I wasn't lying about not asking for this," Lacey said. "What the hell do I do with this? I can't even see how I can get to a *new normal* with this."

"You're obsessed with normal. Get over it," Angele said. The fire began to die down. "You know something had to happen. You couldn't stay in this self-imposed prison forever."

"Are you going to get another drink?" Lacey asked, still seated and even-toned.

"Yes, but not yet," Angele sat down again. "What I'm trying to say is, maybe this whole fugue business with Dinner Jacket is a big plus. Look past all the bizarro-ness of it; at least it's booted you to a new place."

"Yeah, one hundred and eighty degrees from normal."

"Whatever. Do you want another drink?" Angele asked.

"I might, but hold up. Look, I'm not trying to be cagey," Lacey said.

"Yes, you are," Angele interrupted.

"Okay, maybe just a little," Lacey said. She smiled, and Angele smirked, and they were back to the timeworn cadence of their friendship.

"But, look, in much more *normal* terms, work and stuff, I really do think I'm close. I've got to figure out what I would do for a job—but I think I'm close. Do you really think I could get work as a production accountant?"

"Yes."

"Just like that?"

"No," Angele said. "I'd have to get you on as an assistant somewhere first, and it wouldn't pay squat, but once you've got one or two under your belt, you'd be picking up work everywhere."

Lacey pushed back in her chair. "How can you be so sure?"

"The work would be ridiculously easy for you, and you're attractive and even-tempered, and you're accustomed to dealing with outsized personalities. That's a very marketable package. I'm going to the bar." Angele pointed at Lacey's drink.

"Not yet," Lacey said.

✳

Angele never made it back from the bar. After several minutes alone at their table feeling conspicuous, Lacey's phone pinged. A text from Angele: SOMETHING CAME UP. I'LL BE OUTSIDE.

Lacey asked if she should join her. NO. STAY THERE. HAVE FUN.

Lacey looked up from her phone. She saw a room full of near strangers. Eli walked past the far end of the bar and nodded at her. She stared back. After several stricken moments, she glanced down at her clothes. A green linen blouse and khaki pants. She wondered if Eli had sussed out some hidden meaning to her selection.

Yeah, have fun, she thought. *Everyone here's either too self-involved or too creepy.*

She went to the bar, thinking she could pretend to get a drink while she slowly backed up toward the door. If she ran into Angele outside, she'd tell her she had an early morning tomorrow and that she had to go. And why did she need to make excuses anyway? It was Angele who had abandoned her, not the other way around.

Lacey picked the most crowded spot at the bar and looked at her phone, feigning deep concentration. At the same time, her free hand hunted around in her purse for her car key. She couldn't find it.

An instant of panic turned into a frantic pantomime as she patted down her legs. The key was in the pocket of her loose pants. "I'm such an idiot," Lacey said.

"Says who?" said an unfamiliar voice behind her.

Lacey whipped her head around. There stood the Dakota Kid, Kevin Horner. The skin on his neck had cleared up.

"Oh. Sorry. Says no one. Do you need a drink?" she asked.

"That's typically why one walks up to a bar," he answered.

Lacey turned around fully, and saw that Eli was standing behind him. Her defenses shot up.

"Hello again, Eli," she said, her diction crystal-clear and cool.

"Hello," he said. He sounded like a child might, greeting an ancient great aunt seen twice a year. "Kevin, this is Lacey. I have to be somewhere else now."

Eli walked off, robot-like, to the other end of the bar. Lacey made a face.

The Dakota Kid laughed and slid onto an open barstool. The most crowded spot at the bar had miraculously cleared. "Special effects guy. He likes to keep people guessing," the Kid said. He patted the bar stool next to him, addressing Lacey as if they'd been friends since childhood. "I've told him he needs to add a puff of smoke when he decides to do tricks like that. Your name is Lacey?" he asked, his hand out.

"Yes," she said, accepting his hand. "Kevin, right?"

He nodded, a little twinkle in his eye. He knew that she already knew his name, full well.

"Lacey. I love that name. Both gossamer and complex," he said.

Lacey blushed.

"So why are you an idiot?" he asked. He did not seem in a hurry to catch the bartender.

Lacey didn't understand at first. At the moment, she was thinking she was an idiot for letting herself be so easily charmed.

She remembered her car key. "Maybe I'm an idiot for thinking out loud," she said.

"That can be a very dangerous habit. Worse than drinking," the Kid said.

He gestured at the half-empty glass Lacey clutched. "Can I get you another?" he asked.

She was so close to leaving. But she was sure she'd never forgive herself if she let the opportunity for a good story pass through her fingers.

"Sure," she replied. She gave him a sideways glance and smiled.

The bartender was over in an instant, once he saw Kevin Horner beckoning him. He ordered a scotch and soda, and looked at Lacey's glass.

"Vodka tonic?" he asked.

Lacey nodded, impressed. He ordered her a Ketel One and tonic.

Fox had always told her she should never mix a premium vodka. She was delighted at the thought of the drink that was coming her way.

The Dakota Kid leaned in when their drinks came. It suddenly became very intimate. Lacey tried to put space between them, to little avail.

"Why don't I guess?" the Kid said.

"Guess what?" Lacey asked, trying to sound aloof.

"Guess why you're such an idiot," he said. He took her hand by the wrist and turned up her palm. "May I?" he asked.

"May you what?"

He ignored her.

Lacey laughed nervously as he studied the lines on her palm. With his head bent over her hand, she could see the top of his scalp. It was well disguised by hair product and the close-cropped style, but he was starting to go bald. She thought of Nathan, a man probably close to twice his age, and his full head of hair.

"What are you doing?" she finally asked.

He kept his head bent and replied, "Your heart line is what I expected, but your fate line is truly remarkable. You're right-handed, right?"

Lacey had to think for a second. "Yes…"

He was holding her left hand.

"Your non-dominant hand gives better signs of your future."

"You're reading my palm?" Lacey felt stupid as soon as she said it.

He looked her in the eyes and said, "Your head line

indicates that you like to state the obvious." He flashed the movie-star smile.

He returned to studying her hand. "But your fate line—I've never seen one like it. Not everyone has one. And you have a pretty strong one—until it intersects with your heart line. That's where it gets interesting."

"You seem to have quite an arsenal of come-ons," she said. Her attempt to sound witty came off weak.

"You have no idea," he said. "But in your case, it's just a fortunate byproduct." He pulled her a little closer, eyes still on her palm.

"It looks like fate played a strong role in getting you to a point, right to a point where your heart was broken." He looked her in the eyes again. "But then, after that, it splays out, see?" He held her hand up to her face, pointing to a spot somewhere left of center on her palm. She nodded, but had no idea what he was talking about. He traced a finger through her palm. His touch set her spine tingling. Lacey pulled her hand away.

"Relax, sweetheart," he said. "I know what I'm doing."

"I have no doubt of it," Lacey said. She tried to smile seductively, but suspected she looked like she'd developed a sudden palsy.

He laughed. Something seemed so familiar about him. Lacey thought of Steve McQueen in *The Great Escape.* She was trying to craft some sexy way to voice the thought when Eli reappeared, his head popping up over the Kid's shoulder.

Lacey recoiled and cocked her head. Eli's good eye stared at her while the other one floated toward the bar.

The Kid didn't turn around. "I'm sorry, Lacey. It seems we'll have to resume our guessing game at another time," he said. "I *will* find out why you're such an idiot."

"Okay?" she said.

"I look forward to it," he said. He leaned in lightning quick and gave her a kiss on the cheek. The Dakota Kid led Eli through the crowd to the other side of the bar.

Lacey sat, looking at her drink three-quarters full, and tried not to stare in Kevin Horner's direction.

15

Well, what does your palm say about your future? Lacey thought, still looking at her drink. That might have been a good retort. *What does it say about our future?* Whoa, too stalkerish. Unless she could make it sound funny.

She wasn't ready to leave Patton's yet. She needed to sit until she'd made some sense out of her singular exchange with the Dakota Kid. And she needed to figure out how much to tell Angele.

She did not get very far on either count before she heard a voice say, "I figure you owe me a drink."

Lacey tried to contain her excitement, thinking the Kid might have returned. She did not hide her disappointment when she turned to see a familiar face, but one that did *not* belong to Kevin Horner.

She strained to place it. "Excuse me?" she asked.

"At Redd's. You stiffed me," he said.

The Mississippi Charmer, maker of the fifteen-second old-fashioned. Lacey remembered how she'd left the Uptown bar earlier that week.

"Oh shit!" she said. "I'm so sorry! God, I guess I do."

He took the seat recently occupied by the Dakota Kid. "Let's see," he said. "Factor in a few days' interest, plus the labor charge for delivering such a fine drink in such a succinct fashion, I figure it might have to be more than one."

"Why don't we start with one? Make us even," Lacey said.

"I never got your name at the bar," the Charmer said. "You left in a bit of a rush."

"Sorry. It's Lacey." The bartender had come over. "What are you drinking?" Lacey asked.

"Jack rocks, please. And put it on her tab." He nodded his head toward Lacey with a smile.

Lacey took out some money to pay.

Addressing the bartender, the Charmer said, "You're obviously smarter than I am. You know not to let her run a tab."

The bartender cracked a perfunctory smile, took Lacey's money, and moved on.

"Oh, lighten up," Lacey said to the Charmer. "I never do that, I feel really horrible. I should probably give you money to cover that original drink, too."

He smiled, showing off his perfectly symmetrical dimples. "I'm just giving you a hard time. Your drink was paid for."

Nathan. The thought of him put Lacey's stomach in knots.

"Nice," she said. "So you just conned me into buying you a drink."

"I'd hardly say 'conned.' It's one drink. You look like you can afford it."

What is that supposed to mean? she thought. "Who *are* you?" Lacey asked. She looked at her drink and plotted her exit.

"Dan," he said. He held out his hand.

Lacey shook his hand, her nose up in the air. "You a fan of Kevin Horner, Dan?"

"Never heard of him until my roommate started working on this movie. Definitely more happening here than at Redd's," he replied. "Speaking of Redd's, I guess Nate must have done something pretty bad to get you to storm off like you did," he added.

Lacey squirmed. "What do you want, Dan? I got you your drink," she said, glaring at him.

"Oh, chill down, sister. I'm just looking for some gossip," Dan said. He seemed amused.

"Well, I barely know the guy," Lacey said, "and I doubt I'll ever see him again. So you won't get any gossip from me."

"Damn. Yeah, I guess you're too uptight to give any good dish, anyway."

"I'm not uptight!" Lacey said. Her voice sounded shrill.

Mississippi Charmer Dan laughed. "Sounds like I should buy *you* a drink!"

"No, I think I need to go. I need to find my friend," Lacey said.

"Oh, relax. Get another drink, and I'll give you some dish. I won't even ask for any in return. See how generous I am?"

"Yeah, you're a real philanthropist, I can see," Lacey said.

Dan gestured to the bartender, and before Lacey could protest, he put a small overturned plastic cup in front of her drink.

"Fine," Lacey said. "I'm only staying because you're mildly entertaining. And I don't care for any 'dish.' I don't even know the guy. And why are you so interested anyway?"

"It passes the time," Dan said. "I've been bored witless since school ended."

Something in his tone prompted Lacey to ask, "When was that?"

"Two years ago," he answered drily. "So, Nate works nearby," he continued, "and he's been the only person I've seen in the bar under the age of like seventy-five in the past month."

"What does he do?" Lacey asked.

"I thought you didn't care," Dan said.

She brushed him off. "I don't. But it passes the time."

"I think he's like a lawyer, or a title agent or something. All I know is he's not a trial lawyer, and he works in his father-in-law's firm."

Lacey tried to appear only mildly interested.

Dan explained how Nathan had a habit of stopping in to Redd's nearly every day after work for one drink. Sometimes he would buy a scotch but wind up drinking water instead. He would talk about his children, but almost never mentioned his wife. He never spoke about work, but would wax poetic about playing guitar.

"Guitar?" Lacey asked. She couldn't picture it.

"Yeah. Going by what he says, he plays a mean country guitar. Even went to NOCCA or some shit as a kid, might have even toured a little bit with a band in college," Dan said.

Lacey couldn't stop herself from thinking how Nathan and her brother had this pivotal talent in common. They possibly could have known each other growing up, though she was sure Nathan was several years older than Jimmy. And Jimmy, whose style was two thousand miles away from country, never had any interest in attending New Orleans's performing arts school.

"So here I am thinking he's this nice, preppy, middle-aged guy who's maybe going through a standard midlife crisis, thinking about his glory days," Dan said.

Lacey winced at the mention of middle-aged.

"So when he came in looking like he'd been in one hell of

a fight, and asks me to be on the lookout for you, I got real curious," Dan said. "Even more curious when I saw you."

"What's that supposed to mean?" Lacey asked, arms folded across her chest.

"Look, the way he described you, you could tell he was smitten," he said. "And honestly, I'd never heard him speak about anyone in that kind of way, so yeah, I was curious."

"Did you think he was gay?" Lacey asked.

Dan stiffened. "No. I'm pretty sure he's not gay. That's not it—he just never seemed interested in anyone. And you're getting me off subject."

"Excuse me," Lacey said, drawing out the words, inching back on her bar stool.

The dimples reappeared. "You know, his description didn't do you justice. He didn't say anything about a filly-like fire."

"Did you just call me a horse?"

Dan laughed loudly. "Only in the best possible meaning."

Lacey unfolded her arms and put her head in her hands, elbows on the bar. "I'm not sure I want to hear any more."

"Why? It's pretty clear he has a thing for you. Even if you're too uptight to do anything about it, it's at least got to be flattering."

"I'm not uptight," she repeated. The shrill had returned in her voice. "Maybe I just respect the institution of marriage," she added, a notch lower.

"Well, consider you wouldn't be the one cheating," Dan said.

"Who's talking about cheating?" Lacey said, her face peering through her hands. "Plus, the fact that I know he's married would make it cheating."

"Ha! So you've at least thought about it, then," Dan said.

"No! I mean, it's pointless to talk about it at all. I'm glad you found this week's exchange between me and Nathan entertaining. I didn't." Lacey took a long pull from her drink. "So what's up with you and school, Dan?" she asked.

"That's it?" Dan asked. "Shifting gears just like that?"

"Yep," Lacey said. "You promised to give me dish, and that's something I'm curious about."

"Uh-uh," he said. "I already gave it to you. Do you now know more about Nate-who-you'll-probably-never-see-again than you did when I sat down?"

"Yeah. He plays guitar, and is probably not gay. Groundbreaking stuff."

Dan shook his head and smiled.

Lacey wasn't ready to give up. "So you've been sticking around, being bored in your job because…?"

"Oh, no you don't, sister," Dan said. "Maybe some other time, but I think that's all you're gonna get on me tonight."

"How is that fair?" Lacey said.

"It's uber fair!" Dan said. "I didn't go digging around on you and your life's motivation. We were merely sharing information on a neutral third party."

"Neutral. Pah," Lacey said, folding her arms again.

"Aha!" he said. "I do believe Nate Quirk *is* under your skin!"

"He's not," Lacey said. "Or even if he is, he can't stay there. Can we talk about something else?"

"Fair enough," Dan replied. His eyes lit up like he'd just remembered something. "Hey, will you be at that thing on the *Natchez*?"

"The wrap party? I don't know," Lacey said. "I'm not so sure I want to be stuck on a boat for three hours with this crew."

"C'mon, I'll be there. I got off work and everything. Just think of what could happen," he said.

"That's what I'm afraid of," Lacey said. She finished her drink. "It's been real, Dan, but I really do have to go. Early morning tomorrow."

"Yeah, I bet you have something uptight to do, like color-code your summer wardrobe, or alphabetize your recipes or something."

"What does that even mean? And I don't really cook," she said. She cracked a smile.

"Come to that thing on the *Natchez*," he said.

"We'll see."

✳

Pondering the new information about Nathan, she had almost forgotten her encounter with the Dakota Kid.

What a jam-packed night, Lacey thought. She'd opened the front door of Patton's and taken two steps toward Harrison Avenue when she felt a foot on the back of her knee.

She barely retained her balance, and swirled around.

Angele was standing with a two-way radio clutched in one hand, arms folded across her chest.

"I guess three-hundred-and-sixty-degree vision isn't part of your mutant powers," she said. "Not paying attention?"

"Ow," Lacey answered on a ten-second delay. She planted both feet firmly on the sidewalk and returned Angele's glare.

"Who was that you were talking to?" Angele asked.

"What?" Lacey asked. "Who?"

"That little child with the mop of blond hair," Angele said.

"His name is Dan. He works at Redd's."

"That's it?" Angele asked.

"You look like you're working," Lacey said, gesturing at the radio. "You left me in there because of work, remember?"

"I'm on standby," Angele said.

"Are you catching a flight?"

"I can talk now," Angele said, ignoring Lacey's remark. "Did the Kid pull his palm-reader trick?"

Lacey felt her stomach jump. She tried to come up with a pithy retort.

"Yeah, what of it?" *Not so pithy, Lace.*

"Jesus, it just proves my point. Weren't we just talking about you and your fucking naiveté?"

The feeling in Lacey's stomach traveled upward until she felt a burning in her throat. "Nice. You can be so fucking harsh. I bet he wouldn't read yours, for fear of being castrated. Or something." Lacey shifted on her feet.

"Really," Angele said. "Huh. Castrated."

They stared at each other, a showdown on the darkened street, empty save for the patrons still inside Patton's.

"I'm leaving," Lacey said. "Call me when you've calmed down."

"Oh, I'm calm," Angele said.

Lacey shook her head and turned toward her car. She tried to keep her hand from shaking as she reached for her key.

16

For the first time in fifteen months, Lacey sat in St. Daniel's for Mass and was not preoccupied with Fox's death and the repose of his soul. Too many other things were competing for the air space.

Lacey's new start felt irrevocably messy. Angele was mad at her. It wasn't the first time, but it still made her feel awful. And the timing was particularly problematic, because she needed her help in finding a new job.

And she was more confused than ever about her mutant power. Tonti, Cecil, the traiteur lady in Galliano—Lacey knew there was a connection, a connection to *her*. But the more she actually thought about it, the less sense it made.

Underscoring it all, her heart was in tumult. All this mutant-power-fugue business had begun with Nathan. Despite her best intentions, she was beginning to understand that she would not easily be able to dismiss her feelings for him.

Scripture precipitated short bursts of internal processing. An ancient man read the first reading. Lacey knew his voice after so many Masses. It wobbled with age. "But by the envy of the devil, death entered the world…"

His voice broke on the word *death*. Lacey fixated on the word *envy*.

What the hell was up with Angele? Lacey thought. What had set her off this time? Her brief flirtation with Kevin Horner? Lacey had to admit, the thought of making the Dakota Kid her first romantic entanglement after Fox was very tempting. But if it would prompt this reaction from Angele, the juice wasn't worth the squeeze.

Angele was acting jealous. But it didn't feel right. That was not how Angele acted with a crush.

Maybe she'd had her eye on Dan, and she was mad that Lacey had been talking to him. Again, it made no sense. *Dan, the Mississippi Charmer. He knows Nathan.*

Lacey decided to table that thought. She wasn't ready to think about Nathan.

I haven't thought this much about boys since high school. Pay attention, she thought. She tried to focus on the reading, but trying to pay attention only made her think of Eli.

Eli. He had singled her out. Something about his teasing felt like sixth grade. Could he have a crush on her?

Quit thinking everyone's in love with you, she thought. *You're being like Trip.*

Work. She couldn't put it off any longer. The monotony of her workday had been a good balance when Fox was around to make chaos, but now it was only stagnation. It stank like an algae bloom on a drainage canal.

Fox. She returned to a familiar thought. *At least this is one place not haunted by his memory.*

Going to Mass would be harder than it already was if he had ever gone with her. She'd always imagined he would join her in church once they had kids.

Children. She tabled any further thoughts about Fox. The ping, Popp Fountain, their never-to-be children. It was still painful to think about. The pain was not as intense anymore, but she was certain she would always carry its shadow with her.

Deacon Gil read the Gospel. His voice was warm and strong. Deacon Gil was probably older than the man who'd done the first reading. But he didn't carry himself that way. "Christ took away our infirmities and bore our diseases…"

Pay attention, she thought. Christ was a healer. Tonti had said as much after their last dinner.

The incident under the overpass. It felt like a dream. But one of those dreams that was more real than life. Had something supernatural occurred, or had she lapsed into a fugue state?

An answer was there. She felt it in every fiber, but it was unformed.

Please God, she prayed, because she was at Mass and it seemed appropriate, *please make me not be crazy.*

Something had happened, and it had happened with Nathan. A man she barely knew. The man at Mardi Gras World had been a stranger, too, for that matter. But what was it about Nathan that had opened this door?

There was attraction, Lacey thought. *There is attraction.* There's nothing wrong with being attracted to a married man. A man married with children. It's only wrong if something happens.

Something did happen. But not something I have to confess.

What about Jerry at Mardi Gras World? He seemed a nice enough guy, but there was no particular attraction.

Tom and Jerry. Cecil. Cecil knows something. *He knew what I was thinking.* Maybe he knows what this is. Maybe Cecil knows about traiteurs. She latched on to that thought. She remembered reading about how the traiteur's healing powers passed from woman to man to woman and so on. Maybe Fox's mom, whom she had never known, had been a healer, and passed it on to Fox, who had passed it on to her. But that made no sense. Fox had possessed many abilities, but Lacey didn't think healing had been among them. *Traitor*, yes; *traiteur*, probably not.

And what would Cecil know about Fox, anyway? And how would she find him? And would he know why this was happening?

Do I have to know why?

A passing cloud cleared the way for the sun to strike through the stained-glass window, too high above her head to see which saint it featured. A beam of light bathed the empty pew in front of her in shades of crimson and blue.

I don't have to know why. It would be nice, but not necessary. What I need to know is how to manage it.

Like the hand of God, the thought settled her soul. She needed to know how to manage it, whatever it was. That should be her chief concern. Everything else would fall into place. She hoped.

Pay attention. The answer will come.

Lacey shut down for the remainder of the service. She chased away any errant thoughts. A great fatigue settled into the places they might have occupied. She shuffled, zombie-like, in line to receive the Eucharist. She had missed Mass the weekend prior, and knew she technically shouldn't receive Communion, but she ignored that thought, too.

✳

The stampeding thoughts were replaced by one overarching aim: sleep. Lacey filed out of St. Daniel's after Mass had ended, hoping she could make the short drive home without falling asleep at the wheel. She gasped when she felt cold, spindly fingers on her shoulder.

"Imagine seeing you again so soon!"

Lacey turned her head and saw the insect mandible of Dotty Trebuchet jawing up and down.

"Oh," Lacey said. "Hi." She wanted to say, "I didn't know you came to St. Daniel's," but didn't.

Parishioners filed around them as they blocked the walkway outside the church. Miss Dotty launched into a minutes-long soliloquy about Matt and his family, how Matt was so much like her husband, her history with Tonti, and then about everything she had to do in the hours ahead. Lacey stopped her when she heard a familiar name.

"Excuse me, did you just say Esther Mae?" Lacey asked.

"Oh, that's right, I saw you with her at Katie's. I completely forgot about it when you had that run-in with the cockroach in the bathroom," Miss Dotty said, giving her the elevator eyes. "Can you believe, she seemed more alive that night than she had in years? I had really questioned whether she would make it, that annual dinner. She was like another grandmother to me, she's been connected to my family for so long."

The mixture at the table that night at Katie's suddenly made sense to Lacey. "I'm sorry, so what happened?" she asked.

"So we had dinner that evening, and she was so animated and lucid. She had a cab pick her up, and we all thought maybe we just might see her again next year. But then, two days later, she died in her sleep." Miss Dotty shook her head slowly for effect. "I'm so glad I have such a nice final memory of her, though. As I was saying, her funeral is tomorrow, and I have to pick up a ham, and figure out where in heck I'm supposed to deliver it. I'm not really familiar with that part of town." Miss Dotty waved her hand eastward. Lacey raised her eyebrows but kept silent. She suspected Miss Dotty would say the same thing about any part of town that wasn't Lakeview or Uptown.

"I'm so sorry to hear that," Lacey said. "I didn't know her, she just asked for my help that evening. But her name was unforgettable."

Miss Dotty was uncharacteristically quiet. They shared an awkward stare for several moments.

"Well, I should run. Too much to do!" Miss Dotty said. "I didn't know you came to this church," she added as they parted ways. "I'll look for you next time!"

Great, Lacey thought. *Maybe it's time I started going to St. Peter's.* She kept her head down on the short walk to her car. An unforeseen encounter with Miss Dotty was enough for the day.

She stopped, paralyzed, at her car door. She gazed blankly over the hood at the spot where she and Dotty Trebuchet had spoken. Miss Esther Mae had been a new woman after Lacey walked her to the restaurant. The flaming paper towel incident had occurred directly afterward.

You idiot, she thought. Miss Esther Mae had been a third recipient of her fugue-healing thing. She hadn't even counted her in. Angele hadn't caught it, either. Maybe Lacey hadn't told her about Miss Esther Mae, only about what had happened in the bathroom.

Miss Esther Mae *had* been another, and now she was dead.

Lacey locked herself in her car. She remained motionless until the stifling air forced her to start the engine.

17

"Why are you answering your phone this early?" demanded Tonti.

"Tonti, it's hardly early," Lacey said, trying to sound light. She thought of saying something about how she had been up, showered, and already been to Mass, but she didn't have the energy to be clever.

"Did you spend another evening alone last night?" Tonti asked.

Lacey held the phone away and made a face. She cursed herself for answering the call. The only reason she had was her sneaking suspicion that Tonti might divulge a secret or two.

"As a matter of fact, no," Lacey answered. "I was out last night, and actually talked to new people."

"Did you make any new friends? Scratch that question. Obviously not, if you're home alone and sounding so awake this early," Tonti said.

"Tonti!" Lacey couldn't help herself. She tried to recover. "Give me some credit for trying to expand my social circle, like you said."

"I suppose I shouldn't discourage you. At least you're trying. And I'm glad you're awake and sound ready to go."

"Go?" Lacey asked.

"Yes. You're going on a field trip with me."

Lacey thought of her sofa and Ambrose, and her plan to wallow in her thoughts about Miss Esther Mae, the others, and all her burgeoning drama. A "but" was beginning to form, but Tonti cut her off.

"No buts. Be ready in fifteen minutes. John and I will be by to pick you up."

"Can I ask where we're going?"

"To Golden Meadow. John will drop us at the Bay House; he's got some business or other over in Cut Off, he'll be back 'round to pick us up when he's done."

Lacey's heart sank. Tonti was one thing, but no part of her felt up for facing Fox's extended family.

"Relax, child. You'll thank me when we're done. I promise."

✳

Lacey felt like a child, sitting in the back seat of the Cadillac Eldorado with Uncle John in the driver's seat and Tonti by his side. Tonti chattered away. And like a child, Lacey slept in fits. When she awoke, her mind was a million miles away. She wished her body could accompany it.

Every now and then, Tonti would shoot a question back at Lacey, and each time she replied, "I'm sorry, what were you asking?"

Fox's family filled her thoughts as they traveled southwest. The Becnels were a warm but potent force when assembled. And the thought of seeing Fox's father nearly broke her heart.

As if reading her thoughts, Tonti said, "My brother won't be there; he's at the fishing camp."

Lacey snapped out of her fog. "I'm sorry. Which brother?" There were several.

"Big Fox."

"Oh, that's a shame. I would have liked to have seen him," Lacey said. It was only a partial lie.

Fox's father had always made Lacey feel like a favorite. When he compared her to Fox's revered and long-deceased mother, Miss Elaine, Lacey couldn't help but glow. Lacey thought she should ask Tonti about Miss Elaine, something that hinted at her earlier thoughts during Mass. But she couldn't think of a way to ask "Was Fox's mom a healer?" without prompting return questions she wasn't ready to answer.

Lacey was still struggling to form the question when Uncle John pulled into the paved circular drive at the end of a long shell road. The house stood apart from any other, but it couldn't be called "grand." Elevated to accommodate tidal surges, and even with its boat dock and neatly manicured lawn, it was not imposing. It always seemed a bit more on the side of the ridiculous, like a circus performer on stilts.

Lacey had long wondered why they called it the Bay House. The boat dock backed into a bayou, with nothing like a bay anywhere in sight.

Lacey had never heard of Golden Meadow, about fifty miles south of Metairie, until she'd met Fox at LSU. It had sounded idyllic. She'd pictured a thick pine forest clearing to a lovely golden meadow, the Gulf in the distance, with a few stately houses dotting it like some exotic wildflowers.

The first time Fox had taken her there, she had wondered if the Bay House would actually be a standing structure. No forests, just a lonely one-lane highway, the occasional cement box with nary a window housing the local bar, and the smell of the encroaching sea. She had spotted a few mobile homes a distance from the highway. As in love as she was with Fox the first time she visited, she hadn't cared what the Bay House looked like; it must hold some kind of magic if he loved the place so. She had just wanted to experience it with him. Maybe it would be near a beach.

She would quickly discover there were no beaches in Golden Meadow, just bayous and swamps and the great mush that happens when the sea meets alluvial soil. Even so, she was not disappointed the first time she visited to find a standing home instead of a mobile one. The Becnels gathered there on holidays and for several weeks during the summer, most of the caretaking falling to Big Fox and his brother, Uncle. Invariably, each time Lacey visited, someone made a passing comment about the house being in the Becnel family for generations. Which Lacey had never understood, since it appeared to have been built in the 1980s.

Still playing the part of a child, she absently followed Tonti up the drive to the exterior stairwell. Tonti was slow walking up the stairs, exclaiming, "God dammit if my brother doesn't fix that elevator soon!"

There was no elevator in the Bay House.

Lacey finally looked up as they entered the wraparound porch and peered inside. "Oh! It's lovely!"

Someone had been busy on the interior since the last time she had seen it. It had a fresh coat of paint; tattered secondhand furnishings had been replaced with simple, brightly upholstered new ones. Dollar store artwork had been replaced with family photos.

"Would you believe we have Big Fox to thank for this?" Tonti said, with a sweep of her arm. "Got a bug up his ass last year, took down everything, handed off anything anybody might want for sentimental reasons—I didn't want a thing, mind you—and got rid of the rest. Isn't it nice to see it as part of the twenty-first century?"

"Yes, it is. Really lovely," Lacey replied. "Where is everybody?"

"Lulu will be around later; she's out and about."

A bubble of panic formed in Lacey's stomach. Why on Earth was she stranded in the middle of Golden Nowhere with just Tonti and nothing to do for the foreseeable future?

"Let's have a drink and sit out on the porch," Tonti said.

"Tonti, it's only ten thirty."

"Splendid! That's perfect for a little brunch and hibiscus," Tonti said, using a code word for one of her favorite libations.

"I'm not quite ready for champagne," Lacey said.

"Fine. Then go find some cranberry juice and meet me out on the porch."

Lacey watched Tonti grab two champagne glasses—the old-fashioned kind, shallow and flat like a martini glass—and a bottle of cava, and breeze out of the kitchen. Lacey took her time lingering around. She suspected Tonti wouldn't wait for cranberry juice.

Lacey strayed from the kitchen, thinking to use the bathroom, but really because she wanted to snoop. The hallway had bedrooms branching off from it, though "bedroom" was a generous term. "Sleeping porch" would be more apropos.

The hall used to be littered with pictures, too many to take in. But the Big Fox makeover had apparently included a streamlining of the photos. Now there was a neat line of pictures, all in the same size frames, four on either side. One for each Becnel sibling.

Each family was represented in birth order: on one side were the older three sisters, Camille, Amelie, and Tonti, with Uncle finishing up that wall; and opposite Uncle was Big Fox, followed by Lulu, Laville, and Esmé.

She glanced at Camille's picture. She had met her only once, and Lacey saw nothing recognizable in the photo of the young woman before her. Aunt Camille had been in ill health, and had died shortly after she and Fox had started dating.

Lacey turned around to view the youngest Becnel. There was a portrait of an impossibly handsome family, dressed in khakis and loose white oxfords at the beach—Aunt Esmé, the baby of the family, with her husband and children.

Lacey took her time looking at the pictures. The bubble in her stomach tightened into a knot as she wondered what picture Big Fox had chosen to represent his family. There was no standard format. Some had a single photo, some had an artful triptych; Tonti's was a collage, an explosion of photos crammed into an eight-by-ten-inch space.

She turned slowly to see that Big Fox had chosen three pictures, set in a matte as a diagonal slash. Two of the pictures she had seen before. First, the centerpiece, a color photo of Big Fox standing over Miss Elaine with Fox, just a baby in her arms. He was looking down at the two of them with an expression reserved for first-time fathers—pride tempered by a sense of awe (or perhaps abject fear). At the lower left was a picture of Fox when he was fifteen, standing next to a huge marlin. Fox had called the fish Brando. Big Fox had that same photo on a side table at his house, next to one of Lacey and Fox's wedding photos. Big Fox loved to joke that she and Brando were the best catches Fox was ever going to see.

But there was no wedding photo completing this portrait. In the upper right was a young boy of about eight, standing with his hands on his hips, facing a woman in a white uniform, her mouth open as if she was scolding him. But there was unquestionable mirth in her look. And the picture quality was extraordinarily good for the time period—early '60s, Lacey guessed. She figured the boy must be Big Fox, but the woman in the white uniform was a mystery.

She appeared to be in her early to mid-thirties. *My age*, Lacey thought. She was beautiful, too—high cheekbones, a full mouth, and big, dark eyes that held an otherworldliness to them. And something familiar that Lacey could not place.

Worried that Tonti might come looking for her, Lacey cast a quick glance at Lulu and Laville's pictures and returned to the kitchen. She grabbed two single-serve bottles of cranberry juice cocktail from the pantry and met Tonti out on the porch.

"I'm sorry, Tonti—I meant to use the bathroom and got sucked into the portrait gallery in the hall," Lacey said.

"Can you believe that was Big Fox's idea, too? Aren't they gorgeous?" Tonti said. Her glass was nearly empty.

"Yes, they're great. It forces you to linger, I think. Before, I never knew where to focus, so I don't think I ever did," Lacey said.

"Here, child," Tonti pushed her glass at Lacey. "Mix me up a hibiscus while you set yourself up."

Lacey made a cava with a splash of cranberry for Tonti, and a cranberry with a splash of cava for herself. Both met with Tonti's approval.

"So who else is here besides Lulu?" Lacey asked.

"It should just be her and Randy for now. Uncle and Amelie and an assortment of their people are supposed to come 'round tonight, but we'll be long gone by then."

Lacey tried to hide her relief.

"How's Uncle Randy doing, Tonti?" she asked. She remembered the last time she'd seen him, at Fox's funeral, bald and emaciated from his lymphoma treatment.

"Much better! Thank blessed Father Seelos for that," Tonti said, making the sign of the cross.

Lacey played along. "Do you think he's any closer to beatification? Father Seelos, I mean, of course."

"Well I wouldn't think you meant Randy!" Tonti said. "Lulu sent a letter to the archbishop about Randy's remission, so I hope so. At least, she was supposed to. I'll have to check on that."

Lacey hesitated, having nothing further to offer. She'd always found the zealous saint-making missions of her fellow Roman Catholics somewhat bewildering. And she was still fixated on the pictures in the hall.

"Hey, Tonti," Lacey said. "Big Fox's picture in the hallway…"

"Birdie," Tonti replied. She sipped, her eyes searching Lacey over the rim of the glass.

"Birdie?" Lacey asked.

"Yes. You want to know who the woman in the picture is. It's Birdie." Tonti put down her drink and stared at Lacey.

"I don't think I've ever heard of her before," Lacey said. Becnel stories tended to repeat themselves, and Lacey knew many of them by rote.

"There's a reason for that," Tonti said with an air of mystery. "Birdie was only with us about five years," she continued. "She worked for the family when Mamère and Papa had the big house in Galliano. I'm sure Fox had to at least drive you past that."

"Yes, I know it," Lacey said. Fox had pointed it out nearly every time they'd gone to his father's house in Galliano. It was a stately plantation home that, according to Fox, the family had lost to creditors sometime in the 1970s.

"It was a time when Mamère needed the most help, and they had the resources to pay for it. Seven kids, the bulk of them ten and under. She got pregnant with Esmé during that time," Tonti said.

Lacey listened intently. Fox's grandparents were the stuff of legends. They had both died when Fox was a teenager.

"Birdie was an angel," Tonti said. "Literally. I never once saw her lose her temper. I never once saw her bring anything with her into that house but light. Sweetness and light."

"Is she still around?" Lacey asked.

Tonti put down her drink and narrowed her eyes. "No," she said. "But I'll get to that.

Mamère had a lot of spells at that time," she continued. "Birdie was there for all of us when she couldn't be. Foxy was especially partial to Birdie." Tonti nodded her head toward Lacey.

Lacey knew Tonti was digging deep. She wasn't sure she'd ever heard Big Fox called that before.

"We all loved her to the nth, but really none more so than Foxy. And he was her favorite, too. But that was the thing about Birdie. Her way was to sow peace; she never instigated even the slightest spark of jealousy. I think Heaven missed her, and that's why they called her back."

"What happened?" Lacey asked.

"She died in a car accident, a horrible crash out on Highway

One. Head-on collision with a truck coming out of nowhere, going the wrong way."

Lacey went lightheaded. She brought her hand up to her temple. The ever-present, subconscious fear hatched.

"We were devastated. All eight of us. Esmé was about three at the time. I can't say this in mixed company, but I don't think there was a one of us who didn't think we'd have been better off if it'd been Mamère in that crash instead, God rest her soul."

Lacey was silent, her eyes wide.

Tonti topped off her drink with more cava. "As I said, I wouldn't say that to just anyone. I loved Mamère, but she was the most fragile person I have ever known in my long lifetime. It's a wonder we're not more mixed up than we are."

The tension snapped in Lacey. She couldn't help but laugh.

Tonti laughed in response. "You see, that's why I love you, child. I can tell you this deep-seated childhood trauma, mother-drama, and you just laugh."

"I'm sorry, Tonti. That's not it. I mean…" Lacey felt a buzzing in her head. It was difficult to speak. "I mean, I've heard some of the stories about Mamère, but you have a point. I can't speak for the whole family, but you, especially, seem so lighthearted. Unburdened, I guess I mean." Lacey held her hand to her throat.

Tonti smiled. "You play with the hand you're dealt."

Lacey's wheels were spinning. "Tonti, how come I've never heard of Birdie before?" she asked.

Tonti put down her glass, flexed her hands, and gripped the edge of the table. "We all have our different reasons, I guess. Our time with Birdie was something I always kept very close in my heart. I think it was the same for Big Fox. As a reminder of how things can be, how you should be with children. I endeavored to be like her in my own parenting, with mixed results."

"What are you talking about? You're a great mom," Lacey said.

Tonti stared past the screened-in porch, toward a patch of swamp glowing silver in the distance. "You are very sweet, child. For a long time afterward, you know, Camille couldn't bear even the mention of Birdie," Tonti said.

Lacey detected a scent of mulch and decay, and wondered if Tonti was drawing the swamp in with her stare.

"She would get physically ill. I think the loss affected her the most, in terms of responsibility. She felt like she should step into that nurturing role, as the eldest, but she was just not wired for it."

Lacey remembered the stories about the artsy Camille, and thought of the picture of Birdie and the young Big Fox. "Did Camille take that photo?" she asked.

"Yes. It's beautiful, isn't it?" Tonti said. She finally returned her gaze to the porch, and the smell faded. "Lulu and I found that picture when we were cleaning out Camille's house after she died," Tonti continued. "She had this amazing assortment of her photography, very neatly catalogued and stashed in her attic. And the only pictures of Birdie any of us had seen."

"So Big Fox didn't have that picture all along?" Lacey asked.

Tonti tilted her head at Lacey. "Why, no, none of us had copies of those pictures. It was like discovering lost treasure. Lulu and I handed them out to everyone some time after Camille passed. I tell you," Tonti continued, "it brought me, at least, a lot of peace. I had never realized how much I resented Camille for not being able to talk about Birdie, for fear of upsetting her. Not being able to openly grieve was another loss, almost as painful. Finding those pictures—those pictures were Camille's way of caring, I suppose."

Lacey's head was full of car crashes, and grief, and dead Becnels. One especially, on the shore of Lake Pontchartrain. Her esophagus was tight.

"Tonti, you know how they say everyone grieves differently?" Lacey said.

"Yes, it's the truth," Tonti said.

"Well, I think my grief has brought on some stuff that I just can't make any sense of," Lacey said. A bead of perspiration traveled the side of her face.

Tonti nodded with a knowing glance.

"Do you remember the lady at Katie's? The one I helped walk into the restaurant?" Lacey asked, seeing an opportunity.

"Of course. The stately lady a few years my senior," she said with a wink.

"Well, I ran into Dotty Trebuchet today, and she told me the lady—Miss Esther Mae—just *died*, not two days after I helped her." Lacey folded her hands in front of her.

"Oh, God rest her soul. She went home," Tonti said. "Where did you run into Dotty?"

"At St. Daniel's," Lacey said. "But that's it? You don't think anything's weird about her dying?"

"Good for you. I'm glad you're still making it to Mass. Though I'm surprised about Dotty; I would expect to see her at St. Peter's. And no, what would be weird about her dying? She struck me as someone who had lived a full life."

"But she was so frail before I helped her, and then you said it yourself, she looked twenty years younger afterward," Lacey said. She tried to tamp down her measure of shock at Tonti's nonchalance.

"Child, just what is upsetting you about this?" Tonti asked.

"I don't know. What if, what if…I did something to her?"

Tonti laughed. "Like what? Sucked the soul from her body?"

"No! How is this funny?" Lacey asked. "But what if, I don't know, I passed some kind of energy or something on to her?"

Tonti settled, and paused. "Wouldn't that be a good thing?"

"But what if some kind of side effect, an effect of that *energy*, wound up killing her?"

"You're overthinking this," Tonti said, all mirth gone from her face. "And perhaps overestimating your ability."

Lacey wasn't sure she'd heard Tonti right. What insight did she have about her abilities? "Do you know…" she began to ask.

Tonti shook her head and smiled. "I brought you here because I wanted you to see Birdie," she said.

Lacey didn't respond.

"There's something in you that's like her. That's all I know. And something tells me you need to be the Birdie for someone, maybe many someones. I always thought it would be for Fox, but I guess God intended differently," Tonti said. She stood up and walked around the table to Lacey's side.

Lacey, eyes cast downward, knew Tonti meant to embrace her, but she stayed seated. She didn't want an embrace. She wanted no more talk of dead nannies, and she wanted Fox to be living, and more than anything, she wanted her old, normal life back.

Tonti sat next to Lacey and grabbed her hand.

"Child, I can't tell you what's happening, or why. No one can. But look inside yourself. Find the miraculous person that I know is within you. That Fox knew was in you," Tonti said.

Something red washed over Lacey. A lingering feeling that needed to be expressed before it could be expunged. Without thinking, she gripped Tonti's hand, hard, and locked eyes with her. "Who the fuck knows what Fox thought of me?" she said, her voice hissing below a whisper. "I don't know what Fox thought of me. He thought me a *fool.*"

A corresponding wave of calm came over her as soon as the words were out of her mouth. She released her grip and cast her eyes down again. She was disappointed in herself. What had happened to her resolve?

Tonti straightened and laid a firm finger under Lacey's chin, forcing her to look up.

"Lacey Campo Becnel, you listen to me now. Just because Fox couldn't keep his wick in his pants doesn't mean he didn't love you. He loved you like no other. You are the only one he ever wanted as his family. The sooner you accept that, and get over being the victim, the sooner your real life will begin."

Tonti pulled her hand away and placed both hands on her knees. She sat sideways, looking at Lacey's profile. Lacey closed her eyes and sighed. She knew Tonti was right, but needed the validation.

"Do you really believe that, Tonti?"

Tonti rose and stood behind Lacey's chair, placing her hands on her shoulders. "I know it, child. And something tells me you know it, too. Or at least some part of you does. I think it's time you let that part take over."

"I'm sorry I cursed," Lacey said.

Tonti laughed. "I loved hearing it! A sign of fire."

"But still," Lacey said, "I would never want to be rude to you."

"So afraid of your own shadow, child," Tonti replied. "We'll have to find some way to fix that."

18

Lawrence LaSalle felt his burner phone vibrate. It sent a surge of excitement through him, a feeling he almost didn't recognize. He waited a few beats before answering, determined to sound businesslike and not too hopeful. "This is Roark," he answered.

"Yes. We are going to put another feeler out on your client in the next ten days. We've broadened the scope. You should probably take extra measures to hedge the risk." The voice on the phone sounded different from before. The cadence was clipped, Yankee-like.

"Wait, broadened the scope?" LaSalle asked. "How?"

"You're a smart man, you'll figure it out," the Yankee voice said. The line went dead.

Lawrence LaSalle felt the bile rise in his throat again. He was accustomed to demanding clarity from anyone or about anything that sounded specious. It was a hard-won benefit of his status. He was angry that he had no power within this transaction.

He pondered the meaning of the Yankee's message. But he was too distracted, and his thoughts kept leading to one place, the same place they had gone for the past three months—Nathan Quirk's funeral. LaSalle would appear the stalwart fatherly figure to Lisa, and a doting grandfather to the children. He even knew what he would say to the well-meaning individuals who expressed condolences over losing both a son and a business partner: "Nathan truly can't be replaced," he would say. "This is such a tremendous loss to us."

Perhaps they could even hold a private funeral, if the circumstances of his death were tawdry enough. He relished this new line of thought. But he wouldn't want to deprive Lisa of the spotlight of grieving widow.

He suspected Lisa would appear appropriately distraught, but that deep down she would be relieved. Relieved to be free of a choice she'd made that had become burdensome. Oh, she had never confided as much to him, but he knew his daughter. She tired easily, and had probably long ago realized that she had made an inappropriate match. But he had raised her right; she wouldn't consider leaving her husband, certainly not while the children were still so young.

Lisa and the children. That was what the Yankee had meant by "hedge the risk."

Lawrence LaSalle felt nauseated. He'd been so fixated on the demise of Nathan Quirk that he had ignored the full repercussions of his actions. If his death were to look like an accident, what would it matter to those executing the plan if a few others were taken out? He had agreed upon a price for one man, but certainly they must factor collateral damage into their overhead. The full weight of the scenario hit him like an anvil. Had he clearly stated that nothing must happen to his daughter or her children? He had, he knew he had, but what recourse would he have if it went south for any reason?

His office was spinning. He was trying to recalibrate, adjust, hedge the risk, when he heard Nathan enter the main office. He rose from his desk to shut his door, but he was too late. Nathan stood before him, an arm's-width away. It was the closest they had been to each other in several weeks.

Nathan stepped back when he saw his father-in-law. He turned toward his office, then turned his head again.

"Sorry, boss," Nathan said. "You know, since you're up, I have one thing I want to check with you on the Zeringue closing…"

LaSalle blanched. He had always hated his son-in-law's overly familiar tone.

"Is everything all right?" Nathan asked. "You look like you've seen a ghost."

"I may have," LaSalle answered. He recovered quickly. "I'm fine," he added. "The closing is at noon, correct?"

"That's right," Nathan said.

"Can you come back in one half hour? I need to finish the review of the Henderson estate," LaSalle lied.

"Sure. No problem." Nathan turned toward his office. He felt a vibration in his pocket.

Nathan pulled out his phone and read the message that crossed his screen. He debated whether or not to say anything to LaSalle. His determination to keep to the high road won out.

"Actually, I need to run out now to meet a potential client," Nathan said, gesturing at his phone. "But I will see you before the closing."

"Very well. Make sure it's before eleven o'clock. I believe Bruns is the realtor, and he always shows up early," LaSalle said.

Nathan nodded. Bruns had nothing to do with this transaction, but the high road dictated that Nathan let the mistake slide.

19

At Carriere & Associates, Lacey tried to put a name to the way she felt. One word kept returning to the front of her mind: *altered.* More altered than after Fox died. Even more altered than after the first mutant episode with Nathan.

The revelatory trip to Golden Meadow had wiped a layer of gunk from her soul. Lacey suspected both she and Tonti felt a weight lifted, regarding Birdie. Tonti had finally been able to share her feelings about her; and Lacey had finally been able to attach a face—a real person—to things buried deep in her subconscious.

Lacey had forgotten to ask about Fox's mom, Miss Elaine. But the minute Tonti had begun speaking about Birdie, she'd known Miss Elaine wasn't the connection. It was Birdie. It explained her subliminal fixation on car crashes. She still couldn't quite figure how she'd come to acquire her mutant power from a woman who had died before she was born. But being able to place this one crucial piece of the puzzle was empowering.

Sitting at her desk, she didn't feel bored. She felt out of place. Like sitting in a third-grade classroom as an adult at a desk she'd outgrown. Everything in the job she had clung to for so long—the view, her imaginary coworkers, Trip's banal yet oddly comforting obsessions—suddenly felt unnecessary. Elton John was stuck in a feedback loop in her head.

"I've finally decided my future lies beyond the yellow brick road."

Five stories below her desk, a section of River Road was covered with a metal plate. Each passing car sent a metallic thud reverberating up to her ears.

An idea took up residence alongside the song lyric, set to the odd syncopation of that metallic thud. It was not a new idea, but the old arguments against it were no longer valid.

I'm going to quit my job today, she decided.

With the decision came an overwhelming urge to behave rashly. She checked the time: 8:15. Before allowing herself any time to think, she scrolled through her messages to find the last one from Nathan, and texted, CAN YOU MEET FOR LUNCH?

As soon as she'd sent it, she wondered if there was a way to recall it. And since she was soon to be unemployed, she wondered how much money she could make if she developed an app to recall text messages.

Her resolution was firm, she told herself. She only wanted to meet Nathan to elicit more details about what had happened that night. Now that she finally believed it, she wanted to study it. The attraction was inconsequential; it would be subjugated by her desire to learn more about her power.

Minutes passed. She shifted her stare from her phone to her monitor, fingers drumming her desk. Another rash decision: she would write a manual for her replacement. She began to type.

BEST PRACTICES FOR THE ASSOCIATE

1. Be on time. This means any time before 9:00 a.m.

2. Never interrupt Trip. Plan accordingly, because the length of his stories will lead to late nights at the office. Though this only applies to Mondays. His social calendar on the other days of the week has him out of your hair early, sometimes even as early as noon.

3. Never claim to know anyone higher than his social status, even if you do. This is grounds for immediate termination.

4. Watch Rex at Constantinople & St. Charles, neutral ground side. Shout his name loudly. DON'T carry a sign (more grounds for immediate termination). Every year, rain or shine, no exceptions.

5. Protect Marva and Roland at all costs. They are the key to your sanity.

6. Always

Her phone lit up. She felt butterflies in her stomach. She read Nathan's response to her invitation: NOT TODAY :-(

A frowny face? Lacey couldn't decide if Nathan was forty-five or fifteen.

Two beats later, another message appeared. CAN YOU MEET FOR COFFEE NOW?

She didn't allow herself time to think before responding.

Lacey agreed to meet him at Rue de la Course on Carrollton. As she checked her hair and makeup, she kept telling herself, *Don't think. Act.*

She grabbed her purse, and didn't think to close the document left open on her screen.

Lacey ordered a nonfat iced latte and grabbed a table at the back of the airy coffee shop. Though it was only minutes from her office, she did not go there often. She shamefully preferred Starbucks coffee over this local alternative. But she loved the atmosphere inside this café. It was spacious and sunny with the simplicity of a monastery.

Nestled in a shady corner opposite the stairs, she was hidden from view but could easily see both entrances.

A wall behind the stairs, plastered with announcements, held her attention. A flyer for a band playing June twenty-fourth loomed large in the center of the wall. The letters *L*, *V*, and *T* hovered above the date, and the text was superimposed over a faded photo. Lacey trained her eyes on it and recognized it instantly. It was a photo of her brother and his best friend (and bass guitar player) Dave Guidry, when they were about twelve years old.

Lacey pivoted her head toward the side entrance. A tall woman with a baby entered. Not Nathan.

She looked back at the flyer and shook her head. Her brother's latest band was called LeViticum. The venue wasn't listed anywhere on the flyer. She pondered the non-digital guerilla-marketing tactic for Jimmy's "surprise set at the Publiq House." It was rank with his signature. She suddenly missed his stupid sense of humor and his affinity for questionable band names.

The front entrance opened. Nathan. She was disproportionately relieved that it was the entrance farthest from where she was sitting. He was dressed in standard Uptown summer preppy, khakis and collared polo shirt neatly tucked with a belt. He was silhouetted by the early sun behind him, and she could see the definition in his biceps as he closed the door behind him. She cursed herself for noticing.

He walked to the counter and ordered. He glanced toward the back of the shop, but didn't seem to notice her. Lacey felt her reserve falter, and hoped he might get his coffee to go and leave the way he'd come in.

He paid for his coffee and walked straight to her. He stood across from her, towering over the table.

"I thought you didn't want me to call you," Nathan said.

"I don't. And you didn't. I called you," Lacey said.

"I see," he said. He set his coffee down but remained standing.

"You can sit, you know," she said.

"I didn't want to make assumptions." Nathan sat and offered a hint of a smile.

Face to face, Lacey couldn't think of anything to say. *Don't think. Act.* Nothing came to her.

Nathan broke the silence. "So, how've you been? How's the house, how's the beast?"

"If you mean Ambrose, he's fine," she said. She glared at him.

He laughed, loudly. It echoed off the high ceiling. "Listen, lady, you asked *me* out for coffee, remember? It's too late for the cold shoulder."

"I didn't ask you out for coffee," she replied, indignant. "I asked if you wanted to meet for lunch." She smiled, her façade finally cracking. Their eyes met, and her cheeks flushed crimson.

"And I couldn't have been more disappointed that I have a closing scheduled at noon today," he said.

"You look better," Lacey said.

"I am better," he replied. "At least by outward appearances."

Lacey decided not to probe. Not yet. "I'm going to quit my job today," she said.

"That sounds like news," Nathan replied. "I don't even know what you do."

Lacey cast her eyes downward. She couldn't wait for the day she could offer a different response, whatever it may be. "I work at Carriere & Associates," she said.

Nathan laughed. "You work for Trip Carriere?"

"You obviously know him," she answered.

"Mostly by reputation. But yes, I run into him at different places."

Lacey watched the tall woman take her baby out of the stroller.

"You're not in Rex, are you?" she asked Nathan.

"Such disdain," he said. "You sound like you have a moral issue with the grand traditions of Mardi Gras."

Lacey checked herself. "No, no moral issue. But let's just

say, if I get a job that takes me out of New Orleans, I won't miss our peculiar caste system."

Nathan watched Lacey intently. "Sounds like a moral issue to me."

"Easy for you to judge," Lacey said.

"No," he said. "Not really." He changed the subject. "So, are your greener pastures already lined up?"

Lacey sighed. "No. Not yet. I've got some ideas, though."

"That's okay. You're unattached," Nathan said, pausing at the word. "No better time in your life to be jobless. You're young, and capable, and can throw yourself at the right opportunity."

"How do you know I'm capable?" Lacey asked, her tone accusatory.

"Jesus, woman. How did you get that chip on your shoulder? Do we have 'Gone But Not Forgotten' to thank for that?" Nathan asked, smiling broadly.

Lacey remembered his mistaken assumption about her "boyfriend." The red tide came over her without warning.

"Asshole. Who do you have to thank for the pickle you're in?" Lacey regretted saying it as soon as it was out of her mouth.

Nathan was unfazed. "Wow. Good thing I like you so much. Because that was *mean*."

"I'm so sorry," Lacey said, the red tide subsided. "That was uncalled for."

"Noted: lay off the ex-boyfriend talk," Nathan said.

"Yes, please. It can turn me into something I'm not."

"I can see that," he said. He had a look, maybe desire, and a definite light in his eyes she had not seen before. It scared the hell out of her.

"Let me try again," Lacey said. "Thank you for the vote of

confidence. No, I don't know what I'm going to do, but I have a few ideas."

"You see? I told you you'd be on top of this in no time," Nathan said.

Lacey raised an eyebrow at him. "What about you? Are you really so…stuck in your current job?"

"When you work for your wife's father, it presents certain… complications when you start thinking of other alternatives. Add to that your wife's *very connected* father, and two kids, and yes. It gets…complicated," he said. His look went far away.

"I'm sorry, Nathan," Lacey said. "I shouldn't be prying so much."

He returned his gaze to her. "It's okay," he said. "I trust you. You're one of the only people I do trust," he continued. "Kinda sad, huh, when you're someone I just met?"

Lacey struggled to keep her head—and her heart—grounded. "Kinda crazy, I think," she said.

He nodded. "I think that sums up my situation pretty nicely."

Something from the deep surfaced, and Lacey grabbed on to it. "Nathan. Are you still doubting what happened?" she asked.

He was still for a moment. "No. No, I was before I saw you at Redd's. But you were so very real then, and the same now. I've kind of just accepted whatever happened as a new reality."

A new reality. The words rang in Lacey's head.

"How do you explain it?" Lacey asked.

"Explain it? I don't," he said. "I wouldn't even attempt it. I have enough other stuff to figure out."

"You're right," she said. "I'm sorry. Here you are, with someone out to kill you, and I'm bugging you about trying to explain my powers."

Nathan looked over his shoulder, and laughed when he was

certain no one else had heard her. "Another lesson learned: discretion is not one of your strengths," he said.

Lacey looked up and around. "I didn't say that too loud, did I?"

Nathan shrugged. "The acoustics in this place are pretty good," he said. "Are you beginning to doubt it yourself?" he asked.

"Me? No. I still don't understand it, but there've been some other things that have happened. Sort of backs up what you say I did," she said.

"You mean I'm not the sole beneficiary of your magical powers? I don't know how I feel about that," Nathan said. They shared a glance across the table. Lacey's cheeks flushed again.

She hugged her purse to her lap. "I don't know, Nathan. I like what you said—a new reality. I guess that's what I'm trying to make sense of. Somehow I've wound up here, someplace with no road map, and no guide who can tell me what the hell is happening to me."

"I like the way you say my name," he said. His stare was unbroken.

"Are you even listening to me?" she asked, looking over his shoulder, refusing to make eye contact.

"Yes! You're trying to find a road map and a guide," he said.

"No, I don't even think they exist," she said. She felt the heat of frustration.

Nathan leaned back in his chair. "We're in the same boat," he said.

Lacey narrowed her eyes and finally looked at his face. "How can that be?"

"No map, no one to explain what the hell is happening," he answered. He folded his arms.

"Oh," she answered, relaxing. "I see what you're saying."

"And when you look at the end result, the overall impact, how can you even worry?" he said. "Those other… beneficiaries…were they all better off after you did what you did and cheated on me?"

"Quit talking like that," Lacey said.

"Okay. But did you help them, in the end?" he said. He unfolded his arms.

"Yes. Maybe. I guess," she said. She thought of mentioning Miss Esther Mae's demise, but it would take too long. And she knew, from somewhere deep within, that if Nathan were to stop living, her power would have nothing to do with it.

"So maybe you should stop spinning your wheels about how it's all happening, and start trying to figure out how to make the most of it," he said.

Lacey considered, and smiled. "For someone in such turmoil, that was an amazingly insightful thing to say."

He laughed. "Tumult has a way of clearing out the cobwebs," he said. "Believe me, I wish I could wave your magic powers over my whole situation. But I suspect they don't work that way."

They shared another meaningful glance over the table. Lacey was still curious about one item, and it felt like a good opportunity to redirect.

"Nathan, I'm sorry, but—"

"Stop apologizing to me," he said.

"I'm sorry. Can you listen, please?"

Nathan smiled and nodded.

"You said, back at Redd's, that you thought your attackers were waiting for you," Lacey said.

Nathan's smile disappeared. "I did," he said. "I do. I've thought about it. A lot. It's like the pieces of a puzzle."

"How do you mean?"

Nathan looked behind him. "There's not a whole lot I can say. Just, I've been trying to shake off any assumptions I may be holding on to, and look at things cold. As objective as I can get."

"Sometimes it can help to ask for another set of eyes on things," Lacey said, a consequence of her not thinking first.

Nathan softened. "I appreciate that. But I feel like you've risked enough for me already."

He looked behind him again, and lowered his voice. "I've been thinking about motive, and may be on to something, but there's a big missing piece. I don't know enough about our criminal underworld to know how these things may be arranged."

Lacey felt he must be speaking the truth. Would anyone who really knew how the seedy underside of things operated refer to it as the "criminal underworld"?

He looked at her sideways, expectant.

"Sorry," she said. "Can't offer any insight there." Her guard shot up again. *Why would he think I might be a criminal underworlder?*

"It was a long shot," Nathan said. "But I really don't know you at all. Maybe your father, or your…maybe your father was a cop or something. I really have no idea."

"My father was an engineer. Retired now," Lacey said coolly.

"Ah, the chip is back. Please don't take offense. Are you rescinding your offer for another set of eyes?"

"No," she said. "I'm sorry. I guess I really don't know you at all, either."

"If we keep meeting like this, that might change." Another glance, and Lacey felt her butterflies alight.

She sighed. She checked the time.

"Afraid Trip might think you're short-timing him?" Nathan asked.

Lacey laughed. "Well, I haven't quit just yet. But I should think about getting back. I don't want to cut you off, though." *A little too late to say that*, she thought.

Nathan looked at his phone. "No, don't worry. I should get back, too."

An awkward silence settled on their bistro table. The tall lady left with her baby.

Lacey began to rise from the table. Nathan stayed seated.

"Planning to stick around?" she asked.

"I'm not in a hurry," he said.

She stopped and stood next to him, facing him as he sipped his coffee. "I'm sorry I can't stay longer, but I don't think I should linger," she said.

He grabbed her hand with a gentle touch and held it. "Probably not," he said.

Lacey looked at him and pulled her hand away. She struggled to catch her breath as she walked like an automaton to the side door.

20

An oaf stood on the dock. Lacey felt immediately guilty for thinking it, but it was the first word that came to mind. Built like an oak tree, with an unfortunate underbite, he did not look as threatening as his size would signify. Then Lacey noticed the gun holstered at his waist.

Even the wrap party for a made-for-cable movie gets armed security, Lacey thought.

He had a list, but didn't ask for Lacey's name. She strolled across the gangplank without even a nod from the man.

She wasn't even sure why she was there. Angele was still being aloof, but had made it clear she wanted Lacey to come. This would be their first opportunity to talk face to face since their showdown on Harrison.

That was one reason. Lacey needed Angele's help finding a job. She had lost her nerve and had not yet quit Carriere & Associates, but knew it was only a matter of time. She might have an easier time resigning if she at least had a lead on another job.

There was possibly another reason. She thought of encountering the Dakota Kid again. She was excited about the chance, just to continue the flirtation, nothing deeper. But wanted Angele nowhere near when, or if, it happened. That was why she had decided to arrive early.

Walking up a stairway and several inclines, she regretted her shoe selection. She was wearing a new set of peep-toe heels to show off her legs, but by the time she'd made her way to the ballroom, she was teetering.

Only a few partygoers milled about. The largest concentration of people gathered around the sound system. The DJ removed his headphones and pointed out a few things to someone. That someone looked familiar to Lacey. As soon as he turned, she saw the unmistakable profile of Eli.

Good. At least he'll be stuck behind that table and not creeping around, picking on me, Lacey thought.

The Dakota Kid and the Mississippi Charmer were also in the DJ crowd. Lacey wondered how many other states were represented.

She made a beeline for the bar, hoping to remain unnoticed. No chance. The Kid was the first one to spot her. They locked eyes and he immediately split from his crowd.

He looked good. Jeans, T-shirt, jacket. Lacey had hit the nail on the head with the Steve McQueen comparison.

"Who let you in?" he said as he intercepted her.

Lacey arched an eyebrow. "Excuse me?" She tried to come up with a wittier follow-up than "excuse me," but the Kid beat her to the punch. He scooped her up and dunked her, like they were in the midst of a dance. He righted her, and planted a quick kiss on her lips.

"Lacey! I'm glad you're here. We have a game to finish," he said.

"We do?" Lacey asked. Stars sparked in her peripheral

vision. She prayed Angele wasn't off lurking in the shadows.

"Yes! I'm supposed to guess why you're an idiot," he said.

"Maybe I'm not an idiot anymore," Lacey said, unconvinced.

"Ah, but the words came out, less than…what, less than a week ago. The statute of limitations hasn't run out yet," the Dakota Kid said.

"I wouldn't think there would be a limitation on stupidity," Lacey said, realizing she wasn't helping her case.

"For you, there most definitely is. I don't see you being an idiot for more than a week at a time, tops," he said. He had taken her hand and led her to the bar.

"Thank you. I guess?" Lacey said.

"Good. Then it's on," he said. He asked the bartender for a scotch and a Ketel One and tonic.

Lacey, pleased with herself, thought of an opening and took it. "Hey, don't you have some sycophants missing you terribly right now? Why are you so interested in why I'm an idiot?"

"Sycophants, huh? Nice. You use some high-dollar words there," he said.

"You must be fairly sharp yourself, if you know what it means," Lacey said.

"My parents are English teachers," he said. "And if you're referring to my friends, they can be without me for a little while. I'm where I want to be right now, finding out why my production manager's best friend thinks she's an idiot."

"I'm probably an idiot in more ways than one," Lacey said. The Dakota Kid knew the connection between her and Angele. She wasn't sure why that disappointed her. "But knock yourself out, take a guess."

"Let's see," the Kid said. He tapped his fingers on the bar.

"You've got a crush on a younger guy, a real hot property, and you couldn't figure out why you were sitting alone at the end of the bar the other night instead of talking to him," he said.

"Ha! I think this younger guy thinks very highly of himself!" Lacey laughed. "And wait—how do you know he's younger than me?" she asked defiantly.

"I know a few things. I'm full of surprises that way," he said.

"I'm getting that sense," Lacey said. "If you really must know, I think I called myself an idiot because I was panicking about not being able to find my car key, when it was in my pocket the whole time."

"I see," the Kid said. He looked down at the skirt she was wearing and raised his eyebrows. "I can think of only a few places to get lost in that outfit."

Lacey nearly spat out her drink laughing. "Wow," was all she could say.

He smiled, pleased at her reaction. "But I don't buy it anyway. You said there are probably multiple reasons, so I think the key is just a red herring."

"Philosophically, I'm sure there are several reasons," she said, thinking specifically about her reluctance to give notice at her job. "But I can assure you, a crush on a mythical 'young hot property' is not one of them."

"Yet," he said.

Lacey shook her head.

His back against the bar, he crossed his legs and folded his arms in front of him. He looked at Lacey's hands, clasped together on the bar as if in prayer.

Suddenly self-conscious, she dropped them to her sides.

"Don't worry, babe, I saw enough the other night," he said to her, and winked. "So maybe you're inclined to think yourself an idiot because you've let your heart lead you where your head isn't ready to follow," he said. "It's happened before, and you're afraid it's going to happen again."

He said it with an earnestness that made her think it wasn't a come-on. Lacey cocked her head at him. She wasn't sure how to respond. The truth was all she could come up with. "You might be on to something. Am I that transparent?"

The Dakota Kid smiled and looked down at his shoes. A show of humility she doubted she'd ever see again. "Only in the way that anyone who feels is transparent. And for what it's worth, I don't think following your heart is ever a bad idea." At the flip of a switch, the cocky movie star returned. "Plus, you're hardly transparent. You're very vividly drawn," he said.

His hand dropped to her side and caressed the curve of her hip. His fingers tapped gently.

Lacey's wheels started spinning and her breath caught in her throat. She felt completely outshone by the Kid's outsized charisma. It was a familiar feeling.

She quit thinking and kissed him, hard on the lips. He was a little shocked by the move, but wasted no time in returning the embrace. He took control, placing both hands on her hips.

His touch lingered. A finger traced the small of her back, and she imagined her spine lit up like a Christmas tree. He took his time. Lacey couldn't remember the last time she'd made out with someone. She thought of Fox, and a New Year's Eve. It felt like a lifetime ago.

He must have sensed her thoughts beginning to stray. The pressure of his touch intensified. He had a hand nearly under her arm, along the side of her breast, his thumb just brushing against it. It set her pinging.

Something didn't sound right. The music had stopped.

Lacey's head was racing and her heartbeat quickened. But she pulled away when she heard a commotion.

"K-Kevin," she said.

He looked angry.

"Something's happening," she said.

The crowd around the DJ had dissipated and headed en masse to the railing of the boat. They had not yet left the dock.

"I think you're right," he said. "Come with me." He grabbed her hand and pulled her behind him. She took little baby steps in her heels to try to keep up.

He maneuvered his way through the crowd, keeping her in tow. They got to the railing and saw two crewmembers hauling a body up from the water. Eli and Angele were standing by. Angele shot a look full of daggers at Lacey.

Lacey looked in the opposite direction and pulled her hand away from the Kid.

The June evening was thick and oppressive. Lacey took a deep breath and willed the air to be less stifling. She took two steps back.

"Who is it?" she heard the Kid ask Eli.

"Angus," Eli responded, no inflection in his voice.

"Is he dead?" the Kid asked.

"No. I'm going to need your friend," Eli said. He turned his head toward Lacey, but his right eye floated out over the water. She couldn't tell where he was looking.

She tried to back up further, but there was nowhere to go.

"Lacey?" the Kid asked.

Lacey heard nothing else. Eli appeared at her side and led her by the elbow.

The crewmen pulled up the limp, towering body of Angus and laid him out on the deck. Lacey tried not to stare. It was the same man she had seen earlier, the oaf stationed on the dock, who had let her in without checking his list.

Angele stood nearby, arms folded.

A big, wet, lifeless mass. Lacey blanched from head to toe. She couldn't move. She was back on the shores of Lake Pontchartrain, identifying Fox's body.

Eli tightened his grip on her arm and said, "You're going to have to get over that. Come with me. You have to help me help him."

She was struck.

"What? No," she said. "What can I do?"

"Hold his hand," Eli ordered. He pulled her down to the ground and put his ear to the barrel chest of the drowned man.

Eli started chest compressions, but the body didn't respond. Lacey tentatively touched the limp, gray hand. She felt heat, not from his hand, but her own. It radiated up her arm, an almost familiar sensation now.

Lacey fought to maintain consciousness as the fire traveled through her. This hadn't happened before. Or had it? Waves passed through her, and she felt waves buffeting her, like she was treading water in a rough ocean.

She focused on Angus, trying to stay conscious. He had broad, plain features. His underbite more pronounced by a slack mouth. Lacey's knee almost touched his holstered gun.

The waves began to settle. Eli stopped chest compressions. Angus's chest heaved, and he coughed. Fountains of water spewed from his mouth as he violently vacated his lungs.

Lacey released his hand and stood, backing up against the railing of the boat. She felt singed, her only relief her head-to-toe perspiration.

Angus was conscious and coughing. Eli had gotten out of

his way, and through a fog, Lacey saw Angele and Eli talking.

Once again, Lacey felt herself being yanked away and dragged from the crowd. She sailed past the Dakota Kid, a surprised and amused look on his face. He shrugged, and Lacey turned around to see who had hold of her.

Angele. Damn, she was strong for her size. "Walk with me," she said as she pulled Lacey to the aft of the steamboat.

Lacey struggled to regain her feet. She finally did, and as soon as they were out of sight of the crowd, she pushed off Angele.

"What the fuck?" Angele responded.

Lacey felt the red wave rise.

"What the fuck back! What is with you? I could use some help here," she said. Lacey looked up. The enormous paddle wheel at the rear of the boat slowly swayed from side to side as the water lapped at its base.

"I don't know what the fuck has gotten into you," Angele said. "A make-out session with that ridiculous *child*, and then going mutant on some scrub of a security guard. What a fucking waste of energy." The venom in her voice made Lacey wince.

"Jesus, what is your problem?" Lacey hissed. She fanned at herself and tried to catch her breath. "One, I have no idea what happened there," she continued. "Your boy Eli just grabbed me and put me to work, I didn't go volunteering. And second, what about Kevin Horner? Aren't you always telling me to lighten up, be more in the moment?"

"You have no idea of the consequences of your actions," Angele said.

A dredge boat churned past, moving downriver. The boat's lights fell on them for a moment. Angele looked small and sad.

Lacey shook her head. "I don't fucking believe this. I can't do anything right," she said. She kept fanning herself. "And how can you say that," Lacey continued, "about the security guard? Are you really that cold?"

"Say what?" Angele asked.

"That he was a waste of my energy," Lacey said.

"I didn't say that," Angele said.

"Oh, I think you said something about a 'fucking waste of energy' when I don't even know what my energy is."

"Jesus, Campo, it's just a phrase," Angele said. "This guy's been a liability this whole shoot. Look—it's just—he *fell* over. I saw it happen. Like he was leaning over to see something, and poof."

"Jesus, indeed," Lacey said. "Maybe he fainted, or had a stroke or something. Maybe he has health issues. But this is all beside the point. I don't get what you're giving me right now." Lacey turned her back to Angele and walked toward the river side of the wheel.

"Oh, Lacey, shit!" Angele said. She ran to Lacey and shoved her to the ground with the full force of her bodyweight.

Lacey turned her head in time to save her teeth from cracking on the deck. She saw Angele landing blows against her back. She reared up, trying to push her off.

"Wait, Lacey, wait!" Angele said, her hands now gently patting Lacey's back. "Here, roll over." She pushed at Lacey's side. Lacey rolled over.

"Christ, Lee, I think you broke my shoulder! What the fuck?"

"You were on fire," Angele said, kneeling over her, hands on her thighs. She cracked the first smile Lacey had seen all evening.

"Oh, this is funny?" Lacey asked.

"Sort of," Angele said. "C'mon, let's stand you up." Angele offered her hand. Lacey shook her head, but accepted the assist anyway.

The wake of the passing ship slapped against the side of the riverboat. The heavy air smelled sweet. A combination of fuel exhaust and whatever had been dredged up from the riverbed.

"What were we talking about?" Lacey asked.

"Fuck if I know. I guess…I just want you to be more careful, that's all," Angele said. "Especially around this crowd. You have to be careful who you let in."

Lacey patted at her sides, trying to put herself back together.

"Look, I'm sorry about the Dakota Kid," she said. "I didn't know it would put you in such a bad way. I'll back off."

Angele laughed. A chuckle tinged with bitterness. "I could give a shit about him," she said.

Her reaction proved Lacey's hunch about a crush.

"And you're right," Lacey said, changing subjects, "I need to be more careful. Especially if I'm going to start working with these folks and spontaneously combust and shit."

"Have you quit Trip yet?" Angele asked.

"No, no. I will, though. Monday. It's gonna happen."

"I'm not going to make any calls for you until you do, so get on it," Angele said. She was acting like herself again, much to Lacey's relief.

Lacey took a deep breath and pushed her hair back behind her ears.

"Lee, are we done here?" she asked. "I think I need a drink."

Angele nodded. "Yeah." They walked together, back to the crowd.

"So," Lacey asked, "was it like big orange flames or just a little bit of smoke? I knew I felt something."

"It was pretty weird," Angele said, keeping in step. "More like a glow, like embers, with some smoke."

Lacey turned her back to Angele. "How bad does it look?"

"Luckily, the pattern on your top kind of hides it," Angele said. "And it's dark. You'll be fine."

"Easy for you to say."

"I think we just figured out the naked part," Angele said. "I wonder if fire retardant material would make any difference."

21

Eli pulled Lacey aside when she returned to the dissipating crowd at the riverboat's railing.

"Are you okay?"

"Yes," Lacey answered. "I guess."

Awkward seconds passed. His left eye looked at her straight on, making her more nervous than ever.

"Are you going to inquire after Angus?" Eli asked.

"Oh, God, yes, I'm sorry. How is he?"

"He's been taken to hospital. They will test him for signs of a cardiac event. His prognosis is good."

Lacey wondered how he knew that. "Oh. That's good. I guess," she said.

"You guess?" Eli asked.

Lacey folded her arms. "I mean, I'm glad he's going to be okay. But I'm still confused about everything else." And she was. Eli knew something about her ability—that much was obvious. But how? She should have asked Angele.

"You shouldn't be. Have you been paying attention?"

Lacey huffed involuntarily. She looked down at her peep-toe heels.

If Eli was a different sort of person, he might have laid his hand on her shoulder, or laughed and said something reassuring. Instead he said, "Come with me."

Lacey looked up. "What?"

He folded his arms and raised his eyebrows. "You heard me. Let's go."

Lacey looked around for Angele, but didn't see her anywhere.

"No time for stalling," Eli said. He turned and walked inside.

Lacey took a few hesitant steps and felt a hand around her waist. She turned and came face to face with the Dakota Kid.

"Well, that was exciting, huh?" he said.

Lacey shook her head. "Understatement. Where are we going?" she asked.

"I don't know. But he does," the Kid said, gesturing toward Eli.

Lacey had no energy to protest. She would text Angele to let her know where they wound up. And she would work up the nerve to ask Eli how he knew about whatever it was that she did. She'd lost the opportunity with Cecil; she wasn't going to lose another one.

The Kid's arm felt nice around her, but any desire had seeped away. Their moment had passed. Lacey felt herself settling into the friend zone, and everything about it felt right. The Kid pulled his hand from her back to place it on her shoulder. She glanced at it. His hand was dirty with soot.

Lacey sighed heavily when she realized where Eli was taking them. Their driver turned onto Maple Street. Redd's.

What if Nathan is there? Her thoughts turned, and she couldn't stop a wicked little smile from forming. If he was there, he would see her with Kevin Horner. He would be jealous.

Stupid, she told herself. *Nathan is a married man.* A line from a long-forgotten song materialized in her head: *Keep an open heart and you'll find love again, I know.*

She reflected on the source. Tesla's power ballad was pretty catchy, and Jimmy had always liked the band. She had no idea why that snippet of lyric had come to her. Maybe the driver had run over a wormhole that bridged to the stereo in her brother's room twenty years ago.

And she didn't want to find love again. *No, that's stupid, too.* Of course she wanted to find love. Who didn't want love in their life? But not a repeat. She'd already had the head-over-heels tumult with Fox.

A loud rapping roused her from her thoughts. Kevin Horner was outside the car already, knocking on the thick glass of her window and mouthing words. She pulled the door handle.

"Earth to Lacey!" he said as he grabbed her hand and helped her out of the car. "Wow. Where the hell were you?"

✳

They took a booth near the side door, and Kevin volunteered to get drinks. Eli and Lacey sat exactly opposite each other, Eli with his calm Buddha visage, floating eye, and no attempt at conversation. Lacey swiveled her head, attempting to find an opening. He still made her feel wildly uncomfortable, and she was beginning to suspect that was absolutely by design.

There were a handful of people in the place—three guys playing pool, two couples sitting at one of the other booths. They were all younger than Lacey would have expected them to be, and none of them were Nathan.

A young blonde, all skin and bones except for her implants, was tending bar. Kevin took his time getting their drinks.

Eli popped out of his seat and announced, "I'm going to the jukebox." He didn't wait for a response.

When Kevin finally returned, he sat next to Lacey, her purse serving as a divider between them.

Lacey nodded toward the jukebox and said, "He has a pretty unusual way of interacting with people."

Kevin looked confused and answered, "How so?" And then burst out laughing. "It's the genius thing," he answered. "It's almost like he has Asperger's, but without any of the anxiety. He enjoys socializing, but on his own terms."

"Interesting," Lacey replied.

"He likes you," Kevin continued. "He said he thinks you have 'real potential.'"

"What is this, *Pretty Woman*?" Lacey laughed. "Potential as what?"

"Who knows? But it's not the sort of compliment he's likely to make often, I know that."

"Also interesting. So, how's the bartender?" Lacey asked.

Kevin Horner's cheeks tinged red. "Who?" he replied, covering.

Lacey elbowed him in the ribs, a final punctuation to their moment on the *Natchez*. She had gone from potential hookup to wingman in less than two hours.

"C'mon. I've never seen anyone volunteer so quickly to get drinks. We were barely even in the door. She's pretty," Lacey continued after a pause. She could almost see him course-correct. He must think wingman was a good fit for Lacey.

"Well, the sex we had in the office was phenomenal," he said.

Lacey laughed. "It couldn't have been that great, you were only gone a few minutes."

"It was so good it warped space and time." He went shoulder to shoulder with her, and pointed to the doorframe around the office. "You see, you can just make out the blurred edges around the door. Where I warped space and time."

"I've been in that office," Lacey said before she could stop herself. "You'd have to warp space to fit two people in there."

"That sounds like a story," Kevin said.

"Oh, no," Lacey said. "It's not, no story." She folded her arms.

Kevin butted her in the shoulder again. "Ha, it's so totally a story! I want to hear it."

"It's a story not yet ripe for the telling," another voice said.

Eli. He appeared and took his seat opposite them.

"Yes, thank you," Lacey said, freaked out by his observation. "And it's not even a story."

"It will be," Eli said. His eye floated toward the jukebox.

"Dude, knock off the Yoda routine," Kevin said. He pushed his beer in front of him.

Eli took a sip, and a rare smile passed over his face as a new song started. It was LeViticum's cover of "Time Passages."

"Nice choice," Lacey said to Eli. *Jimmy will appreciate the support.*

"Do you know the original?" Kevin said. "I just heard it recently for the first time. It sounds *nothing* like this version."

"I have to disagree," Eli said. "It's the same structure, just taken to a minor key."

"If that meant anything to me, maybe I would agree with you," Kevin said.

Lacey was glad their attention had shifted elsewhere. "Which version do you prefer?" she asked.

They both agreed on the current version. "Me too," Lacey said.

Eli said how he wished LeViticum had incorporated synthesizers into their version, but short of that, thought their version was superior. That launched an animated discussion of whether it was okay to change the lyrics when covering a song, with Kevin staunchly opposed, and Eli taking the pro position.

Lacey settled into the role of devil's advocate, on this and most of the other topics that came up into the wee hours of the morning. She was surprised by how comfortable she felt with them. Her need to interrogate Eli lost its urgency. The artful burn marks on her back were hidden from view, and she felt no ill effects.

Kevin's trips to the bar increased as the crowd dwindled, even though they were well set for drinks. Sometime south of two a.m. he repositioned himself there permanently.

Alone with Eli, some part of Lacey thought she should grab the opportunity. She went to speak, and stifled a yawn instead.

"I'll make sure you get to your car," Eli said.

Lacey looked at him and nodded. "Let me tell Kevin goodbye."

The bartender's back was turned. "Guess I'm going, then," Lacey said as she approached Kevin.

"No!" Kevin said. "We're having too much fun."

Lacey ignored his comment and half smiled. "I'm kind of sorry I forfeited my turn for her," she said above a whisper, nodding at the bartender. "But I like her, though."

Kevin Horner looked very excited. "Three way?"

Lacey laughed and shook her head. "Jesus, you are bold!" She kissed him on the cheek. "I don't share the spotlight. 'Til the next time?"

"You can count on it." He jumped off his barstool and grabbed Lacey in a big bear hug, lifting her off the ground.

Back on solid footing, she walked toward the door.

She flipped her hair, looked over her shoulder at the once and future Dakota Kid, and said her sexiest "Bye!"

The look on his face said everything Lacey wanted it to.

At the threshold, Lacey stopped short. Tesla's "Love Song" began to play. She turned around, but the Kid had already reengaged with the bartender. Before her, Eli waited on the sidewalk.

"Is your song selection still playing?" she asked Eli.

They stood side by side. He turned his ear, and then nodded without looking at her.

"Big fan of Tesla?" she asked, staring straight ahead.

"I like how they chose their name," he answered, as if that was what everyone should like about the band.

Lacey had never thought about it before. They had always been grouped in her head as one of an amalgam of hair bands for which her brother had an inexplicable affinity.

She bit. "What's behind their name?"

"They named themselves after the inventor Nikola Tesla."

"Oh! Geez. I never made the connection before."

Eli turned to her with a disappointed look. "They are all around you, if you would only see them."

A car pulled up, the same one that had delivered them. Eli walked around to speak to the driver.

What does that mean? Connections are all around me?

Did he know that song was in my head earlier? Lacey was dumbfounded.

Eli came back and opened the door for her.

"Reggie will take care of you; she'll make sure you get to your car safely," he said. He stood like a sentry, blocking her way to the passenger seat. "Have you been to the New Orleans Healing Center?" he asked.

"No," Lacey answered. She had never heard of it, but the name struck her.

"You should go," Eli said. "There's much for you to learn. Good evening, Lacey." He stepped out of her way.

Time froze as she lowered her head to enter the car. She turned to look at Eli. "Goodnight," she said. Eli was already through the door of Redd's.

The driver, Reggie, had a voice tinged with caramel and a lovely complexion. "Back to the *Natchez*?" she asked.

"Yes, thank you," Lacey said. She buckled herself in, surprised that her body was in the car when her mind felt all over the place.

Lacey stared straight ahead, replaying her exchange with Eli. And it came as quickly as a light switch. Eli's bald head, his cryptic demeanor, his seeming ability to read her thoughts.

Eli was Professor X.

22

On Monday, Lacey was ready. She would go in late to the office, tender her resignation, and if Trip wanted her to leave immediately, she would go to the New Orleans Healing Center. She would go there today even if he didn't usher her out the door.

But she was certain all would go as she imagined, with Trip expressing dismay but taking it in stride. Trip's Jaguar XK was in his designated spot, so she knew he was there. She ran through her script for the millionth time as she rode the elevator up to the office.

She turned the key to the front door, strode to her desk, and prepared to drop her purse and head straight into Trip's office. But his office door was shut. That was the first sign all would not go as planned.

The antiquated HVAC system in their building worked best when it could cool the space without the obstacles of closed doors. It was not so unusual for Trip to enclose himself in his office in the winter to tend to secretive Rex duties, but in the summer months he was too delicate a flower to withstand the heat.

Lacey sat at her desk and watched the river. Nary a ship in sight. She checked the phone and saw all lines were open. She trained her ear, and heard Trip in conversation with a female voice. Even more peculiar. Lacey booked all his meetings, and if he happened to arrange something himself, she was sure to hear of it because he would brag incessantly about his independence.

She opened a spreadsheet and pretended to study it. She kept her eyes on the screen when Trip's door opened, looking over with a casual head-turn after a moment. A pretty girl seemed to hang on Trip's every word. With her black hair tied up in a long ponytail, and her basic black business suit, she looked like the casting-call version of a fresh-out-of-college job applicant. There was a slight sheen on both their faces, and Trip's white button-down showed a widening sweat stain. Pretty Pony shook Trip's hand, smiled broadly at Lacey when she saw her at her desk, and walked out the door.

Trip stood in his doorway, an unusually steely gaze aimed straight at Lacey. She raised her eyebrows, and he shrugged his shoulders and motioned her into his office. He fooled with the thermostat just inside his doorway.

"Who was that?" Lacey asked in the most innocent, non-accusatory voice she could muster.

"Your replacement," he replied.

Lacey's stomach fell.

Trip smiled at her reaction. Which did nothing to make Lacey feel better.

"Have a seat," he said.

She took the nearest of his well-appointed leather guest chairs, noticing only too late that it was still wet with Pretty Pony's sweat. *At least she's human*, Lacey thought.

"Well, that didn't go as planned," she said, loud enough for Trip to hear.

"I'd imagine not," he replied as he left the thermostat and came around the desk.

He sat and said nothing, obviously amused. Lacey imagined canary feathers poking out the sides of his mouth.

Lacey asked, "Did you know I was planning to resign today?"

Trip laughed. "Were you actually going to do it today? That's brilliant."

Lacey couldn't hide her shock. She wasn't sure what confounded her more—that Trip might be more perceptive than she'd ever given him credit for, or that he'd actually taken the initiative to hire someone without her assistance.

Her stomach sank even further at an errant thought—had Nathan revealed her plans to Trip? He'd said they weren't friends, but they ran in the same "social circles."

Never one to play out a joke too long, Trip cleared his throat, like he was coughing out a feather. "Best Practice Number Three," he said. "Wait, which one was that one, again? 'Never interrupt'? Or was it 'Never claim to know anyone higher…'"

He trailed off when he saw the desired reaction on Lacey's face: beet red, eyes wide with mortification.

"Oh shit!" she said as she put her face in her hands.

And it began. Her breath came in short gasps, her head trembled. She looked up and faced Trip, laughing hysterically.

He looked at her uneasily.

"God, I'm so sorry, Trip, that was a joke, I was bored! I had no idea—I never intended—I can't believe you actually saw that!"

Trip took a pregnant pause, letting Lacey settle.

"Honestly, Becnel," he said, "I would never had guessed you had that caustic edge to you. I might be more impressed than hurt."

That was hardly caustic, Lacey thought. She even considered saying it aloud, now that there was truly nothing to lose.

"Really, Trip, I am *so* sorry," she offered instead.

"Becnel, think about it. You know, and I know, it's time. Not to be indelicate about this, but I knew after you lost Fox that it could only be a matter of time before you sought out new employment."

"It's time," Lacey repeated his sentiment.

"Yes. But I was waiting for you make the first move. I certainly couldn't push you out, a recent widow. Besides the legal ramifications, what kind of insensitive prick would that make me?"

Lacey laughed involuntarily.

"Don't answer that," he continued. "So I happened to see your 'employee manual,' snooped around, and saw the start of a resignation letter open on the same screen."

Lacey was horrified at the thought of Trip looking at her computer, even though she knew he had every right. What else might he have seen?

She tried to play it off. "I'm curious, Trip, why didn't you say something to me about it? We could have come to this point sooner, and maybe I could have helped you recruit."

"Well, Becnel, I think that qualifies as 'none of your beeswax,'" Trip said, delighted by his use of colloquialism. "But in the interest of honoring our nine years together, truth is, this thing with Katelyn just materialized. You know of Evan Long, don't you? Katelyn is his associate's daughter. Evan owes him, I owe Evan. Katelyn graduated cum laude from USL, she wants to stay in the city, have a good job, but have the flexibility to plan her wedding."

"Sounds familiar," Lacey said as she reminisced about her first interview with Carriere & Associates, about ten months before she married Fox.

"Exactly." He finally seemed to lighten up.

"And it's ULL, you know," she said.

"Pardon?"

"It's not called USL anymore, it's the University of Louisiana at Lafayette now, ULL. Maybe she won't think you're an insensitive prick if you refer to her alma mater by the proper name."

"Hmm." He seemed not to hear her. "And as far as not approaching you, I didn't want to spoil your surprise. I knew it would be coming, and wanted to let you tell me in your own right."

"So much for that," Lacey said.

"I would like to maximize whatever time we have left," Trip said, ignoring her comment. "You can give me at least six weeks, can't you? To train Katelyn?"

Six weeks? It felt like forever.

"When does she start?" she asked.

"Oh, let's see," Trip glanced down at a note on his desk. "Not until August fifth. There's some sort of nonsense about a trip to Europe. I tried to force her to start sooner, but she said something about a graduation present, and her parents having planned for five years, if you can believe that."

Probably planned and saved for five years, Lacey thought.

"Yes, I can believe that," she replied. "It shouldn't be a problem, Trip. I don't exactly have things lined up on my end yet," she said. It was liberating to be so candid with him.

"What are you thinking of, if you don't mind me asking? Were you thinking of staying in New Orleans?"

Lacey tried not to wonder why he was being so solicitous.

"I'm thinking of getting into film production. There seems to be so much work going on in the city, so maybe I could work here, but I'm also pretty free to travel now."

Trip's face darkened. "You know, Gus Savin has a hand in that business."

"I'm not surprised by that," Lacey said. "It's a big business. Some investors might be attracted by the 'glamour' of it all."

"Should I consider investing?" Trip asked. She knew he was now playing their old game. He wasn't interested in her answer; he merely wanted to stake a claim against Savin.

"I'll keep an ear out for any opportunities for you," she offered, forcing a smile.

"There's a sport," Trip said. He had moved on to some new distraction on his desktop monitor. Lacey recognized the cue and rose from her sweaty chair.

Her back turned to him, she had nearly escaped his office when he asked, "By the way, Becnel, who are Marva and Roland?"

Lacey rolled her eyes and put a hand to her mouth. "Nothing. No one. It was all just a joke."

✳

"He actually said 'insensitive prick'?" Jimmy asked.

When Lacey tried calling her brother on a whim and actually got him, she couldn't believe her luck.

"Yes! Those words came out of his mouth!!"

"Well, think about it, Budgie," he said. She could hear him

chewing on something. "It's not really that surprising how this all played out. His office—you—your position, the whole thing. It's all window dressing for him, you've said as much yourself."

"Yeah, I know," she nearly shouted over the hands-free in her car. "It's all there so he can have a semblance of a vocation. A profession to put on his tax returns. But still, I guess I'm just disappointed in myself."

"Why?"

"I hate being surprised," she said, stopping at a red light. "I was so sure how the whole thing would play out."

"I'm gonna offer a few words of brotherly advice, Budge," Jimmy said. Lacey knew she wouldn't be able to keep him on the phone much longer.

"Go ahead."

"Leaving this job is just one kind of negotiation. You'll have to get used to that," he said.

"Get used to what?"

"Negotiating. I'm guessing you haven't had much experience with it. At least, not at work."

"No, I guess not." The light turned green.

"The thing about negotiations is that the only way to prepare is to prepare for anything. People can conceal lots of things in their day-to-day life, but when it comes down to negotiating something important, they'll reveal their true colors."

"But we don't think Trip's job is important to him. And my position, certainly not."

"The actual work, no, but the appearance, yes," Jimmy said. "The illusion is paramount to him—that his chumleys in Rex perceive him to be active in some sort of business and have employees. That's important."

"How can you live so far away and know so much?"

"New Orleans's bullshit social-Uptown-deb scene turned out to be a pretty good primer for the music biz."

Lacey couldn't let one thing go. "Chump, what if he hadn't known I was planning to leave already? Do you think he would still have done this?"

Jimmy laughed. "Christ, Lacey, you've got to stop overthinking this thing. Think about where you are—you're in a good position."

"I am?" Lacey wasn't convinced.

"Quit being a ninny," he said. "Look, you've still got six weeks' salary coming, and you know you can short-time him in a big way. Hell, you could probably insult him to his face now, now that you're not essential to the illusion anymore."

"That might be fun."

"That's the spirit. You've just taken your first step into a larger world," Jimmy said, channeling Alec Guinness.

"I'm so glad I caught you. Do you think I'm too old to complete the training, Obi-Wan?" Lacey asked, finally getting over herself.

"No. You're the perfect age. But probably not reckless enough."

"Ha! I'll show you! I can learn."

"We'll see. I'll run you through some exercises Saturday."

"Can't wait!"

The call disconnected, and Lacey thought about seeing her brother. Happy anticipation was quickly replaced with panic. How was she going to tell him about her mutant power?

23

Lacey parked along St. Claude, in a neighborhood undergoing a New Orleans-style gentrification. She crossed the street and stopped at a small, grassy lot. It contained a driftwood sculpture that looked like the bones of a dinosaur. An arch composed a makeshift entryway, two unmatched wooden beams connected by a ten-foot-long tree branch along the top. Etched into the bark with a crude hand, the sign read UNIVERSAL GARDEN. She had read that the building she was headed toward had once been a store called Universal Furniture.

On the other side of the street, near her car, a man shuffled past. He looked like an old-time hobo; all he was missing was the stick and bandana attachment. Lacey thought of Fox.

He would have had a fit if he knew she was heading into this neighborhood alone. She smiled at the thought and gave Fox a mental "fuck you."

The exterior of the New Orleans Healing Center was painted a warm orange hue. She felt like she was entering a giant peach. A wave of calm passed over Lacey the instant she walked through the door. Sculptures were on display in the great atrium, some suspended from the ceiling, some firmly planted to the floor. The diffuse afternoon light broke through high windows; a few folks carried yoga mats.

Lacey thought of Eli and wondered how he knew this place. She thought a little further and realized how little she knew about Eli at all. She didn't even know where he was from. Was he really Professor X? If so, the upside was that he could help her figure out her mutant powers. But the downside worried her—did she really want someone that far up into her thoughts? She needed Magneto's helmet. Maybe they sold something like it here at the Healing Center.

She lingered at a directory sign, hoping an answer would magically appear. A yoga studio, a co-op grocery, a credit union, a bookstore, an interfaith worship center.

Bingo. The occasion called for a quick prayer, Lacey decided. She wandered up to the interfaith center on the top floor.

She entered a small studio space, empty except for big cushions arranged on the floor. Glass doors opened onto a rooftop terrace. Ominous storm clouds gathered to the south, beckoning her outside for a closer look. A downpour threatened, the pleasant breeze saturated with the scent of the coming rain. She drew in a deep breath.

Thank you, God. She began her "gratitude" prayer. *What am I grateful for?*

For being alone, at the moment. Too many new people were entering her sphere. Too many people who seemed to know more about what was going on than she did. Trip hiring the new girl.

Small potatoes, she thought. *Move on.*

Eli. Eli sends her here, she follows mindlessly.

Tonti, sharing new, deep, dark secrets from the Becnels' past.

Nathan, occupying too many of her thoughts.

What was going on, and why was she allowing these people to run her?

Keep an open heart and you'll find love again, I know.

That song.

Sorry, God, for the '80s music. I really am trying to pray.

Was she keeping an open heart but losing her mind?

She was grateful for her brother. She would see him tonight. She could tell him everything. But would she? It would be worth it. He could help ground her.

She peered south, willing herself to focus on the storm clouds. If she was *in* the clouds, she'd be able to see a great swath of southern Louisiana. Metairie, where she'd got her start. Galliano, where Fox had had his beginnings. Galliano, which she hadn't known existed until she met Fox. Further back, Big Fox, and the mysterious Birdie. Birdie, whom she hadn't known existed until six days ago.

A terrible accident. Her irrational fear of losing someone in a car crash. Birdie.

Pay attention. Eli's words came to her.

She thought of every change in her life since Fox had come into it. She thought of everything that had happened since Fox had left her life. Most of it in just the past two weeks.

Pay attention.

She'd healed Nathan underneath the overpass. In the shadow of Popp Fountain. She knew she had, though she didn't understand it. She knew it in the same way she knew her heart was beating. Popp Fountain, where Fox had told her of the ping. The ping. Fox had said everything became clearer, for just a little while.

Forget Fox, seek the ping. Pay attention.

Birdie had possessed the same ability. *Ping.* Birdie, somehow, had passed it along before she died. *Ping.*

But how the hell do I fit into this? Why me?

Birdie had saved the Becnel children, if Tonti was to be believed. Or at least helped them not be ruined. And who knew what else she'd done while she was alive?

Still doesn't answer why me. And if so, what am I supposed to do with it?

There have been others now. Tom and Jerry. Angus the security guard. And, Miss Esther Mae. Now dead. *Ping.*

Am I grateful for this, whatever it is?

Lacey took another deep breath, and felt a fat water drop fall on her ear. She opened her eyes and saw the rain upon her. She hurried back inside, wet from only a few seconds of exposure.

The ferocity of the downpour kept her inside the Healing Center for over an hour. She was on the verge of something, some realization that remained elusive. She spent most of that hour in the bookstore.

Several copies of the *Bhagavad Gita* were displayed next to a stack of New Testaments—St. John's. She was drawn toward a section marked "Healing." She read the back jacket of a book written by a woman who credited her internal healing power with curing her of cancer. Another book on Olga Worrall, who was known for her healing abilities. Another book on famous despots throughout history who claimed to have healing powers.

Lacey Becnel doesn't make a good despot name, she thought. *Maybe the Dark Lace?*

"I don't think that's your path, young Lacey," she heard a baritone voice say.

A man with a mass of dreadlocks stood like an oak across the stacks. She knew him. Cecil.

That can't be a coincidence, she thought. *Remember, you want to ask him something.*

She couldn't remember what it was.

From his height, Cecil could see the despot book she was holding in her hands. He smiled his giant sun of a smile, and it lit up the shadowy bookstore.

Lacey smiled in return and wondered if Eli had known Cecil would be there. Did they know each other?

"Cecil," she said. "Do you know this place?"

"Of course," he answered. "Do you not?"

"No, no. Someone told me about it, and I thought it was time to check it out."

"Indeed," he said. "Once again, we meet over books." He moved like Treebeard around the shelves and stood beside Lacey.

"Oh! That's right." Lacey felt like she was in a trance.

"Books are helpful for finding direction," he said. "But you must know how to seek it."

"I…I think that's what I need," Lacey stuttered. "I don't know what's happened to me."

"Life has happened to you, young Lacey," Cecil said. "Same as it happens to all of us. People around us die, people around us are killed, we get injured, we are all subject, this is ordinary."

Lacey wasn't sure if Cecil was speaking, or if she was hearing him in her head.

"What you're concerned with," he continued, "what you *should* be concerned with, is what you're becoming. That is extraordinary."

"What am I becoming?" Lacey asked, a little too loud. A goateed hipster behind the checkout counter looked up from his book.

"That is for you to find out," Cecil answered, a register lower. "No one will be able to tell you. Be suspicious if they do."

Lacey considered this. "I think I would trust you if you told me," she said under her breath.

Another full-powered smile. "Careful with that trust, young Lacey. It gives you much strength, but it can also get you detoured," he said. "I left two things at the counter for you. They will enlighten your search. Remember, your story has multiple strands. They are knitting together, now, to form something truly unique in the universe. Seek out those who are knowledgeable."

He stepped toward Lacey and enveloped her in a bear-hug embrace. "It's time for me to go," he said.

It was the last thing Lacey remembered him saying before the tidal wave hit her. A wall of images, much more powerful than the ones from her last Cecil encounter at Mardi Gras World, crashed down upon her: A woman's face, now familiar. A bloody crash scene. Fox's father. A young man in Army fatigues. All these images—with their corresponding narratives—coursed through her impossibly fast. In a millisecond, all was revealed. But like a sneak peek through a curtain, the veil came down just as quickly.

Lacey stood alone, drenched with sweat. The goateed counter man stared at her. She willed her leaden body to walk behind a shelf to escape his attention. She focused on a copy of the Bible. Where had Cecil gone? She hadn't even seen him leave. She tried to focus on the flood of images, and strained to retain just one tiny portion of the knowledge. The woman's face. Why was it familiar?

Big Fox. Birdie. The woman was Birdie.

At Mardi Gras World, Cecil had said his auntie practiced "light magic." Birdie had been Cecil's aunt.

That had to be it. So she had a living connection to Birdie. Cecil had to know more about her. But Cecil was so elusive he might just as well be a ghost.

But still, it's more than I knew when I came in here.

Almost sleepwalking, Lacey walked to the counter. Cecil had said he'd left something for her.

She faced the hipster behind the counter. His expression had turned friendly. He held up a book.

"He bought this for you. Said to make sure you didn't leave without it," he said. His voice had a lilt that did not match his surly countenance.

Lacey looked at the book. *The Hidden Reality* by Brian Greene. The subtitle read *Parallel Universes and the Deep Laws of the Cosmos.*

He dropped it into a bag. "There's something else, too, just a bunch of photocopied pages he brought. They're in this bag, too." The hipster's perpetually annoyed look returned.

Lacey snatched the bag from his hands. "Thank you." She scanned the pages. They looked like some sort of family history or genealogy, dense with names and dates. No sign of any personal note from Cecil.

She walked out of the bookstore, eager to be out of the eye of the man tending the counter. She read the book jacket as she headed toward the exit of the New Orleans Healing Center. It was about science and quantum physics. Physics was the one subject she'd struggled with in school.

Great, she thought. *So, I possibly have Cecil's family history and a book on quantum physics. All this stuff might as well be written in Latin.*

When she stepped through the doors of the New Orleans Healing Center, the sun had come out, turning the air to steam. She swore she heard a chime behind her, from the direction of the bookstore. A light, clear, *ping*. In that moment, she decided to accept it as a good omen, and not try to track down the source of the sound.

24

Lacey noted the time as she pulled out her phone: 9:30 p.m. She was annoyed and relieved. Annoyed that her brother hadn't told her to expect the crowd of about twenty or so youngsters milling about his tour bus. Relieved that her energy wasn't flagging. Usually by this time of night, sleep was the only thing on her mind. But she was amped up. She felt like she could be up for the next thirty-six hours.

"Are you here?" Jimmy answered.

"Really, dude? When did you get a fan club?" Lacey said.

Jimmy laughed. "Sibling rivalry gives you a convenient memory, Budgie. I've always had one. Hold on, I'll send Helga out."

"Fine." She ended the call.

The crowd of teenagers all turned in hushed attention, like a colony of meerkats, as the door to the tour bus opened. There was audible disappointment as a broad-shouldered woman exited the bus. She had brassy blonde hair tied in a braid, and her black polo shirt was tucked into functional black chinos. Lacey immediately understood why Jimmy called her Helga.

Lacey turned her shoulder to the crowd. Helga had no problem spotting her. She approached and faced Lacey head-on and asked, "Who are you here to see?"

"Jimmy Campo."

"And what's your name?"

"Lacey."

The correct code word cracked the ice on Helga's façade. She smiled and held out her hand. "Lacey, I'm Amy. Come with me."

Lacey smirked as she fell into step beside the woman. She was sure her brother, probably the whole band, had never called this woman by her given name.

Helga opened the door to the bus and ushered Lacey up the steps. Jimmy was sitting in the driver's seat, hands on the steering wheel, playing distraught and asking, "How am I gonna keep this thing above sixty?"

"Pop quiz, hotshot," Lacey responded, lapsing into their movie quote language.

Jimmy's hair was long again, and he had lost the extra weight he'd been carrying on his six-foot-two frame the last time Lacey had seen him. He jumped out of the driver's seat and lifted Lacey off the top step and set her down beside him, hands on both her shoulders.

"How ya doing, Budgie?!?" he said.

Lacey had figured she'd find her brother in his good preshow mood. It could break either way before a performance. If it had been the dark one, he wouldn't have asked her to come by before the set.

"Man, I've missed you!" Lacey said as she gave him a hug. "This tour is agreeing with you; you look really good."

"I think I might finally have this figured out. I've been

managing to keep up my workouts on the road. Surprisingly, this isn't as easy at thirty-six as it was at twenty-five."

"Yeah, big surprise, Chump. Getting older sucks," Lacey said.

"Where's Gellee?" Jimmy asked.

"She had to work tonight. She's going to try to make it for your set," Lacey answered. Angele had texted Lacey her change of plans. There was still a slight chill between them.

"You want something to drink, Lace?" Jimmy asked, his back to Lacey.

The interior was more spacious than she had expected. Jimmy was blocking her view, but she could sense people milling around in the back of the bus.

Lacey replied, "Just some water if you have it, please."

"Have a seat, I'll get you some."

There were two recliners to Lacey's left, and a padded bench opposite. Lacey guessed the well-worn black recliner was where her brother spent most of his time, probably opting to sleep there over what appeared to be a sleeping cabinet a little further back. She took a seat on the bench.

All the windows had dark wood panel shades on them. The look of the bus was an uncanny match to LeViticum's sound—a lot of retro elements combined in a very twenty-first-century way.

Someone emerged from the back, not her brother. He was tall—but not as tall as Jimmy—and leaner, wearing black jeans and an Avengers T-shirt. Shaggy, rust-brown hair and an angular face. He looked ready for the stage. He walked up to a charging laptop, but turned his attention to Lacey when he noticed her.

"Hey," he said with an approving smile and piercing blue eyes. Lacey detected a bit of brogue in that one word.

"Hello," she answered. When he didn't turn his attention away, Lacey stood up, her hopes plummeting. She had wanted to debrief Jimmy on her supernatural state now, before his set. This new guy would make it impossible.

"You're Jimmy's sister," he said.

Definitely sounds Irish, Lacey thought. "Yeah, that's right. Are you new to the band?"

She had a good idea of who he might be, and was glad her level of annoyance gave her an edge of cool.

"Yeah, that's right," he returned. "I'm Trevor," he said as he held out his hand.

He had a very firm handshake, but the real force came from the twinkle in his eye. Trevor was clean-shaven, but Lacey thought with a little bit of facial scruff he'd be one tall leprechaun.

"You a Marvel fan?" Lacey asked, gesturing at his T-shirt.

"What, this shirt? I just thought it looked cool."

Lacey narrowed her eyes at him, not sure what kind of small-talk would succeed.

Trevor's face broke out in a wide grin. His mouth was as sexy as the sound of the words coming out of it.

"God, I love Americans," he said. "You have the hardest time detecting irony. So much fun."

"How do you know I'm American?" Lacey asked. It was all she could think to say.

Trevor laughed outright. "You're hilarious!"

Lacey considered. His personality was a definite shift from the oblique indifference she'd come to expect from Jimmy's other bandmates. With Trevor Toomey as lead singer, LeViticum had achieved breakout status. There was definitely some sort of alchemy at play.

"Lay off her, Seamus." Jimmy popped Trevor in the shoulder with a water bottle.

"Sorry about the water bottle, La," Jimmy said. "We're trying to be green, but I couldn't find a clean glass. Figured you could at least take this inside."

"Good for you," Lacey said, smiling. This streak of conscientiousness was new. Lacey remembered her conversation with their mother, and the unmentioned girlfriend.

Jimmy took the reins before Lacey could ask anything about it. He put his hand on Trevor's shoulder and said, "Don't mess around with my sister. She's fragile."

"Oh, right," Trevor answered in a thick accent. "The poor widow Campo."

Lacey snapped to attention. She sensed she was about to be the butt of an inside joke. Old family war games. Her window was closing fast to jump in and turn it around.

"It's not Campo. It's Becnel," she said. *A bit weak*, she thought.

"The widow Becnel sounds like it could be one of the ghosts at the Myrtles Plantation," Jimmy said.

"Nah, go further south," Lacey replied. "Somewhere with more Cajuns."

"I still have yet to hear a real Cajun accent," Trevor jumped in. "All I know is that people down here seem to have a harder time understanding me than in California, or up on the East Coast. I don't get that."

"People don't leave southern Louisiana," Jimmy said, "and people don't move here. They don't get your accent because they don't have the diversity you get on the East or West Coast."

"Hold the phone, Chump!" Lacey said.

"Who talks like that?" Jimmy replied.

She moved right past the put-down. "Excuse me, but you've been away from here for a really long time. A *lot* has changed. There has been such an influx of new blood since Katrina. You can't make that blanket statement about here anymore."

"Maybe," he said. "But the character of the people you encounter here hasn't changed. The ones who grew up here. They're gonna make a big deal over an Irish accent, more than they would other places."

"Maybe," Lacey replied. "But if that's the case, I hope that never changes. At least you know where you stand—it's better than someone listening to you, not understanding a word, and pretending that they do."

"Let's talk more about me and my accent," Trevor said as he grabbed Lacey's hand and pulled her down onto the bench, sitting right next to her, a little too close.

Jimmy checked the time on his phone and eased into his recliner. Lacey shot her brother a pleading look.

"He's harmless, Budgie. Like a puppy. Give him a quick pop on the nose if he gets too close."

Lacey angled toward Trevor and gave him a short snap on the nose with three fingers.

"Ow!" he said as he shifted, only slightly, away from her. "I hope that doesn't leave a mark; that will look terrible on stage."

"What a baby," Lacey chided. "That wasn't hard enough to leave a mark."

"Can we try again?" he said with a twinkle.

"Where did you find this guy?" Lacey asked her brother.

"Wandering the rolling green hills outside of Dublin. Naked. With a harp," Jimmy replied.

Lacey felt a pang at the naked crack. She tried to cover. "Was there a pot of gold nearby? And perhaps a rainbow?" she asked.

Trevor interjected. "That's not how it went at all. I was introduced to the band by me agent, Darby O'Gill. It was all very businesslike, and we sealed the deal with pints of Guinness."

"He must be good. I can't see Dave putting up with this foolishness otherwise," Lacey said.

She had known Dave Guidry for half her life. She could honestly say she'd never heard the man speak more than twenty words to her at any one time.

"Dave? No, Dave loves me," Trevor replied. "It's Paco who can't stand me."

"Paco? Paco's a teddy bear! You must be a real asshole," Lacey said.

Lacey had only met Paco Nocente, the drummer, a handful of times, but he still felt like another brother to her.

"Where is he, anyway?" she asked. "I want to say hi before y'all start."

"Not here," Jimmy answered. "Went out for a walk. He's trying to quit smoking, winds up walking for hours sometimes instead. He'll walk straight to the set."

"You see?" Trevor said. "I'm no asshole. He doesn't like me because he's trying to break his nicotine addiction."

"He's right," Jimmy continued. "Paco kinda doesn't like anybody right now."

"I don't believe it. All the same, I could see how Lucky Charms here would grate on the nerves of a Zen master. Much less a poor soul trying to quit cigarettes," Lacey said.

"Just wait 'til you get to know me. My lucky charms might surprise you," Trevor said as he winked at Lacey.

Lacey lifted her hand to give him another pop in the nose, but he grabbed it instead and gave it a swift kiss.

"James, is it time?" Trevor asked.

"Yeah," Jimmy said, rising from the recliner. "Lacey, you'll probably want to stay here. Wait for Helga to get back and she'll walk over with you."

"I don't need an escort," she said.

"Trust your big brother. It'll be less hassle."

Lacey formed her fingers into the shape of a *W* aimed at her brother.

"How old are you?" Jimmy asked.

"It's just a number, Chump," she said.

She gave him a little wave as he and Lucky Trevor Toomey exited the bus. She crossed over and looked through the window. She wondered where Dave Guidry was, but only for a moment. She knew he must already be at the set. His tendency to obsess over the details of stage, sound, and lights had saved her brother on more occasions than she could count.

The crowd had grown in the last twenty minutes. Trevor clicked his heels in his last step off the bus, an oddly graceful movement.

Helga and another black-garbed security guy stood several paces behind Trevor and Jimmy as they shook a few hands and signed a handful of autographs. Trevor kissed one young girl on the cheek. Lacey imagined that girl would not wash her face for a week.

Lacey calculated when she'd be able to talk to her brother alone. Another three hours, at least. *Shit.*

As they sauntered out of sight, Lacey thought about magnetism. Her brother had always had it, and this newly discovered Irishman had it in spades. The Dakota Kid had it, too. Was that *their* mutant power?

25

Jimmy had been right, of course. Lacey did as she was instructed and waited for Helga before walking over to the Publiq House. An attempt at polite conversation yielded Helga's point of origin—Nebraska—but nothing more. They were interrupted by the approach of a pack of intrepid teenagers.

The boldest one, a solid-looking girl—too old for the pigtails she wore—came within inches of Lacey and asked, "Are you Jimmy's sister?"

There was no threat in the girl's words, but Lacey was glad Helga was there just the same. She placed a gentle hand on the girl's shoulder and moved her outside Lacey's boundary.

Pigtails took it in stride, her anticipation unabated. She was ready to prove that she had correctly inferred Lacey's relation to the band, knew all there was to know, and was, indeed, LeViticum's biggest fan.

With Helga's implicit blessing, Lacey responded to Pigtails that she was Jimmy's sister. When Pigtails and two of her companions asked for her autograph, Lacey again looked to Helga.

Helga looked amused and shrugged. She had not spoken since "Nebraska."

She signed "Lacey B" on the only blank space left on a T-shirt full of autographs, and again on the back of a picture of the band. She was proud of her attempt to make her name sound hip.

Helga helped Lacey navigate the rest of the crowd, and led her inside through a backstage entrance.

"Do you need anything further from me, Lacey?" Helga asked.

Lacey saw Dave Guidry fiddling with a soundboard. *Pay attention*, a voice in her head said. She looked over at Helga, and realized she surely had one thousand better things to do than wait for her reply.

"Oh, no, Hel…Amy, thank you very much for your help. I'm good from here," she said.

"Ten-four," Helga replied, and disappeared into the recesses of the building.

Lacey eyed the bar at the end of a long passageway. As she made her way through, she called out to Dave Guidry.

"Hey, Dave."

He looked up, his pointy face registering annoyance, then recognition.

"Hey, Lacey," he answered with a nod of his narrow head, and then returned his attention to the soundboard.

Eighteen more words and he's at the record, Lacey thought.

Lacey found a spot at the middle of the bar, which afforded a decent view of the stage. Her mutant powers must have magically opened up a seat for her, because the place looked like it was at capacity.

"How's the talent?" Lacey heard a familiar voice in her

ear, from behind. She whipped her head around and saw Angele.

"Lee! Did you finish up earlier than expected?" Lacey made a conscious effort to smile and inject warmth into her voice.

"Yeah, just about everyone left today," Angele said. She had to shout to be heard. "I need to stay on a few days to wrap some things up, but my sixteen-hour days are behind me."

"Great!" Lacey said. "I'm glad you're here. Jimmy will be happy, too."

Angele didn't respond. Her eyes scanned the room and she said, "The short, fat guy ratio is too high in New Orleans. I hate that."

"Wow!" Lacey said. "Harsh. So harsh. What if those short, fat guys have hearts of gold?"

"Who's to say tall, attractive men don't have hearts of gold, too?" Angele replied.

"I guess California's a better place to find that out," Lacey said. "I'd imagine the ratio is better there."

"Definitely fewer fat guys," Angele said.

"Oh! Speaking of attractive and tall, I met Trevor Toomey. He's kinda dreamy."

"Yeah, I've met him," Angele said. "You know I don't mix with musicians."

"Maybe I'll add him to my list, then," Lacey said.

Angele shot her a look full of daggers.

Whoops, Lacey thought. *Maybe that was too soon after the Dakota Kid fiasco.* She was relieved when they were both distracted by a tall guy down the bar. Lacey looked at Angele.

"Yep, I've got it. Waiting for a turnaround," Angele said. "He could be a two-face."

Lacey wondered how Angele was able to keep her eye on

anything. Standing, her vantage point came barely a foot over the bar.

Megadeth's "Train of Consequences" started to play when the tall man finally made his turn. Lacey caught his profile and the blood rushed out of her head, settling somewhere below her stomach. "Oh shit," she said.

"What?" Angele still seemed annoyed with her.

"Lee, that's Nathan," Lacey said. "That's Dinner Jacket," she added when Angele didn't immediately register his name.

"Jesus. He looks like someone's dad," Angele said.

The space next to him had cleared, and they were both afforded a better look. He was dressed older than he should have been for the venue, a T-shirt tucked into a pair of shorts, neatly belted. With loafers. It was a look that would have worked for brunch.

"Well, he is someone's dad," Lacey said. "Poor guy. Good thing he's big enough to defend himself." Lacey swore internally. Why did she feel sympathy for him?

"Still, if you look at just the T-shirt and face, not bad. Doesn't look as old as you said he was," Angele said. Her annoyance had dissipated.

"What the hell is he doing here?" Lacey asked.

"Does he know your connection to the band?"

"No. I've never told him about Jimmy."

"Maybe he's a fan, then." Angele glanced at Lacey and shrugged.

Before Lacey knew what was happening, Angele turned toward Nathan and closed the distance as best she could.

"Hey, Nate! Nathan!" Angele shouted.

Lacey hid her face with her hands. "Jesus! Please stop."

"You'll thank me later," Angele said.

"Highly doubtful."

Nathan looked a little confused but not displeased when he glanced at Angele. He didn't know her, but didn't seem to mind being called out by a pretty female. Angele gestured for him to join her. He paid for his drink and pardoned himself through the crowd.

He only noticed Lacey when he was inches from her.

"Hey, Nathan," she said with a slight lift of her head.

"Lacey!" His expression was somewhere between panic and joy. He went in for a hug, but the crowd was too thick to allow for it, so he put his hand on her shoulder instead. He looked over at Angele.

"Nathan, this is my good friend Angele Lee," Lacey said.

Angele wore her innocent face. "It's nice to meet you," she said. "I've heard a lot about you."

"Really?" Nathan said. His panic dissipated and he raised an eyebrow at Lacey.

"Sorry," Lacey said. "It was her idea to call you over here."

He looked at Angele. "I'm glad you did. Nice to meet you, too."

"So, Nathan, what are you doing here?" Lacey blurted out.

"I've been here," he said, now relaxed and confident. "What are you doing here?"

"You've been here?"

"Yeah. I was here for Cat Ballou's set earlier. I'm without family for a few days, so decided to stay out and see what LeViticum is all about."

"Huh," Lacey said. "Will you excuse me for a second?" She hustled off in the direction of the bathroom.

"You'll have to forgive her," Angele said to Nathan. "She doesn't get out much."

"So she says."

"So you're without family?" Angele asked.

"Yeah, they're in Destin. I'll be joining them in a few days, our annual summer vacation," he said.

"Why aren't you with them?" she asked, never one to tiptoe around anything.

"Oh, you know. The place opened up early, so my wife decided to extend the trip on the front end. I couldn't get off work," he said unconvincingly.

"Huh. That sucks," Angele said. "How was Cat Ballou?"

Nathan's demeanor changed instantly.

"Phenomenal," he said. "I wasn't sure how I'd feel about her straying toward rock, but she blew my mind."

"I'm sorry I missed it," Angele lied. "Sounds like you're a follower."

Lacey reappeared, head and shoulders hovering right above Angele's shoulder.

"She's my ex-girlfriend," Nathan said. He looked at Lacey for a reaction. She was stone-faced.

Angele, eyes forward and surveying the crowd, replied, "That sounds like a story!"

"Sounds like I'm trying to make myself more relevant than I really am," Nathan said, his mood notching down again. "She was my high-school girlfriend. We used to play in a band together."

"Well that's kind of cool," Angele said, more disinterested by the second. "To have that kind of history with someone who's become famous."

Lacey grinned. There wasn't one shred of sarcasm detectable in Angele's voice, but she knew the response was loaded with it.

Lacey angled in to regain her seat at the bar. "Sorry, hot

flash," she said. The look on Nathan's face made her wish she'd said anything but that as an excuse.

"You're too young for hot flashes," Angele said.

"Well, I'm better now," Lacey said, trying to play it all off.

"Now it's my turn to run off," Angele said, looking toward the far end of the bar. "I see a line on my next gig. Ping me later." She said a perfunctory goodbye to Nathan and scurried away.

"Good luck," Lacey called after her.

"What does she do?" Nathan asked.

Lacey looked at him, realizing she was alone with a family-less Nathan in a crowd of three hundred people. She struggled to keep the composure she had stepped away to regain.

"She causes trouble, is what she does," she answered under her breath. "She works in film production," she said a little louder, putting on her game face. "Her last production is wrapping up right now."

"Huh. Maybe that's work you could do," he said.

She tried not to be mad at him for being so interested in her life.

"You pay attention," she said. "Yeah, I'm kind of working that angle, hoping something turns up soon. So, why are you without family?"

"Oh. I was telling your friend, they started our vacation early, I'll join them in a few days," he answered without looking at her.

"Oh," Lacey said. He did not sound excited.

"Good thing your friend saw me," Nathan said, changing the subject. "Now you don't have to watch the band alone."

The chip on Lacey's shoulder flared up. "Why do you have to be with somebody to listen to a band?" she said. "It's like a movie, it's not like you need someone to talk to while it's going on. Why do people freak out when someone shows up alone anywhere?" She regretted the words as soon as they were out of her mouth.

"Lacey, are you coming to my defense again?" he asked.

"No!" she said. "No, I mean, it was unintentional if I was. It's just not that big a deal."

"Oh, I think it is," Nathan said. "I think when you go to a movie or a concert with someone, it's because you want to share the experience with them. So maybe," he continued, "there should be more sympathy for people who show up somewhere alone. Because they have no one they want to share it with." He looked pointedly at Lacey. He was clearly playing.

She laughed. "Don't look at me like that! I *know* you're not that pathetic." She went to touch his arm, to emphasize her point, but thought better of it. "Plus, you're alone by choice. *And* you know someone in the band. I have no sympathy."

"Maybe I called five friends to see if they wanted to join me and had no takers," Nathan said.

"You have five friends?" Lacey asked. She meant it as banter.

Nathan smiled. "No, not really. Maybe once upon a time, but not anymore."

"There you go again, being pathetic. I don't believe a word of it," Lacey said. She picked up a new line of conversation. "And I only believe Cat Ballou is an ex-girlfriend because it's too preposterous to believe otherwise."

Lacey remembered reading somewhere that Catherine Bourgeois, a.k.a. Cat Ballou, had gone to NOCCA, probably around the same time he had.

"Preposterous?"

"Yes. Preposterous." Lacey was having fun. Her caution was slipping.

"Good word. But what about you?" Nathan asked. "I wouldn't have pegged you as a fan of LeViticum-style music."

"You don't know me that well," Lacey replied, and left it at that. "Do you talk often?"

"Who?"

"You and Cat."

"No," Nathan said. He looked thoughtful. "Very rarely. Although I did get to see her before her show tonight. It was nice. There's a shorthand you get to use with people you were close with."

"How short a shorthand?" It sounded a lot more seductive than Lacey had intended.

Nathan looked at her, not understanding at first. "What? Oh! No. That's barking up the wrong tree."

"Really? Old girlfriend, your wife out of town?" Lacey asked, a tinge of resentment in her tone.

"No, no, no." Nathan went on the defensive. "She just got married. Met the guy briefly, he seems all right. They have a couple of kids together already; we talked a little about them."

Lacey tried to display the appropriate amount of interest, but was exceedingly distracted. Hearing Nathan talk about a long-ago girlfriend, she imagined him younger and less buttoned-down.

"You know what she said to me?" Nathan asked.

She shook her head and tried to shake off whatever it was she was feeling.

"Cat said she could tell something was 'massively different' about me. Different in a good way. Like I was coming back to the person she'd always expected I would grow up to be when we were young."

"She didn't expect you to be the way you are now?" Lacey asked.

"Whoever does?" he answered. "I'm not quite sure I followed what she meant, but on a really deep, gut level, I think I do."

The distance between them had become nonexistent. It was hard to hear anything—the house music was rising in volume the closer it got to show time—but Lacey heard Nathan loud and clear. The heat between them was now palpable. Lacey grabbed the back of her neck, attempting to dissipate the blood flow.

Nathan stared at the curve of Lacey's arm. He took a step back, as much as the crowd would allow, and turned his attention toward the floor.

"I'm going to get a drink," he said. "Can I get you anything?"

It took Lacey several seconds to respond. "No," she said. "I'm good."

Nathan nodded, distracted, and turned toward the bar. He turned back almost as quickly, an unreadable expression on his face. He moved in toward Lacey, grabbed her elbow to anchor himself, and put his lips an inch from her ear. The back of his hand touched her breast.

"Don't forget I've seen you naked," he said.

He let her go as quickly as he'd grabbed her, flashed a full-on bedroom smile, and turned his back to her.

26

Lacey watched Dave Guidry at the back of the darkened stage. He had escaped the attention of any fans, dressed all in black with a ball cap shading his eyes. He was making adjustments to the drum set. She wondered if Dave even had any fans, and if so, if they would be upset that they were missing this nonperformance sighting.

She had just regained her breath after the near-miss kiss, or whatever it was that had passed between her and Nathan. She was glad to have the distance from him, but it did seem like he had been gone an extraordinarily long time just to get a drink.

Trying to appear nonchalant, she turned her head toward the bar. She found Nathan, or rather his back. They were now separated by ten feet and at least twenty people. Nathan appeared to be talking to someone, someone big, who looked more out of place at the Uptown, college-crowd venue than he did. She saw a full head of dark hair, slick with gel, shaved above the ear, and a white T-shirt sleeve tight on a bulging bicep.

They moved away from the bar together. Lacey thought absently that if they both left the bar, equilibrium might be restored at the Publiq House. But then Nathan turned his head.

He didn't see her, but in a split second, Lacey saw the panic in his eyes. The back of her neck felt tingly.

Pay attention. The words echoed in her brain, propelling her forward as she followed Nathan and the stranger through the crowd. She had no idea what she would do if she caught up to them. She realized that was an unlikely outcome, anyway, when they reached the doorway and she was still ten feet away and surrounded by a sea of people.

Lacey felt like she was drowning when a hand grabbed her shoulder from behind. She whipped her head around, angry at being stopped.

"Let go of me!" she said. Her anger dissipated when she saw that it was Helga.

"Lacey, what's going on?" Helga asked. Her tone was soothing and even.

"I think my friend, someone I know, is in some kind of trouble," she said.

Helga kept her hand on Lacey's shoulder. "Show me," she said.

Lacey pointed to the door, and Helga instantly moved to point position. "What does your friend look like?" she asked, voice raised.

Lacey was embarrassed to describe him, and was glad Helga couldn't see her face. "Uh, he's probably six foot or a little over, big, but fit. He's wearing khaki shorts with a belt, and a solid, dark-colored T-shirt, maybe black. Dirty blond-brownish hair."

With Helga leading the way, they sliced the crowd and covered the distance to the door in seconds.

Far down the street, Lacey saw a white T-shirt and a black

T-shirt. The men wearing them were standing beside an ancient-looking sedan, a Lincoln or Cadillac.

"That's him!" she said.

Nathan was slumped. White T-shirt, hand on Nathan's bent head, pushed him through the car door.

"Stay here," Helga said. She looked Lacey directly in the eye when she said it, and Lacey knew it was a non-negotiable command.

Helga moved rapidly down the street, not walking and not quite running. It was almost like she was levitating. The sedan started a slow roll toward her.

A gun appeared in Helga's hand, and she nailed both front tires and the driver's side rear with three quick shots, just as the car was attempting to pick up speed. She shouted for Lacey to stand clear as it passed in front of her.

Lacey would later find out that Helga kept her gun in an ankle holster, but at the time she produced it, it appeared to have popped up straight from the ground.

An explosion of sound erupted from inside the Publiq House. The whining guitars of LeViticum's heavy metal cover of "Time Passages."

The car bumped and scraped to a stop just five yards past where Lacey stood. A scrawny, unkempt man drove the car. He looked like a cornered animal. White T-shirt was in the passenger seat, and looked very angry. Nathan was in the back seat, passed out.

Helga used her magical moving powers again—one moment she was forty yards away, shooting out tires, the next she was standing by the passenger door of the car, about to get charged by White T-shirt.

The cornered animal attempted to pull a semiconscious

Nathan from the back seat. The last thing Lacey remembered hearing from her brother's set was Trevor's lead vocals.

He sounds really good, she thought as she ran to the car. The sound from the Publiq House faded over the short distance.

Lacey heard the man with his hands on Nathan speaking as she approached. Either to himself or Nathan, she wasn't sure. His sinewy limbs looked a lot more powerful close up. He gave off the stink of an animal, too. Lacey thought of a weasel.

"Fuck it all," the Weasel said, "I wasn't supposed to do any heavy lifting with this job. Fuck it all."

He was too focused on Nathan to see Lacey. She saw Nathan's leg rise and kick the Weasel in the groin, and then Nathan's arms were forward, like a zombie, going for his neck.

The Weasel let out a high-pitched howl and bolted from the car. The edge of the car door caught Lacey above her eye as he fled out of sight.

"Oh, fuck!" Her response to the pain was involuntary. She held her hand over her eye and looked in on Nathan.

"Are you okay?" she asked him. The question felt remarkably innocuous.

"Yeah," he replied. He rubbed his head and sounded like he'd just woken up.

"You're bleeding," he said when he looked at Lacey.

She felt something dripping in her eye. She'd thought it was sweat. "Yeah, maybe." She pressed her sleeve to her forehead. "Come on, we need to get you out of there."

Nathan scooted out of the car, and Lacey peered over the vehicle's roof, looking for Helga. She saw two figures brawling in an alley between two old storefronts.

"Where did he go?" Nathan asked.

"Who?"

"That guy, the driver," he said.

"I don't know. He scampered away pretty quickly."

"He was one of the guys from the first time," Nathan said, looking first at Lacey, then searching the horizon. "The one who wouldn't shut up."

"I don't know," Lacey repeated. "But the other guy is still here."

She walked toward the alley. A capricious street lamp flickered on and off, illuminating the tight space like a slow strobe. Lacey heard a single shot ring out. It was like the sound from Helga's gun before, but with more echo.

For the second time that night, Lacey found herself at a full sprint, this time toward the sound of that shot. She heard another one, the light flicked on, and she saw a figure falling backward. Dread torqued her entire body as she feared the fallen might be Helga.

The light flicked off. Lacey willed her eyes to stay open and blood free as she searched the darkness. After an interminable interval, the light came on again. Helga was on her back, but with her head raised and gun still poised. It was the man in the white T-shirt who lay in front of Lacey, a single bullet hole centered precisely between his eyes.

"Idiot," Helga said as she put down the gun and clutched her leg. "He shouldn't have come after me."

Lacey looked down at the dead man. She gingerly stepped over the body and felt a fleeting flash of danger, noticing another gun next to the lifeless hand. She felt like she was crossing the border between two warring nations—two places where the rules were diametrically opposed, and you crossed between at your own peril.

Once clear, she rushed to Helga. A pool of blood was

rapidly growing beneath her. She looked quickly at the dead body, and saw it wasn't coming from him.

"Amy, you're hurt!" Lacey said as she knelt beside her.

"Just grazed, I think," Helga replied. She sounded like she was sleeping.

Lacey put her hands over Helga's leg. Helga let her hand slip and lay her head down, and Lacey could feel the pulse of the blood as it poured from the wound. There was a hole in Helga's black pants, and Lacey hooked in two fingers and ripped away a sizeable section to get a better look. A palm-sized hunk of flesh appeared to be missing from her thigh.

Lacey's stomach jumped into her throat, her head went light, and she was overcome by a profound sadness. She could feel the life ebbing away from Helga's body, and some part of her was trying to remember how much blood loss a person could sustain and still stay alive. And what was it that ran through the leg? The femoral artery? If these things were things she even knew.

Lacey's hands began to tingle, a heat radiating up her arms. She kept her hands on Helga.

"That feels nice," Helga said.

Lacey became unbearably hot. Fire was coursing through her veins, her lymph nodes, her neurons. It wasn't painful. It was…engaging.

There was no pain, only heat. Her clothes were an impediment. She remembered what had happened on the riverboat, the smoking blouse. Always keeping contact with the wound, she started to rip away her clothes. With one hand, she pulled off her blouse. Her bra, a yoke, needed to go. Off it came.

She stood. She had already wriggled out of her sandals.

Keeping a bare foot on the wound, off came her skirt, and her underwear. Everything must go.

Now fully naked and blood-smeared, she crouched at Helga's side, both hands on the wound. Heat radiated from her, and she glowed like the afternoon sun on the walls of a sandstone church. Helga's blood flow eased, the size of the wound shrunk. Lacey felt nothing but a slight spark at the center of her brain. Like a thought trying to form.

Both Lacey and Helga were out of their heads and didn't realize they were being watched. Nathan stood against the alley wall, his eyes fixed on Lacey.

He hadn't understood, until that moment, that the light radiated *from* her. He remembered the light from that night under the overpass, but had been barely conscious when Lacey had worked on him. In the weeks that had passed, he had convinced himself that the light must have been an illusion, a fevered vision brought on by his damaged condition. No, the light *was* her. He stood, mesmerized.

Lacey felt something like a small stone atop Helga's leg. It was hot and it burned her palm. She brushed it off with a quick, mindless gesture—like she was shooing a fly.

A thought finally took shape in Lacey's head. She thought she must have hallucinated the size of the injury, or been in shock after her first sight of the wound. She looked down at Helga's leg, and one hand easily covered the damage. Only a trickle of blood oozed from it. Old scar tissue covered a large area above it. Knowing Helga's occupation, she figured it was from some other injury sustained in the line of duty.

"Lacey, what are you doing?" Helga's voice was low, but more alert than before. "Where are your clothes?"

"I don't know," she replied. She was overwhelmed by déjà

vu. That sense of waking from a wonderful dream. A sense of completeness.

Her déjà vu slipped away as she looked down at her naked body, felt a hand on her shoulder, and looked up to see Nathan Quirk's face.

"Why does this keep happening?" she said to him with a look of utter resignation.

Nathan experienced his own rush of déjà vu. "C'mon, let's get you dressed," he managed to say, his voice raspy and barely above a whisper.

Lacey let Nathan assist her, too drained to feel any sense of modesty.

Helga struggled to get to her feet.

"Wait," Lacey said. "You shouldn't—"

Her words were cut off by the shrill of a siren. Nathan moved to help Helga stand. Something by Helga's foot caught Lacey's eye. The small stone that had burned her palm. It was a spent bullet. Lacey picked it up—it was still warm to the touch—and stuffed it in her pocket.

In less than a minute, the alley was filled with strobing red and blue lights.

27

"You should go to the hospital," Lacey said to Helga.

Lacey looked at Nathan. "You too. You probably have a concussion."

They were sitting in Jimmy's tour bus, under the watchful eye of an impossibly fit uniformed NOPD officer. Lacey wanted to ask her how much longer they would have to wait for the homicide detective, but it had taken a major feat of diplomacy just to get to the bus. She didn't want to press her luck.

Helga was resting on one of the recliners, a towel underneath her leg, and sipping a protein drink.

Lacey and Nathan were beside each other on the sofa. She wanted more distance from him, but both her energy and her resolve failed her.

"If this takes much longer…" Lacey began to say. "I'm really concerned about your leg."

"Lacey, stop," Helga replied. "I will get myself checked out as soon as we're done here. Quit nagging."

Nathan nodded at Lacey.

She blew a breath out of pursed lips and folded her arms over her chest.

She felt her phone vibrate in her skirt pocket. A text from Angele: Show's letting out. Where the fuck are you?

Lacey looked at the policewoman, who was staring through the windshield of the bus. Confident she wasn't being watched, Lacey typed, very discreetly, More fugue business. Stay clear of the bus. Will call you later.

Nathan, eyes closed, put his hands on his knees like he was ready to stand up. But he stayed seated, opened his eyes, and said, "I haven't thanked you yet. Either of you."

"That's two you owe me, junior," Lacey said, smiling. Nathan didn't seem to get the reference.

"But," she continued, "you really owe our friend here."

Lacey swept her hand toward Helga. "Amy" didn't sound right, and she didn't want to perpetuate the nickname, so she settled for calling her nothing. "If she hadn't stopped the car," Lacey said, "I'm not sure…" She didn't follow through on the thought.

Nathan looked at Helga. "Thank you," he said. He sounded earnest.

"You're welcome," Helga answered. An almost imperceptible smile turned up one side of her mouth as she closed her eyes and fell silent.

✳

Lacey opened her eyes when she heard the bus door open. She wasn't sure how long she had been asleep. Helga was standing at the front of the bus, talking to someone.

Helga, fatigued in both her face and her gait, approached Lacey.

"Is the detective here?" Lacey asked.

"No," Helga said, returning to the recliner. "It's Jimmy."

Lacey shot up from the sofa. Nathan looked up at her.

"NOPD won't let him in," Helga said. "He wants to talk to you."

"Will they let me go out?" Lacey asked.

Helga nodded and closed her eyes again.

"Okay, good," Lacey said. She avoided Nathan's gaze as she moved to the front of the bus. She glanced at the police officer. She returned a disinterested stare.

Jimmy looked like a bored teenager waiting for school to let out. Trevor was standing with him. He smiled sweetly at Lacey as she came down the steps.

Everything bottled up inside Lacey began to uncork at the sight of her big brother. Still bloodstained and looking worse for the wear, Lacey felt tears stream down her cheeks.

Jimmy walked to her. "Jesus, Lace. Are you all right?"

He grabbed her in a hug.

"Just peachy." She laughed through the tears. She held on to the embrace for a little while.

She stepped back and saw Trevor watching her intently. Lacey tried to cover. "God, I'm so sorry. We took over your bus!"

Trevor shrugged, and Jimmy answered, "Lacey! Get over it. We don't need the bus. What the hell happened?"

Lacey looked nervously at Trevor.

Jimmy turned to him. "Go on ahead, Toom. I'll meet up with y'all in a few."

Trevor nodded. He walked to Lacey and kissed her, gently, on the top of the head. He poked his head inside the bus, and someone handed him a wallet and a phone.

He gave Lacey and Jimmy a tip of an imaginary cap, and walked off into the night.

"Where did you find this guy again?" Lacey laughed through the last of her tears.

"So, what's going on?" Jimmy asked, ignoring her question.

Lacey stepped away from the bus and led Jimmy toward the wall of the opposite building. She looked up at him and said, "A friend of mine was kidnapped tonight. Helga intercepted the whole thing and killed a guy in the process."

Jimmy processed the information. "But something happened to Helga, too. She wouldn't tell me, but I could tell. Is she okay?" he asked.

"Well, that's the thing," Lacey paused, careful with her choice of words. "Helga got shot, too. I think she lost a lot of blood. She won't go to the hospital until we're finished here," Lacey added, her voice rising in pitch.

Jimmy nodded. "That woman is a machine. Quit worrying about her, Budge, I'll take that on." He shifted his weight. "Who's the friend?" he asked.

"This guy, Nathan. He's in the bus right now."

Jimmy raised his eyebrows and shifted on his feet again. "Was the guy alone?"

"Who?" Lacey asked.

"The dead guy, the kidnapper."

"No," Lacey answered, touching her forehead. "There was this weaselly dude, the driver. He ran off. The little fuck hit me in the head with the car door," she added under her breath.

"When did you start cursing so much?" Jimmy asked.

"Lay off." Lacey folded her arms.

"You didn't get that bloody from just that cut," Jimmy said, eyeing her blood-streaked legs.

"No," Lacey answered. "That's from Helga." She clasped her

hands before her and looked her brother in the eye. "Yeah," she said. "Jimmy, something's happened. Something on top of all this kidnapping and homicide stuff."

Jimmy quit moving and waited for her to continue. His fidgetiness passed to Lacey.

"Something's going on with me," she said, "like some kind of power. Something manifesting. I think I got it from Fox. Or from Fox's family. I don't know. I can't really describe it, but I might be able to heal. There are these Creole healers called traiteurs; there might be something there. I might have healed Helga's gunshot wound. I don't have it figured out yet."

Jimmy raised his eyebrows again.

"You think I'm crazy," Lacey said, shaking her head. "I know, I might be losing my mind. But I never thought a psychotic break would feel like this."

"Like what?" Jimmy asked, calm as a Buddha.

"Like, right," she said. "There's something about the way I feel when it's happening, and right after it happens. Everything feels…right. Like the way things are supposed to be."

They stared at each other for a moment until Lacey cast her eyes to the ground.

"I don't think you're crazy," Jimmy finally said.

"You don't?"

"No." Jimmy finally relaxed into a normal stance. Lacey finally caught her breath. "So, tell me about what happened with Helga," he said.

Lacey wiped at her brow. "She and the guy were in the alley." She gestured in that direction. "I was helping Nathan… my friend…out of the car when I heard a gunshot. When I got to the alley, I saw the guy—definitely dead—and then Helga, on her back. There was a lot of blood pooled around her. I remember seeing her leg. It looked awful. Like a fresh shark bite." Lacey paused, temporarily reliving the moment.

"But now it doesn't?" Jimmy asked.

"No. The wound looks a lot smaller than I remember, and it looks like she has some old, bad scarring."

"And you think you had something to do with that?"

Lacey got defensive. "Yes. No. Yes, I know I did," she said finally, arms crossed.

Jimmy laughed. "Relax, Budgie. I believe you. I'm just trying to get a picture. Do you, like, lay hands on the wound and stuff? Is there any 'Praise Jesus' involved?"

"No," Lacey said, still defensive. "At least, I don't think so. I kind of black out, or go into a type of twilight."

"That's a little scary," Jimmy said.

"You don't know the half of it," she answered. "Anyway, it feels more like science than religion. Like I'm channeling some sort of energy. Like a conduit."

"Maybe that's what those religious wackos feel, too," Jimmy said.

"Not helping," Lacey said.

"Actually, believe it or not, the thing that's got me stuck is you running toward the sound of a gunshot," Jimmy said. "That's pretty bold. Almost reckless, one might say."

"I don't know, Chump. This is all new to me. Who's to say I didn't have this in me all along? This kind of bravery."

"I'm not saying you've never been brave. Just cautious. Especially after Fox."

Lacey shrugged.

"You said something about Creole healers. Do you think you're part of a special breed?" Jimmy asked. "Like *Highlander*?"

"No, at least I hope not," Lacey said. "Remember he got thrown out of his village."

"And there were lots of beheadings, too," Jimmy said. "You'd probably want to avoid that. You said something about 'a power manifesting.' That made me think of the Quickening."

Lacey paused. "Yeah, maybe. There's a lot of heat. It's happened twice now. Actually more than twice, but two really big, definite times."

"What was the other time?" Jimmy asked.

"Oh," Lacey's defenses went up again. "Well, I don't remember everything. But it was that guy, Nathan. I found him underneath the I-610 overpass by my house."

"Jesus! Who is this lowlife?" Jimmy asked.

"I barely know him! I don't think he's a lowlife. I think he's just caught up in something bad, some bad mojo, maybe." Lacey realized she still had no idea why this was happening to Nathan. And he had tried to tell her, too.

"Whatever. But Helga got shot because of him, too. And someone got killed. Did you come here with him tonight?"

"No! Geez. Settle, please," Lacey said, trying to assuage her brother's protective streak. "You know I was supposed to come with Angele. I ran into Nathan inside, purely coincidental."

"I don't believe in coincidences," he said. "You said 'more than twice,'" he added.

"Well, I think," Lacey replied, relieved at the change of subject. "There may have been other times, but just not as big. If anything happened, it was super quick and not dramatic. I'm not entirely certain I did anything to help."

Jimmy was in deep thought. "Like earthquakes," he said.

"What?"

"In California. Sometimes you feel these minor, quick tremors. You're not sure whether it's a truck passing or an earthquake. The big everything-shakes-for-more-than-a-minute ones happen a lot less frequently."

"Huh. What's this got to do with me?" Lacey smiled. She rolled her neck, her shoulders feeling suddenly unencumbered. She should have known her brother would take her news in stride.

In the direction of the alley, a group of people began to break up. Lacey sensed the detective might soon be upon them.

"Hey, Chump? There's something else kind of weird," Lacey said.

"Kind of? Because the rest of this isn't weird at all?" Jimmy asked.

"I know. Stay with me, here. It's when the 'big ones' happen. I think I have to be naked." Lacey kicked at a pebble at her feet. "Or, I don't know if 'have to be' is right, but somehow I end up that way," she added, still fascinated with the ground.

A lightbulb snapped on over Jimmy's head. "Like the Hulk?" he asked, grinning.

"Oh stop it!" Lacey said, finally looking up. "I don't bust out of my clothes, no," she said. "It's more like Superman, except I have to change into my birthday suit."

"That could get inconvenient," Jimmy said.

"Ya think?" Lacey looked down at her feet again. "No more comic references come to mind?"

"No," Jimmy said with a toned-down smile. "I'm sticking with the Hulk."

"What about the X-Men?" Lacey asked. "They're the first thing I thought of. And if I have to be non-flesh-colored, I'd rather be Mystique than the Hulk."

"No way," he said. "Mutants are born that way. Same thing with the Immortals. And Superman, too."

"Maybe I was born with this," she answered lamely.

"Uh-uh. You said you think you got this from Fox. It's something that happened to you, so that makes you the Hulk. Fox was kinda like gamma radiation," he added.

"Not sure where to go with that," she said.

They stopped talking as a rumpled, barrel-chested man in an ill-fitting suit coat approached.

The detective had a hard time opening the bus door. Lacey and Jimmy stood behind him, glanced at each other, and Jimmy spoke up.

"Sir, yeah, the door's a bit tricky." It wasn't.

The detective stumbled as he stepped aside and let Jimmy get the door. Inside, Helga bolted upright from her chair. She and Jimmy spoke for a few moments. Lacey noticed her brother was only an inch or two taller than Helga.

Nathan also stood and stepped away from the sofa. He looked much bigger standing than he did seated, filling a small space near one of the windows.

Lacey got her first good look at the detective when he finally made it to the deck of the bus. The man was shambling and looked like he had just gotten dressed, and not done a great job of it. The buttons of his shirt were misaligned, leaving one collar higher than the other, and the opposite shirttail longer. The jacket thrown over it was wrinkled. She prayed he'd remembered the zipper on his pants.

"So who do we have here?" the detective asked. The alcohol on his breath permeated the bus.

Helga took the line of fire. "I'm Amy Hoskins, Ridgeline Security. Detective…?" He had shown a badge to Jimmy and Lacey, but no one knew his name.

He looked exasperated, and flashed his badge again. "It's Aucoin. Detective Aucoin. Where the fuck is Officer Stiles?"

"In the back for a moment," Helga answered.

Detective Aucoin shook his head. It seemed like he might fall over from the effort.

"I need the names and identities of everyone involved," he said.

Helga indicated herself, Nathan, and Lacey, and the detective pulled out a notebook.

"Who are you?" he asked Jimmy.

"I'm her brother," Jimmy said, nodding his head at Lacey, "and this is my bus."

"You can't stay here," the detective said, agitated and about to get in Jimmy's face.

Lacey harkened back to evenings with a drunken Fox, and put into practice some well-used tactics.

"Detective Aucoin!" Lacey said forcefully, without any hint of emotion. She approached him with her hands out and lightly touched his forearm, which was hanging slack at his side. "We can separate while you question us. The bus has several compartments," Lacey said. She wasn't sure if that was true.

The detective looked at her as if he was seeing her for the first time, and looked down at her hand on his arm.

Lacey's hand grew warm, and she felt a tingling sensation

radiate up her arm. She pulled away as soon as she realized what was happening. Why would a drunk need healing? The effect of the alcohol would wear off on its own.

Nathan, Helga, and Jimmy stared at her. She put her hand up to her cheek to feel if she was flushed.

The detective ran his hands down his shirt to straighten it, noticed it was misbuttoned, and attempted to pull his jacket closed over his protruding belly. "I'm sorry," he said, addressing Jimmy. "Is there a private room here?"

Jimmy looked at Lacey and raised his eyebrows. "Yes, Detective," he said.

The detective pointed at Helga. Lacey winced as she watched her limp toward the back of the bus. An awkward silence settled over Lacey, Jimmy, and Nathan.

Jimmy eyed Nathan. Nathan took the opposite approach and held out his hand, with all the confidence and poise of a friendly business meeting.

"I'm sorry, we haven't met, with all this. Nathan Quirk."

Jimmy accepted. "Jimmy Campo."

The impossibly fit Officer Stiles reappeared and shut down any further conversation. Jimmy approached her, and after a brief conversation retrieved his laptop from the recesses of the bus and sat next to Lacey.

Lacey stared at the blinds on the window opposite. She closed her eyes, the easiest way to avoid Nathan's gaze. She focused on the sound of Jimmy typing, and tried to clear her mind.

When she opened her eyes, Nathan was emerging from the room with the detective. Helga was gone.

Crap! How could I have fallen asleep? Lacey thought.

Lacey looked at Jimmy. "Did Helga—" she started to ask.

"In the ER waiting room at UMC, as we speak," Jimmy said. "She's fine, she's been texting updates."

"Okay, good."

Nathan stopped in front of them. "Detective Aucoin's ready for you, Lacey," Nathan said.

Lacey nodded. Her steps toward the back of the bus were weighted with dread.

The detective was wedged into a cramped cubby opposite the toilet. His notebook was on a ledge in front of him. There was only one place to sit, and he motioned for Lacey to take it. He remained standing.

"Stacey Becnel, correct?" he said without looking up.

"Uh, it's Lacey," she said. "Lacey, with an *L*," she added when he didn't seem to understand.

"So, what happened to you tonight?" he asked.

She started by trying to explain why she looked so bloody. The detective didn't seem interested in her appearance. So she tried recounting, as plainly as she could, everything she remembered after walking out of the Publiq House. She didn't get very far before the detective countered nearly every sentence she spoke with a question:

"Why did you start running toward the alley when you heard a gunshot?"

"Did you look at the body when you passed it?"

"Did you see anyone fire a weapon?"

"Where was Ms. Hoskins's weapon?"

"When did Mr. Quirk appear on the scene?"

"Did Mr. Quirk show any signs of struggle?"

Lacey answered every question truthfully, flat, and with no hesitation. She only faltered when the detective asked how long she had known Nathan.

"Is there something you know about Mr. Quirk that you're not telling me, Stacey?" he asked, cutting her off.

Lacey flared. "No, Detective Aucoin." She emphasized his last name.

He stared at her. "It's not salient, anyway," he said, moving on. "But I will tell you, Stacey, we could finish up quickly if you could be more substantive in your answers."

"But I—" Lacey stopped herself. She looked down at her shoes but imagined jumping up, overturning her flimsy chair, and stomping out of the bus and into the night. It took every ounce of grace she possessed to say, "Okay."

She squared her shoulders and raised her chin. He looked over his notes, then asked about the driver of the car.

Hoping she was almost done, she chose her next words carefully. "He was a very slight man, no taller than me, five seven, and maybe one hundred and fifty pounds. He was dressed poorly, like he might have come in off the streets. He was driving the car, and the man who is now dead was in the passenger seat, and Mr. Quirk was in the back seat. I got a better look at him after the car had stopped. He hit me with one of the rear car doors, and then fled down an alleyway."

The detective considered her statement. "Did he intentionally hit you with the car door?"

Lacey thought before answering. "I can't speak for what he may have intended, but it did seem he meant to stop my forward progress by pushing me with the door."

The detective scribbled something in his notebook. "I might need you to give a detailed description of this individual. I will have someone contact you in that case."

Lacey sat expectantly. He finally looked up at her. "You can go," he said, uninterested.

Lacey walked, zombified, out of the cubby. Her desire of just a few moments ago—to bolt out into the night—had completely abandoned her. Jimmy sat in his chair, still accompanied by his laptop. Nathan was gone.

Everything felt foreign to her. There sat her brother, but he was the brother she knew the least, the famous rock star. She sat on the little sofa opposite Jimmy, like she was taking a seat on a bus full of strangers headed to unknown destinations.

Jimmy looked up from his screen. He had a pair of glasses resting on the bridge of his nose.

"You okay, Budge?" he said.

The detective lumbered past them without a word. He motioned to Officer Stiles at the front of the bus, and they both left.

Lacey giggled. She looked at her brother, and the glasses made her laugh outright. He stood up and walked to her side.

"Okay, you are definitely not all right," he said.

"I'm sorry," she said. "Nervous letdown, I guess. How long have you needed glasses, Chump?"

He pulled them off his face and set them atop his head. That made her laugh more.

"Just wait," he said. "They're in your future, too. You'll rue the day you laughed at me about them."

"Who talks like that?" she said, the automatic, movie-quote response. "Chump, I need to get home," she continued.

"Do you need company?" he asked.

"No, I'll be good. The beast will protect me. Plus, he's probably wondering where I am," she said. "But I will accept an escort to my car."

"You shouldn't call your new boyfriend that," Jimmy said, needling her as he grabbed his phone.

"He's not my boyfriend! And I meant Ambrose, Chump."

Jimmy tilted his head at his sister and shook it slowly.

"Really? Okay, glad we cleared that up," he said.

"Shut up," she said, shaking her head in return. "Will you just get me to my car already?"

28

Safely in her car and almost home, Lacey was taken by surprise by the phone call. There was something unfinished between her and Nathan, she knew, and she had checked her phone at every stoplight for a text.

A text would have been some punctuation on a dramatic evening. A period. Nathan chose an exclamation point.

"Very clever," he said, his voice echoing through the car's speakers.

"What are you talking about?" Lacey said.

"You hear about my connection to Cat Ballou, but you don't think to mention that your brother is in one of the hottest bands around?" Feedback interspersed his words.

"I don't like to hang on my brother's coattails," Lacey said.

"If you were trying to make it as a musician, I could see how that might be valid," he said.

"What do you want, Nathan?"

He wasted no time. "Will you meet me for a drink?" he asked.

"No," Lacey said. "I don't want to go anyplace that would

still be open at two a.m. And I think you should go get your head checked out," she added.

Nathan laughed. "In more ways than one, probably. But no."

"I'm concerned you might have a concussion," Lacey said. "You were passed out."

"I'm not up to dealing with the graveyard shift of the ER," he said. "What do you have at your house? Can you make me a drink?"

"Wow. That's bold," she said.

"Please?"

She knew she did not want to be alone. And the thought of having Nathan Quirk back at her house thrilled her. She hated herself for it.

"Yeah. Okay," she said with a good dose of resignation. "Do you remember where it is?"

"I remember. See you soon."

Silence filled her car after he hung up. She could feel the blood rushing through her head.

She was only a few minutes from home, and started running through a mental checklist. It had been a long time since she'd had a visitor. Angele and her parents didn't count. And neither did the first time with Nathan. That had been out of need, not invitation.

She pulled into the driveway and saw Ambrose's giant form rise in the lit window. *He will need to go out, and stay out,* she thought. He couldn't have the run of the house tonight. Luckily, everything was clean.

As she put the key in the front door and heard the jangling dog collar, she stopped herself. No more checklist. She hadn't issued an invitation to her house; Nathan had invited himself. Her house, and her dog, were the way they were going to be.

She greeted Ambrose, patting him down and checking him over. He stood, poised and stoic. She realized how much she would want him nearby when Nathan came calling.

As she emptied her pockets, the evening's trauma came crashing back in on her. There was the bullet she had magically drawn from Helga's leg, and her money and ID, wet and red with blood.

"Oh, Jesus."

Ambrose followed her to the guest bathroom and stood watch outside the open door. The mirror confirmed her fears. The hair on the right side of her head was matted with dried blood, the eye below it was swollen. She touched her head and could feel a bump.

I can't believe no one said anything to me, she thought.

She opened the faucet and washed her face and worked the blood out of her hair. She grabbed a wide cloth headband, which could do double duty by pulling her hair back and serving as a bandage. She tentatively touched her swollen eyelid, and tried to will her fiery feeling to work on herself. She closed her eyes. She felt foolish—and vain—for trying to heal herself. Her fingertips tingled.

Ambrose rushed away when the knock on the door came. Lacey grabbed some mouthwash, took a swig from the bottle, and gave herself one last check in the mirror. "I'll be damned," she said. Her eye, though still swollen, seemed less so. She left the bathroom, but froze five feet from the front door.

I don't want this, she thought.

There was another knock, and Ambrose answered with a single bark.

I don't know what I want, she rethought, and resumed her way toward the door.

"Stay," she said to Ambrose.

She opened the door to find Nathan holding a daisy. He had pulled it from her garden.

"Good evening, ma'am. May I come in?" he asked.

She cocked her head at him. "You're not a vampire, are you? Asking for permission to cross my threshold?" She regretted the words as soon as they came out of her mouth.

"I'm no vampire," he said, laughing. "But…"

Ambrose growled. Lacey took the daisy from Nathan and locked the door behind him.

"Ambrose!" she scolded, inwardly praising him. "You remember Nathan. Greet Nathan."

He quit growling and blew air out his nose. He held up a giant paw. Nathan leaned over to shake the dog's paw. He winced as he straightened up.

"What is it?" Lacey asked.

"Nothing. Just seeing stars."

Lacey shook her head. "This is not smart. You probably have a concussion, and I'm covered in blood. And we just saw a man get killed, for Christ's sake."

Nathan stood and stared, anchored to the floor. "Would you rather be alone?"

Lacey shut her mouth. She shook her head again, slowly. "It's too much," she said.

"Yes," he answered. "It is. All of it. And I don't want to be alone either. I want to be with someone I trust."

Lacey felt too vulnerable, and Ambrose sensed it. She shot laser eyes at him to keep him from growling again.

"Why don't we have that drink, then," she said, walking away. "Do you drink bourbon?"

"I prefer scotch," he said.

From the wet bar, Lacey blew the dust off a bottle of Glenfiddich 15. She held it up behind her and asked, "Is this okay? I don't know scotch."

She turned around when Nathan didn't answer. He was still anchored to the same spot by the door, facing Ambrose.

"Ambrose! Go to bed," Lacey said. The dog let out another massive sigh and retired to his bed in the corner.

Nathan still didn't move.

"It's fine, Nathan, he's not going to hurt you," Lacey said.

"It's not that," he answered, staring at Lacey.

He finally took a few steps forward and asked, "Did the house come with that?"

"What are you talking about?"

"Was the bar that way when you bought the house, or did you have it put in?"

"Oh," Lacey said. Her mind drifted to negotiations with Fox over the wet bar. He'd eventually won her over with unfulfilled promises of elegant dinner parties with witty and charming friends.

"It was put in," she answered in a low voice. She pivoted, looking for tangible signs of Fox that might have caught Nathan's attention. She found none.

She held up the bottle of scotch again. "Are you okay with this?"

"Definitely," he answered, released from whatever spell he had been under. "That's a good scotch."

She rinsed out two rocks glasses in the sink and dried them off before opening the ice maker. "Ice?" she asked.

Nathan leaned back against the edge of the sofa, arms folded. "No thanks."

She shut the ice maker. They were both neat.

She handed him his drink before pouring herself a half inch of Blanton's. Nathan moved closer.

"It's almost like a shrine," he said, running a finger along the dark granite countertop and eyeing the well-stocked shelves.

"Don't say that," Lacey said.

"Why not?" Nathan asked. "Am I in Gone But Not Forgotten territory?"

Lacey preferred the petrified Nathan to this version. The last thing she wanted to do was talk about Fox.

"Yes," she answered curtly. "We bought this house together, and the wet bar was his idea. But now he's gone, and it's mine. Why are we talking about this? Who was that guy?"

"What guy?" Nathan asked.

"The dead guy," Lacey said. "The one who tried to kidnap you."

"Jesus," Nathan said, stepping back. "I don't know who he was." He set his drink on an end table and ran the palms of his hands across the sides of his head.

"What did he say to you?"

"Not much," Nathan said. "He got up really close to me at the bar and said he had something to tell me about my kids. Then he pressed a gun hard against my side and told me to walk to the exit."

"Did he use their names?" Lacey asked.

"Yes."

"Shit," Lacey said. "I'm sorry. Have you… I mean, are they okay?" She was unable to express herself clearly about his family.

"They're fine. They were asleep when I talked to Lisa."

"Oh," Lacey said. Her stomach cramped. She wasn't sure

she'd ever heard his wife's name before. "Did you tell her what happened?" Lacey asked.

"No," he said. "I pretended to be drunk and emotional and got her to assure me that the kids were safe."

"Oh," Lacey said. She thought of his "someone I trust" remark and her stomach tightened more.

"You know, that one guy was the same," Nathan said. "The driver. Except he wasn't driving the last time."

"The last time?" Lacey asked.

Nathan looked at her square and almost smiled. "Yeah, the last time I almost got killed until you came to my rescue."

"Oh."

"He was the one who wouldn't shut up, the time before. This time, he was still saying a lot, just not as loud."

Lacey nodded. "He was saying something I couldn't hear when I got to the car. I thought he was a junkie. Or at least he kinda seemed like he might be on something." She thought "junkie" sounded too judgmental. Or maybe outdated.

"I have no doubt," Nathan said.

Lacey thought back to their unfinished conversation at the coffee shop. She'd been so preoccupied with her own "whys" that she hadn't considered Nathan's. She felt foolish and self-absorbed.

"What dark secret are you harboring, Nathan?" she asked. "Why are these people after you?"

Nathan finished his scotch in one long swallow. "Would you mind?" he asked as he reached for the bottle behind her.

"Go ahead," she said, stepping aside.

Now face to face with her, he asked, "Did you know Gone But Not Forgotten's family?"

"Yes," she said. "Why is that—"

He cut her off. "Can you imagine how there could be someone so obsessed with him, and so disappointed in his choice of you, that they would rather make you disappear?" he said. There was an intensity to his look that belied his casual tone.

"Is that it?" Lacey asked. "You think someone in Li—your wife's…family wants to kill you?"

Nathan shrugged.

"Well that's… God, that's awful," Lacey said, realizing anything she could say would sound like understatement. "When you work for…"

Nathan set his drink down and nodded.

"Oh," Lacey said.

His own father-in-law is trying to kill him. The words sounded surreal in her head.

"You can see how that might put some additional strain on an already taxed marriage," he said.

"I don't know what I can say, Nathan," Lacey said.

"Maybe we should quit talking, then."

Nathan braced his hand on the counter next to his drink. He positioned himself like a guard between the couch and the bar, blocking her passage. He stared at her.

The knots in Lacey's stomach tightened. She looked down to avert his stare, and saw her legs and feet streaked with blood.

"I really need to take a shower," she said, her voice cracking. "I feel like I'm tracking blood everywhere."

He nodded. "Don't let me stop you."

"You're blocking my way to the bathroom."

He stepped aside, silent, never taking his eyes off her.

"Thank you," she said, eyes still cast down. "Make yourself at home. I'll only be about ten minutes."

✳

Lacey's head was buzzing. She wasn't sure she wanted it to stop. She stared at the dark stone tile floor of the master bath as she dropped her clothes.

She opened the faucet and water sparked from the rain showerhead. She spread her arms and still didn't touch the walls of the shower. She tried to make her mind empty, letting the water wash off all thoughts, all experiences. She looked down and saw water, streaked with red, circling the drain.

She looked up, and her breath caught in her throat. Nathan stood in the open doorway. He walked toward the shower and set his scotch on the sink counter.

Lacey thought of trying to cover herself, but stood, motionless, under the water. She was transfixed by the color of his eyes. They were hazel with flecks of green. How could they stand out so much through the spray of the shower? Had she even noticed them before? She looked down again, to break the spell, and saw that he was barefoot. Where had he left his shoes?

He must have read her thoughts. "You said make yourself at home," he said.

Lacey raised her hand to turn off the water.

"Don't," he said. He walked into the shower, shirt and shorts still on. Lacey noticed then that his belt was gone, too.

"What are you doing?" Lacey said, laughing.

Nathan did not laugh, his expression solemn. He touched her face, above her hurt eye.

"Is this okay?" he asked.

She knew he wasn't asking about her injury.

Lacey knew all the reasons it wasn't okay. She tried to summon just one of them, some incontrovertible truth she could hold in front of her like a solid granite rock that would block the path they were headed down. But all she felt was water drops on her skin, and a needful impulse, and the only truth available to her was her response: "Yes."

He closed the short distance between them the instant the word was spoken. His lips met hers, tender at first, then the pressure intensified as he began to envelop her. Something flamed inside Lacey, her pilot light ignited. His hands slid down past the small of her back. A sigh escaped her throat and she removed his shirt, now thoroughly soaked. A heavy slap sounded as she threw it to the shower floor.

He answered with his own firm slap, square on her buttocks. Lacey gasped and ran her hands over his chest and torso. A new sensation arced through her as she sensed the power and strength beneath his hard body. She marveled at how Nathan could be ten years older but have a body ten years younger than Fox's.

Her finger traced the line of light fur that angled down to his navel, and she passed her hands over the centerline of his shorts. She could feel him, already hard, swell even more underneath.

"Take them off," he said into her ear, his teeth brushing her lobe.

She obeyed, unfastening the button and the zipper, and placed her hands on either side of him. She slid both shorts and boxers past his hips. Out of habit nearly forgotten, she moved down to put her mouth on him as he stepped out of his shorts and kicked them behind him.

"No," he said. He put a finger under her chin and led her back up to her full height. He kissed her, gently again, then less so. He pulled back slightly and smiled. "Me first."

He moved down, stopping to flick his tongue over the nipple of her left breast. Her sense left her. He moved to her other side, his hand replacing his mouth. The pressure of his hand sent surges through her body. Her head reared back.

It was only a prelude to the feeling to come, as he moved to his knees. With the water running down her, and then over Nathan's head and down his back, his tongue explored her. Lacey made a sound she didn't think she had ever made before. He brought her to the brink, and then pushed her over it. She braced her hands behind her, fingers slippery against the wall of the shower.

He stopped and stood up, leaving Lacey panting. She kissed him and he pulled her close, his hand holding her head against his chest. She felt some sense return, at the same time she felt him hard against her.

Nathan pulled back just enough to look her in the eyes. He had a melancholy sweetness that melted Lacey's last ounce of steel.

"I want you," he said.

"I know," she said with a laugh. "Uh, I've been out of the game for a while," she said, questioning whether she had ever really been in it. "I don't think I have any kind of protection around here."

She knew she didn't. She had thrown out every last stashed condom she'd found after Fox had died.

"I'm fixed," he said, his voice revealing a sense of urgency.

"Oh," Lacey said, unsure.

"Seven years ago, after my second was born," he said. "I've only had one partner for the last fifteen years," he added. His mouth moved to her neck.

What reason do I have to believe him? she thought.

His teeth grazed her ear. The slight prick of pain convinced her.

I've trusted him this far.

He felt her relent, and he lifted her up onto him, without any obvious effort. She wrapped her legs around him, her back against the cool, wet wall. She felt the crush of wet body to her front and stone wall to her back. And then, in an instant, she felt Nathan inside her.

"Oh, fuck me," Lacey said. Her voice fell off.

He responded with labored breaths and surprisingly melodious grunts. It sounded like he might break out into song. Lacey marveled at the rhythm and his strength. How long could he keep her suspended like this?

When he gently placed her back into a standing position, Lacey thought they were done. She turned off the water.

She turned around to face Nathan, and he placed his hand on her shoulder. He pushed her against the wall of the shower with a firm and sudden movement. With his other hand he felt her, still flooded at her center. The swift transition heightened the sensation.

He used that hand to guide himself into her. Before, he must have channeled some of his strength into carrying her weight. This time, she felt his full force. She extended her arm behind her head to keep it from banging into the wall. Something that had been caged a very long time, in both of them, was released.

Nathan's strange melody faded, silent as he drove into her repeatedly. Lacey's head echoed with a sound.

Ga-dunk.

Like repeating anvils, syncing with each thrust he made into her. Lacey called out, a wild spirit escaping her through her vocal cords. When she felt him come inside her, she responded in kind, her cry sounding a flash of light that sparked in the center of her brain.

That light wiped out everything. Lacey felt like her reset button had been punched. Her mind a blank, she stared at Nathan, eyes wild.

He turned away and grabbed towels from the rack outside the shower. He went to Lacey, her back still against the wall, her head now down and staring at the drain. He wrapped her in a towel, as he would a child.

"You're burning up," he said, startled.

"It'll pass," she answered. She knew what had transpired. "How's your concussion?" she asked.

He smiled. "Please relax. I don't have a concussion. God, I feel great, actually."

He lifted his hand to touch the side of Lacey's face, but her look told him to pull back. Her eyes searched his face.

Nathan caught on.

"Oh. Really?" he said. "You think you just, uh, did your thing?"

She lifted her shoulders, felt some normalcy return. "I think I just had an out-of-body experience, is what I think," she said.

Nathan laughed involuntarily. "I'm just that good, baby."

Lacey moved away from the wall of the shower and wrapped her towel around her. She smiled at him and said, "You're a jackass." She bent down to pick up his clothes from the floor of the shower. She wrung them out.

"Seem like a good time for housekeeping?" Nathan asked.

"Unless you want to leave here wearing some remnants left behind by Gone But Not Forgotten, I thought I'd put your clothes in the dryer."

"Who says I want to leave?"

Lacey stood and faced him. "You'll leave," she said. "Eventually." She caught her breath as something caught her eye. The scar on Nathan's shoulder. She hadn't noticed it through the spray and their activity in the shower.

"What is it?"

"Nothing," Lacey said. "Is that—" she reached her hand to his shoulder.

He caught her hand. "Yes. It's from that night."

"Does it still hurt?"

"No," he said. "Maybe just a deep ache occasionally. Like it's something I got a long time ago." He released her hand and let her touch his shoulder. Her fingers moved gently over the scar.

"It *looks* like something from a long time ago," she said. She peered around his shoulder to his back and saw a smaller pockmark on the opposite side.

"The bullet went through you," she said. *Not like I would've remembered if I'd drawn a bullet from him anyway,* she thought.

"Yes," he said, solemn as a graveyard. "Your—your thing, this ability, is pretty miraculous, you know."

Lacey sighed. "I don't feel miraculous." She moved past him and out of the bathroom, her movements deliberate. In the dark hallway, she was overcome.

A torrent of images cascaded upon her. She closed her eyes and braced her free hand against the wall, but they would not stop. Time ceased. Each image felt like it was burned into her retinas:

An older man she did not know sitting in a spacious office. The same man sick in bed.

Fox as a child visiting his mother's grave.

A country highway and an old, white truck, its front end folded over the cab and a slash of blood on the door.

A mountainside retreat, whitewashed stone reflecting the light from lanterns hanging in the trees.

Lacey inhaled deeply and opened her eyes. How much time had passed? Had someone else's life flashed before her? She willed herself to take one step, then another, until she approached the laundry room.

She caught her reflection in the mirrored Schlitz beer sign that hung in her kitchen. Her eye was no longer swollen. The cut above it appeared no more than a scratch.

29

Lacey closed the dryer door.

"Oh God!" she said as she turned around. "You scared me!"

Nathan stood in the doorway of the laundry room in nothing but a towel, his arm braced against the frame in a model pose.

"That was not the reaction I was going for," he said. He positioned into a bodybuilder flex, exaggerating every movement.

Lacey wasn't sure if he looked so good to her *because* he was trying to be funny, or in spite of it. Her head was in a spin cycle, alternating between a weightless, untethered amazement and a massive, anchored sense of shame.

She was determined to mask it. "You okay?" she asked.

"Best I've felt in five years." He went to her and circled his arms around her waist. The shame threatened to suffocate her.

She squirmed. Her gaze kept returning to the burden basket on the wall. "You, ah, have really never…strayed before?" she asked.

He kept his hold on her, but his expression lost its ease. He didn't answer.

"I know I shouldn't be asking, but really, I'm not fishing," she said, the words streaming out of her in a fast pitch. "I'm just… I'm just curious. You said five years, and I know you've been married for longer, and, well, you know Gone But Not Forgotten?"

"No, not personally," he said. "But yes, I know I'm not supposed to bring him up for fear of releasing the Incredible Hulk."

Lacey's eyes grew wide. She snorted out a laugh and thought of her brother. Jimmy didn't believe in coincidences. What were the odds of two Hulk comparisons in one night?

"What is it?" Nathan asked.

"Nothing, I'll tell you later," she said. "Let me try to finish what I want to tell you."

Lacey relaxed. "Gone…he and I were in a relationship for a very long time," she said. "My whole adult life, really. I found out after it had ended that he had been cheating on me the whole time." The words sounded foreign to Lacey as they came out of her mouth.

"Shit," Nathan said. He kept a loose hold on her.

"Tell me about it."

"Did you kill him?" he asked.

"What?" Lacey said, stiffening.

"I've figured he's gone in the literal sense," Nathan said. "Just a feeling."

"So you've figured he's dead, and that I killed him?"

"The dead part, yes, but no, I don't really think you killed him," he said.

Lacey worked her way out of his embrace and backed up against the washing machine.

"That's pretty deductive of you," she said. "Yes, he died last year. And no, I didn't kill him."

"Well," Nathan said, bracing himself against the doorframe again. "I also figure you were married to him."

"Oh yeah?" Lacey said. "How do you figure that?"

"Your last name's different from your brother's."

"You pay attention to details."

"Yes," he said. He looked sad and sweet. "I'm sorry he cheated on you, Lacey. I can't imagine why he would go elsewhere, when he had you."

"Don't say that," she said.

"Why not?"

"Because it's too much flattery. Because you don't know me that well. Maybe I was a shrew and drove him away."

"I hope you don't spend too much time believing that about yourself."

Lacey turned her head toward the laundry room window. She didn't want to talk about Fox anymore.

"You know, I don't even feel like I've been tempted before," Nathan said. "Before you. Things with my wife were actually pretty good, early on."

Lacey returned her gaze to Nathan. "What happened five years ago?" she asked.

"Nothing. Nothing happened. It's when my youngest started preschool. I think that's just when things started to… decay." His words had a ring of finality to them. And Lacey knew, on a gut level, exactly what he meant.

She moved toward him and said, "I'm sorry."

"For what?"

"For asking." She took his hand and gave it a quick kiss, and led him out of the laundry room to the bedroom.

✳

She awoke not knowing how much time had passed. Light was starting to punch through the frame of her bedroom window shades. She could feel Nathan fast asleep at her back.

That was nothing like it used to be, Lacey thought. Maybe her resentment of Fox, and their shared sense of decay, had enhanced the chemistry between her and Nathan. Then again, she had never saved Fox's life. That could have something to do with it. She searched for the right description.

We fucked like champions, she thought. Angele might appreciate that. *Angele. Shit.*

Yes, she could tell Angele. Angele would not judge, at least not in this instance. But the thought of bringing this, whatever it was, outside the secure and intimate world of her home on Florida Boulevard deflated her. She didn't want the interlude to end, and that scared her more than anything.

She eased out of Nathan's arms, grabbed a camisole and some cotton shorts, and snuck out of the bedroom. She refused to look back at him.

On her way to the laundry room, she heard Ambrose barking. Ambrose didn't bark—not at passersby, not at the trains, and not at the squirrels and possums and raccoons that frequented the neighborhood. The most he spoke was a single acknowledgement, a yes or no "woof." Something wasn't right.

She went into the guest bathroom and stood on the ledge of the tub. She peered through the clear panes of the window, above the frosted ones. She saw Ambrose in the side yard, standing at attention, barking through the fence. A car moved slowly down the street. The early morning light was low, and Lacey struggled to make out anything distinct about the car. It looked like a cop car, painted a dark color. It disappeared down the street. She didn't see a license plate.

Ambrose remained stationary at the fence. Lacey hurried to the kitchen door. Ambrose came running as soon as he heard it open.

"You're a good boy," she said, rubbing his head. *And I'm an idiot*, she thought.

She gave Ambrose a treat and asked him to keep watch at the front windows. He nodded his giant head and shuffled to the living room.

Nathan's an idiot. We're both idiots. Had he been followed? What had happened to the weaselly junkie who'd got away? Could he have followed Nathan here?

What if the car had been there all night? Why hadn't the cops told Nathan that someone might still be after him? Maybe they had. She didn't know what had transpired between him and the detective. She stormed into the bedroom to find Nathan sitting up, hands behind his head, eyes closed.

"Nathan!" She used the same tone she used to command Ambrose.

Nathan opened his eyes and looked at her lazily.

"Why did you come here tonight?"

"I thought we established that already," he said. "Three times." He was pleased with himself, which only made Lacey angrier. He got out of bed and stood to the side of it, baring his full frontal. "What's wrong?" he asked.

Lacey couldn't help but stare. It was the first time she had seen him flaccid, and he was still impressive. She shook her head and reminded herself why she was so angry. "I just saw a suspicious car," she said.

"A suspicious car?"

"Yes, no license plate, moving slowly down the street," she

said. "Ambrose was watching it. What if you were followed here? How could you not know to be more careful? Do you want me to get killed, too?"

He blew out a deep breath and walked toward her. "I told you I didn't want to be alone."

"But why come here?"

"You didn't want to go out." He was now directly in front of her. He grabbed a strand of her wavy hair.

"Stop it." She pushed his hand away.

A stray sunbeam caught the side of her face. It illuminated a previously hidden thought. Lacey's expression fell. "You're using *me*, for protection?" she asked.

"When someone's trying to kill you," he replied, "it's pretty handy to have the company of a healer."

Lacey turned her back on Nathan.

"Oh God," she said. She held her head in her hands. "How could I be so stupid?"

"Lacey. Stop it." His placed his hands on her shoulders. She wanted to shrug them off, but couldn't.

"Stop it," he repeated. "Yes, I thought I could be followed. But I had nowhere else to go."

She heard a different tone in his voice. The flippant air had dissipated, and his guard was down.

"I don't believe that," she said.

"I don't care. It's the truth. And I knew you, at least you, would be safe here."

She turned around to face him. "How can you say that? How can you know that?"

"That dog would kill anyone who tried to hurt you, including me," he said.

Lacey let out a tight laugh, despite herself. "That may be

true. But having sex with me seems like a pretty lousy way to keep watch."

"Would you rather I bored you with stories from my doomed marriage and my father-in-law who is trying to have me killed?" He stepped back and folded his arms. He eyed her up and down. "Jesus. You're even more beautiful when you're angry. I didn't think that could be possible."

"No you don't." She stared at him. "You can't disarm me with charm. I know those tricks."

"I don't care. It's the truth.

"Lacey. Listen to me," he continued. "Things are very…" He stopped, searching for words. "Very uncertain for me right now," he said. "And there's no real way for me to…repay you, ever repay you, for what you've done. For what you've meant."

"Repay me?" Lacey asked.

"You've saved my life," he said. "Multiple times."

"Nathan, it doesn't work that way," she said, confused.

"Do you know how it works?" he asked.

"No, but I'm pretty sure sex as a remittance puts all this at a fairly base level," she said.

Nathan laughed, finally relaxing into his words. "That's not what I meant. Can you accept, just possibly, that last night was a culmination of something?"

Lacey was silent. The danger outside was still present, but it felt muffled by the danger standing in front of her. It heightened her feelings as she listened to Nathan.

He sensed it. He moved toward her and put his hands on her hips.

"My life, and what I have to face down, is kinda awful right now. Outside of this," he said, caressing the side of her face. "Let me have this. Let me have you. Now."

Lacey surrendered with a swift and sudden kiss to his lips.

After a fourth and final coupling, they both knew it was time. At six fifteen a.m., the street outside was bright and unthreatening. Kravitz's crape myrtles had blossomed overnight, the rainbow of colors stretching toward the eastern horizon. Lacey pointed out where she had seen the car. She and Nathan both looked up and down the street before he stepped out onto her front porch.

They made no movement to embrace or touch each other. Lacey stood in the doorway, mute. Nathan turned to her, his hand behind him, holding on to the open door.

He looked anguished. "I love you," he said. He didn't wait for a reply. He turned his back to her and walked down the front steps, and didn't look back.

30

Lacey was overloaded, wired and tightly so. More than an hour had passed since she had watched Nathan get in his car and drive away. Time was crawling and barreling down on her, all at once. She wondered if his declaration had been the desperation of a man who might meet death around the next corner. She wondered if she'd ever see him alive again. If she did, she thought she might want to kill him.

She lay on the sofa, trying to sleep. Her attempts were futile. Needing to accomplish *something*, she put on running shorts and a T-shirt and grabbed Ambrose's leash.

She and Ambrose set a leisurely pace. Possibly for the first time ever, Lacey hoped she would see Kravitz outside. He did not disappoint. He was on his porch in an undershirt and boxers, cigarette resting in the ashtray, cup of black coffee next to it. Gabi rushed down the steps to greet Ambrose. Lacey relinquished her hold on Ambrose's leash and let the two animals do their dog greetings.

"What's happening, Mr. Max?"

"Pretty quiet morning, here," he said, sounding more gravelly than usual. "Surprised to see you out this early."

"Yeah, it was kind of a late night last night," she said, knowing he knew full well the hour she'd made it home. "My brother's in town; I was Uptown, watching him and his band."

"Huh! That wasn't him who left here this morning, was it? I would have said hello."

Here we go, Lacey thought.

"No, Mr. Max, that wasn't Jimmy," she said. "That was a friend of mine; he needed a place to stay."

"Huh. Nice car he has."

"Which car?"

"You don't know what kind of car your friend drives?" Kravitz asked. He took a pull off his Camel. "The silver Lexus."

"Oh, yeah, sorry," Lacey said, rocking from side to side on her feet. "He wasn't parked on your grass, was he?"

"No, no, he was over on your side. No problem."

Well, that's one helluva relief, Lacey thought. "Hey, Mr. Max," she said, "I saw some other car pass down here pretty early, driving real slow. Did you happen to see that one?"

"Don't think so. What did it look like?"

"Black Lincoln sedan or something—kinda looked like a cop car, but dark colored."

"Uh-uh. Didn't see it."

Just my luck, she thought. *The one thing I need that nosy bastard to see, he misses.*

"Oh. Okay. Was just afraid it might have been somebody up to no good, casing the neighborhood. If you didn't see it, though, I'm not worried. Must have just been a random passer-through."

"I'll let you know if I see anything like that."

I know you will, Lacey thought. She called Ambrose back to her side. "Thanks, Mr. Max," she said. "You gonna take Gabi to the dog park later?"

"Nah. It's supposed to rain today."

"Oh, okay. Guess I better get Ambrose walked before it hits."

"Yup."

"Okay. Have a good day, Mr. Max."

"You too, little Lacey."

She hastened her pace as she approached Orleans, eager to get out of Kravitz's line of sight. She took one note of solace from her conversation—it was unlikely that the suspicious car had been there all night. If the car had been parked in the vicinity for any length of time, Kravitz would have seen it from his wraparound porch.

She made the walk a quick one. On their return, a gust of wind came up like a scout from the coming storm. The crape myrtles shivered in the gale. Lacey and Ambrose were pelted with flower petals. The wind blew out the cobwebs of paranoia about Nathan and suspicious cars.

"This is insane," she said aloud. Ambrose looked up at her. "Don't you think?" she said in response to his gaze.

In reply, he broke free of her grip on the leash and ran the rest of the way home, bounding up the steps and waiting for her at the front door.

"Ambrose!" she shouted. She ran to catch up with him. "What was that about?" she asked the giant dog as she put her key in the lock. Ambrose nosed in the door ahead of her and stood by the side table, where she'd left her phone.

Lacey looked at the phone and saw a two-word text from Angele: CALL ME.

"Thanks, Bro," she said to the dog. She gave him a double-handed scratch behind the ears before calling Angele.

Angele rarely wasted her time with hellos, but this time, she picked up the other line by just saying: "You!"

"Good morning to you, too," Lacey replied.

"Listen, first things first," she said. "You've got a job, if you want it. Production accountant, Syfy movie in California—San Luis Obispo—you'll be working with a friend of mine, Lynn, who's pregnant and wants a backup. She'll budget in a salary for you. This is one of those opportunities you'd be a fool to pass up. I hope you're not going to be a fool."

"I'm in," Lacey answered without hesitation.

"Wow. That's it?" Angele said. "No whining about what you're going to do about the oleander plant in the side yard that needs attention?"

"It's not an oleander, it's a Japanese elm, and I'll figure it out," Lacey answered. "I've got to do something, Lee. And getting out of town sounds kinda good right now."

"Well, that was easier than I thought," she said. "Expect a call from Lynn in the next few days. Her name is Lynn Batzer. Next thing. What the fuck happened last night?"

"Too much to say over the phone."

"Give me the Navajo code version," Angele said.

"Oh Jesus," Lacey said. "Okay. Somebody went after Nathan. I freaked out, got one of Jimmy's bodyguards to help me find him. We did, and now somebody's dead. I went into X-Men mode, but not for the dead person."

"Somebody's dead?"

"Yeah. Nathan thinks someone from his wife's family is out for him. I guess it was a hired goon?"

"Hired goon?" Angele's tone was biting.

"It's a fitting description," Lacey said. "Or, at least it was. Jimmy's bodyguard, Helga—"

"I know her," Angele said.

"Okay. Helga got hurt, and I went into my fugue state. The full-body fugue state."

"You went naked again?"

"Yeah. If you keep interrupting, I won't be able to finish." Lacey paused, and when Angele didn't say anything more, she continued. "However it turned out, Helga got better. I think she lost a lot of blood, though. I have to make sure she's okay."

"I'm going to interrupt if you don't stay on track," Angele said.

"Fine. Me, Nathan, and Helga had to wait around to talk to the cops. It was several hours, at least. That's when I got the text from you. Jimmy came by with Trevor after their show, Trevor kissed me on the top of the head and left. I looked like hell, too—all bloodied, and my eye was hurt. Jimmy stayed with me while I had to wait for the cops. He and Nathan sort of bowed up against each other. That's the end of that part."

"Move to the next part," Angele said. "I don't have much time."

"Right," Lacey said. "Well, once we were all clear, Nathan called me while I was driving home. He invited himself over. He left about two hours ago."

Silence.

"That's it?" Angele finally replied. "Dinner Jacket just leaves your house, and that part gets two sentences?"

"I think it was three."

"No you don't. I'll need more than that. Was it all talk, or was there action?"

"There was action."

"Good action?"

"Yes. Phenomenal," Lacey said. "I'm going to have a hard

time putting it behind me. Putting him behind me."

Angele laughed. Her abrasive, staccato laugh. "You might want to be careful how you word that," she said.

"Doesn't matter, since you're the only other soul on Earth I'm ever gonna tell about it."

Angele switched gears. "Is there going to be any trouble with you leaving the state to take the job with Lynn?"

"Shit, I don't know," Lacey said. "I don't think so. I hope not. I think someone followed Nathan here last night. I'd feel a whole lot safer out of town."

"That's another important detail you left out," Angele said.

"Yeah, so I saw this car with no license plate going down Florida early this morning. There was a guy who got away last night, the driver."

"Well that sucks," Angele said.

"Understatement," Lacey said. "Yes, I need to talk to the detective about that guy anyway. I'll check about leaving town and any hearings and stuff when I talk to him."

"Good," Angele said. "You know, I didn't get any details about the timing. Lynn might need you this week; it could be next month. You'll have to be ready to get your ass out there whenever she tells you."

"Okay." Lacey felt the conversation was about to come to a close.

"Are you going to be okay?" Angele asked.

Lacey laughed. "What would you do if I told you no?"

"Ignore it," Angele said. "You've already buried a husband. Mutant powers, police involvement, and a little roll in the hay with a doomed lover are just the next chapter. You can handle it."

"Thanks for the vote of confidence."

"Bye," Angele said, and disconnected before Lacey could say

anything else.

Lacey plopped down on the couch and dropped her phone on a pillow. The prospect of new employment succeeded in staking some limited real estate in her head. She hoped it could overtake Nathan Quirk, who occupied every other thought.

She knew she didn't love him. She hadn't known him long enough. She wasn't sure what she felt for him. Attracted, crushed? *In* love? But she had no right to feel those things for another woman's husband.

And everything he was going through—it was beyond toxic. Last night had to be a bad side-effect from that. Last night had been a big, glorious, overwhelming mistake.

Make a list, she told herself. *Make a plan of what you need to do to leave town. Make yourself useful. You have no power, no say in whatever becomes of Nathan. Sort of like Fox. They're both gone. Fox is dead. Nathan should be dead to you.*

She wished she could believe that.

She rose from the sofa to grab her laptop. She'd need to know what kind of clothes to pack for San Luis Obispo.

When Lacey heard the knock on her door Sunday evening, her heart jumped into her throat. Even though she knew it had to be her brother—they had spoken earlier and she was expecting him—a big part of her longed to see Nathan back at her door instead.

Jimmy shook to dry himself on the front porch. The promised rain did not disappoint; it had been coming down all day.

The Avengers was on TV, and Jimmy made a beeline for the recliner. "Is watching this like homework, now?" he asked.

"Wait," Lacey said, ignoring his remark. She draped a towel over the recliner. "Here you go. How is Helga doing?" she asked.

"She's fine. She left the hospital before I did," Jimmy answered. "Do you remember Rocky Anselmo?"

"Sort of," Lacey said. Jimmy could not go anywhere in New Orleans without running into a friend—old, new, or otherwise.

"He works as a cardiac nurse there," he said. "I was catching up with him on his break, and Helga got released. You know the ER doc thought the wound on her leg was months old?"

Jimmy looked at her sideways and flexed himself like the Incredible Hulk.

Lacey rolled her eyes. "I'm glad you think all this is funny. So Helga—Amy—is okay?"

"Like I've been telling you, Budge, that woman is beyond tough. She's fine."

Ambrose settled next to the recliner. When it came to rock-star adoration, the dog was worse than Jimmy's teenage groupies. Jimmy stretched his long arm over the arm of the chair and stroked the dog's head.

"What are you going to do with him when you go to SLO?" Jimmy asked.

"SLO?" Lacey asked.

"San Luis Obispo, Budge."

"Oh. I'll catch on," she said. "He's coming with. I'll need to find a place to rent that'll accept him."

"He could stay with me in Mar Vista if you have any problems," Jimmy said. "I'm going to be home most of July, and I know a good dog-sitter if your stint goes longer."

"Who's the dog-sitter?" she asked, her tone leading.

"A neighbor," Jimmy answered, not picking up the subtler question. "Lives right across the street. Dude's always on me about how much business he's missing out on since I don't have a dog."

"Oh," Lacey said. She tried the direct route instead. "So who are you dating that you told Mom about?"

"Ha!" Jimmy said, his eyes still trained on the television. "I should have figured Irene would blab."

"You know it," Lacey said, also keeping her eyes forward on the TV. "But I would have been mad if she hadn't. This is important stuff."

"You're such a girl."

"And better looking than you, too," Lacey said, the words coming to her like muscle memory.

"I should hope so."

"So?" Lacey asked when their decades-old taunt had run its course.

Jimmy got out of the recliner and headed toward the bar. Ambrose got up and left the room. "You want anything?" he asked.

"No thanks. Knock yourself out."

Jimmy poured himself a scotch. His back to Lacey, he finally spoke. "She's from Baton Rouge," he said. "She went to LSU."

"And you met her out there?" she asked.

"Yeah. She's really smart, Budge, she runs a development department at Fox," he said, all sarcasm erased from his tone. "But she still acts like she's from here."

"How do you mean?"

"She hasn't gone all California."

Lacey wasn't sure what he meant, but thought she might

find out soon enough.

"What's her name?" she asked.

"Monica."

"And how long have y'all been going out?"

Jimmy didn't respond. "Why do women always ask that?" he finally asked.

"Because it's important," Lacey said. "Most women have to deal with the relationship half-life. If the relationship ends after a couple of months, no biggie, it'll be out of your system in a month—six weeks if you're extra sensitive. Years are a weightier matter."

"Women are insane," Jimmy said. He crossed the room, drink in hand. He perused the stack of books on the side table by the recliner.

"No, we're just wired differently," Lacey said.

Jimmy pulled a book from the stack and returned to the recliner. "So, does that relationship logic still pertain to Fox, even though he's dead?"

"Hell, yeah," Lacey said. "I've got at least another three years of half-life purgatory before I can truly say I've moved on."

Jimmy considered. "Maybe I shouldn't have been so hard on your friend the doucheboat, then."

Lacey laughed at the word. "Who?"

"Your friend from last night."

"Nathan?"

"Yeah. Doucheboat."

Lacey couldn't keep herself from giggling. "Okay, this being completely none of your business, but if you're reconsidering your opinion of Nathan, why?"

"Because I would assume new relationships can accelerate the 'half-life,'" Jimmy said. "And you're a fine one to be telling me it's none of my business."

Lacey finally turned away from the TV and faced her brother.

"Uh-uh," she said. "You told Ma about Monica, that makes it my business. You just happened to meet new friend Nathan by circumstance. I wouldn't have told anybody about him yet."

He turned toward Lacey. "Yet?" he asked.

"I mean ever," she said.

She did not think Nathan's marital status would bother her brother as much as it did her. But something in his look told her otherwise. She wanted to drop the subject, quickly.

"I'm still kind of shocked Ma found out about your girl before I did," Lacey said. "It must be serious."

"Eh, I'm still trying to figure it out," Jimmy said, his eyes back on the TV.

"So how long's it been?" Lacey asked.

"We've known each other a while now," Jimmy said, "but I guess we started going out about a year ago."

"Jesus, I suck," Lacey said. *Pay attention.* The words stung. How much had she missed, cocooned in her own grief, her own problems?

"You've had a lot going on," Jimmy said.

"Other than a dead husband, and up until about two weeks ago, not really."

Jimmy stood up and gripped the back of the recliner, stretching his limbs.

"You'll get to meet her before Irene does, if that makes you feel any better," he said.

"It definitely does. When?" Lacey asked. She watched her brother. He reminded her of a three-toed sloth.

"We'll come up and see you at some point. SLO is awesome."

They stopped talking to watch Bruce Banner wake up naked in a pile of rubble. Jimmy nodded at the TV, then at Lacey.

"I'm *not* the Incredible Hulk!" she said, suddenly sounding like an eight-year-old.

Inspiration struck. "Why can't I be Wolverine?" Lacey asked, her voice returning to her thirties.

Jimmy sipped his scotch. "Huh. I guess you do have the healing thing going on."

"That's right! And I can be tough," she said. She stood up and began to stretch, too.

Jimmy laughed.

"Pretty sure I've never heard Wolverine complain about the relationship half-life," he said. "Plus you look more like Jean Grey than Wolverine."

"Wait," Lacey said. She was into it now. "Wolverine might never have specifically complained about the relationship half-life, but pretty much his entire life has been ruined by his feelings for women. And I'd rather be Dark Phoenix."

"You can't go by the movies for Wolverine," Jimmy said, dismissing her argument.

"Hell, they even talk about relationships in *Highlander*," Lacey said. "Scottish-Spaniard-Egyptian Sean Connery tells MacLeod not to fall for a mortal, it'll break his heart."

"You're thinking about this way too much, Budge," Jimmy said. "I still think the Hulk is the best." Inspiration struck Jimmy, too. "She-Hulk!"

Lacey huffed. "You're a chump."

Jimmy angled his three-toed arms out in front of him. "That's my name, don't wear it out."

Lacey looked down at her feet. "You know, I told you everything I know so far about this thing last night. But I still feel weird about how it all went down. I wasn't expecting to have another incident again before I told you."

Jimmy had a half smile on his face. "You know, Lace, that's how life goes sometimes. When the things that are supposed to happen start happening, you can't really put on the brakes. You shouldn't want to."

"You think this was supposed to happen to me?" she asked.

Jimmy laughed. "No, not *this*, necessarily. But I've always wanted something special for you, because you are special."

Lacey was surprised by Jimmy's tone. She tried to brush it off. "Yeah, special needs, maybe."

"No doubt," he said. "But let me be serious for just one more minute. Look, some part of you was hidden when you were with Fox. Now, you seem more alive than I've seen you in years."

"Does freaked out count as more alive?" she asked.

"That's temporary, Budge. You'll get past that. I'm actually kind of excited about all this. Yeah, it's supernatural and defies explanation, but how cool is it?"

Lacey laughed. "I'm glad you think so."

They watched the rest of *The Avengers* together, Jimmy taking every opportunity to make cracks about Lacey's mutant power. She took it as a good sign. He left after the movie ended.

Lacey picked herself up from the couch and paced the living room. She was disappointed in herself for being so self-absorbed and not asking more about Monica. Although it was a good bet that Jimmy wouldn't have offered much more information, even under questioning.

She grabbed the towel from the recliner, and was stopped by the book Jimmy had left on the chair. The quantum physics book Cecil had bought for her.

Pay attention, she thought. Her encounter with Cecil at the Healing Center had been buried underneath everything that had occurred in the past twenty-four hours. She picked up the book and remembered the photocopied genealogy. She had stashed it in a drawer, intending to study it further when she had more time. She pulled it out and returned to the couch, letting the towel drop to the floor.

31

After a barrage of missed calls and text messages, Lacey finally pinned down Tonti. She had a thousand questions for her, the most prosaic being how to look after the house while she was away.

Tonti would be at happy hour, Tuesday evening, at Mondo in Lakeview. Lacey expected a host of Tonti's contemporaries, and planned to show up very late. Hopefully the herd would thin as the hours wore on.

Lacey arrived at the well-appointed restaurant at seven forty p.m. Tonti and one other woman remained at a table for six at the back. Lacey recognized the woman's mandible, and suddenly heard the cicadas outside.

"Fashionably late, child!" Tonti exclaimed. She maintained her regal seated posture while Dotty Trebuchet stood.

"Look at you!" she exclaimed, and held out her arms to Lacey for a hug.

"Hi, Miss Dotty," Lacey replied. Her words and the half embrace felt awkward. "Miss Dotty" didn't suit her.

"You're so fit! I didn't notice when I saw you the last time," Dotty Trebuchet said.

Nice backhanded compliment, Lacey thought.

"Isn't she beautiful?" Tonti interjected. "She runs all the time, even did when Fox was around. Keeps her in fighting shape."

The mention of Fox caught Dotty Trebuchet off guard. It was a reaction Lacey recognized well. Bringing up the dead, especially amongst people who only knew them at arm's distance, could cause them to lose their footing. Lacey secretly praised Tonti for doing it.

Dotty Trebuchet recovered. "Oh, Matt's not as active as he used to be, not since Jenny had the twins," she said. "I can tell he regrets it, but he still looks good; he must have his father's metabolism. Thank God he didn't get mine!"

Lacey imagined the beefy Matt Trebuchet she'd known in college as a bony insect. She stifled a laugh.

Dotty Trebuchet looked at her Rolex. "I really do need to get going! I have to get to the north shore; I'm watching the twins tonight. I can't wait until Matt moves back over here. He thought they'd try it—get more house for the money and all that—but they both hate it. They're trying to get back over here before the twins start kindergarten; they want them to go to Newman."

Way more information than I need, Miss Dotty, Lacey thought. "Oh, okay," Lacey said. "Well, it was nice seeing you."

"You, too! Keep up the running! It suits you!"

Lacey glared at Tonti as Dotty Trebuchet walked through the door of the restaurant.

Tonti smiled. "Oh, she's a right Nigel, all right."

Lacey wasn't sure what that meant, but it didn't sound complimentary.

"Have a seat, child."

"Should we maybe go to the bar?" Lacey asked. "They look kind of crowded in here; it looks like they could use the table."

"Relax, dear, they will not kick us out. We have this little gathering here about once a month. Half of the table are investors, so we get some consideration. Thank God you came; there's only so long I can tolerate Dotty Trebuchet one on one."

Lacey laughed as she sat. "Why do you stay friends with her, then?"

"I thought we covered this," Tonti said.

A server appeared, just in time to spare Lacey.

"Robin, I'm afraid you'll have to put up with me for just a little bit longer," Tonti said to the server. "Could you be a dear and bring another bottle of the Duval-Leroy? And a glass for my niece here."

Lacey looked at the empty champagne flute in front of Tonti and thought of protesting, but didn't have the energy.

"Would you like to look at the menu?" Robin asked Lacey.

Lacey looked at Tonti. "I am a bit peckish…"

"Go ahead, child! I have nowhere to be."

"Yes, please, that would be great," Lacey said.

"There's only one thing of Dotty Trebuchet's that I'm a little envious of," Tonti said.

"What's that?"

"Grandbabies."

For the first time in a very long time, the subject of babies did not make Lacey's chest tight. Instead, it served as the perfect segue to a topic that had been on her mind for three days.

"Tonti," Lacey said. "Did Birdie have children?" She already knew the answer, but wanted to hear Tonti's recollection.

Tonti looked thoughtful and held her tongue. Robin returned with a bottle, a fresh champagne flute, and a menu.

"I'll give you a few minutes to look it over," she said as she popped the cork and filled both glasses.

"Do y'all need anything else right now?" Robin asked.

"No, you're fantastic, darlin'," Tonti responded. "Just come back in a bit to feed my precious baby here."

Tonti was unusually silent. Lacey regretted how she'd brought up the topic of Birdie. "I think I know why you're asking that," Tonti finally said.

"You do?"

"She didn't," Tonti said. "As I grew up, I came to think that might have been why she was so attached to us. We were the children she never had."

"Was she married?" Lacey asked. Lacey wasn't as sure about that one. The genealogy was confusing at points.

"Yes. I only ever saw her husband once—at her funeral. Mère almost didn't let us go, but I think Papa insisted. He took Amelie, Uncle, and me. Camille refused to go. Big Fox wanted to go so badly, but Papa told him he was too young."

A slow change came over Tonti. She looked decades younger.

"I vividly remember Papa talking to Birdie's husband," she continued. "I was afraid to go near him. He was seated in the front row of the church, and he looked so severe and so sad. He stayed seated while Papa talked to him, standing up. I saw later, as everyone filed out of the church, that he walked with a cane. It seemed like walking was a great labor to him."

Robin checked in. Lacey quickly glanced at the menu and ordered the Mondo burger.

"Did you go to the cemetery?" Lacey asked after Robin departed.

"No. Papa said burials should be for family. I wanted to say that we were her family, but Amelie knew what was about to come out of my mouth and she grabbed my hand and stopped me. Which I suppose was for the best. It wasn't the place nor the time to trigger Papa's temper."

Lacey took advantage of the pause in a pause in Tonti's story. "Did you ever meet any of her relatives?"

"No," Tonti said. "I remember she talked about a brother; I think he lived somewhere out by Lafayette. But I don't remember ever meeting him. I'm sure he must have been at the funeral, but I don't remember. I was too young to think of things like that."

Lacey drew in a deep breath. "I think I've met Birdie's nephew."

"How splendid!" Tonti said, unfazed. "How on earth did you come to make the connection to Birdie?"

Lacey shook her head slowly. Tonti completely confounded her.

"It's sort of a long story," Lacey said. "It began when he came to the office to pick up a donation of books, and he drafted me into some volunteer work…" Lacey decided to redirect. "Long story short, I ran into him again recently, and I didn't know why at the time, but he gave me all this old paperwork, and from it, it seems pretty clear that he's Birdie's nephew."

Tonti nodded.

"You don't think that's a little coincidental?" Lacey asked.

"I don't believe in coincidences. God doesn't believe in coincidences, child."

That was enough to hear to make Lacey keep going. "Do you remember how you said there's something in me that's like Birdie?"

"Of course, child. Are you learning more about it?" Tonti

asked Lacey like she might ask a college student about Plato's *Apology*.

Lacey chuckled. "You could say that. Do you also remember how I asked you about that healer lady down in Galliano?"

Tonti narrowed her eyes. "I think so. But how do those types of charlatans have anything to do with Birdie? Or you, for that matter?"

Lacey decided to skip over how she'd seen the word *traiteur* directly behind the name Roberta Henriette Meeks in the genealogy. Everything in the narrative about Roberta Meeks indicated that she was Birdie.

"Nothing," Lacey said. "Just the healing part. I think Birdie was a type of healer."

Tonti sipped her champagne silently. Lacey searched her face for any clue of affirmation, dissent, any acknowledgement whatsoever. She was tempted to divulge all the gory details of her burgeoning ability just to prompt an answer, or at least a reaction, out of Tonti.

Robin returned with Lacey's food, just in time to spare Lacey from the growing awkward silence.

Lacey thanked Robin and stared at the plate.

"Are you thinking you can absorb the food by osmosis?" Tonti asked.

"No," Lacey said, looking up. "But do you think this is all crazy? That Birdie was a healer…and that maybe I am, too?"

Tonti cracked the barest of smiles. She didn't look like herself. "No, not crazy, child. Miraculous, maybe. Extraordinary, certainly."

Lacey picked up a French fry and traced the outline of her plate. "I can't shake the feeling that you know more about this than you're letting on," Lacey mumbled.

"Oh, child, that's just nonsense." Tonti's normal persona returned. "I was too young to know anything about Birdie, other than how she treated me and what she meant to us. And your connection to her has always been nothing more than a feeling to me. Something soul-deep that I can't really explain. I'm actually delighted that you're proving my intuition right!"

Something in Tonti's tone broke the spell. Lacey thought about her desire for answers. What was more important, knowing the *how,* or knowing what to do with it? She exhaled. "So you're satisfied with that?" she asked. "You don't want to know the details?"

"Child, I *always* want to know the details. But everything about you right now tells me you're not ready to divulge them. You might not even know how. Don't let me add to your stress, especially when you have other news you need to tell me."

"Other news?" Lacey asked.

"That's why you're here, isn't it?" Tonti asked. "To tell me goodbye for a while?"

Lacey had to stop herself from throwing her arms up into the air. "How did you know that already?" she asked.

"Subtlety, child," Tonti said. "Or lack thereof. I could hear it in your messages on the phone."

"Wow," Lacey said. *There's definitely something to Tonti's intuition,* she thought. "Well, you're right," Lacey continued. "I'm going to California."

Tonti looked like the cat that swallowed the canary. "What will you be doing?" she asked.

Lacey finally started eating. In between bites, she explained that she'd be working on a movie set. "I'm not sure how it's all going to work yet, but I should only be gone for a few months. I need your advice on a few things."

"What are you going to do with that giant of a dog?"

"Ambrose is coming with me," Lacey said definitively.

"They'll let you do that?"

Lacey wasn't sure who "they" were, but she was certain of one thing—she needed Ambrose with her on this upcoming adventure.

"I've still got to figure that one out, but yes, I'm planning on taking him with me. But what should I do about the house?" Lacey asked. "I don't think I'll be gone long enough to rent it out, and I don't think I want to do that anyway. But I'll need someone to check in on it occasionally. My parents are too far away."

"Consider it done," Tonti said.

"Oh no, Tonti, I didn't mean to trouble you with it!" Lacey said. "I just figured you would know people—especially a gardener—who could keep the outside in shape."

"Yes, I do know people," Tonti said. She refilled her glass. "So leave it to me to determine when they need to be called. You won't mind if I have the occasional cocktail on your front porch, will you?"

Lacey laughed. "Not at all. If you don't mind being the target of Mr. Max's spying."

"I look forward to it. You have a fabulous front porch. And there's something I love about watching the trains. Makes me feel so connected. Time and distance and all that."

"But truly, Tonti, I don't want to put you out with this."

"Child, relax. Your house is five minutes away, I have no regular schedule to keep, and it will make me feel like a million dollars to help you out this way."

"What about Brazil? Won't you be gone for a while yourself?" Lacey asked, proud of herself for remembering.

"That's not until November, child, don't fret," Tonti said. "Where in California?"

"San Luis Obispo," Lacey said. "It's somewhere between Los Angeles and San Francisco."

"I know it!" Tonti said.

Lacey finished up her food while Tonti chattered about a trip she'd made up the Pacific Coast Highway when the boys were little. She tried to remember a specific detail about San Luis Obispo. "There's something about butterflies," she said. "I'll have to look it up and tell you about it."

Lacey dabbed at her the corners of her mouth with a napkin and wondered if she could take her leave. She was about to say something about hating to eat and run when Tonti took another serious turn.

"Lacey, back to Birdie," she said. "I don't know why she didn't have children. I don't know whether it was because she couldn't, or just didn't. And I'll never know."

Lacey felt her breath catch in her throat.

"But I can't imagine that her gift was in any way connected to that," Tonti said. "It breaks my heart that you and Fox never had children, but it would have broken my heart even worse to see those children lose their father. Sometimes the miracle is in what doesn't happen."

Lacey's eyes welled up. She glanced down at the three forlorn French fries left on her plate. From across the table, Tonti grabbed Lacey's hand.

"Oh, child. Don't despair," she said. "And don't think of your gift in terms of what it might take from you. Pay attention, and see what it manifests instead."

Lacey looked up, a faint smile on her face. She thought of Eli.

"You know," Lacey said, "I have a friend who's been telling me that a lot. To pay attention."

"Your friend is right. Your time in your chrysalis is over. It's time to spread your wings and engage with the world around you."

Still thinking of Eli, Lacey asked, "You're not hiding any distant Birdie relatives from me, are you?"

Tonti smiled and shook her head. Lacey's phone lit up. "Look, child, there's the world wanting to engage with you," Tonti said.

Lacey looked at the number. The area code confirmed it was a call about the new job.

"Tonti, I'm sorry, I really should take this."

"By all means, child." Tonti watched Lacey step outside to the restaurant patio, and smiled. She downed the drink remaining in her glass and asked Robin the server to close out her tab.

32

A large container ship floated down the Mississippi River. Lacey watched from the fifth- floor picture window at Carriere & Associates. She marveled at its fluid, even pace toward an inevitable destination. She didn't once think of its origin.

Twelve days from now, she would be in California. On July tenth, she would be far away from that ship, Trip's office, every vestige of her former life. Twelve days didn't feel like enough time to tie up all her loose ends—train Trip's new employee, make arrangements for the house, pack—and yet it still felt like an eternity.

Lacey's replacement at Carriere & Associates, Katelyn, was going to Europe in July and would not start working for Trip until August. Trip wanted Lacey to return then, to train Katelyn. Lacey attempted to explain why that would be impossible, that she would be on a job thousands of miles away, but gave up when she saw that Trip wasn't listening.

Instead, Katelyn had agreed to come into the office for several days before she left for her vacation. She had been there yesterday, and was scheduled for a few more days upcoming. But today, Lacey was alone.

Lacey liked Katelyn. She was competent, and excited about her imminent wedding, and nearly apoplectic about her trip to Europe. Lacey was confident she would learn the intricacies of working for Trip Carriere in short order. She thought of introducing Katelyn to Marva and Roland, but decided it was best to let them introduce themselves.

Putzing around the office by herself, Lacey tried to stop smiling. She had no reason to feel so upbeat—she had a never-ending list of things to do before leaving town, she had no idea what her days in California would hold, and she was certain there was some major thing she would forget to take care of in New Orleans. She suspected the latter concern was related to Nathan, still ever-present in her thoughts. She did not want feel so happy, thinking about their night together, but couldn't deter the feeling.

Maybe my mutant powers have severed the tie between my heart and my head, she thought.

Her mutant powers. She thought of the time between June ninth and July tenth. Between June ninth and today, for that matter. That was the true eternity. How altered she had become, in less than a month's time. Was there more to come? The incident with Nathan—the first incident—had happened June tenth. Or, more precisely, the wee hours of June eleventh. But she now knew the significance of June ninth.

The incident. She separated herself from thoughts of their most recent night together, and remembered Nathan's deepening trouble. That finally wiped the grin off her face. Lacey thought of Detective Aucoin. She had been waiting to hear from him—he had said something about possibly needing a description of the Weasel. But there had been no word, and Lacey had been too busy to follow up of her own accord.

Lacey resolved to call him today and tell him about her upcoming departure. Jimmy and Helga had left yesterday. Helga was bonded through her company, but Lacey wasn't sure how that worked or if it had anything to do with her being able to leave town.

She would collect her thoughts before calling the detective.

Lacey grabbed a notepad, placed it next to her monitor, and squinted at the glare. The sun had caught a corner of the picture window, sending a high-intensity laser beam directly to her desktop. She looked into Trip's empty office. Cool and shady.

He had been in the office earlier, and she didn't expect to see him again today.

She grabbed the notepad and Detective Aucoin's card and sat at Trip's massive desk. She made a list of the questions she wanted to ask. Then she made a list of items she'd need to buy this weekend. Next was a list of utilities and services at the house she'd need to set up for autopay. Lacey was about two-thirds of the way through a list of essentials to pack when she heard the front door open.

Crap! What is Trip doing back so soon? she thought. She jumped up and grabbed her things, returning everything on his desk to its proper order. She went to one of the bookshelves and pretended to take inventory.

When he didn't bellow his usual greeting or come straight to his office, she turned and looked out to see someone who brought an instant wave of nausea to her insides.

The Weasel stood, unsteady, waving a gun at the vicinity of her head.

She cursed herself for not activating the lock on the office door. She had even set a reminder to do it. *Your lack of focus is going to get you killed*, she thought.

"Grab your things like you were going to leave the office at the end of the day," he said. The words flowed out in a garbled heap.

"What?" Lacey asked. An automatic response. She touched her forehead where he had hit her with the door.

"Get. Your. Shit. Close up so no one will wonder where you are."

An animal stink permeated the air. Sweat and stomach acid and bad breath. Lacey swallowed.

"Where are we going?" she asked. She struggled to keep her tone even. *Speak to him like an animal,* a voice inside her head told her.

"To finish a job. You're the bait. Hurry it up. Now." He was agitated, thumping his free hand against the side of his leg.

"Okay. Okay. I can't leave my phone in here; my boss will know something's wrong."

She held her hands up and pointed toward Trip's office. Her phone—and Detective Aucoin's card—were on the bookshelf.

"Fine. Just hurry the fuck up! Wait." He held the gun up and approached. The stench was overpowering. "Need to make sure you don't try anything."

The Weasel held the gun inches from the back of her head as she grabbed the phone and palmed the card.

✳

Lacey gripped the steering wheel harder, trying to stop her hands from shaking. The Weasel had forced her to drive wherever it was he intended.

Maybe he's smarter than he looks, she thought. *Makes me drive, so I can't use my phone.*

She took a deep breath and instantly regretted it. *I know something's wrong with me. I should be afraid for my life, but I'm more concerned with how I'm going to get the smell of this man out of my car.*

Something told her to stop talking to herself and start talking out loud. "Where are we going?" she asked. She had an idea of where.

"It's close. Just follow my directions."

She thought of faking some kind of car trouble, but they approached their destination before she could work out any reasonable scheme.

He instructed her to parallel park next to an enormous pothole. Her phone was in the loose pocket of her linen jacket. If she could get three seconds out of the Weasel's sight, she could dial Detective Aucoin. She was afraid she wouldn't have time to explain everything if she dialed 9-1-1.

He grabbed her arm, keeping the gun out of sight but jammed into her ribs. Her heart sank when she saw the wooden shingle on the building across the street: LaSalle Title.

A clear and pleasant bell tinkled when the Weasel pushed Lacey through the front door. The reception desk was empty.

Thank God, Lacey thought. She turned her head to the Weasel and was thinking of something to say to persuade him to leave, for them to leave together, when she heard a voice from the back of the office.

"I'll be right there."

Nathan. He was already out of his office and in the hallway. "Sorry, our receptionist just stepped…"

Nathan stood frozen in the hallway. Lacey read the look on his face, and it scared her more than being kidnapped at gunpoint.

"Keep steppin'," the Weasel said. His voice was low and surprisingly calm.

Nathan walked out into the foyer.

"You can let her go," he said. "I'm coming."

"No!" the Weasel said, his foot tapping. "You're both in this now. I have a job to finish."

"What job?" Nathan asked, his voice raised. He was stalling.

"What the fuck do you mean, what job?" The Weasel gripped Lacey's arm tighter and pointed the gun at Nathan. "The job you keep fucking up!"

"C'mon man, think about it. It's broad daylight," Nathan said. "There are neighbors all around here. We can leave here together, and not look suspicious."

Beads of some kind of amphetamine-fueled sweat formed at the Weasel's hairline. He looked like he was trying to think. The strain threatened to overwhelm him. A tremor formed in the hand holding the gun.

A floorboard creaked at the back of the office. Nathan closed his eyes and sighed.

"What the fuck was that?" the Weasel said. "Who is that?"

Lawrence LaSalle had stepped out into the hallway. He saw, or maybe smelled, the Weasel, and bolted back into his office and closed the door. The sound of something heavy being pulled across the floor echoed through the building.

The Weasel hadn't factored in another potential witness in his addled brain. He bolted down the hallway, past Nathan. Nathan tried to get his hands on him, but he slid right through them, like a wily rodent escaping into the underbrush. The Weasel slammed the full force of his underweight body against LaSalle's door. It budged an inch.

Nathan grabbed him by the shoulders, and he swung around, gun still in his hand, now pointed squarely at Nathan's head. Nathan held up his hands and backed off.

"Who is that in there?" the Weasel said. His eyes were rings of black against a blood-splattered canvas.

"It's no one," Nathan said. "He didn't see you. It's not important."

"Fuck that! I'm trying to cover my tracks here, and finish the job."

He kept the gun trained on Nathan, and butted himself backward against the door. Each attempt brought the screech of metal against wood.

Through the door, they could hear LaSalle talking to someone, his voice panicked. Nathan knew it wasn't the police.

The Weasel knew no such thing, and his fear fueled him.

"What do you mean, the job's been canceled?" LaSalle said. The desperation in his voice strengthened Nathan's resolve.

The Weasel turned his head, and Nathan looked at Lacey, still in the entry foyer. She was concentrating on her phone. He nodded vehemently toward the door. Now was her chance; the Weasel had his hands full.

Lacey looked up at him. Still maneuvering her phone, she backed up and quietly stepped out the door. No one heard the bell over the commotion in the hallway.

Outside his father-in-law's door, Nathan's standoff with the Weasel was about to end. Inside, LaSalle wasn't speaking anymore.

The Weasel opened the barricaded door just enough to wedge his body through. Nathan followed. Lawrence LaSalle was sitting at his desk, both hands holding a gun, pointed at the intruders.

"Fuck!" the Weasel exploded. He spun around, wielding his gun in a circle.

"Where's the girl? Fuck!"

After two-and-a-half turns, Nathan bodychecked the Weasel, hoping that his equilibrium was off kilter. The Weasel went down, finger on the trigger.

Nathan saw the discharge from the gun before he heard the retort. He lurched forward as he watched the next two seconds unfold in slow motion. The gun dropped to the floor. Nathan pinned the Weasel on his side, and the gun his father-in-law held fell from his grip.

LaSalle looked down, bewildered. He held his palms to his stomach, then held them up to his face. They were a brilliant, slimy red.

He looked at Nathan. Nathan kicked the Weasel's gun behind the desk and released him.

The Weasel scrambled through the door. Nathan went to his father-in-law. He felt a rush to his head when he saw the amount of blood.

"This wasn't supposed to happen," LaSalle said.

Nathan picked up the handset on LaSalle's desk and dialed 9-1-1. He heard a siren not far away.

"You're going to be okay," he said. "I'm calling for help right now."

The door to the office pushed open further, and Lacey came through, a wild abandon driving her. Two simultaneous feelings stopped her just inside. She steadied herself against the doorframe.

First, relief. Nathan was standing, alive, apparently intact.

Second, déjà vu. She had seen most of this before; the man at his desk, the office. Before, when she and Nathan had been together.

"I heard the gunshot," she said, her voice cracking.

She sensed the man at the desk was losing consciousness. She choked her emotions, put them out of her way. She went to the man without thinking, a heat rising inside of her. The man did not move when she put her hands on him.

He looked her in the eyes as he started to slip sideways. He was confused.

"This wasn't supposed to happen," he said to Lacey.

"It's okay," she said. "We'll try to help you."

Lacey pushed her sleeves up, frustrated. Nothing felt right. She didn't know what to do. How had she known what to do the other times?

Nathan was on the phone with 9-1-1, also frustrated. She looked up at him.

"Nothing's happening!"

"We have a medical emergency," Nathan shouted. "A man has been shot."

Lacey pulled one of her hands away from the injured man and held the back of it against her forehead. It was cold. There wasn't even a bead of sweat along her hairline.

"Nathan, it's not working! Why isn't it working?"

LaSalle slumped over the side of his chair, eyes open, nonresponsive.

Lacey put both hands on his bloody stomach, thinking at least she could apply pressure. He didn't move, and it didn't feel like a body. It felt like a lump of runny clay.

She looked back at Nathan, a slight shake to her head. He put the phone down, grabbed her hands, and pulled her upright.

"I don't think there's anything you can do," he said.

A chorus of sirens grew louder, then stopped.

33

Lacey sat in a small room on a decaying sofa in the Second District police station on Magazine.

Nathan had been put in handcuffs and taken ahead of her. She rode with Detective Aucoin, who'd set her aside and told her to sit tight. She saw Nathan from across a hallway being led to a room. She turned her head to avert his stare.

She thought of the dead man, Nathan's father-in-law. She was convinced that Nathan had told her the truth—that the gun had gone off while it had still been in the Weasel's hands. But the only people who could say for sure were either dead, or in police custody.

The room was closing in on Lacey. She got up from the sofa and peeked through the blinds of the room's one window. It offered a view of the station's interior. For some reason, Lacey thought of the officer on the lakefront, the day Fox had died. The kind woman with the bright eyes. She had brought Lacey back from the brink once before. Lacey looked for her now, hoping she was available to do it again.

The door opened. Lacey looked up, expecting to see Detective Aucoin or some other police officer. Instead, there was a familiar shaved head and stocky form clothed in functional attire. She felt an instant of strange comfort at the sight of those perfunctory pockets.

"Eli," she said. No other words would come.

"How are you, Lacey?" He took a chair opposite her sofa.

"I'm not good," she said. "Why—how—are you here?"

"I'm here for you," he said. "The how is inconsequential."

She stared at him.

"We're going to be working together," he said. He pulled his phone from a pocket in his cargo shorts and set it on his oak-limb of a thigh.

"We are?"

"Yes."

Lacey's mind flew in a thousand different directions.

"I will be in San Luis Obispo, working on the same production as you," he said after a pause.

"Oh." Her thoughts funneled to a different concern. "Do you know anything about what just happened?" she asked. "Do you think it's going to keep me from being able to leave New Orleans?"

"One of the things you're going to learn," he said, "is about being present. Leaving for San Luis Obispo is not the present. What is the present?"

Lacey bristled at his tone and looked up at a stained ceiling tile. "A dank room, waiting to give a statement about a death I just witnessed?"

"Better," he said.

"Glad you think so."

Eli glanced down at his phone.

"There was an earthquake in Papua New Guinea," he said. "There's a tsunami warning for a good portion of Australia."

Lacey struggled to make sense of anything coming out of Eli's mouth.

"Oh," she said. "That happened just now?"

"Yes. The present."

"Um, okay. Do you know someone there?"

He didn't answer right away. His intense hawk eyes peered at her, his lazy right eye staring behind her. *Doesn't everyone know someone in Papua New Guinea?* Lacey imagined him saying.

"No," he finally said.

He glanced down at his phone again, picked it up, and scrolled through something.

Guilt and misery sat like a fifty-pound weight on Lacey's chest. Eli's obtuse conversation didn't help. She struggled to breathe.

"Do you realize that not even Jesus could heal everyone?" he said.

Lacey felt her throat close. "What?"

"Considering he lived for thirty-three years—according to biblical lore—yet death and disease continued around him. It's not as if the march of life ceased while he was on Earth."

Lacey placed her palm against her sternum and pressed. "Eli, what are you talking about?"

"Lacey, when we first met, I told you to pay attention. Have you done this?"

She felt a wave of electricity wash over her head. It made her nauseated. "Yes," she answered, her voice a notch above a whisper. "Yes. And things have happened, and I don't understand any of it."

"That's a false statement. You're beginning to understand it." Eli gripped his phone and stood. He moved to the side of the sofa and braced one arm against the wall.

Lacey didn't turn. She stared at an abandoned coffee cup across the room.

"Not everyone is meant to be healed," he said to the side of her face. "Have you wondered whether you could have saved Fox if you had reached him sooner? Or been with him when he had the heart attack?"

Lacey jerked her head to him. "How do you know that? How do you know about Fox?"

Eli was placid. His floating eye tracked off to the right. "I pay attention."

Lacey stopped herself from following the gaze of his eye. She was afraid she might see Fox's ghost standing there.

"I know I didn't have this ability then," Lacey said, calmer. "But if I did, could I? Do you know what I can do? Could I have saved Fox?"

Eli took a deep breath. He had the expression of a PhD student trying to explain particle physics to a room full of second-graders.

"Lacey, I can't tell you that. I can't see that way. But I can tell you this: some things, some threads, are meant to manifest. Your greatest challenge will be identifying those threads, and releasing those you were never meant to touch."

Lacey blew out a breath. It didn't help. Her eyes filled.

Is everything I've done so far wrong? she thought.

"You misunderstand me," Eli said. She whipped her head back to him.

"Your power won't work on those whose threads are complete. Whose 'time has come,' might be another way to phrase it," he continued. "It will be hard for you to accept that."

"So the man today, the man who died," she said, "there was nothing I could do about it?"

"I wasn't there, Lacey, I don't know. But if you tried, and nothing happened, you should take it as an article of faith that you were never meant to have anything to do with his life."

A gurgle escaped Lacey's throat. "An article of faith?" she asked.

"Faith is just one of infinite variables at play here. It's one I know you can relate to."

They both turned to the door. Words were being exchanged just outside, not loud enough to be discernible. Lacey recognized Detective Aucoin's blustery cadence.

Eli continued, unfazed. "Pay attention to this, Lacey: Faith is only one variable, and the one I know the least about. There are other elements involved—the actions and reactions of time, space, and the physical world—this is where my expertise lies."

Lacey looked at him, eyes wide. *He really is Professor X*, she thought.

Detective Aucoin put his hand on the doorknob, and Lacey decided to ponder Eli's mutant expertise later. "Okay, Eli, since you know all about time and you're trying to keep me concerned with the present, what should I say to the police?"

"Tell them the truth. Tell them what happened."

"What about the other part? Why my hands were bloodied?"

One side of his mouth curved. Lacey guessed he was smiling.

"Tell them the truth," he said. "Tell them you were trying to stop the bleeding." His expression transformed into Buddha-like contentment.

"Oh. I guess that is the truth," she said.

"Weren't you?" he asked. "Trying to stop the bleeding?"

"Yes. I see what you're saying," she said.

Articles of faith and space-time continuums aside, Eli had a way of making the present much simpler and less scary.

Detective Aucoin bullied his way into the office. "Are you ready, Stacey?" he asked. He stopped cold when he noticed Eli. "Who are you? How did you get in here?" the detective said.

Eli held his finger to his temple, Professor X-style. "I'm Lacey's boss," he said. "I came to find out why she was missing work."

The detective looked off into the distance for a moment. "Oh. Okay. This won't take long. Follow me Sta—Ms. Becnel."

34

Lacey focused on the back of the man's head in front of her. A ring of white fringe surrounded a constellation of age spots on a weather-beaten skull. "God's Trumpet," she deemed him, for his refrains and responses could be heard throughout St. Daniel's. She suspected it was because he was deaf.

Most Sundays, Lacey liked to sleep in, so she was an infrequent attendee of eight a.m. Mass. But the rare times she made it, God's Trumpet was always there. She had snuck into the church around 8:10, and hadn't realized she had chosen a seat so close to him until it was too late to do anything about it.

She cradled her face in her hands so she could surreptitiously cover her eardrums when it was time for the congregation to speak.

What am I thankful for? she thought.

Eli, definitely. She was convinced he had Jedi mind-tricked Detective Aucoin at the police station. The detective had been respectful and concerned in every subsequent encounter. Lacey's interview with him after LaSalle's death had been anticlimactic. He'd asked her what happened, she'd told him, and then he'd told her she was free to go. Eli had been gone by the time she was done.

She'd had the sum total of two calls from Detective Aucoin since. The first telling her she was free to travel until the Weasel's trial. The second time he told her the trial would not be until sometime in the fall.

The Weasel. She wasn't grateful for him, but grateful that she hadn't lost her life to him.

His name was Edmund Robert Villere, his mug shot a disturbing and ubiquitous visual on the Internet and in the antiquated newspaper. He had been charged in the murder of Lawrence LaSalle, whose death had been characterized as terrible collateral from a botched robbery attempt.

"Lord, hear our prayer," God's Trumpet shouted from the pew ahead of her. Lacey added her own voice to the refrain, but continued her own private liturgy.

What am I thankful for?

Helga, most definitely.

Helga had saved Nathan's life, and most likely Lacey's, too. Who knew what might have happened if Lacey had faced the hired goon solo? No one had come forward to claim the body of that man, who had outstanding warrants against him in ten states. NOPD had concluded that Helga had acted in self-defense, so she was free and clear.

Free and clear. Nathan?

She didn't know what would become of Nathan. All she knew of his fate had been pieced together from the news. Reports of Edmund Villere's crime noted Nathan on the scene at the time. How her presence had escaped the media's attention, she wasn't sure, but she was eternally grateful. She suspected Eli had everything to do with that.

The death and funeral of Lawrence LaSalle had dominated the news for weeks, the story angle focusing on the senseless tragedy, the seemingly random violence, and LaSalle's legacy. She saw Nathan in sound bites; a shot of him speaking about the tremendous loss, him in a dark suit at the funeral, standing next to his wife. How could he say anything about the real story?

Could she trust that Nathan had told her the real story? If LaSalle had hired the Weasel to kill Nathan, how come the Weasel hadn't known LaSalle?

It made her head hurt thinking about it. Angele figured that the whole thing had been contracted and subcontracted multiple times, and that Edmund Villere was an ambitious but incompetent sub-sub-subcontractor. At least, that was how it usually worked in the movies.

It still felt so unreal.

She prayed for the repose of Lawrence LaSalle's soul. Whatever he had done in his lifetime, it was over now, and she hoped he might now find respite.

She marveled at fate. She had not sought out Nathan, or the drama of his life. Yet she had been drawn into it all the same, forever linked by the circumstances of her first healing, and now her part in his marital infidelity. She prayed for forgiveness for any harm that transgression might have brought to Nathan and his family.

Transgressions. Fox.

She missed him. It was like a scar; she knew that longing would always be with her. But it felt different; there had been some fading. It felt more nostalgic, a warm flush of memory of a time long ago, a childhood time. She thought of how her crazy, mad love for him had drawn her into the Becnel family, made her a Becnel. Made her Tonti's niece.

How thankful am I for Tonti?

Hard to quantify. No, impossible to quantify. She prayed that Tonti remain in good health for twenty more years, at least.

Tonti and Fox. (And Angele). The only people who'd crossed her consciousness at this Mass that she'd known for longer than a month. Everyone else, all new. With a new job, and an open future, how much wider would her life be a month from now?

Seek out those who are knowledgeable, young Lacey.

Cecil! she thought. His words appeared in her head so suddenly that she looked around, thinking he might be nearby and have telepathed it. She didn't see him.

None of this would have happened without Cecil. The momentous date of June ninth, and Cecil. The genealogy he had given Lacey was peppered with the word *traiteur* amongst a plethora of dates. Aside from dates of births, marriages, and deaths, when a traiteur was marked, there were two additional dates. Lacey figured they were the dates the ability was acquired, and when it was shared. The date common between Roberta Henriette Meeks—Birdie—and Cecil Augustine Session occurred one spring when Cecil was a very small boy. April thirtieth. Before that, there was a common date between Birdie and her father, and between him and an aunt.

But for Cecil Augustine Session, next to the typed date of April thirtieth was a handwritten one: June ninth. The day he'd showed up at Carriere & Associates and picked up the books.

Why had he chosen to share this with Lacey? Only he knew the answer to that question. Lacey already knew there was much more to the ability than the traiteur tradition. She had not found anything on the Internet about traiteurs healing bullet wounds. And there was the quantum physics book that still made no sense to her. Maybe her mutant power warped the space-time continuum or something. Cecil had told her to seek out knowledgeable people—Eli definitely seemed to fit that bill. And she would get to spend time with him in California.

Two things felt clear to Lacey. She felt them *soul-deep,* as Tonti might say: one, her immediate path should be to learn what she could do, what was within her power; and two, she would see Cecil again. Perhaps when she did, she'd be ready for his answer.

Thank you, Cecil, she mouthed silently. *Thank you for choosing me. I think.*

"Peace be with you," God's Trumpet shouted at her with an outstretched hand.

Lacey shook it gingerly, not wanting to crush his frail and gnarled fingers. "And with your spirit," she mumbled.

✳

Lacey walked up to Communion with her purse. She chose a pew at the very back of Church when she returned; easier to make a quick getaway. And it put some distance between her and God's Trumpet.

Waiting for Mass to end, she tried to remember what the Gospel was about and couldn't. She chastised herself for being so self-absorbed. But then cut herself some slack. It had been a very eventful few weeks.

She waited until the closing hymn had finished. Leaving before then would be two errors in a row, arriving late and then leaving early. She needed better karma than that. She walked out with the crowd.

As she approached the parking lot, Lacey noticed God's Trumpet speaking to a man close to her age. The younger man was attractive, with nice eyes and a kind expression. Remembering Angele's admonition, she looked at his left hand as she passed and saw a ring.

Oh well, she thought.

She didn't notice that God's Trumpet was speaking to the man at a normal volume.

35

Lacey's departure was imminent. All arrangements had been made, certain services suspended. She had rented a place for her and Ambrose to stay in San Luis Obispo, sight unseen. She was in a strange limbo, occupying these last few remaining days in the house as she had done for years—walking Ambrose, doing laundry, maintaining the yard. Knowing that she would return, but suspecting that she would be wholly changed by the time she did.

In a strange way, it was another goodbye to Fox. They'd started their life together in this place, this home on Florida Boulevard. When she and Ambrose came back to this house, they would bring a world of experiences and memories totally separate from Fox. She would bring the rest of her life back here.

The rest of her life had already begun, truly, on June ninth. All that had transpired since had placed an impenetrable layer of sediment over the traces of Fox. He was a stratum that told the history of another age.

Love will find a way. The Tesla song had not vacated her head. It bubbled up to the surface during quiet moments. She was beginning to hate it.

Lacey tended to some weeds in her side garden, trying to ignore the song and the potent mixture of dread and hope that filled her. She knew the nugget of dread that sat at the base of her esophagus was directly related to Nathan. She tried desperately to let hope hold the balance.

She told herself that was the sole reason she had contacted him—to tie up that loose end and leave town on a positive note. Despite what she told herself, she knew their relationship would not be tied up anytime soon. Tugging at some dollar weed, she checked her watch.

There hadn't been a full day of sun since the Fourth of July. Torrential downpours during the holiday had ruined the plans of thousands of New Orleanians, but Lacey had used her time spent indoors wisely. She and Ambrose were nearly all packed and ready to go.

The bench Lacey chose was dry. From her vantage point inside the Besthoff Sculpture Garden, she could just make out Robert Indiana's red and blue *Love* sculpture. Tesla provided the audio in her head.

She moved to the opposite side of the bench to face a tree instead.

She saw a young couple entering the garden with a baby in a stroller, and winced like she had been jabbed with a hot poker.

The intermittent spells had become so frequent that Lacey had devised a name for them: residuals. They felt like lingering connections with the people she had healed. Psychic or spiritual or what, she didn't know.

She could see things, usually right upon waking, that she couldn't connect with any part of her life. A few days ago, she'd awoken with a young girl in her mind's eye, maybe ten years old, white-blonde hair, the scope of her rifle trained on a ten-point buck up in some mountainous place. She'd known it was Helga.

She knew she'd had a vision of Lawrence LaSalle in his office; it had come to her after she'd first made love to Nathan. Now she forever equated it with his death.

Other residuals connected to Nathan had come since she'd last seen him: being present at the birth of a child. It had happened twice now, and each time she'd felt a distinct anguish.

A walking path traced the borders of the lagoon at the center of the garden. The family with the stroller meandered along it. The late afternoon heat was oppressive. Lacey took a sip of the iced tea—unsweetened—she had purchased from the café at the museum. Even in the shade of the tree, her pink sleeveless blouse and khaki shorts were beginning to stick to her.

"You look like you're trying to give someone the slip," a voice said behind her.

She whipped around. She'd been so preoccupied with the young family that she hadn't even thought of checking the other direction.

Nathan was there, in a polo shirt and shorts, a rose in his hand. He looked leaner than he had the last time she'd seen him. His eyes were very tired, too. As drained as he appeared, he couldn't suppress a smile.

"I didn't do a very good job of it, I guess," Lacey answered.

Iced tea in hand, she opened her arms in a halfhearted

attempt at a hug. He responded with an embrace like she was a long-lost treasure, hidden away and finally unearthed. Even in the heat, she was reluctant to disengage.

"Nathan," she said, breaking off. "How are you?" She knew the words were weak.

"Better," he said. He looked down at his hands, remembered the rose. "Here, this is for you."

"Thank you," she said. "Did you take this from the botanical garden?"

He laughed. "You got me."

"I think City Park frowns upon such things."

"I think I can handle a little heat from the City Park police. Bring it on."

She twirled the rose in her fingers, careful to steer clear of the thorns. "I bet you could."

She looked up at him, her eyes asking the question she couldn't bring herself to voice.

"I'll tell you what I can, but give me just a minute first." He took her hand. "It's really good to see you," he said, his voice cracking on the first syllable. He pulled her over to the bench. "Interesting choice for a meeting place."

"Can't think of a better place. It's about as private as you can get in a public space," Lacey said. She pulled her hand away from his and reached down below the bench. "Here, I got you some iced tea. I don't know how you drink it; I have some sugar and sweetener if you like it that way."

"That was sweet of you," he said. He held the Styrofoam cup in both hands, rolling it back and forth without drinking.

Lacey looked forward and stretched out her arms, trying to check the time on her watch without being obvious.

Nathan turned to her. "Do you have someplace to be?"

Lacey blushed, another bloom in the heat. "No, no. I don't have anywhere to go."

"No hot date that you lined up as an excuse to get away from me?"

She felt her ire rise. "No, unfortunately. That was a good idea, though—I wish you would have mentioned it sooner."

"I would have. I've been a bit…busy."

Their backs to the oak tree, they sat separated by only an inch. Nathan blocked Lacey's view of the *Love* sculpture.

She had picked the only vacant bench in the area. Silent sculptures, their plaster white and rough, populated the other seats. She stared at the human form on the bench opposite, a man with half-formed features and folded arms.

Far off, past the downtown skyline, heat lightning brightened the sky. The lagoon caught its reflection.

"Whoa," Lacey said. Not able to stand the silence any longer, she asked, "So, what's going on? What happened?"

"You don't know?"

"Other than all the stuff I saw about your father-in-law's funeral in the news, not much. And I know that the Wea— Edmund Villere is in custody."

"Well, here's what didn't make the news," he said. "I'm out of a home, soon to be unemployed, and barely escaped a murder charge." Nathan wouldn't look at her. He ripped the lid off the Styrofoam cup and downed half his iced tea.

Lacey bit on the easiest question first. "Where are you staying?"

"My parents. Who are thrilled over the whole situation, I'm sure. Their forty-four-year-old son crashing and burning up their nice, quiet retirement."

Lacey hadn't known how old he was. "Where do they live?"

"Uptown, on Danneel Street. Same house I grew up in."

"I'm sure they're more understanding of your situation than you think," she said.

"You don't know my parents."

"You're right." Lacey stood. "Nathan, I'm so sorry I couldn't do anything that day. That's one of the reasons I wanted to see you, to tell you how sorry I am. I'm still learning how this thing works. You wouldn't be in this situation if I'd been able to…help your father-in-law."

Nathan looked up from his cup. "Are you joking?" he asked.

Lacey stepped back and folded her arms. "No, I mean it. I…" her voice quit as she felt a stranglehold on her esophagus.

"Lacey, I wouldn't be alive if it wasn't for you. We both know that. And if you had saved him, I'm deadly certain he would have finished the job that you kept interfering with. So, no, my current situation is temporary." Nathan stood. "And preferable to being dead, which is permanent. The shit of it all," he continued, "is that I had finally confronted him that morning."

Lacey unfolded her arms. "You confronted your father-in-law?"

"Yeah." Nathan shook his head slowly. "I told him I knew he was involved in an attempt to kill me—multiple attempts—and that I would bring the evidence forward unless he was willing to work out a compromise."

"You have evidence?" Lacey asked.

Nathan stepped closer to her. "You're not very good at card games, are you?"

Lacey didn't understand his question. She felt very dense.

"Like him," Nathan mused. "He was a terrible poker player. I think that's one of the many reasons he despised me."

Lacey was as stone-faced as the whitewashed figures at her back. "Because you could beat him at poker?" she asked.

"He never could read a bluff," Nathan said.

Lacey stepped one foot toward, then away from, Nathan. "What are the odds?" she said.

"Of what?" Nathan stood, still as a statue.

"Nothing," she said. She returned to the bench.

"No, what are you getting at?"

Lacey looked up at Nathan, but avoided his eyes. "Well," she said, "from what I can tell, Villere is an addict and not that smart. And I know he was acting alone, at least on that day." She stopped herself from saying "on that day your father-in-law was killed."

"I don't know how I know it," she continued, "but I just do. No one would send that guy off alone to complete a job."

Nathan walked toward the bench. The distance between them disappeared.

Lacey took a deep breath. "So what are the odds that he would wind up killing your father-in-law on the same day you confronted him?"

Nathan shook his head. "One to one," he said.

He bent down before her and took her hand. She let him. "Look, Lacey. Things were coming to a head. I knew someone was trying to have me killed. And I knew my father-in-law was behind it. I had to do something. And that man—Villere—was always the wild card."

Lacey pulled her hand away and held it against her chest.

Nathan wouldn't allow it. He grabbed her shoulders, gently. "Lacey, no. I had nothing to do with Villere. I would never, ever, do anything to put you in jeopardy. I've told you that before. I meant it then, and I mean it now.

"Look, you're not following me at all," he continued. He stood. "All this crap was happening then. So the odds were good that all the pieces would come together, sooner rather than later. And the truth is, he set all this in motion. Whether Villere was acting alone on that day or not, it all began with some deal my father-in-law made."

Lacey looked at the ground. "So you think he got what he deserved."

"Christ, Lacey. No. Do you really think that about me?"

She looked up, held his gaze for two seconds, and stood. "I honestly don't know you that well, Nathan. And you just said if he had survived, he would have tried to finish the job on you. So it wouldn't be out of line for you to think he's better off dead."

"No," Nathan said. He towered over her. "This is not what I wanted to happen," he said. "I wanted never to see him again, to be free of him, but I didn't want him to die. That would make me as bad as him, and I don't want that."

"What do you want?" Lacey asked.

Nathan inhaled, relaxing his shoulders. More heat lightning lit up the sky.

"A life that's my own," he said. "To be an example for my kids. To raise my kids."

Lacey nodded. She backed up toward the bench. "I'm still unclear on some things," she said. "Did your wife throw you out? And you said you barely escaped a murder charge."

"Yes," Nathan answered. "And not quite. That was a bit of an exaggeration."

Lacey scowled. "That's not something I would exaggerate about."

"Let's just say I was under some intense pressure until all the crime scene results bore my story out," Nathan answered. "And Villere got the light on him."

"He confessed?"

"I don't know. I just know the heat was off me."

Lacey remembered the moment she'd run into the room and seen LaSalle dying. She still wanted to know what had transpired in the moments before. But something told her the less she knew, the better.

After a moment, Lacey asked, "When did you move in with your parents?"

He returned to the bench. "It's still in process. Lisa and the kids have been staying with her mom. It's not far from our house."

"How is Mrs. LaSalle doing?" Lacey felt a sort of bond with widows. Or at least an obligation to inquire.

"Okay," he answered. "Better than you would think. She, believe it or not, is more understanding than Lisa."

"I'd believe it," Lacey said.

"I want split custody, right down the middle, and I think my mother-in-law might just be the voice of reason there," he said.

Lacey chose her words carefully. "I hope so. For the kids' sake." She wanted to take his hand, but didn't. "I'm sorry, Nathan," she continued. "Breaking up a family is awful enough on its own, without all," she paused, "without all this other stuff."

The sun sunk behind him. He closed his eyes and took a deep breath. "I've been doing a lot of soul-searching," he said. "I never realized the depth of my father-in-law's contempt for me." He opened his eyes and looked directly at Lacey. "I never thought he was bad man. I still don't. And what I can't figure out is what did I do? What did I do to drive him to this?"

Lacey wasn't sure if he was fishing for sympathy. She felt compelled to offer it, even if he was. "Don't say that, Nathan," she said. "You can't think like that."

He stared at her, wordless. A man in a skiff motored by in the lagoon, the engine at a low idle. His wake left waves lapping across the walkway.

"Look. I don't know what your relationship with him was like. Or your relationship with his daughter, either. But think of your worst argument, with either one of them. Was it worth losing a life over it?"

"No," he said. "That's what I don't understand. I don't know what I did to deserve this."

"Don't go down that path, Nathan. It's a slippery slope. People you love will do things that confound you. The best you can do is know your own heart." The words surprised Lacey as she said them. But she could feel the truth of them. She took Nathan's hand.

He stared at his hand in hers, and looked up into her eyes. She inched backward in her seat.

"I'm going to be out of town for a while," she said. She lifted her voice, trying to inject some levity. "So I won't be around to get you out of any more jams." She pulled her hand away and rested it on her hip.

Nathan straightened. "Oh yeah? What's up?"

"I got work on a movie. Production accounting. Out in California. But it's not permanent. I'll be back when it's over."

"You're an accountant?" he asked.

I guess there's a lot we don't know about each other, Lacey thought.

"No," she laughed. "At least not a CPA. But I've done a lot

of accounting work for Trip, and it's something I'm good at."

"You see? I told you you'd find something quickly. You need to have more faith in yourself," he said. "Know your own heart," he added with a wink.

She missed a beat. She wanted to turn the attention away from herself. "I'll be back for the Villere stuff, whenever that is," she said, stumbling over her words.

The lights in the walkway came to sudden illumination. Each had a patina of sheen covering it in the stifling air. Nathan stared at Lacey, mute. Neither was inclined to move. The heat, or something more internal, paralyzed them both.

Lacey wanted to articulate something about her feelings for him, but the words wouldn't come. He'd said he loved her, what felt like a lifetime ago. But she could not bring herself to say it in return. A seed of that feeling was inside her, but it wasn't ready to bloom.

"Strange, magical things are happening," she said instead. "My part in your story is something I still have trouble fathoming."

He looked at her. Sun glinted off the towering stainless-steel sculpture embedded in the lagoon, swirling light patterns above his head.

"How is it that I encountered you under the 610 overpass that night?" she asked. "Why am I a part of this horrible time in your life?"

Nathan made a lightning-fast movement. He pulled her in from the waist and kissed her—slow, hard, long. Lacey's breath was stolen in that first instant. She gave in to the kiss, falling into the connection. She knew it was this intimacy she had longed for—this kiss was why she had contacted him, despite all her reasons otherwise.

He finally pulled back and placed a hand on her leg, close to her knee. He smiled, looking more relaxed.

"So, how long will you be gone?" he asked.

"Oh. I'm…I'm not sure." Lacey struggled to stop her head from spinning. "Anywhere from eight weeks to three months is what they told me," she finally said.

Nathan nodded. "I might just be starting to get my life back in order by then."

"I'm nervous," Lacey said. She was too preoccupied with the next few months to think about what might happen after she returned.

"What are you doing with the hound?" Nathan asked.

"Ambrose? He's coming with me. Really, he's the only thing keeping me grounded about this massive step I'm taking." A flash of inspiration came to Lacey. She thought of her house vacant with only Tonti looking after it, and poor Nathan moving in with his parents.

She banished the thought almost as quickly as it had appeared. It left her too exposed to whatever it was Nathan was still going through. She decided saving his life twice was generosity enough.

"Maybe I need a dog," Nathan said.

"How would your parents feel about that?"

Nathan laughed. "Yeah. One thing at a time, I guess."

"Right."

"So, I probably should be going," Nathan said. He made no attempt to leave Lacey's side.

"I…I just wanted to follow up on you," Lacey said, feeling the need to say something. "And to let you know I was going to be out of town for a while. You have my number, right? In case you need anything, related to your situation?"

"Yes, I have your number," he said. He laughed under his breath. "I think this undertaking is going to be a big deal for you. You might not want to come back. I think it's great."

"I'll be back," Lacey said. "How could I leave all this?" She swept her hand in what was meant as an ironic gesture, but the sculpture garden looked especially enchanting in the falling light. The irony was lost.

"We'll see," Nathan said. He stared at the blazing sunset. "I'm going to be fine, Lacey. I just have to keep up my stamina and get things set up through this…transition."

"Transition sounds right," Lacey said. "I think that's a good way to look at it. For both of us."

Nathan exhaled and stood. "Where is your car? I don't want you walking through here alone in the dark."

"You don't think I can handle myself?" Lacey asked.

"No, I *know* you can handle yourself. But I was raised better than that."

"I'm right outside the gate," she said as she stood. She looked down and straightened a wrinkle in her shorts.

Nathan touched the side of her face. She gasped at the surprise. He tucked her hair behind her ear and rested his hand on her cheek.

"God, you are beautiful," he said. "In every possible way."

Lacey was mute. She didn't believe it, but she didn't mind hearing it. Not from him.

He kissed her again. This time without the element of surprise, but with the force of possession. There was an urgency coursing through him, and she felt it pass through to her. *Remember me, remember this,* she felt resounding inside her. *As if I could forget,* she said to herself. She placed her hand on his shoulder and pressed gently.

"I should go," she said.

He nodded slowly as he broke off. He looked her straight in the eyes, almost through her, and said, "I meant what I said."

"I know," she said, and smiled. She grabbed his hand and said lightly, "C'mon, Romeo, it's time to say goodbye. Walk me to my car."

His intensity slipped away, and he relaxed. "Which way?"

"It doesn't matter; either way will get us to the gate."

He asked her where in California she would be, and said he had been to the central coast once. It was beautiful, he said. Lacey wondered if Nathan had multiple personalities, so quickly had his mood gone from soul-baring to walk in the park.

"So what's the movie about?" he asked.

"Huh?"

"You said you're going to be an accountant on a movie, right?"

"Oh," Lacey said. "I've been told it's a coming-of-age story with elements of magic and light."

"What does that mean?" he asked.

Lacey laughed. "Exactly. I have no idea. I guess I'll find out."

Through the sculpture garden they exchanged theories about the different works they passed—the upside-down man who rang like a bell, Renoir's *Venus*. The talk was small, but deep down, she knew she would forever after associate this place with Nathan. A beautiful place full of abstract expressions—some resonant, some head-scratching. It suited their relationship.

At Lacey's car, there was no kiss, no embrace, no further confessions of the soul. Nathan placed his hand on her back to help her in. She smiled and said goodbye. He stepped back as she fastened her seatbelt and started the engine.

Looking forward, she jumped when she heard a loud tapping at her window. She rolled it down.

Nathan leaned in. The soul-baring intensity was back. "I'll see you again soon." He tapped the roof of her car like it was a taxi, turned around, and walked away.

ABOUT THE AUTHOR

ANNE McCLANE writes sci-fi and paranormal fiction. She is a New Orleans native who spent sixteen years out west before returning home to embrace the mysteries of the Mississippi River Delta. She has many years experience in publicity, public relations, and marketing, which has provided a fine primer for writing about the speculative, abnormal, and outrageous.

You can find her science fiction stories on Amazon, in the anthology *Just a Minor Malfunction….* Learn more at her website: **AnneMcClane.com**

OTHER BOOKS IN THE TRAITEUR TRILOGY:

Book Two: The Trouble on Highway One—Lacey seeks answers on California's Central Coast

Book Three: The Conclusion on the Causeway—Back home in New Orleans, Lacey finds her calling